After studying English at university, Nell Pattison became a teacher and specialised in Deaf education. She has been teaching in the Deaf community for 12 years in both England and Scotland, working with students who use BSL. Nell began losing her hearing in her twenties, but still refuses to wear her hearing aids. She lives in North Lincolnshire with her husband and child. *The Silent House* is her debut novel.

THE
SILENT
HOUSE

NELL PATTISON

Published by AVON
A division of HarperCollins*Publishers* Ltd
1 London Bridge Street
London SE1 9GF

www.harpercollins.co.uk

A Paperback Original 2020
3

Copyright © Nell Pattison 2020

Nell Pattison asserts the moral right to
be identified as the author of this work.

A catalogue copy of this book is available from the British Library.

ISBN: 978-0-00-836176-1

This novel is entirely a work of fiction. The names, characters and
incidents portrayed in it are the work of the author's imagination. Any
resemblance to actual persons, living or dead, events or localities is entirely
coincidental.

Typeset in Sabon by Palimpsest Book Production Limited, Falkirk,
Stirlingshire

Printed and bound in UK by CPI Group (UK) Ltd, Croydon CR0 4YY

MIX
Paper from
responsible sources
FSC™ C007454

This book is produced from independently certified FSC™ paper to ensure
responsible forest management.
For more information visit: www.harpercollins.co.uk/green

For Albert

Prologue

There was someone else in the room.

Jaxon rubbed his eyes groggily. Light from the lamppost outside was spilling through the gap in the curtains, and he could see the shape of a grown-up standing by the door. Who was it? He couldn't tell, his eyes blurred with sleep.

Only half awake, he rolled out of bed and patted his little sister Lexi in the bed next to his. He poked her to see if she was awake, but she didn't move. His other sister, Kasey, was asleep on the other side of the room, her chest rising and falling.

Go back to sleep, the grown-up signed.

Jaxon looked down at his hands, which glistened with something dark and sticky. He saw the same dark stuff on his sister.

Why won't Lexi wake up? Jaxon signed, his confusion over Lexi's lack of response eclipsing his concern about who was in his room.

The grown-up turned to look at the little girl in the bed. They stood over Lexi for a moment, and Jaxon saw their hands moving frantically over her body. They stepped back, one hand raised to their face, then bent over as if they were about to be sick.

Jaxon was too sleepy to resist when the grown-up pulled him out of the room and into the bathroom. They didn't turn the light on, but used a torch to check none of the red had got on his pyjamas, before carefully washing his hands. The light blinded him, keeping the grown-up in shadow.

Did I do something wrong? he asked.

Back to bed now. Don't tell anyone. It's a secret, okay? Their hands shook as they signed to him.

He nodded again, allowed himself to be led back to his bed. Lexi still had stuff all over her, but maybe they would clean her up next. As he drifted off to sleep, wondering who had been in his room, he didn't notice the adult was still standing by his bed, head bowed and shoulders shaking.

They let out a howl of anguish, but nobody in the house heard.

Chapter 1

Saturday 3rd February

'I'm the interpreter,' I said clearly, as I leant over the police tape. My breath fogged in the cold morning air as I spoke. I pulled out my ID badge and waved it at the nearest uniformed officer, a luckless PC who was clearly having a hard time keeping the nosy neighbours back. He only looked about twenty, his eyes bloodshot from tiredness. The card I handed him was my expired ID from the last agency I worked for, the photo an old one. My face had rounded out in the years since it had been taken, but the brown eyes and long dark hair hadn't changed. I hadn't got around to having something new made when I went freelance. I'd been putting it off, out of a fear it'd jinx my fledgling business. The main thing was that it still opened the doors I needed it to.

Those three words were usually met with a look of relief on emergency call-outs, and this time was no different. The PC waved me over to the edge of the crowd and lifted the tape for me to slip under. I could feel the eyes of the onlookers on my back, wondering why I'd been allowed passage. I assumed they were neighbours, their attention drawn by the lights of the emergency vehicles; few people would be passing through this area of Scunthorpe on a Saturday morning, and if they saw police here they wouldn't be inclined to stop.

'Wait here, please,' he instructed me, leaving me on the pavement as he approached the house.

There were officers in white paper suits milling around in the doorway. Other uniformed men and women moved amongst the crowd, notebooks in hand. It was seven on a Saturday morning, didn't these people have better things to do, instead of gawping? A shiver ran through me as a memory surfaced, but I pushed it back down again.

I hovered halfway along the path, unsure if I should go up to the house or stay where I was. The street was typical for that part of Scunthorpe. Rows of identical council houses squashed together, the gardens and exterior walls in varying stages of disrepair. There were neat gardens, clearly loved and tended; there were front yards that were more like the municipal tip in miniature form. How could people cope, living in such disarray?

Past the houses to my left, the road sloped downwards to meet a large patch of waste ground, which stretched away towards the imposing silhouette of the steelworks, jagged against the dark sky. Much of Scunthorpe had been built on the garden city model, but nothing grew amongst the rubble. The street lights enhanced the shadows and for a moment I thought I saw movement. Probably a fox.

In full daylight, the houses on this street looked shabby and rundown, but in the gloom of the winter morning they were bathed in the eerie blue glow of the police car lights. Three cars, lit up but with their sirens off; an ambulance, paramedics moving around inside it but with an air of despondency rather than urgency. It was serious, then.

A phone call first thing in the morning never brings good news. Within an hour of my mobile buzzing me awake, I was pulling up six houses down from the address I'd been directed to. I couldn't get any closer because of the police cordon holding back the gaggle of inquisitive neighbours, pyjamas and slippers visible under their coats. I glanced at the windows nearest to me and saw signs of more observers – corners of curtains pulled back, silhouettes at dark windows. None of them would have known what was happening. Even I had been given the barest of detail, and I wouldn't know more until I went inside.

I ran a hand through my bed hair. I had been on call for the emergency services for six months, and in that time I'd learnt that the people who needed me at short notice would prefer me to be quick rather than smart. If I turned up to a regular job in the afternoon looking like that I probably wouldn't get much repeat business, but when it was an emergency call-out for the police, all bets were off. Still, my professional life was dogged by that little voice in the back of my mind saying that nobody would take me seriously, and my dishevelled state did nothing to quieten it. I grabbed a brush from my bag and tried to sort my hair out while I waited.

The white-suited officers in the entrance to the house had dispersed, leaving a couple with their arms around each other, and I felt a jolt of concern as I recognised them. Alan Hunter, and Elisha . . . I couldn't remember her surname. So, if it was their house, what had happened there? As I watched, the pair separated. There was blood on Elisha's clothes, but she didn't look hurt and the paramedics weren't with her. Alan's eighteen-month-old daughter, Lexi, was my sister's goddaughter. As I pictured her, a horrible thought struck me. Where were the children?

I'd waited for long enough. I needed to know what had happened in that house, and I looked around for a police officer to ask. At that moment, a dark-haired woman came out of the house and marched straight up to me, her hand outstretched.

'DI Forest. You're the British Sign Language interpreter?' Her suit beneath her white overalls was rumpled, but her eyes were sharp.

I nodded. 'Paige Northwood.' At least she gave my job its correct title. Most people called me 'the signer', or worse, 'the signing lady'.

'Come with me. We need to collect some clothing and the woman isn't cooperating.'

'What's happened here? I need context,' I told her as she hurried away from me back towards the house.

DI Forest waved a hand dismissively. 'We don't have the full information. That's why you're here. Right now we need to collect this evidence then get this couple to the station.'

Gritting my teeth in frustration, I followed her. At the door, Forest handed me my own protective paper suit to put over my clothes. After I spent a minute wrestling with it, she ushered me inside. The front door led into the living room, and I could hear voices and footsteps overhead. DI Forest took me straight through a door opposite, into a rear hallway. A door to my right led to the kitchen, and the stairs were to my left. Alan and Elisha were now standing at the foot of the stairs, clinging to each other once again.

The hallway was sparsely decorated – laminate floor, magnolia walls. It reminded me of the house I'd grown up in, another one with the drab decoration of the local housing association. No photographs, no artwork, just a small mirror halfway along the passageway. At the foot of the stairs, by the back door, was a scooter. It looked about the right size for a five- or six-year-old – probably Jaxon's, Alan's oldest child. There was a strange smell in the air – a fuggy mixture of cigarette smoke, marijuana and something else, something more organic. At the top of the stairs I could see figures moving around, but the landing was in darkness, hiding their features.

The phone call that morning had been very curt, simply saying that there had been an incident with a deaf family and the police needed a British Sign Language interpreter immediately. They gave me the address, but no information about what had happened or who was involved. I realised I was shaking as the potential seriousness of the situation hit home: from the amount of blood I could see on Elisha's clothes, someone must have been seriously injured. It was mostly on her sleeves and chest, but I could see smudges on her pyjama bottoms too, probably where she'd wiped her hands.

One of the paper-suited officers was trying to explain something to Elisha, waving a large brown evidence bag in front of her and pointing to her clothes. The woman pleaded with her, but Elisha shrank away; the officer looked at DI Forest and shrugged. I recognised Elisha from the Deaf club, and I spotted a flicker of recognition on her face when she saw me. She was only in her early twenties, as far as I knew, but at that moment she looked much older. There were dark circles under her eyes, which darted back and forth between the two police officers.

'Please could you explain to Miss Barron that we need to take her clothes for evidence? She is allowed to go and get changed, but we need to take those clothes with us. She and Mr Hunter then need to come with us to the station so we can take their statements and their fingerprints.'

'Whose blood is it?' I asked Forest, but she frowned at me and jerked her head in Elisha's direction, as if to say get on with your job. I gave Elisha what I hoped was a supportive smile, trying to keep the fear from my face, and signed the detective inspector's request. Alan had his arm around her, protectively, and looked unwilling to let go. Whenever I'd seen Elisha in the past, she'd been well turned out – not overly dressed up, but neat, as if she looked after herself. This Elisha looked like a different woman. Her brown hair was a mess, half of it falling out of her ponytail. She was wearing an old pair of pyjamas with a couple of holes in. She had probably just got out of bed when it happened, but still, I was surprised by her appearance. Whatever had happened must have been traumatic, to have wrought such a change in her.

As I signed, Alan's knuckles whitened and Elisha grimaced. She shook her head in answer to the request and hugged herself tightly.

'She's refusing,' I told them.

Forest frowned at me again, as if I were the one saying no. 'That's not an option. Her clothes are evidence and we need to get them from her, one way or another. I don't have time for this,' she added with a hiss.

Elisha was surrounded by hearing people making

demands she didn't understand because they weren't using her language, not because she wasn't capable of carrying out their requests. I felt for her, and wasn't surprised she was shutting down. Looking at the exasperation on the officers' faces, I decided it would be best to take the firm approach and get this over with quickly.

You need to give those clothes to the police, now. Doesn't matter that you don't want to, you have to. Go upstairs, get changed and give those clothes to the police. Now.

I was rewarded with a long stare then finally a shrug. Alan narrowed his eyes at me, but his grip on Elisha's shoulder loosened and his arm dropped to his side.

'You come upstairs with me?' Elisha asked. Her speech was soft, and the detectives looked surprised to hear her reply.

I checked it was okay with the officers, then nodded.

'Wilson, take her upstairs to get changed, then send the interpreter back down to me,' Forest snapped as she moved back towards the living room.

When her back was turned, I rolled my eyes, but followed the officer and Elisha upstairs to her bedroom.

There was a flurry of activity on the landing as we climbed the stairs, and a door slammed, so by the time we reached the top there was nobody there. My unease grew.

'Please could you take your clothes off and put them in this bag,' the officer asked Elisha, clearly relieved to have me interpreting.

Elisha nodded and pulled a clean t-shirt out of a drawer. I averted my eyes while she changed, but the officer continued to watch her.

'I need to know – what happened here?' I muttered to the officer as Elisha changed, but she shook her head.

'DI Forest will fill you in on anything you need to know. I can't discuss it.'

I decided not to push it. The officer took photographs of Elisha's clothing before bagging each item separately. Once I had heard the two paper bags rustle, I turned around, swallowing hard when I realised that Elisha still had a smear of blood across her forehead, going up into her hairline.

'Thank you,' the officer said, and nodded to me. 'DI Forest would like you to return to the living room. Elisha, you can go back and join Alan.'

'Sure,' I replied, quickly translating this for Elisha.

We stepped out onto the landing and were descending the stairs when I heard a door open behind me. I leapt in fright as Elisha let out an unearthly wail, and I realised she was saying a name.

'Lexi! Lexi!'

I turned around on the stairs, expecting to see the little girl. Instead, I saw the open door to the other bedroom and, beyond the officer in the doorway, a toddler bed. My legs went from under me and I fell onto the step. Lexi was lying on the bloodstained mattress, her lifeless eyes open and staring.

I gasped and covered my mouth to stop myself retching, and the officer in the doorway turned, noticing us.

'Shit, get that door shut,' I heard someone say, then our view was obscured once more.

The officer who took us upstairs muttered something under her breath, then guided Elisha towards the stairs, but I was in the way. I wasn't sure if my legs could hold

10

me, so I swivelled around on the step and squashed myself against the wall so they could get past.

I clasped my shaking hands around my knees and swallowed several times to get rid of the bile in my throat. Lexi was dead. Lexi had been killed. How was I going to tell Anna? My sister doted on her little goddaughter.

Elisha ran down the stairs and flung herself at Alan, sobbing as she pressed her face into his chest and clung to him. Alan just stood there, his face blank, not even putting his arms around her. He looked up the stairs and our eyes met, but I looked away quickly. I felt another stab of fear when I thought about his other two children – where were Jaxon and Kasey? Were they dead too?

I needed fresh air, so I forced myself to move. As I stood, someone came out of the smaller bedroom and walked past me on the stairs. It was a different female police officer also dressed in a white paper body suit. She had a large evidence bag in her hand, and she shielded it with her body as she squeezed past me. When she turned, I got a clear view of the bag and its contents: a teddy bear. I remembered taking Anna shopping to buy it when Lexi was born. Its fur was so soft.

I followed her down the stairs, and as she moved into the light in the hallway I saw a dark stain on the bear's foot. Blood. There was blood on Lexi's teddy and they were taking it away for evidence. The room lurched and I stumbled towards the open back door in my haste to get outside, where the rush of cold air precipitated a violent reaction and I vomited onto the cracked patio. Shaking, I sank down onto the doorstep, spitting out the last of the bile in my mouth. What the hell happened in that house?

The officer I knew only as Wilson appeared next to me

and handed me a bottle of water. I gave her a grateful smile and rinsed my mouth out, then took a big gulp.

'Sorry, you shouldn't have seen that.'

I made a strangled noise that was somewhere between a laugh and a sob. 'This isn't the sort of job I normally do.'

'Are you okay? Do you know the family?'

I glanced up and saw a wary look in her eyes. I knew there was a potential conflict of interest, but I nodded anyway. 'I know them vaguely from the Deaf club. I know Alan's ex, Laura. Lexi and Jaxon's mum.'

Laura was good friends with my sister, Anna, and I'd known her since I was eighteen. I'd occasionally spent time with Lexi in the last eighteen months, and another wave of horror hit me as I thought about her.

I swallowed and took a deep breath. 'My job can involve working with people I know, in sensitive situations. The Deaf community is small, and you won't find a local interpreter who doesn't know them. I just hadn't expected to arrive here to find out a child is dead.' I swallowed the bile that yet again rushed to the back of my throat, and continued: 'When I'm on call it's usually hospital work, telling doctors what happened and where it hurts. Nothing like this.' I did my best to keep my voice steady, professional, but it cracked a little at the end. I held back the information that Lexi was my sister's goddaughter. Even in my shocked state, I knew I wanted this job; I had to know what had happened. I didn't want the officer knowing the full truth of how close I was to this, in case she told the detectives and they called a different interpreter.

Wilson flashed me a brief smile. 'I understand. Are you okay to continue?'

I nodded. There was no way I'd let them replace me. I needed to be there.

She led me back into the house and through to the living room. As we entered, DI Forest frowned, but the man with her smiled warmly and introduced himself as DC Singh. Alan and Elisha had disappeared, either into the kitchen or outside with another officer, I assumed.

'We need to get back to the station and take statements,' Forest said.

'I'm ready,' I said.

'Normally we would have asked you to meet us there, but the communication barrier has slowed things down. Now you're here, hopefully we can get on with things.'

Forest turned on her heel and walked out of the front door, leaving Singh looking a little awkward. He gestured for me to follow, then directed me to where Alan and Elisha were waiting.

I explained the situation to them, and once I was sure they were going to cooperate, I ducked under the police tape and walked back to my car. There were still some onlookers milling around, and I could feel their eyes on my back as I walked away. As I unlocked my car door, I realised my hands were shaking, and I rested my head on the steering wheel before I set off for the police station, taking deep breaths. What the hell could have happened to that poor little girl? And how was I going to tell my sister?

Chapter 2

On arriving at the police station, Alan and Elisha had their fingerprints taken. I interpreted the detectives' explanation that it was for elimination purposes, but Alan continued to look wary. The officer taking their prints looked them up and down then spoke slowly, with an unnatural sing-song tone to her voice. When Elisha looked to me for clarification of what she'd said, the officer sighed and went through her exaggerated instructions again while I cringed behind her. Only when Elisha snapped, 'I'm deaf, not stupid,' did the officer shut up and let me take over.

It took an hour to get everything sorted, and before they were ready to take statements I found myself sitting in a waiting room, reading the same five posters repeatedly. I considered sending Anna a message, to break the news to her, but I decided against it. Hopefully she wouldn't find out before I was finished at the police station, then I could call her and tell her face to face. I pressed my lips together to stop my jaw trembling as I imagined my sister's pain at the death of her goddaughter.

Singh brought me a cup of coffee, which I drank gratefully despite its murky grey colour. I'd been to bed late the previous night, anticipating a weekend lie in, and I was finding it hard to stay awake.

'Before we begin, I'll give you the basic background.' Singh sat down opposite me and rubbed the bridge of his nose before continuing. 'I'm sure you realise this is a very serious situation. We were contacted via the emergency text service just after six this morning, saying a child was dead. CID were called in due to the suspicious circumstances, and myself and DI Forest are part of the incident team who'll be dealing with the case from now on.

'There are two adults who were present at the time the child's body was discovered: Alan Hunter and Elisha Barron, both of whom are deaf. There are also two other children, who haven't been harmed.'

I let out a breath I hadn't realised I'd been holding. At least Jaxon and Kasey were okay.

'The dead child's name is Lexi Hunter. She was staying with her father for the weekend, although normally lives with her mother. Her brother, Jaxon, and half-sister, Kasey, were asleep in the same room when it happened.'

The implications of what the children might have witnessed stunned me for a moment, but before Singh continued I held up a hand to interrupt him.

'Where are they? Jaxon and Kasey?'

'We contacted the duty social worker, and they're being cared for. Jaxon should be back with his mother shortly, although we'll need to arrange to interview him in a couple of days.'

15

Drawing in a sharp breath, I wondered how Singh could deal with things like this every day. The prospect of interviewing a six-year-old about the death of his sister sounded awful. I knew I should tell him that I already knew the family, but I didn't want him thinking I shouldn't be working on the case, and I let the moment pass.

'We need to establish what happened and what Alan and Elisha can tell us, but we need to take their statements individually,' Singh continued. 'They've been reluctant to be separated until you were here. We'll need to speak with Lexi's mother once we're finished here, as well.'

'Does she know? Laura, has someone told her?'

'Yes,' he replied, his deep voice reassuring me. He either didn't notice my slip, showing I knew Lexi's mum's name, or he let it go. 'We sent officers over as soon as we were given her address. Her mother is also with her.'

I knew Laura was living with her mum, so at least she had her there for support. From what I'd heard, Bridget Weston was a strong woman, so hopefully something like this wouldn't break her completely, devastating as it would be for the whole family. I worried how Laura would ever cope with a tragedy of such magnitude.

DI Forest approached as Singh finished filling me in. 'Is there anything else you need to know before we begin?'

I swallowed, not wanting to ask but needing as much information as they could give me. 'How did Lexi die?'

Forest grimaced, her mouth pulled tight in a straight line. 'There will have to be a post-mortem. Until we have the results, I'm afraid we can't discuss it with you.'

I bit back a response. There must have been more she could tell me, but I couldn't bring myself to push for it yet. As the interviews progressed, there'd be things I didn't want to hear, but it was my job. I'd been present during some of the most private moments of people's lives: I'd been there when a doctor told someone they had cancer; I'd had to inform a client that his wife was filing for divorce; I'd worked with social services, in homes and in court, when children were being placed under child protection orders or were being removed from their families. I had learned to deal with not being able to talk to anyone else about my work, about the things I heard and experienced, but in nine years I hadn't learned to separate myself emotionally from my clients and their experiences. When I understood my clients' emotions, it helped me to interpret them more accurately, reading their facial expressions and body language to help me modulate the tone and inflexion of my spoken English translation. This empathy never made my job any easier, though.

Forest led me through to an interview room where Elisha was sitting at a table, hands clasped around a cup of tea. I smiled in an attempt to reassure her, then sat down opposite her so she could see me clearly.

'Elisha, we need to take your statement about what happened to Lexi. Do you want the BSL interpreter here?' Forest asked as soon as we were all settled.

I was surprised at the question, but then I remembered the confusion when Elisha spoke at the house. Many deaf people speak as well as use sign language, often combining the two, and others don't sign at all. I treated every client differently, depending on how they chose to communicate.

'Yes, please. I don't always understand people speaking.'

You want to speak, or you sign and I speak for you? I signed to Elisha.

She wrinkled her nose as if she were thinking, then signed, *You speak.*

I relayed this to the detectives, and Forest nodded at Singh to continue.

'Okay, Elisha. Paige will interpret for you, and we're videoing this interview,' Singh began, indicating the camera. 'Do you think you can tell us what happened?'

Elisha's eyes darted around the room for a moment, then finally she looked at me so I could interpret Singh's question.

I told you in the emergency text, she signed with a frown. *I found Lexi in her room. I don't know what happened.*

'I understand that, but we need a lot more information about what happened, now that we have an interpreter.'

I explained this to Elisha, adding in that the police needed to do it properly. Still, she looked distressed. *I don't want to talk about it.*

I interpreted this and DI Forest sighed briefly before she replied. Didn't she know that Elisha could read her frustration in her body language?

'We need to hear it from you, exactly as you remember it. It's important we find out what happened to Lexi.'

Elisha closed her eyes for a moment, then started to explain.

I woke up early and went to check on the children. There was blood on Lexi's head, and on her bed. It was all over her. I checked, and she wasn't breathing. Elisha looked at the floor, and I wondered why she was so defensive, what she was scared of.

'Why don't we start from last night,' DC Singh suggested, his calm tone contrasting starkly with Forest's. 'What time did Lexi go to bed? Start from there.'

Elisha pinched the bridge of her nose, then covered her face with her hands for a moment before she responded. She was terrified.

The children went to bed at nine. They all sleep in the same room when Jaxon and Lexi are staying. We've only got two bedrooms. She glared at Forest as she signed, as if the detective inspector was somehow responsible for their lack of living space.

'How often do Jaxon and Lexi stay?'

Most weekends.

Singh made notes as I translated. 'And when did you next go into the room?'

I checked on them every half hour, maybe every hour. Jaxon takes a long time to go to sleep, so I had to check he wasn't disturbing the girls.

'What time did he go to sleep?'

Elisha shrugged, then looked down at the floor again. Her arms were wrapped tightly around herself. It had been mild for February, but there was a chill in the room that morning.

She gave me an imploring look. *I don't think I can do this.*

I interpreted this and Forest pursed her lips. 'Give us as much information as you can, but we may still need to ask you some more questions when you've finished, if there's something else we need to know.'

For a moment I thought Elisha would refuse; she looked to the door, as if she were contemplating leaving, but eventually she nodded.

Alan went out to the pub, so I put the children to bed at nine, then went back downstairs. I kept checking on them every half hour until they were all asleep. One time

I went in and Jaxon was under his bed, but he went to sleep around eleven, I think. I checked on all three of them, and Lexi was fine. I saw her mouth move as she sucked her dummy. She paused. *I went to bed then. I woke up around two, but I didn't go back into the children's room until this morning.*

'What time did Alan come home?' DI Forest asked.

Around two. That's why I woke up.

'Would you normally check on the children in the night, if you woke up?'

Maybe.

'Did Alan check on the children when he came upstairs?'

Elisha's eyes darted to the side and she fidgeted for a moment before she replied. *Alan didn't come upstairs. We had a fight because . . . because he was really drunk. I made him sleep on the sofa.*

The two detectives exchanged looks and DC Singh made a note of this before gesturing for Elisha to continue.

She picked at her fingernails for a moment. *As soon as I got up this morning, something didn't feel right. I went to check on the children again, and Lexi was lying on her front, with her head on one side. Her hair was in her face, but I brushed it out of the way. Her eyes were open and my hand felt sticky. I could see blood on her clothes, on her bed. The back of her head was all covered in blood.* Tears slid down Elisha's face as she looked at her hands, which were shaking.

I shuddered at the memory of Lexi's body, some of the blood clearly visible from where I had been standing. I wished I could blank it out, forget what I saw, but I knew I never would. DI Forest shifted in her chair, and asked Elisha to continue.

I knew she was dead. I reached down to touch her, to make sure. That's how I got her blood all over me. Elisha sniffed and swallowed, more tears threatening to spill over. From the shape of the bloodstains on her clothes, I thought she had probably picked Lexi up and held her close.

Her face looked . . . strange, she continued. *I don't know if something happened to it, or if it was just because she was dead, but her face was the wrong shape.* She shrugged, unsure of how to express herself further. She swallowed again.

Someone did this while I was asleep. How could someone come into my house and do this? Why couldn't I have woken up? Elisha's words made me shiver at the thought of someone walking around the house, knowing they couldn't be heard. I thought she was going to carry on, but she wrapped her arms around herself again and shook her head to indicate she didn't want to say any more.

'What about Jaxon and Kasey? Did you check on them?'

It took a moment for me to get Elisha's attention, but in the end she took a shuddering breath and looked at me.

Of course I checked on them. They were both asleep. Kasey didn't wake up, but she was breathing deeply. Jaxon woke up when I touched him. He looked confused, not scared, so I don't think he saw what happened. He didn't understand what I was doing.

'Is that when you contacted the ambulance?'

Elisha nodded. *I've got the emergency SMS on my phone, see?* She dug her phone out of her pocket to show the detectives.

Singh made a note of something, then leant forward. I definitely got a good cop, bad cop vibe from those two.

'Did you tell Alan what had happened?'

When I interpreted this question, Elisha pressed her lips together so tightly half her face went white. She nodded, then her eyes flicked towards the door again.

'Was he awake?'

She shook her head, but offered no more information. Singh wrote something down, but didn't push the point.

'We want to ask you a couple of questions about Lexi now. Would that be okay?'

Wiping her eyes with the torn cuff of her jumper, she agreed.

'Did you look after her a lot, when she and Jaxon stayed over?'

Quite a bit. Alan's very busy, and I have Kasey, so I usually have the three children together.

'Have you noticed anyone behaving strangely around Lexi recently?'

Elisha frowned and shook her head. *I don't know what you mean.*

'Has there been anyone acting suspiciously, doing anything that worried you, around the children?'

No, nobody. Well . . . She paused mid-sign, and I thought she was going to carry on, but she just shook her head.

Singh looked at me, but Elisha stayed still and didn't sign anything else.

DI Forest cleared her throat. 'We need to wait until the results of the post-mortem confirm cause of death. That's why we need as much information as possible right now.'

Why would someone kill Lexi? As I interpreted this, I realised Elisha was asking me, her desperate face appealing to me for an answer to make sense of what happened. The facade she had been putting on slipped, then crumbled. She reached a hand up to her head and dug her fingers into her scalp, rocking as she sobbed. I laid a hand on her arm, but I knew I couldn't offer much comfort.

When her sobs subsided, she looked back at me again. *She was a beautiful little girl, always happy.* The tears still rolled down her cheeks, and she buried her face in her hands.

I could feel my own emotions churning. I hadn't had time to process the thought that I was working with the police as part of a murder investigation. I agreed with Elisha – surely nobody would have any reason to harm a young child?

Singh flipped back a couple of pages in his notes. 'You said that Alan slept on the sofa because you had a fight. Did he stay there all night, or did he come upstairs at all?'

Elisha glanced at the door yet again and chewed her lip for a moment. *He stayed downstairs. I don't like it when he gets really drunk, so he slept on the sofa.* She didn't make eye contact with me when she signed this, and I got the feeling she wasn't telling the truth, but I could hardly say that to the detectives. I didn't think she could take much more of this questioning. She was perched on the edge of her chair, poised for flight.

She started to sign something to me, but I was distracted by a knock on the door. A uniformed officer opened it and beckoned Singh over with an apologetic grimace. The two men bent their heads together and muttered to each other for a moment before Singh nodded and followed him out of the door.

Chapter 3

I'm Deaf, but I'm not deaf. Growing up, I was the only hearing person in my family, which makes me Deaf with a capital D. I was always part of the Deaf community, and BSL was my first language. Being Deaf is a cultural identity, not simply a term for hearing loss. You can have full hearing and still be considered part of the Deaf community. I can't put my finger on when I started to slip into the role of family interpreter. It was the easiest way to get anything done; I translated the world for my parents and my sister, before email and texting made communication more accessible. I never intended for it to be my job, though. It was something I fell into for convenience, then never found my way back out of. Most of the time, I didn't mind it, but certain jobs made me rethink my options.

The fear in Alan's eyes as Singh had left the room set my adrenaline pumping, and when I looked down, I could see my hands trembling. Forest, Elisha and I waited in the interview room, the tension palpable. Elisha rocked on her chair, pulling her hair out of its ponytail so it fell over her face. Using her hearing aids, I wondered how much she could hear of the commotion outside the door.

After a few minutes, Singh stuck his head around the door. 'Miss Northwood, can we have your assistance, please?'

I explained to Elisha where I was going, then slipped out, heart hammering with trepidation. Calming down traumatised clients wasn't part of my remit. In the corridor, Alan sat on the floor, with his back to a wall and his knees raised. He squared his jaw and glared at Singh and the other detective who were standing over him, his eyes rimmed with red, but he didn't move.

'Mr Hunter has calmed down sufficiently, I think. Please could you explain to him that we'll take his statement as soon as we've finished with Miss Barron, then we will take both of them to stay somewhere else.'

I did as Singh asked, and Alan grunted in response. *I don't care about the statement. I want my children back. Social services can't take my children. Jaxon and Kasey are staying with me.*

Singh nodded when I had translated. 'Of course, I understand your concerns, but we have to check them over to make sure they're okay. They could have witnessed a very traumatic event. It's normal for us to contact social services when something like this happens.'

Why? Alan was tense, but I could see the pain on his face, and I understood. Someone had taken one of his children from him, and he desperately wanted to see the other two, to reassure himself.

26

'Mr Hunter, someone murdered one of your children only a few hours ago. It is in Jaxon and Kasey's best interests that we make sure they haven't been harmed.'

I was surprised by the tone in Singh's voice, but his stern facial expression did the trick, and Alan's head drooped. He screwed his face up; I thought he was trying not to cry.

'Now, we need to finish taking Miss Barron's statement, then we'll speak to you. DC Benson will take you back to wait in an interview room.'

I translated, and Alan nodded, so Singh and I went back into the room where Elisha and Forest waited. Elisha jumped backwards in her chair when the door opened, and looked relieved when she saw us. I wondered who she'd been expecting.

We went over Elisha's statement, and she agreed to everything. For a moment, I thought she wanted to add something, but she dropped her eyes from mine and we left the room.

The two detectives compared notes, and I was shown to a waiting area. A couple of minutes later, Elisha was also escorted in, but I didn't make eye contact with her, bending down to pull a bottle of water out of my bag. It could feel strange, ignoring a client in the middle of a job, but there was nowhere private to have a break and I desperately needed one. If it hadn't been such a horrific situation, I might have looked for another coffee, but it didn't feel appropriate to go wandering around the station, somehow. Water would do.

I could hear the detectives muttering in the hallway, but they didn't look my way. Checking my phone, I wondered again if I should call Anna. She was a night owl like me, but it was gone ten so she'd probably be awake. I told myself I was putting it off for her sake, when really a part of me hoped she would find out from another source so I didn't have to be the bearer of such terrible news.

After waiting for about ten minutes, I got up to stretch my legs. The police station chairs weren't chosen for comfort, and I needed to get some blood flowing if I wanted to stay awake. Forest and Singh had disappeared, and I stood in the doorway and glanced down the corridor. A couple of uniformed officers were walking past, and as they did I caught a snippet of their conversation.

'. . . sick, bashing a little girl's head in like that.'

'People like that shouldn't have kids if they can't protect them. Imagine not knowing someone was in your house, in your kid's bedroom.'

The world started to spin, and I needed to grab on to the door frame for support. The PCs suddenly noticed I was there, and one stepped forward to check I was okay. I shook him off and stormed up the corridor looking for Singh and Forest. Trying several doors, I found them in an office, leaning over a desk. I was so desperate to know exactly what had happened, I didn't care if I was interrupting them.

'Is there a problem?' Forest asked, looking at Singh even though I knew she was talking to me.

'What happened in that house? What happened to Lexi? Who could have done this?' I blurted it out before thinking.

Forest's face darkened and the atmosphere became noticeably colder. 'We can't discuss the particulars of the case with you.' The set of her jaw told me she expected that to be the end of the discussion, but I couldn't just leave it there.

Breathing deeply to try and stop myself from shaking, I stepped closer to her.

'I have been thrown into this situation with no information, no warning about what I was going to hear. Thanks to your officers I've seen the body of a dead child, something that I will never forget. I need to know what happened!' I knew my voice was becoming shrill, but I didn't care any more. I trembled as the image of Lexi's battered body rose unbidden in my mind, and I took some deep breaths.

'Miss Northwood, we have already said—' Singh began, but I cut him off.

'Tell me, please!' My voice broke and I let out a strangled sob before covering my mouth with my hand.

The detectives stared at me in silence for a second before Forest took a step towards me. She was invading my personal space, but I didn't move; I wouldn't let her intimidate me. I focused on my breathing and tried to swallow down the lump in my throat.

'Miss Northwood, if you continue to overstep the boundaries, we will be forced to employ someone else. Do I make myself clear?'

The iciness of her tone brought me to my senses. Of course they couldn't tell me what happened, however much I wanted to know. Mumbling an apology, I backed down, taking a step sideways and leaning on the door. I wiped my face surreptitiously, embarrassed at losing control. Forest looked as if she was about to say something else, but Singh headed her off. He indicated for me to follow him out of the room, and the three of us walked to the interview room in silence. I found myself hoping the next interview would be quick and straightforward; the emotional strain was taking its toll on me.

Alan Hunter was a big man, and when I saw him folded into one of the chairs in the interview room, I was worried it might break. He was tall as well as stocky, with close-cut hair that was prematurely greying. I knew he was older than Elisha, but I was pretty sure he was only in his early thirties. He looked wired, his eyes bright and alert, which surprised me, considering what had happened and the fact that he'd allegedly been up late drinking then had slept on the sofa.

'Mr Hunter, I understand this is a very upsetting and distressing experience for you, but it is important that we take your statement about what happened last night. Any information you can give us will help us to find out what happened to Lexi.'

I don't know what happened. Maybe it was an accident.

I translated this for the detectives while Alan sat bolt upright in his chair, flexing his fingers.

'We won't know anything for certain about how she died until the post-mortem is complete,' Forest said. There were dark circles beneath her eyes, and I wondered what time she'd been called out.

Alan scowled but didn't respond, so Forest continued. 'Where were you when Elisha discovered Lexi had died?'

He shrugged, but didn't offer anything further.

'You weren't in bed,' Singh said, trying to draw a response.

His upper lip twitching, Alan tapped his finger to his nose.

'None of your business,' I translated.

'Mr Hunter, we are trying our best to help you. We want this over with as much as you do. If you don't talk to us, it prevents us from finding out what happened.'

At this, Alan spread his hands before replying. *I went out to the pub. I'd had a bit to drink, so I decided to sleep on the sofa. Elisha gets grumpy with me if I wake her up. Happy?* I tried to convey the angry sarcasm of Alan's body language in my tone of voice.

Singh made a note of his response. Forest looked like she'd just bitten a lemon, and I noticed her eyes narrow as she formed her next question.

'Elisha told us that the two of you had an argument when you came home, and she refused to let you upstairs. So, which is it?'

Fine. She said I was too drunk. She was pissed off, so I slept on the sofa.

'Did you go upstairs after she was asleep?'

No! Alan jerked forward on the chair as his anger and frustration poured out. *I know what you're trying to say, but I would never hurt my kids.* His hands moved so fast I could barely keep up, his signing unclear because of the sheer emotion behind his words.

It's her fault! It's Elisha's fault that Lexi is dead. She should have looked after her better. She should have checked on her. She was supposed to check on the children, to make sure they were okay, but she didn't. And now Lexi is dead! And someone has taken my other children away.

Alan's face contorted with rage, but tears flowed down his cheeks. Singh and Forest looked comical, with matching raised eyebrows, taken aback by the sudden outburst. Singh leant over to whisper something in Forest's ear, and Alan glanced at me for a translation.

31

I shrugged. *Can't hear*, I signed to him.

'Why didn't you check on the children yourself?' Singh asked.

When I interpreted this for Alan, he made another jerky movement and I instinctively sat back.

I was drunk and she made me angry. I passed out on the sofa before I even thought about going to check on the kids, he replied eventually. His face fell as he realised he couldn't put the blame on Elisha without assuming equal responsibility.

He looked up, as if something had just occurred to him. *Someone must have come into the house and killed her. A stranger. Why didn't I wake up? How did they get into my house?* I was finding it increasingly difficult to follow his signing – I was tired and he was erratic, the worst possible combination.

'That is a question we wanted to ask you. First it was Elisha's fault, now it's a stranger who just wandered off the street into your house, upstairs and into your children's bedroom? How do you think this stranger got in? None of the doors appeared to have been forced.' Forest couldn't hide the scepticism she felt, and Alan could read it on her face as clearly as I could.

I don't know! I don't know what happened. My little girl is dead. There was a long pause before Alan shook his head. *Don't you understand how hard this is for me? Someone was in my house, and I didn't protect my children. I should have protected my little girl.*

I was still translating his signs when he got up and stormed out of the room, slamming the door so hard I felt the wall behind me shake.

Singh turned to Forest. 'Do you want me to go after him?'

Forest stared blankly at the door for a moment, then shook her head. 'We'll bring him back in once we've got the results of the post-mortem. We can't do any more until we've got some evidence.'

Singh nodded his agreement.

'With his record, we might be safer bringing him in anyway. They'd better find the murder weapon soon,' Forest muttered, glancing over the paperwork in front of her. She looked up and appeared startled when she realised I was still in the room. That wasn't unusual – people get into the swing of a conversation and forget the interpreter is there.

'Thank you, Miss Northwood, you can go. We need to speak to Laura Weston later today, though, if you're available?'

I was surprised she'd want to employ me again, after my earlier outburst, but I flashed her a professional smile and handed over my card with my mobile number on it. 'Of course. Just let me know what time.'

She nodded and I got up to leave. Singh shook my hand and ushered me to the front door.

'We understand this is a difficult situation, such a tragedy in a close-knit community. A word of warning, though. DI Forest won't put up with you speaking to her like that again,' he told me once we were outside. The meaning was clear in his voice: I could keep the job as long as I remembered why I was there. I nodded and thanked him, and he flashed me a smile before heading back into the station.

Standing at the edge of the car park for a moment, I rubbed my eyes and tried to wake myself up enough to drive home. I thought about Jaxon and Kasey, how they were coping with this, and if social services had managed to find a support worker who could sign. Maybe Jaxon had been taken back to Laura's. I couldn't imagine what it would be like for them, too young to understand what had happened to their sister.

I left the shadow of the police station behind me and walked across to my car. It was bright yellow, the only splash of colour on the grey street. Before getting in, I paused, hand on the door, and looked back. My heart picked up its pace as I realised I was being watched from the entrance to the station. I couldn't tell who the silhouette belonged to. For a moment I stood there, hoping it was someone who happened to be leaving behind me, but the figure remained motionless, facing in my direction.

After a moment, the figure pushed open the door, and I realised it was Alan Hunter. He lit a cigarette, not taking his eyes off me. It was probably coincidence that he'd followed me outside, but I shivered nonetheless. Without waiting to see if he was watching me leave, I climbed into the car and got out of there as quickly as I could.

Chapter 4

I got home just before twelve. Luckily, it was a quiet weekend for me, and I had no jobs booked in for the day, although I knew the police would call me when they wanted to interview Laura. I was so desperate to get out of the station, I'd left before they could be specific about when. Kicking off my shoes, I flopped down onto the sofa, my mind whirring. What the hell had happened in that house? I hadn't processed the true horror of the situation, but as I sat there it started to sink in. Alan and Elisha had been the only adults in the house. Could one of them have killed Lexi? I felt sick at the thought.

I sat there for nearly an hour, trying to come to terms with what happened to the little girl my sister loved so much. A sudden noise startled me: my work phone was beeping, and I wished I'd put it on silent. I ignored it, needing coffee first.

I padded through to the kitchen, grabbed a mug and loaded a pod into the coffee machine. As it whirred away

I rubbed my eyes; I knew my involvement with this horrific situation was far from over. At least the money was good. A call-out on a Saturday was one and a half times my normal hourly rate, and every bit I could put towards my credit-card bills was welcome.

If I had to do more of those interviews, I knew I'd be forced to listen to the details about how a little girl died. I wouldn't ever be able to forget the sight of Lexi's body. Bile rose in the back of my throat and I took a gulp of coffee to force it back down. If anything, the scalding liquid made it worse. Think of something else, I repeated in my head. Think of something positive.

Wool and scraps of fabric were scattered over my kitchen table, with most of the space taken up with a half-finished wet felting piece. I didn't finish my textile design degree, and after several years in a controlling relationship, I'd lost touch with the things I loved to do. Recently, I'd been trying to get back into it, to work on my skills again, but it could take me months to finish something. I turned my back on it and went through to the living room.

I'd just settled myself on the sofa with my coffee when my phone rang again. My heart sank until my brain caught up: the ringtone was different, which meant it was my personal mobile. I dug it out of my bag and saw Anna's avatar smiling at me. She and my deaf friends used video calls to chat, but sometimes I wished they didn't have to see my face.

Anna was studying for her PhD at University College London, at the centre for Deafness, Cognition and Learning, and she taught several classes a week. Putting on my best fake smile, I answered, but as soon as Anna's face popped up I knew she'd heard. Her blonde hair was lank and straggly as if she'd been running her hands through it, and her face was tear-stained.

Paige, I have awful news. Lexi's dead. Murdered. Someone killed Lexi! Anna burst into tears again as she signed.

I didn't know what to say. If I admitted that I knew, technically I'd be breaking confidentiality, and I couldn't let that get back to the police. On the other hand, she was my sister, and if I pretended I didn't know, I would be lying to her.

Even now she was twenty-eight, I felt the need to protect Anna. She was still at school when Dad had died and I'd left university to support Mum. Then when Mum got cancer I did everything I could to keep Anna at uni, to stop her repeating my mistakes. By the time I was twenty-two, Mum was gone and we only had each other.

Chastising myself for not being brave enough to tell Anna myself, I nodded. *I know, I heard. It's horrible. Who could do something like that?*

I feel sick, Anna said, and from the colour of her face I could believe it. *I think I should come up and help Laura.*

I know, I know, I signed, doing my best to soothe her. *But she's got her family with her and she probably doesn't want anyone else at the moment. And you've got classes to teach. Keep in touch so she knows you're there for her, but give her space. I can't imagine what she's going through.*

Anna nodded and sniffed, pulling a tissue from somewhere off the screen. *It's just such a shock.*

I know, I know. I didn't know what else I could say. She didn't question where I'd heard the news from, and

I didn't want to give away the fact that I had inside knowledge about the case, so I tried to change the subject. *How are you? Are you busy at the moment?*

She shrugged. *A bit. I can't think about it today. I really think I should come up and spend some time with Laura.*

Why don't you give it a few days, let things sink in a bit? She probably won't want to see anyone right now, anyway.

Anna looked like she was about to protest when the jangling sound of my work phone distracted me. I had forgotten that was what disturbed me earlier.

I'm sorry, I signed. *I have a call about work. I need to go. Love you.*

Anna frowned, suspicion furrowing a line between her eyebrows, but I hung up before she could question me.

'Hello, Paige Northwood.' I tried to sound professional, hoping whoever was calling didn't realise how reluctant I was to engage with work after what I'd witnessed earlier.

'Miss Northwood, it's DC Singh. We'd like to call you back in, if that's okay? We'd like to use the same interpreter whenever possible, to limit the number of people who know the details of the case.'

Despite giving the detectives my card earlier and encouraging them to call me, the last thing I wanted to do now was leave the comfort and familiarity of my flat. The horror of Lexi's death loomed large in my mind, and the knowledge that I'd kept quiet about my connection to the family made me uneasy. I found myself wishing they could find another interpreter, but I couldn't afford to turn down a job at the moment.

'Any interpreter you book will be bound by client confidentiality,' I said, the phrase tripping neatly off my tongue. I'd said it so many times before. People were always worried about sharing their personal information with a third party, and seemed to think I was going to gossip about their hernia or their child's school report down at the Deaf club. Needless to say, I always had better things to talk to my friends about.

'Nevertheless, we'd prefer you when possible,' Singh said smoothly.

I rubbed a hand across my face as I leant on the kitchen table. 'Fine. Is this to take Laura Weston's statement, as you said earlier?'

'Yes, a family liaison officer has been with her this morning. We need to ask her a few questions, and we'd rather not have a family member interpreting.'

I assumed he was talking about Bridget, Laura's mother. I had never met her, but Anna had told me plenty about her. According to my sister, she was besotted with her grandchildren, but could also be immensely overbearing. I pictured how she might have taken over the conversation, answering the officers' questions instead of interpreting Laura's answers. Anna and Bridget didn't get on, and one of the reasons was my sister's regular attempts to help Laura be more independent of her mother.

Singh reeled off the Westons' address, although I already knew it. I'd been there a few times to drop Anna off as Laura had been living there ever since Alan left her for Elisha, when both of the women were pregnant.

'Right. I'll be there in about half an hour.' I dropped my phone onto the table as I hung up, knocking a couple of bills onto the floor.

* * *

As I drove, I tried not to think about what the job would entail if I continued working for the police on this investigation. I'd never worked with CID before, only ever with uniformed officers when a deaf person had their house burgled, and I couldn't say I was enjoying the experience. There was so much pain coming from the family, but I couldn't offer them any reassurance, or help in any practical way other than as a mouthpiece for them. I'd already found myself wondering about the evidence the police had gathered, or what the post-mortem would reveal, but I wouldn't be privy to any of that detail.

The Westons' house couldn't have been more different from the one I had been in just a few hours earlier. It was situated on a new build estate behind a small retail park, where there was a supermarket, various fast-food outlets and a budget chain hotel. The identical houses had identical gardens, all kept neatly, as if the owners were in competition with each other.

I was greeted at the door by Bridget. Even though we hadn't met, I felt I knew a lot about the family. The walls of the hallway were lined with family photographs – Laura and her two brothers, as well as all of Bridget's grandchildren. No photos showed Laura's father, who had never been around for as long as I'd known her.

The frames stretched up the stairs as well, and I knew there would be more in the living room. Closest to the door, I spotted a photo of Laura with her arms around Jaxon and Lexi, the little girl grinning for the camera while her brother scowled. I breathed in sharply as the tragedy of it struck me once again.

Bridget stared at me for a moment after I introduced myself, to the point where I became uncomfortable under her gaze. 'At least it's someone Laura knows,' she said at last. Her face was made-up impeccably, but there was a red puffiness around her eyes from where she'd been crying, and her smile looked forced. Her dark hair was cut in a severe bob, but there were loose strands sticking out at the back, the smallest indicator of the turmoil she must have been going through.

'I'm so sorry, Mrs Weston, I just can't imagine . . .' I tailed off, because all the platitudes sounded meaningless in the face of the horror of what had happened.

Bridget nodded, pressing her lips tightly together to stop them trembling. She waved a manicured hand towards the living room, her bare wrist looking starkly pale. I took the gesture to mean I should go through.

The room had two cream leather sofas taking up most of the wall space, and they were pointed towards a huge flat screen TV. Unlike their counterparts in the Hunter household, the sofas were spotless. As I'd expected, the walls contained more family photos. In the corner there was a space between two photos, with a faded square left on the wall. I assumed a photo of Lexi had hung there; maybe Laura was clinging on to it.

Laura was sitting on one of the sofas, next to a woman I assumed was the family liaison officer. She didn't move when I entered.

DI Forest was there too, standing to one side of the giant screen. She looked decidedly more uncomfortable there than she had in the Hunter house, and I wondered why that was. Maybe she found it easier to deal with bereaved parents if she suspected them of something? I pushed the thought to the back of my mind – it was none of my business who was a suspect and who wasn't. It hadn't even been confirmed how Lexi died, although what I had seen and heard didn't leave me in any doubt that it was violent.

'Miss Northwood.' Forest nodded at me. Turning to Laura, a smile flickered across her face but it was soon gone.

The family liaison officer was probably outranked by Forest – I didn't know the full ins and outs of it all – but I could see she wanted to say something.

'Why don't we sit down, Detective Inspector?' I suggested, hoping that if I could reduce the tension, the interview would be a bit easier. The family liaison officer beamed at me; she had an ally.

Forest looked at the empty sofa as if it might bite her, then perched on the edge of it. I sat next to her, angled so I could see Laura. I took the opportunity to have a proper look at her. She was wearing jeans with a hole in the knee and a hoodie that was at least three sizes too big. Her head was hunched down into the neck of the jumper, as if she wanted to pull the hood up and disappear into it, pretend none of us were there and this hadn't happened.

Laura glanced up at me again and I gave her what I hoped was a reassuring yet sympathetic look. There were dark circles around her eyes, but they weren't as striking as the eyes themselves, which looked dead and glassy. She looked right through me, and I wondered if she was in any state to answer Forest's questions.

'Thank you for allowing us to talk to you, Laura,' Forest began, her voice taking on a gentle quality that surprised me. 'I know this is very hard for you, but we need your help so we can find out exactly what happened to Lexi.'

I interpreted all of this for Laura and she nodded, but didn't add anything.

'Why was Lexi at Alan's house this weekend?'

She goes every other weekend. She and Jaxon both go to their dad's house. Laura's signing was slower than usual, and her body language was muted.

'When did they go over to Alan's?'

Last night. I took them to the Deaf club, and we met Alan there.

'And when should you have picked them up?'

I had to sign this one twice, as Laura kept looking down at her lap, picking at a thread that was coming off the edge of her hoodie. Between answers, she buried her hands in the pocket, seeking comfort and protection.

He brings them back on Monday morning, in time for Jaxon to go to school. Sometimes Sunday night if he's working early on Monday. She's always happy when she comes back. She had a beautiful nature, my little Lexi. I was so lucky to have her. My angel child, with her curly hair. She was always so good. Laura's gaze remained unfocused as she talked about her daughter, and I found myself picturing Lexi the last time I saw her alive, giggling in a soft play ball pool.

The family liaison officer hadn't spoken, and I still hadn't heard her name, but she was watching Laura like a hawk. I wondered how long she'd allow the questioning to go on for, though she might not have had any power to overrule Forest.

'Was anything different about this weekend?' Forest continued, still in that gentle voice.

Laura frowned at me and signed, *What? Different how?*

'Different in what way?' I interpreted.

'Was anything happening at your house, or at Alan's? Were you going out, doing anything special?'

Laura shook her head, then shrugged.

'Where were you last night?'

Here, with Mum. We watched a film.

'Were you both here this morning when the police came round?'

Yeah. Mum was going to do some shopping but she hadn't gone out yet. Laura swallowed and I saw tears well up in her eyes. *Alan was out last night, wasn't he?*

'Yes, for a while,' Forest replied.

Were my children in bed? Who was looking after them? She was more involved in the conversation now, more like the Laura I knew.

'As far as we know, the children were in bed, yes. Elisha Barron took care of the children while he was out.'

Laura pulled a face. *Left them with her.* The last word was signed sharply, her face twisting with a bitterness that surprised me. *He doesn't think about our children.*

'What do you mean, he doesn't think about the children?' I heard the subtle change in Forest's voice as she latched on to something that could be useful.

Laura sank back onto the sofa and shrugged. *I don't want to tell them.*

I interpreted this, and Forest frowned at me, confused.

'Laura doesn't want to tell you what she means,' I explained. 'And now she's saying to me that I shouldn't be telling you that.'

My job is to interpret everything you sign, you know that. It's what I'm here for, I explained to Laura, speaking at the same time so the police officers knew what I was saying. Laura gave a one-shouldered shrug, which I knew was the closest I'd get to an apology.

44

Forest sighed and sat back a little on the sofa. 'You don't have to tell us anything, Laura. You don't have to talk to us at all. But anything you do tell us might help us to find out why your daughter was killed.'

The sign for 'killed' is drawing a finger across the throat, and it brought a vivid picture of Lexi's body into my mind. I felt a shudder of revulsion at having to sign this, but I kept my feelings to myself and got on with my job.

Alan does what he wants, and he doesn't care about the children. Sometimes he changes his plans and tells me he can't see Jaxon and Lexi, then someone tells me he's getting drunk or going away with his girlfriend.

I picked up on the fact that Laura referred to Elisha as 'his girlfriend' rather than naming her. Was she trying to pretend Elisha didn't exist? Was she still bitter that Alan left her for another woman? From the look on her face, Forest had also noted it.

'Do you have arguments, you and Alan?'

Laura gave that one-sided shrug again. *Sometimes.*

'What do you argue about?'

I just told you. Alan doesn't care about the children. He does what he wants. He needs to see his children.

'Okay,' Forest said, making some notes. 'When you argue, does it ever get physical?'

I signed this for Laura and she queried my sign, so I checked with Forest. 'Can you be more specific about physical? Laura isn't sure what you mean and I don't want to paraphrase without it being your words.'

I signed Forest's response, keeping it basic to get the point across: *You and Alan, do you ever hit, kick, slap, punch? Ever fight?*

45

Laura shook her head.

'What about when you were together? Did Alan ever slap or hit you?'

Again, she shook her head, though I was sure I saw some hesitation in her eyes. I couldn't give my interpretation of body language, though. That sort of guesswork was too inaccurate for such a serious situation.

'Two years ago, you reported him for assault, but then withdrew your statement.' Forest didn't frame it as a question, but watched Laura's reaction when I interpreted it for her.

I tried to keep my shock from my face. I didn't know about this, and I wondered if Laura had told Anna.

Laura's face coloured slightly, but she gave her head a quick shake. *No, it was a mistake.*

Forest paused to let Laura continue, but she didn't add to what she'd said.

'Has he ever hit the children?'

This time Laura just stared at me after I relayed the question to her. It was a blank stare, not one of disbelief or fear, just empty. It was as if someone had turned off what little light there was remaining.

She turned to look at Forest, then looked back at me. *Did Alan kill Lexi? Did he kill my little girl?*

'We don't know anything at the moment. I'm sorry, Laura. The post-mortem and evidence from the house will tell us more. We just need to find out about all of the people who might have been involved in her life.'

The look Laura gave Forest showed she was thinking the same thing as me – if they didn't suspect Alan, why ask such a direct question?

It must have been him, or Elisha. They were both in the house, weren't they? One of them did it.

46

'We're still gathering evidence.'

Laura shook her head. *No, if someone was in my house and hurt one of my children, I would know. It was one of them.*

She set her jaw defiantly, and Forest tilted her head as she looked at Laura appraisingly.

'What about Elisha? Have you ever fought with her?'

Laura waved her hand in a dismissive gesture. *I don't know that woman. I don't know her.*

'What do you mean, you don't know her? She and Alan have been together since before Lexi was born. Don't you see her when Alan has the children?'

Wrinkling her nose as if she'd smelt something rotten, Laura explained. *Yes, I see her, but I don't talk to her. She's a slut. She stole him from me. She fucked him when he was mine.*

In the years I'd been an interpreter, I still hadn't got comfortable translating other people's swearing. I did my best to use an appropriate tone of voice for what was being said, to match the client's body language, but I was inwardly mortified at having to repeat certain words in front of the police.

Laura rubbed a hand across her face, and I could see how much this was taking a toll on her.

I don't know what else I can tell you. I don't know what happened. Who could have done this?

She started to cry again, and the family liaison officer put an arm around her. Forest was about to speak when we heard the phone ring in the hallway, and a moment later Bridget came in.

'That was a social worker on the phone. We can go and pick Jaxon up now.'

47

Laura looked at Forest.

'I think we'll call it a day,' the DI said, checking her watch. 'Thank you for speaking to us, Laura, we know it must be very difficult for you. If you think of anything else that might be important, however small, please let us know. I'll leave you my number so you can text.'

Laura nodded her thanks, then left the room with Bridget.

'Paige, can we check your availability for the rest of the week?' Forest asked. 'We need to interview Jaxon, though not for a few days.'

'I don't usually book jobs in for Sundays, so I'm free all day tomorrow.' I pulled out my diary and she noted down the times when I would be available for the rest of the week. I had very few appointments booked in, and felt my face grow warm with embarrassment. Going freelance hadn't been as easy as I'd expected.

'Good. It's likely that we'll need you.'

'If sessions are going to be more than an hour, you really should book a second interpreter. Either that, or plan in rest breaks.' I wanted the job, but I also didn't want to be overworking myself, or letting them work me into the ground.

'That's fine, we can arrange that.'

I didn't know which option DI Forest meant, but by that point I didn't care. If I did well, there was a good chance I'd get regular police jobs in future. The hours wouldn't be sociable, but my work had been far from regular since I went freelance. I had to get the work wherever I could. There was still a voice in the back of my mind telling me I couldn't go it alone, that I should go back to the agencies, but I did my best to ignore it. I knew who'd put that voice there, and it was about time I got rid of it in the same way I'd got rid of him.

Nodding a quick goodbye to Forest and the family liaison officer, whose name I never learned, I headed back to my car and home again for the second time that day.

16 hours before the murder

I don't see why he should continue to have them every other weekend, Bridget said as Laura packed the children's bags.

It's what we agreed, Laura replied.

But if you're going to tell the court that you're worried about his care of the children, how will it look if you're still letting him look after them on a regular basis?

Laura put down the socks she was balling up and glared at her mother. *If I don't let him see the kids, he'll use that against me in court. And anyway, you're the one who's worried about his parenting, not me.*

Bridget pursed her lips and didn't respond. When she realised Laura wasn't going to pay any attention to her, she went downstairs. Laura sat down on the bed and sighed, double checking the clothes she'd packed for Jaxon and Lexi. She'd told Alan he should keep some clothes for them at his house, but he said it was easiest if she packed them everything they needed and he sent it back on Monday. Of course, God forbid he or Elisha should have to deal with a little extra washing, or spend any money on his children. She bit her lip as tears welled up in her eyes.

The baby monitor on the side vibrated and flashed, so she went through to Lexi's room to see the little girl wide awake and smiling. Laura picked her daughter up and held her close, kissing her curly head until she began to wriggle, then took her downstairs.

In the living room, Laura got some toys out and put Lexi on the floor. Bridget stood in the doorway with her arms folded for a moment, before signing, *It'll be time for her lunch soon.*

Laura took a deep breath and forced a smile onto her face. *I know, Mum.*

Just don't let her get too involved with playing, that's all. She'll get upset if you take her away from her toys before she's ready.

If she's hungry she'll be fine.

I've told you before, you can't let her dictate when she's going to eat all the time, Bridget said, coming into the room and moving a glass that Laura had left on the coffee table. *You need to get her into a routine.*

Laura didn't reply. She knew there was no point arguing with her mum. Bridget had raised three kids herself, so had plenty of experience, she knew this, but she also wished her mum would let her get on with parenting in her own way. Her brothers lived far enough away that they only saw each other every few months, and she often envied them their freedom. Not for the first time, Laura told herself it was time to move out. She could go on the waiting list for a council house, but while she was living with her mum there was no chance she'd get anything, and she couldn't face the idea of making herself homeless with two kids. Unless she got a job, she wouldn't be able to afford to rent privately, even in the poorest areas of Scunthorpe. Finding a job that was accessible as a BSL user wasn't easy, and last time she'd worked none of her colleagues could communicate with her, which had made her achingly lonely.

She watched Bridget playing with Lexi for a moment, talking to her but not signing. Laura had given up using hearing aids when she was sixteen and started sixth form at the school for the deaf, and had never expected her children to wear them: another parenting decision Bridget constantly picked at. Both Jaxon and Lexi were profoundly deaf, and BSL was her chosen mode of communication with them. She'd stood her ground on this one, though she hadn't succeeded in getting Jaxon into a school for the deaf yet. That was her next battle to fight with her mother, but she didn't have the energy for too many arguments at once.

Once she'd got Lexi into her high chair and was feeding her, Bridget started again. Laura knew her mum liked to wait until she couldn't get away.

We need to start taking this seriously, Laura. What if Alan contests what you're saying in court? What if he turns it around and tries to get custody himself? There was fear in Bridget's eyes as she signed this.

He wouldn't do that, he can't look after them the whole time.

Of course he can't, but you can't trust him, Laura! He's a dangerous man, you know that. It's not safe to let him have the children!

Laura stared at her mum. *Calm down, he's not going to do anything that puts them at risk.*

How do you know that? Everyone said that about your aunt and uncle, but look what happened!

Laura carried on feeding Lexi and let Bridget rant. She'd been bringing up her aunt and uncle and their failure as parents more often recently. It was her fault, for telling Bridget about that conversation she'd had with Anna. She wondered how much her mum had been dwelling on it.

The two situations were completely different though; her aunt and uncle were both alcoholics who neglected their child. Alan had his issues, she knew that, but he wasn't a danger to their kids. Part of her still cared for him, and she knew if he wanted her back she'd go. Oh, she'd hesitate for a while, telling him things had to change and he couldn't just expect her to come running, but in the end she'd give in.

You're not paying attention to anything I say, are you? Bridget stood up and looked down on Laura where she sat at the table. *I'm going to call your solicitor, we need to move things forward.*

No! Laura stood up and grabbed Bridget's hand as she reached for the phone. Lexi looked up at them both from the high chair, a piece of apple clutched in her little fist.

Why not? What aren't you telling me?

I don't want to talk about this now, Mum, Laura replied, looking at Lexi.

Bridget glared at her. *Laura.*

Fine. I'm going to hire an interpreter for my solicitor's appointments. I want to go on my own next time.

Why? Bridget frowned. *You want to shut me out, after everything I've done for you?*

Laura sighed. *You know that's not true. But I'm an adult, I need to do this for myself. You and the solicitor talk to each other and you don't explain everything to me. I should be the one making the decisions, but you're doing it without consulting me.*

I have never done such a thing! I've always taken your wishes into account . . .

That's the point, Laura interrupted. *Taking my wishes into account isn't good enough, you're not letting me be independent and do this for myself! I don't even know if I want full custody any more. Alan's not a bad father. I might put a stop to the whole thing.*

Bridget stared at her for a moment, her lips pursed, then she took a step back and held up her hands. *Fine. Fine. Do it all yourself, if you don't want my help I won't bother. I just hope you don't end up regretting it.*

She flounced out of the kitchen before Laura had a chance to respond.

Chapter 5

Sunday 4th February

The next day, I was back in the same interview room to finish taking Alan's statement. I was starting to find the drab walls oppressive and wondered if they were deliberately designed to make the occupants uncomfortable.

Being back in the police station unearthed some memories I'd kept buried for many years. I had rarely had any involvement with the police before Lexi's death. The first time I'd been inside a police station was after the death of a girl I knew. Caitlin was only eight when she died on an outing with a large group from the Deaf club. At the time I'd been one of the only hearing people present, so I found myself acting as an interpreter until they could find someone qualified. After the initial details were clarified, the case took weeks to get going because of the struggle to get interpreters. That experience was the reason I ended up going freelance. Sometimes social workers and the police needed two or three weeks' notice to book a BSL interpreter, and crises can't wait that long. Going freelance meant I could be on call for those services, and my intention was to try and ensure nobody had to wait that long to have their voice heard. If I'd told Forest my connection to this family and she'd sent me away, they'd probably still be waiting to take those first statements – I told myself this was why I'd kept it from the detectives, nothing to do with my own burning desire to know what had happened.

I had never intended for interpreting to be my career; I fell into it as a way to earn money after Dad died, to make sure Anna could go to uni, but I always intended to finish my own textile design degree. That never happened, and when I made the decision to break away from an agency and go it alone, I accepted that it never would. I regularly found myself frustrated by the lack of support I could offer my clients. I acted as a mouthpiece for them, but I hadn't yet succeeded in creating greater deaf awareness amongst the services they used.

Pulling myself back to the present, I focused on the interview ahead. Alan Hunter was there to finish giving his statement, and I'd been provisionally booked by the police for the following three days. I knew I had to remain professional, but I was exhausted after broken sleep plus another three emotionally draining calls from my sister.

Whenever I had seen Alan before, he'd tended to swagger and make his presence known. The change in him was startling: he was hunched over the table in the interview room as if he were trying to curl up into a ball. His eyes were red, his hair was a mess and his skin looked yellow with fatigue. Part of me felt sympathy for him, then it struck me that he was most likely a suspect. Forest and Singh both looked very serious, and something about the atmosphere felt different from when they took the first half of his statement yesterday morning. Wondering what they might have discovered since then, a jolt of revulsion coursed through me.

'Mr Hunter, we want to talk to you about the night of Friday the second of February, the night your daughter, Lexi, was killed.' Forest's face was impassive as she began. 'Can you tell me what happened that night?'

Alan watched me with dead eyes as I translated the question, then screwed his face up and looked down at his hands. He shrugged.

'We need you to tell us what happened that night,' Forest repeated.

Alan didn't look up, so I waved to attract his attention, and he finally looked at me.

I don't know what happened, he eventually responded. *Someone came into my house and hurt Lexi. I don't know why.*

'Start at the beginning. Elisha told us you went out to the pub, is that correct?'

He nodded. *I went back out after I picked up the kids at the Deaf club. I was there with some friends. We had a few drinks, talked about football. That's all.*

'Did you see anything strange during the evening on Friday? Anyone hanging around your house who shouldn't have been there?'

I thought Alan was about to sign something in response, but he shook his head.

'Have you had any concerns about people around your house on any other night, anyone watching your children or behaving strangely?'

Again, he seemed to think for a moment before shaking his head.

'Is there any reason for you to believe someone else had been in your house on Friday night?' Singh asked, his smooth, deep voice a complete contrast to Forest's clipped tones. They were back to that good cop, bad cop thing again; I'd thought it only happened in films. Singh still looked pretty severe though, and it was the body language and facial expression that would give Alan the impression he needed.

No, Alan replied with a frown. *What do you mean?*

'You said someone must have come into your house and killed Lexi. Did you see anyone in your house? Was there anything that made you think someone had been there?'

Like what? He looked wary as he processed Singh's question.

'Had anything been moved? Had a window been broken, or a lock forced?' Forest asked, her eyes boring into him. I knew the police would have found any evidence of a break in. Were they asking Alan about it to try to catch him in a lie? I caught my breath at the thought.

I don't think so, he replied, slowly shaking his head. *But it must have been a stranger.*

'Why do you say that?' Forest asked, her voice razor-sharp.

Alan stared at her for a moment. *It wasn't me. It wasn't Elisha.*

'So if it wasn't you, or Elisha, and there was no sign of a break in, how did this mysterious person get into your house?'

There was a long pause after I interpreted this question, as the meaning behind it sank in. Alan started to shake his head, slowly at first but quickly gathering speed, then he put his face into his hands and began to sob. I raised my eyebrows at Forest.

The detectives gave Alan a minute or two to compose himself before they continued.

'What upset you so much?' Singh asked once Alan had blown his nose and was looking at them again.

Hunter fidgeted for a moment before responding. *I was thinking about Lexi. I was thinking about how someone came into my house and killed my little girl, and I didn't even wake up. Someone took her life away. I'm never going to hold her or play with her again. Any father would be upset. Lexi was my little girl, and I blame myself for what happened.*

Singh's face displayed a sympathetic smile. 'Of course, we understand this is very distressing for you. Still, we need you to answer our questions.'

Okay.

'Is there anyone you suspect might have hurt Lexi?'

No. I don't know anyone who would do this.

'Have you recently had any arguments or disagreements with anyone? Someone who might want to take revenge?'

Alan's jaw tensed, but he shook his head.

'Elisha was upstairs at the time Lexi was killed.' Forest sat back in her chair and folded her arms, this statement more powerful than any question she had asked.

There was a long pause before Alan responded. *I don't know what you're trying to say. Elisha would never hurt Lexi. She's so upset, she can't eat or sleep. She blames herself, too. She blames herself for not waking up when there was someone in our house. Elisha loved Lexi, she would never do anything to hurt her.* As he signed this, he became more agitated, his face reddening.

Forest watched him for a moment, but he didn't sign anything else, lapsing into a stubborn silence to match hers. After an uncomfortable length of time, she nodded and moved on to the next question.

'When Elisha came down to tell you what had happened to Lexi, did you go upstairs to see for yourself?'

Alan nodded. *I didn't believe her at first. I thought maybe she was wrong, Lexi was just sleeping.* He hung his head.

'And when you knew your daughter had been killed, did you have any immediate thought about what might have happened, or who might have done it?'

There was a long pause. Hunter looked shifty, his right knee bouncing up and down as he looked anywhere but at me or the two detectives.

Should I have a lawyer here with me?

'You're not under arrest, Mr Hunter. We just need to make sure you've given us your full statement about Friday night.'

Does that mean I can go? I've finished telling you what I know.

Forest screwed up her mouth into a grimace, but nodded. 'You can leave whenever you want. If you think of anything else, anything at all about that night, please let us know.'

Alan asked again for clarification that he could leave, then got up and walked out before anyone could say another word.

Before I left the station, DI Forest confirmed that they wanted me to be on call for the rest of the week, in case they needed to conduct more interviews. Tomorrow, they were going to have to interview Jaxon, and I didn't relish that task. How could I ask a little boy if he'd seen who killed his sister?

I had the rest of the day free, and once Forest signed my time sheet I headed home. Just under half an hour later, I pulled up outside my flat. I was hoping I could manage to have the rest of the day to myself, but as soon as I got out of the car I realised that wasn't going to happen. Anna was sitting on the doorstep. She got up as soon as she saw me walking up the path, and I noticed the large bag next to her.

Why didn't you tell me you were interpreting for the police?

I didn't know what I could say. *You know I have to keep my work confidential.*

Anna frowned but didn't reply. I raised my eyebrows, looking pointedly at the bag. She shrugged, answering the question I didn't even need to ask.

I'm moving in.

Chapter 6

It didn't take Anna long to get settled in my spare room; my flat was essentially her second home. The scant amount I'd inherited from our parents had just about covered the deposit for it. When my last disastrous relationship had imploded, leaving me with virtually nothing, I thanked any god that was listening that I'd managed to keep the flat in my name.

After Mum's cancer left us parentless, I could have moved away, or gone back to university, but something held me back. I told myself I wanted to keep family roots in North Lincolnshire, in case Anna ever wanted to move back from London, but I think I was scared. While I'd always had more than my fair share of responsibility in our family, I'd found myself supporting Mum and Anna financially when Dad died. I signed up as an unqualified interpreter to make sure we had some money coming in, then did my qualifications at weekends. Without our parents, I didn't want to feel like Anna and I would become rootless, and I felt a huge weight of responsibility towards her. She carried on her studies in London, and I made sure she had a home to come back to each holiday. It was never the same as it had been before Dad died, but I worked hard to keep us from crumbling.

Can we go for a walk? she asked me once she'd unpacked her bag. *I need some fresh air.*

I agreed, and the two of us bundled ourselves up in coats and scarves and went out into the chilly afternoon air. North Lincolnshire is a mostly rural county, and I'd chosen to buy a flat in one of the villages outside Scunthorpe. It was only a ten-minute drive from the industrial town, but the difference in the landscape was striking. Here, it would only take us a couple of minutes of walking before we found ourselves in open fields, stretching away as far as the eye could see.

The cloudless sky was a crisp, pale blue and our breath fogged in front of us as we walked through quiet residential streets towards the church, until we turned down a lane. The houses soon petered out, leaving a farm to our left and open fields to our right. We hadn't gone far, but we'd soon left most of the sights and sounds of the village behind us. In a few hours, the stargazing conditions would be perfect, with clear skies and very little light pollution. As it was, the two of us walked without chatting for another five minutes, until we reached the community sports field.

You knew before I called you yesterday, didn't you? Anna asked when we finally stopped.

I nodded and leaned back against the gate. *I gave my details to the police when I went freelance. They called me out to the house first thing yesterday morning.*

Anna squeezed her eyes shut for a moment, and a tear

rolled down her cheek. She looked out over the field for a couple of minutes, where a small group of boys was playing football.

Why didn't you tell me? You should have called as soon as you knew. Anna was always direct, and I should have expected her reaction.

Because I'm a coward, I admitted. *I knew how devastated you would be, and I didn't want to be the person who made your heart break.*

That's crap, Paige. I found out through Facebook. Do you have any idea how horrible it is to get news like that via social media?

I hung my head, ashamed of myself for putting my sister through that. *I'm so sorry.*

She nodded, and I knew I was forgiven. Anna wasn't the sort to bear a grudge, and there were far greater things to worry about.

I only talked to Laura on Friday. She called me while she was at soft play with Lexi. Then just a few hours later . . . Anna shuddered and didn't finish the thought.

We stood next to each other for a moment, lost in our own thoughts, until she turned, squared her shoulders and looked me in the eye.

What's happening now? Have they arrested anyone?

Nothing like that. They haven't even released the results of the post-mortem yet. It could have been anyone. I scuffed my toe in the gravel by the gate and stifled a yawn. I was shattered, emotionally wrung out.

Why won't they say what's happened? You can't pretend it was anything other than murder, not like with Caitlin.

I gave my head the smallest of shakes; I wasn't prepared to talk about Caitlin.

When did you last see her? Anna asked me. For a moment I didn't realise she was talking about Lexi, but then I noticed she had her keys in her hand. The keyring had a photo inside it. Lexi, with her thick dark curls framing her face, giggling. Her natural state of being.

The time you took her to soft play, just before Christmas.

Anna nodded. *She loved it there. Whenever I looked after her, I'd take her there while Laura spent time with Jaxon. There was nothing she didn't enjoy. Lexi was the happiest child I've ever known. Completely the opposite of her brother.*

I nodded, remembering the way Lexi giggled as she climbed and rolled, Anna lifting her up and tickling her, or burying her under the ball pool. She'd slept all the way home, exhausted by all the fun she'd been having. There wasn't a single grump or grizzle out of her the whole day.

I hope the police find who did this, she said. She stepped away from the fence and stared at me, the same determined stare I remembered from when we were children and she had a challenge ahead of her. I started walking again, feeling the need to move.

I just can't comprehend how something like this could happen. Why would someone kill Lexi? Anna asked, as if I were keeping the answer from her, but I had asked myself the same question dozens of times.

An image floated through my mind of a cuddly bear with a bloodstained foot. There were too many unanswered questions, and I didn't know what to think. I wanted to believe that this was something that couldn't have been prevented, a tragic accident, but that wasn't possible. Both Alan and Elisha seemed evasive. Were they trying to cover something up, hoping they wouldn't be

held responsible? If they were the only people in the house
. . . I couldn't bring myself to finish the thought.

Anna had always been good at picking up on my
emotions, and I knew she could see the turmoil going on
behind my eyes. She kept pace with me, putting an arm
around me, and we walked like that for a while. I knew
she'd be thinking the same things as me, but it was too
much to process.

When we were nearly back at the flat, she stopped me
and turned me to face her.

What do you know? she asked, her eyes searching my
face for information.

I shook my head. *I can't tell you about it, you know
that.*

Please, Paige. I have to know what happened.

*You don't. It won't make it any better. Anyway, it's
confidential. I have to be professional about this.*

I won't tell anyone, she implored. *Please.*

I shook my head. *No.*

She looked like she was going to ask again, but thought
better of it. I was glad; I was stressed enough as it was. If
I was going to be involved in the investigation, I hoped it
moved quickly. There was only so much of it I could take.

For the rest of the day, Anna and I caught up, talking
about anything we could think of other than Lexi. Her
ghost was there with us, in the room, but we managed
to avoid the subject until the evening, when we were
hopping around Netflix and sharing a bottle of Pinot
Grigio.

There are loads of rumours flying around online, Anna
told me, scrolling through her phone.

66

What about?

Lexi. Who might have done it; why they did it.

I frowned at her. *Facebook isn't exactly the most reliable source of information, is it?*

She shrugged. *It's still interesting to know what people are saying. I can't get information from anywhere else*, she said pointedly, but I didn't take the bait. She'd piqued my interest, though, and I tried peering over her shoulder, then gave up and opened my laptop so we could have a better look.

Someone, presumably one of Laura's friends, had set up a page entitled 'RIP Lexi', where people had been leaving messages for Laura and her family, offering their sympathy and expressing outrage. It was all very banal, like when there's a terrorist attack or a natural disaster and everyone rushes to write 'Praying for Paris' as their status, as if it will send mystical healing energy across the sea to whichever city's afflicted.

Anna logged into her account, because it was her friends who were discussing it rather than mine, and I couldn't access their pages. Clicking on her notifications, she pointed out that someone had added her to a group called 'JFL'. I told her to click on it, intrigued.

It was a secret group. The description read 'Justice for Lexi. The police need to know the truth about Alan Hunter and lock him up.' Well, at least it was unambiguous. I wondered who set it up, because there was a good chance they could be done for libel, by the looks of what people were saying.

There was a real mix of posts, most of which fell into that same meaningless sympathy category, then a few attention seekers, and some who seemed to think of themselves as private investigators. A few all caps rants were thrown into the mix:

ALAN HUNTER IS A DRUGGIE AND SELLS DRUGS TO KIDS HE SHULD NOT BE ALOUD TO LOOK AFTER KIDS.

This is ridiculous, I told Anna, and she nodded but carried on scrolling.

I skimmed the posts as she scrolled. Most were concerned with Alan's drug peddling. Everyone in our community knew he was a minor dealer, so I was sure the police must have already known something about it. Maybe evidence would come to light during this investigation that they couldn't ignore.

I don't think there's really anything useful on here, I told her, but she shook her head.

Look at this one. She pointed to the screen.

It was a post from someone called MB – I had no idea who it was, but I was sure they must have been connected to the family in some way, from what they'd written. I read the post through a couple of times.

'The paper has more information about how Lexi died. The police need to connect the dots with Alan Hunter's previous arrests.'

That was it. Just two sentences, but they left me with far more questions. Clearly, this person had intended to be cryptic, but he or she had no replies to their post, so either people were ignoring it or they didn't know what it meant.

Do you have the local paper? Anna asked.

No, but we should be able to read the story online. I'd given up my pretence that I wasn't interested beyond my professional connection to the case.

Did you know Alan had ever been arrested? Anna asked.

I remembered what Forest had said about Alan having a record.

Not before this happened, I told her, opening a new browser window and pulling up the site for our local paper. It didn't take long to find the stories about Lexi, as it had been on the local news the night before and all the front pages that morning. Something that shocking wouldn't be ignored by the media.

Poring over the most recent article, it didn't take me long to find exactly what MB had been talking about in that mysterious post.

'An unnamed source has reported that Lexi suffered blunt force trauma from a heavy object, some time late Friday night or in the early hours of Saturday morning. Witnesses are being questioned, although no arrests have been made at this time.'

Blunt force trauma? You said they didn't know how she died. Anna gave me a hurt look, as if I'd deliberately lied to her.

I don't know anything about her cause of death, I insisted. *I didn't think they had the post-mortem results yet.* I'd seen the blood all over Elisha and the teddy bear, as well as a brief glimpse of Lexi herself, but there was no way I was going to tell Anna about it. She didn't need that image in her head any more than I did.

What has this article got to do with Alan? What did that post mean about his previous arrests? Laura never told me Alan had been in trouble with the police, even after he left her for Elisha.

Anna pulled up the secret group again, looking for MB's

post, but she couldn't find it. I took the laptop from her and scrolled up and down the page a few times, wondering if it had been bumped down by people commenting on other posts, but it definitely wasn't there.

Where did the post go?

I shrugged. *Maybe they deleted it, or whoever the group admin is got rid of it?* I did a quick search for the screen name, but no profiles came up. What could have happened in the space of a few minutes to make someone delete their post?

It's gone.

It can't have just gone. Anna grabbed the laptop and searched again, but came up with nothing.

Maybe it was deleted because it was libellous?

Anna gave me a dismissive wave of her hand. *How can we find out why Alan was arrested before?*

Thank God for the internet. I didn't fancy traipsing down to the library and looking through old copies of the paper, or whatever it was people used to do before we had this handy worldwide database of cat pictures and porn.

To begin with, we searched for his name, but that brought up far too many results for us to wade through. There were an awful lot of people called Alan Hunter in the world – hundreds on Facebook, at first glance. So we added further search terms to narrow it down: Alan Hunter deaf Scunthorpe. We spent the next ten minutes trawling through articles about deaf football – it seemed Alan was a pretty good player until he suffered an injury.

Trying again, we searched for 'Alan Hunter deaf Scunthorpe arrested' and hit the jackpot. It was only a small article, from three years earlier, but the gist was clear: Alan was suspected of attacking a man in the street, a man who allegedly owed him money. How had this man been attacked? He'd been clubbed with a heavy object.

A cold feeling washed over me as I thought about the implications of what we'd read, and from the look on Anna's face I could tell she was thinking the same thing. Clearly, this was exactly the connection MB wanted the police to make. Alan's daughter probably died after being hit with a heavy object. Alan had a history of attacking people and bludgeoning them. I couldn't find out if Alan was charged and spent any time in jail, as the article didn't specify, so I wondered if he was released. Maybe that was why MB's post was taken down, because Alan wasn't actually convicted? So was this MB person just a troublemaker, another of the people convinced Alan must have killed Lexi, or did they know something about that night?

Anna tried a few more times to get information out of me about the case, but I stood my ground. It wasn't just because I needed to keep things confidential; I didn't think it would do Anna any good to know what I'd seen and heard. She had been here less than a day, and I was already worried about how far she wanted to involve herself and interfere. I knew I was already in too deep, but I hoped by keeping Anna close I could prevent her going the same way.

15 hours before the murder

Alan finished work on the lorry's tyre and checked his watch. Carefully putting his tools away, he wandered down the road outside the yard before he lit his cigarette. Whatever others might think of him, he wouldn't break his employer's safety rules by smoking that close to the petrol tanks.

It was Friday, which meant he'd have the kids for the weekend. He really needed to speak to Laura and change the arrangement, they were bloody hard work. Surely one weekend in three would be enough? He loved his children, of course, but sometimes he wanted a bit of time without them. Good job Elisha was good with kids.

He stubbed out his cigarette and was about to walk back up the road to the haulage yard where he worked when a black Fiesta pulled up next to him. It had a large spoiler on the back, black wheel trims and yellow filters over the headlights, none of which hid the fact that the car had seen better days.

Rick Lombard wound down the window and Alan looked towards his workplace, debating whether to ignore him or have a conversation.

What are you doing here? he asked at last, sauntering closer to the car but staying far enough away that if anyone asked, he could say the driver was lost and asking for directions.

I've got the stuff.

And you thought you should come to my workplace and tell me that? Alan clenched his jaw, holding in his anger.

You never answer your phone, Lombard replied with a shrug.

Alan shook his head and started to walk away, but Lombard got out of the car and caught up to him. Feeling a hand on his shoulder, Alan spun around and glared at the other man, who was significantly shorter than he was.

Get your fucking hand off me, he signed, knocking Lombard's hand away in the process.

Don't think you can threaten me, Hunter. I don't give a shit about your reputation. We had an arrangement, and I came here to tell you I've done my side of the deal.

The two men stared each other out for a moment, until Alan took a step back. *We're not going to have a problem, are we?* He looked Lombard up and down, his nostrils flaring. He'd kept out of trouble recently, but his fingers were itching for a fight. He'd made a deal with the slippery bastard but he didn't like him, so he'd be more than happy to give him a kicking.

After a moment of tension, Lombard gave a casual

shrug. *No, no problem. Let me know when you're ready to look it over.*

He turned and walked off, kicking up gravel as he went. Alan watched him leave and wondered if he was going to regret making this deal.

Chapter 7

Monday 5th February

I was looking after two little girls, and I left them playing nicely in my living room while I went to the kitchen to get them some snacks. Before I could open the cupboard, a terrible scream brought me rushing back through to see a faceless figure standing over them both, a hammer raised above their heads. I watched in horror as the two girls scratched and kicked their attacker, but I couldn't move or make a sound to stop it.

When my alarm went off I sat bolt upright, sweat dripping off me despite the frost on my window. I rolled over to turn it off, and knocked a glass of water off my bedside table. Swearing, I jumped out of bed and rescued my phone charger from the rapidly spreading puddle. As the nightmare faded, I recognised the two girls for who they were: Lexi and Caitlin.

I checked my work phone, but there were no new calls or messages. Still, I had a busy day ahead of me – Forest had booked me for Jaxon's interview, followed by a further chat with Laura. After that, I thought, I'd need about twelve hours' sleep, though I expected I'd get more questions from Anna later. When she'd turned up, I thought she would add to my problems, but it had been nice to have some company last night. I wasn't sure I wanted her getting involved, but some of the things we'd found out online had set my brain ticking.

Dragging myself to the bathroom, I frowned at the tiny lines forming at the edges of my eyes. I was only thirty, but I was sure I'd gained more wrinkles in the last six months than was natural. I really needed a break, but that wouldn't happen until Lexi's case was solved. Forest warned me that they should have the results of the post-mortem by this morning, so they would be telling Laura how Lexi died. How had the local paper got hold of that information so soon? A shiver ran down my spine. Thinking of Laura, I checked my watch and realised I needed to get a move on.

Can I come with you? Anna was standing in the hallway, dressed and ready to go.

I sighed, exasperated. *You can't. You know you can't.*

Please, Paige. I'm her friend who happens to be visiting. That's all.

It's Jaxon's interview first. I can't just bring you with me.

Her face fell. *She won't be in the interview, will she? Can't I just wait with her, keep her company? I promise I won't do anything to mess up your job.*

Chewing my bottom lip, I thought about it. It would be good for Laura to have a friend there.

Fine. This is just about you being Laura's friend, though. Okay?

Of course!

I hated myself for thinking about my reputation at a time like that, but it was too important not to mention. I knew Anna was smart enough not to do anything to jeopardise my career, but I had to make sure. It might be better if we didn't tell the police she was my sister, but I didn't know how long I could hide my connection to the family.

I'd been given the address of a different building in town, which the police used when interviewing children and other vulnerable witnesses, and I was jittery by the time we arrived. Whilst I'd spent a little time with Lexi, I didn't really know Jaxon, and I was used to interpreting for adults. I'd seen him a few times but he'd never acknowledged that he recognised me. Would he respond to me?

DC Singh met us at the door and I introduced Anna by her first name only, explaining that she was Laura's friend and was going to keep her company while Jaxon was interviewed. He nodded his agreement and led us through to a room where Laura was sitting, desperately trying to get her son's attention.

When Laura saw Anna, her face lit up, and the two of them hugged for a long time. Anna sat down to talk to her friend, so Singh took me aside.

'The need for interpreting makes this interview a little complicated. Normally, when we interview children, the officer conducting the interview will be in one room with the child and usually with a social work officer, with a notetaker observing in an adjoining room. We decided it was best to use someone Jaxon is familiar with for communication, and for you to be in the adjoining room, to support the notetaker by interpreting what Jaxon and the communicator are signing. Is that okay?'

I tried to wrap my head around what he'd said. 'So I'll be watching, but I won't be in the room?'

'Yes.'

'Who's communicating for Jaxon?'

Singh nodded his head at the doorway, through which I could see Forest talking to a woman with frizzy hair. 'That's Hannah Lachlan. She's a communication support worker, and she works with Jaxon at school.'

I watched as the woman's glance darted nervously around her, and I wondered if she'd drawn the short straw. I understood their reasoning for using someone Jaxon already knew, and if I was honest, I felt a bit relieved. I had no idea how Jaxon would respond to me.

Singh led me through to a room with a large window overlooking an interview room. The other room was set up with comfy chairs and a colourful playmat with toy cars on it, as well as a stack of paper next to pots of pencils and crayons. The window fascinated me, knowing that we could see whoever was in the next room, but they couldn't see us.

Hannah Lachlan also followed us in, and Singh introduced us. A moment later we saw a door open in the other room, and DI Forest led Laura and Jaxon inside.

'Miss Weston is going to help Jaxon to settle in the room first, before you go in, Mrs Lachlan,' Singh murmured to us. I wondered if sound could pass through the mirrored glass, or if he was just being cautious.

The communication support worker chewed her lip and nodded. 'I hope he's okay. Just thinking about what he might have seen . . .' She shivered and her voice tailed off. Tension radiated off her.

'Have you worked with him long?' I asked, curious, but also hoping to relax her by getting her talking.

She nodded. 'About eighteen months now. He's in a mainstream school, so he needs someone to sign for him all the time. We're doing our best for him.' Hannah Lachlan spoke quickly, gabbling and stumbling over her words. She bit her lip again, as if conscious that she shouldn't say more than was professional.

Singh cleared his throat, then flashed a smile at Hannah Lachlan before escorting her into the next room. At the same time, another woman entered the room I was in and introduced herself as the notetaker. So many people required to take a statement from one six-year-old boy. I hoped it was useful, but I also hoped for Jaxon's sake that he'd been fast asleep and hadn't witnessed his sister's murder.

As I watched Laura leave her son with DI Forest and Hannah Lachlan, Singh joined me again. I was surprised that she was the one conducting the interview, as she was far less approachable than the DC, but she was a higher rank.

'Jaxon, we want to ask you some questions about Friday night, when your sister Lexi was hurt.'

I watched Hannah Lachlan try to get Jaxon's attention, but he was looking around the room at the cars. She tried waving, and tapping his arm, but he stubbornly refused to look at her until she moved to kneel in front of him, and even then his eyes slid away from her. She simplified her signing to get the message across, and I interpreted exactly what she had signed for the notetaker.

At first, Jaxon didn't respond. He grabbed some of the crayons and began to scribble on one of the pieces of paper, holding four crayons together to make a multi-coloured scrawl. He got off the sofa and knelt in front of the table, bending low over the piece of paper. Hannah Lachlan tapped him and signed the question again, shooting a worried look towards DS Forest.

Jaxon slammed the crayons down on the table. *I sleep. Lexi sleep. Kasey sleep. Lexi head all blood.*

I interpreted this word for word for the notetaker, instead of converting it into a full sentence. BSL has a very different grammatical structure from English, and the meaning of a sign can change depending on how it's signed or the facial expression used. When interpreting, you use all of the information available to translate it into standard English, exactly as you would if you were interpreting a spoken language. In this case, however, I didn't want to be accused of adding to the meaning of Jaxon's statement. While I did this, Hannah Lachlan told Forest what he'd said.

'Was there anyone else in the room?' Forest asked.

I woke up. Lexi on bed all blood. Elisha told me stay there, go tell Daddy.

'Did Elisha tell Daddy, or you?'

Jaxon picked up a black crayon and scribbled with it, pressing so hard it snapped in his hand, then he threw it down on the floor. *Elisha. Told. Daddy.* He signed this without looking up, his signs jerky, with pauses in between. Suddenly, he swept all the paper and the pots of crayons onto the floor, making Forest and Hannah Lachlan jump.

Jaxon climbed onto the sofa, standing up on it and jumping up and down. Hannah Lachlan got up and took his hand, encouraging him to sit down again, which he did, kicking his heels on the base of the sofa.

'Jaxon, was anyone else in the room? Did you see any other person in your bedroom?'

He sat still for a moment, and signed very clearly. *Bad man killed my sister Lexi.*

Forest leant forward slightly. 'Did you see a bad man?'

Jaxon shook his head, and I heard Singh exhale as if he'd been holding his breath. *Grandma said.*

There was a pause, but he didn't sign anything else.

'What did Grandma say?' Forest asked.

Grandma told me bad man. Bad man killed my sister Lexi. Jaxon looked at Forest as he signed this, then turned to the car mat, pushing his communication support worker out of the way to get to it. He began to play with the cars, and refused to look around when Hannah Lachlan tried to get his attention again.

Picking up a car, he pretended to drive it around the mat, then across the floor towards Forest. He drove it over Forest's feet, up one of her shins, across her knees then back down to the floor, then clambered onto the sofa again. He ran the toy car along the back of the sofa, then stood on the cushion and traced a pattern up the wall with it. Hannah Lachlan moved forward to try and get him down again, but he spun around and flung the car at her, striking her just above her eye. She cried out, and Forest got up to help her, but Jaxon just carried on playing with the other cars.

'I think that's enough,' Singh muttered as he rushed out, and I watched the scene in the room as he ushered Laura in and she scooped up her son.

Behind me, the notetaker packed up and left, but I continued to stand behind the mirrored glass, shock at Jaxon's behaviour rendering me inert. As Laura led Jaxon out, he pointed at the bump already forming on Hannah Lachlan's face and laughed. Laura looked mortified, and hurried him out of the room.

'Well, that was livelier than I expected,' Forest said, and I realised she was talking to Singh. They were the only people left in the other room now, and they didn't know I was still in the side room, listening. I should leave, I told myself. I couldn't stay there and listen to them. But I didn't move.

'I think Bridget Weston has coached him about what happened, so I don't think what he's said is going to be of any use to us.' Singh shook his head in exasperation.

'I think you're right. Plus I don't think anyone would accept that interview as valid. His behaviour could have been caused by distress and trauma.'

'Given what we've heard about his behavioural problems, I don't think that was completely out of character. I suppose we should have been better prepared.' Singh picked up the folder that was sitting on Forest's chair and read for a minute, letting out a low whistle. He looked up at Forest with a raised eyebrow.

'He's only six.'

'I know.'

I knew that if Forest caught me listening in on their conversation, she'd fire me on the spot, but I couldn't resist. Nobody would give me any information, so I had to find ways of keeping myself informed. At least, that's how I justified it to myself.

Singh blew air out of his cheeks as he read the file, his eyebrows threatening to meet his hairline. 'And he did all this?'

Forest nodded. 'And apparently every time the school try to address it, Bridget Weston turns it around on them. Tells them they're not supporting him properly, he's frustrated because he's not being stimulated, people can't communicate with him, and so on.'

This exchange didn't surprise me. I could picture Bridget insisting Jaxon wasn't to blame for his own behaviour. I was desperate to read that file and find out what had shocked Singh.

'They need to get someone to assess him, get to the bottom of why he behaves like this. Now social work are involved with the family, perhaps they can push through some referrals. It could be something serious.'

The detectives shot each other a look, and I dreaded to think what they were implying.

'Hannah Lachlan seems to be the one who gets it in the neck the most,' Forest continued. 'The school had to send her on a course so she's allowed to physically restrain him if necessary. The woman looked terrified. I wondered if we were going to have to postpone, get another communicator.' Forest grimaced. 'And now for another shit job.' She waved another sheet of paper at Singh.

'Post-mortem results?'

I took a deep breath. I had been dreading this part. On the other side of the glass, Forest nodded.

'How much do we need to share with the mother?'

Forest rubbed her face. 'Enough that she knows what happened, but no more.'

'Right. I'd better speak to Paige,' Singh said, his glance flicking to the mirror.

My heart leapt into my mouth and I lunged for the door, dashing into the corridor and leaning against the opposite wall. I hoped I looked casual, but the door hadn't quite closed when Singh stepped out into the corridor. He looked from the door to me and cocked his head on one side ever so slightly. I felt a blush begin to rise up my face and prayed he wouldn't notice.

'We need to chat with Laura,' Singh said to me, 'give her a bit more information, but she asked if she could take Jaxon home first.'

I assumed Hannah Lachlan had interpreted that request, but didn't trust myself to speak until my heart stopped racing.

'Can you meet us there in about half an hour?'

'Of course.'

He turned to leave, but I stopped him. 'Is it okay if Anna comes too? She wants to help Laura, if she can.' I held back from telling him she was my sister; I thought Singh would probably give me the benefit of the doubt, but I had no idea how Forest would react.

'Sure, as long as Laura's happy for her to be there.' He gave me a sad smile and walked off, leaving me trying to process what I'd heard about Jaxon. Was his behaviour in there a reaction to the death of his sister, or was there something deeper at the root of it?

Chapter 8

The journey to Laura's house was far too short. As I drove, Anna tapped away on her phone and it set my teeth on edge. I wasn't ready for the post-mortem results, wasn't prepared to hear the information the police had to share, or to interpret it for a grieving mother. At that point I wished I had chosen a different career path. When we arrived, we sat in the car for a few minutes, until I saw another car draw up outside the house, and Forest and Singh stepped out.

Come on. We have to do this, for Laura. And for Lexi, Anna signed then squeezed my hand. She was right. I was really glad she was there, if I was honest with myself.

As we walked up the path, I introduced Anna to DI Forest, leaving out the crucial fact that she was my sister. Forest nodded and said, 'She'll probably need all the friends she's got.'

A sombre cloud hung over the four of us. I looked up at Bridget's house, identical to those either side of it. I felt like it should stand out, look different because of what they'd lost.

She opened the door before we reached it. She had clearly been watching out of the window, waiting for us. Her black hair was clipped back out of her face so it looked a little less severe, and she was wearing a green striped top under a white blouse with a matching white skirt. Her arms were folded, and the heavy gold rings on both hands gleamed against her tanned skin.

'Morning. Laura said you were on the way.' Bridget didn't smile as we approached. I knew she had very little to smile about, but even so I had expected a slightly warmer greeting. Then again, she never approved of Anna as a friend for Laura – according to my sister, she was far too bad an influence, in Bridget's eyes. Anna was confident and outgoing, which as a teenager had meant she could be cocky and sometimes rude. But more importantly, she knew her own mind, and encouraged Laura to be her own person instead of blindly following what her mother told her to do.

'Would you mind letting Laura know we're here?' Singh said, his voice reverentially quiet.

I swallowed nervously as I thought of the conversation to come, wondering what they were going to say.

Bridget's mouth was set in a straight line and she didn't say anything, just turned around and climbed the stairs to fetch Laura.

'There's a social worker here too; she came back with Laura,' Bridget said over her shoulder when she was halfway up the stairs. Maybe this was the source of her displeasure. 'She'll look after Jaxon while we talk.'

I'd been under the impression that Bridget would look

after her grandson while the detectives spoke to Laura, but I didn't speak up. I got the feeling it would be difficult to prevent Bridget getting involved.

A couple of minutes later, the two women came back downstairs, and we all crowded into the living room. Bridget sat in one of the two armchairs, and motioned to Laura to sit in the other. She did as she was told, and Anna perched on the arm, hovering over her protectively. I noticed a look pass between Forest and Singh, suggesting they weren't happy with Bridget staying. Still, neither of them said anything about it.

'Laura, thank you for speaking to us again today,' Singh said. I hoped he was going to be leading the interview; I much preferred his gentler style to Forest's brusque one.

Bridget got straight to the point. 'What have you learned? Why are you here? Laura told me Jaxon was incredibly upset after you interviewed him. I don't think you should be putting such a little boy through that.'

'We know it was a difficult morning for him, but it was important for us to find out if he'd seen anything. He's been through a traumatic experience, even if he was asleep when it happened, and it's vital we work with you to make sure he gets the support he might need in the coming weeks and months.'

Bridget sniffed, but she didn't reply to Singh's attempt to appease her.

Singh looked around at all of us – there were six of us in the room, and I wondered if he felt like Poirot at the point of the big reveal. I nearly laughed at my own mental image, and I realised how tired I was. I bit the inside of my lip to bring myself back to the moment.

'Are you sure you want so many people here?' Singh

asked Laura. Realistically, the only people he could banish from the room were Anna and Bridget, and I couldn't see either of them complying willingly. I interpreted the question for Laura, and she gave one sharp nod, which I took as her consent to everyone staying. She probably wanted to get on with it. Bridget didn't look at me and I wondered why she seemed so opposed to me being there. Did she see me as usurping her role in Laura's life? Or did she want to control what Laura told the police?

Forest cleared her throat and took over. 'I'm afraid we have some difficult news. The results of the post-mortem showed that Lexi died as a result of several blows to her head with a heavy object.'

Anna grabbed Laura's hand, but she pulled away to sign.

It was on the internet. It said blunt force trauma. I didn't believe it.

Forest grimaced. 'I'm not sure how that information came to be leaked to the media, and I'm sorry for any further distress it caused.'

I kept swallowing as I interpreted, in an attempt to shift the lump in my throat.

Bridget stared down at the floor, her lower jaw trembling. 'Who did this?' Her voice was quiet, and she didn't look up, but I could feel the weight of emotion in her voice. 'Do you know who did this?'

'Not yet. But we're gathering evidence and doing what we can to find out what happened.'

Bridget thumped the arm of her chair and I jumped. Laura looked askance at her mother.

'That's not good enough! We need to know what bastard did this! Who would kill a toddler? What sort of man would do that?'

'Mrs Weston, I am so sorry for your loss,' Singh said, soothing her as best he could. 'I know this is a hugely distressing time. The family liaison officer will be able to offer you support while we investigate. I promise you, we'll do all we can.'

Sniffing, Bridget wrinkled her nose at him as if she thought his words were worth nothing. 'It shouldn't take long. I always knew Alan was trouble, from the day Laura started dating him. I never thought he was capable of something like this, though.'

'We're still processing evidence and conducting interviews,' Forest said, her voice stern. 'There have been no arrests at this time, and we can't make any assumptions about who it might have been.'

Stop saying it was Alan until we know more, was what she was trying to say. I thought back to Singh's comment about Bridget coaching Jaxon. Had she told him a bad man killed his sister to try and lead the police towards his father?

Laura had sagged against Anna, but Bridget was still sitting upright, her fists clenched so tightly her knuckles were white.

I want you to find who killed Lexi, Laura signed.

'We'll do our very best,' Singh replied. 'Now, I want you to think. Is there anyone who might have wanted to hurt Lexi, or anyone who might want to hurt you or Alan?'

'Of course there's nobody who wanted to hurt her, she was a child, a baby!' Bridget said, her voice quivering. 'And why would anyone want to harm Laura? It's Alan you need to be looking at.'

Singh looked back to Laura and repeated his question.

'Can you think of anyone who might have had a reason to do this?'

Bridget sat forward in her seat. 'I've just told you the answer! Why are you insisting on asking the same question over and over again?'

'Mrs Weston, you need to control yourself if you want to be present in this interview,' Forest said in a low voice.

'I have every right to be present. Laura is my daughter!'

'Laura is an adult, Mrs Weston, and we are fully within our rights to ask you to leave the room if you continue to interrupt in this manner.' Forest's eyes flashed dangerously and I was worried she and Bridget would come to blows, if not today then at some point in the investigation.

Throughout this exchange, I continued to sign what was happening, while Bridget threw me dirty looks. Laura was wide-eyed. Eventually, she reached up and put a hand on her mother's arm.

It's okay, she signed, and I interpreted this for Forest and Singh. *Mum, you need to sit down, calm down. I want to help them.*

'Why are you interpreting that?' Bridget snapped at me. 'She was talking to me, not them.'

'I'm here to interpret everything,' I explained, trying to stay patient. 'If you want to have a private conversation, you need to leave the room.'

She glared at me, but she sat back down.

'Can we get back to the question?' Forest asked testily.

I repeated the question for Laura and she bit her lip. *I don't think anyone wants to hurt me, but maybe Alan.*

'Someone wants to hurt Alan, or Alan wants to hurt you?' Singh asked for clarification. Bridget let out a huff but didn't say anything.

Someone might want to hurt Alan. Some of the people he knows are . . . not nice people.

'Can you be specific? Which people? What's not nice about them?' Singh pressed.

Laura shifted her position and picked at the corner of a fingernail. *I don't know all of their names, but I think some of them deal drugs.*

Forest scribbled in her notebook, then asked, 'Did Alan take drugs when you were together?'

She shrugged. *Sometimes.*

Bridget made another huffing noise. I wondered how long Forest would put up with her behaviour – it seemed inevitable that she would be asked to leave the room at some point.

'Would he take drugs when the children were in the house?'

She nodded, dropping her eyes to the carpet. *He would invite people over and they would drink and smoke weed. Sometimes they'd take pills.*

'Do you know what the pills were?'

Laura shook her head. *I don't know.*

'Of course she doesn't know. Laura has never taken drugs,' Bridget piped up.

I had known it was only a matter of time before she interrupted again. The woman was incapable of keeping her mouth shut.

Singh looked directly at Laura, ignoring her mother. 'Did you ever take drugs with him?'

She looked uncomfortable, and resumed picking at her nail.

'I told you, no! Don't come in here and accuse my daughter of being as bad as that man. She's grieving, she doesn't need this.' Bridget thumped her hand on the arm of the chair again and Forest glared at her.

'Mrs Weston, one more outburst like that and I will ask you to leave the room. We're asking your daughter, not you. We need Laura's answers, not yours.'

Exhaling hard, Bridget fell silent again.

Not when I was looking after Jaxon, Laura admitted. *But sometimes when he was staying here with Mum. But I haven't done anything like that since Lexi was born, since Alan and I split up.*

Bridget shot her daughter a scandalised look; I wasn't surprised Laura had never told her this before. For once, Bridget seemed to be lost for words.

'Okay,' Singh said, offering Laura an encouraging smile. 'And these friends of his, you can't remember any names?'

She shook her head. *There were lots of them. Always coming in and out of the house. I didn't pay attention, I didn't want to know them. I just wanted to look after my children.*

'Don't worry, this could still be useful,' Singh said.

I knew he was trying to be reassuring. Forest looked sceptical, though that could have been her default attitude.

'Are you protecting someone, Laura?' Forest asked.

Bridget stood up again, her fists clenched at her sides. 'I've had enough of this. We've both answered your questions and now you're suggesting my daughter had something to do with this. I want you out of my house!'

Before Forest had a chance to reply, Laura grabbed her mother's wrist. *No, I want to talk to them. We have to tell them what we know. I need to know what happened. Someone killed my little girl!*

Forest was on her feet too. 'Mrs Weston, I think it's

time for you to leave us with Laura. We need to complete this interview, and I'd rather do it here than at the station. You can wait in the kitchen and we'll speak to you later.'

For a brief moment I thought Bridget was going to swing for Forest, but she curled her lip and stalked out of the room. Laura's mouth was a round O of surprise, whether at her mother for not arguing or herself for standing up to her, I wasn't sure. I expected Forest to send Anna out as well, but instead she sat back down to face Laura.

'Can we get back to the questions, please?' Forest was irritable, and I couldn't blame her. Bridget's interruptions dragged everything out unnecessarily.

I'm not protecting anyone. If I knew Alan had something to do with this, I'd tell you. He doesn't tell me what he's doing any more. I ignore him on Facebook, we're only friends so we can share pictures of the children. Laura looked more relaxed once her mother had left the room, and her signing was more fluid. *I didn't know anything about what he was doing on Friday night after I left the Deaf club.*

'So you weren't in his house that night?'

No. Why would I be there?

'Have you ever been inside his house?' Forest continued without answering Laura's question.

Laura frowned. *Sometimes, when I drop the kids off or pick them up. But we're not friends. I don't sit down and have a cup of tea. I just go for the kids.*

Singh nodded slowly and Forest made more notes in her book. I wondered what they were angling at, but I couldn't ask. Technically, I shouldn't have been given any extra information about the case. I had to know enough to be able to interpret the interviews in context, but I knew I wouldn't get details of everything else that went on behind the scenes. I couldn't be involved in the gathering of evidence, or the interviews with any hearing witnesses or suspects.

'Now, can I ask about your court case, Laura? Can you tell me about that?'

I was surprised. I didn't know what he was talking about, but I did my best to keep it from showing on my face.

I'm seeing a solicitor about custody.

I hadn't known about this, and whilst it wasn't my sister's responsibility to tell me everything that was going on in her friends' lives, I was surprised she hadn't told me when we'd been talking about Lexi.

'Why did you decide to do this now?'

Laura shrugged. *I wanted something from the court to say when Alan should see the children, because sometimes he changes our plans. He's meant to pick them up then texts me at the last minute to say he can't. I'd had enough. I want them to tell him he has to see his kids every week or something.*

Forest pursed her lips. 'You wanted to keep joint custody with him?'

Laura shifted on her chair, curling her feet up underneath her. *That's all I want.*

'But someone else wants something different?' Singh asked, picking up on Laura's hesitation.

She nodded. *Mum thought I should ask for full custody. She thinks Alan isn't a good father.*

Singh did his slow nod again. I wondered if that was what he always did when he was thinking and needed a moment to process before he spoke again. Or perhaps he did it to encourage an interviewee to speak more, giving them an empty space to fill.

If it was the latter, it worked, because Laura continued: *She told the solicitor he wasn't a good father, that he didn't look after the children properly. She made some things up about Jaxon coming home in dirty clothes, or Lexi being left to cry for hours, but I don't know if the solicitor believed her. I don't know how she would know those things. She helps a lot with the children now I live here, and that's really good, but how would she know what happens in Alan's house?*

When we split up . . . She twisted her face up as if she were searching for the right words. *When Alan cheated on me, Mum stopped Elisha in the street and shouted at her. I didn't want her to do anything like that again. I don't like Elisha, but it wasn't her fault. Alan was the one who cheated. Elisha probably didn't even know he was with me. Mum can shout at Alan if she wants, but it's not fair to shout at Elisha.*

Laura's response surprised me. She suddenly seemed a lot more open, and it wasn't lost on me that she was now using Elisha's name. Alan managed to get Laura and Elisha pregnant within a couple of months of each other, and it was only when the strain of trying to deal with two pregnant girlfriends got too much that the truth emerged. I remembered it well, because it was plastered all over Facebook. Anna loved a good gossip, and she called me with an update most days, sometimes twice a day. You'd have thought they were a celebrity couple, the way she got involved in the tiniest detail.

'Okay. And you were here all night on Friday?'

Laura nodded and gave me an exasperated look. *I've told you that. I was here on Saturday morning when the police came to tell me about Lexi. I'd been here all night!* Without warning, she burst into tears, and I wondered how long she'd been holding them back. It was awful that she had to deal with the situation, but as it turned out, Laura could cope far better under pressure than I had expected. Her reliance on Alan and then Bridget had led me to assume she couldn't manage on her own. Despite how he treated her, despite the lies and the cheating, she always took him back, and I had to admit I'd seen that as weakness.

The detectives turned their backs to us and muttered something I couldn't catch. It was a tactic they'd quickly developed, so they could discuss something without me interpreting it. I didn't mind, though it would have been easier if they'd left the room.

'Thank you for your time, Laura. We can leave it there for today.' He turned to Anna. 'Could we now ask you some questions, as you're here?' Singh said. I signed their request for Anna, who nodded and checked with Laura that she'd be okay.

Laura gave her a flat smile. *I'll be fine. Say goodbye before you leave, though.*

Of course, Anna told her.

Laura went out, leaving the four of us in the lounge.

How can I help you? Anna put on her best respectable face, which I knew she was doing for my benefit. I raised an eyebrow at her, and she smirked slightly, but luckily the detectives didn't notice. The last thing I wanted them to think was that we were making light of the situation.

'Can we take your name and contact details first, then we can get in touch with you if necessary?'

Anna and I looked at each other. I knew there was no way we could hide it any longer. She wrote her name and number on the piece of paper Singh held out to her, then slowly slid it back to him. He glanced at it, and I could see the moment realisation dawned on his face. Forest took the paper off him and glared at us.

'Anna Northwood. So, you're sisters?' She looked between the two of us, my sister slim and fair, I heavier and dark, but on closer inspection she must have noted the family resemblance.

'We should send you straight home and take you off our books,' Forest continued, then let out a huff of frustration. 'But we need you right now. You should have revealed this conflict of interest at the beginning.'

'I barely know the family,' I replied, hoping to explain myself. 'Laura is Anna's friend, that's how I know her.'

For a moment I thought Forest was going to continue to argue, but after a long pause she nodded at Singh to continue.

'We just wanted to know if there was any information you could give us that might be of use,' Singh said, settling back on the sofa. 'How do you know Laura?'

We were at school together, for sixth form, Anna replied. *I was at Lincoln School for the Deaf right from when I was in reception, but Laura moved up here from London when she was sixteen. She had sign support in school down south, but she didn't have many friends because very few people could sign, so when it came to college she insisted on going somewhere she'd have a deaf peer group.*

'Do you know of anyone who might have harmed Lexi?'

Anna thought for a moment. *I'm not sure. There are lots of things going around in my mind, but it's hard to know what's relevant. I keep thinking about Lexi, and what a sweet little girl she was. How could anyone do this?*

She sighed and rubbed her nose. *When Lexi was born, I really wondered how Laura was going to cope. Alan had left her for Elisha, who was also going to have a baby around the same time, and she'd moved back here with Bridget. Bridget's fantastic in many ways, but she can be very controlling, and I was worried Laura would start to . . . lose her identity, I suppose. And then there's Jaxon.* She gave me a meaningful look, eyebrows high on her forehead.

Forest looked between us. 'What about Jaxon?'

He's always been hard work, Anna explained. *He's a very difficult child and needs a lot of attention. You saw it this morning, Laura told me what happened. I was worried that Laura wouldn't have time for the new baby, and Lexi would end up being ignored, or she'd be as much trouble as Jaxon.* Anna's face softened, and her eyes shone with tears. *But she wasn't. She was sweet and loving and beautiful, and never any trouble. She hardly ever cried, and when she did it was really easy to soothe her – usually she just wanted a cuddle, or a nappy change.*

For a moment, she sat and stared at her hands, and I knew she was remembering the time she spent with Lexi.

I don't know anything that could help you with this investigation. I worried about Laura a lot when she was with Alan, and I was concerned he might be abusive, at least emotionally, if not physically. But being a controlling partner doesn't mean you'd murder your own child, and I don't want to suggest it was him. I can't process this at the moment, I'm sorry. She glanced at me. *If I think*

98

of anything else, I'll let you know, but I don't know how I can help.

Singh gave her a gentle smile. 'Don't worry, we just wanted to make sure we spoke to you while you're here. I understand it's a very difficult time for you, being close to Laura and Lexi.'

Anna nodded, and a single tear escaped. She wiped it away quickly, but I moved over and put a protective arm around her. I shouldn't have let them speak to her, not without being prepared for it. Lexi's death was a huge shock for her, too.

'Thank you for your help,' Forest said, pocketing her notebook.

She and Singh got up to leave, and Anna and I went into the kitchen. Bridget was sitting at the breakfast bar, her jaw clenched, and I wondered if she'd said a word to Laura since she left us with the detectives. Laura was making tea and offered us a cup, but I deferred to Anna, who shook her head.

We'll leave you in peace.

I'm not feeling very peaceful, Laura replied.

Anna gave her a huge hug. *I'll come back to see you tomorrow, okay?*

Laura attempted a weak smile, but it didn't reach her eyes. She was going through the worst thing a mother could ever face. There probably wasn't much room in her mind for anything else.

When we pulled up outside my flat, we sat in the car for a few minutes and I rested my head on the steering wheel, hit by a wave of confusion and emotion. My work and family lives were starting to overlap in a way they shouldn't, and I wasn't sure how to stop it. I liked to compartmentalise, to separate the different areas of my life, but they were blending together because of the case, and it had only been three days. What if it went on for weeks, or months?

After Caitlin's death, I thought I would be able to cope with anything, but I was struggling to manage. Her face kept appearing in my mind, merging with Lexi's, and I couldn't stop the memories surfacing. I had so many buried emotions that they were bound to leak out at some point, but the main one I felt was guilt. Knowing what put Caitlin at risk, could I somehow have seen Lexi's death coming?

I gave Anna a quick hug and she got out of the car so I could drive to my next job, a social services meeting I'd had booked in for a few weeks. I wanted to devote all of my mental energy to Lexi's murder, but I couldn't afford to turn down other work. I hadn't had any time to eat lunch, and my stomach complained at me. When I arrived in town, I found myself a parking space but didn't think to check my phone. I ran to the social work offices only to discover the meeting had been cancelled. Only then did I notice the voicemail that would have saved me a lot of time and effort. I had to put a clause in my contracts stating I still needed to be paid if jobs were cancelled at short notice, or sooner or later I'd fall behind on my mortgage payments. There was no way I wanted to go through such dire financial difficulties again.

Half an hour later I was back at home, frustrated and annoyed. Anna made me a coffee as I slumped over the kitchen table. The pressures of the investigation were eating away at me, and I realised that was why I was so angry at myself. I was having nightmares that led to a lack of sleep, and was living on adrenaline. Interpreting is tiring work, requiring constant concentration in order to listen to what's being said, process it and interpret it correctly whilst maintaining focus on the conversation. That's why we normally work in pairs for anything that will take more than an hour, allowing each person to sign for fifteen or twenty minutes, then have a break while the other interpreter takes over.

Why won't they book a second interpreter? Anna asked, reading my mind.

I've told them they need to, but they haven't been able to get anyone else at short notice.

But it's not fair, them asking you all the time.

I rubbed my eyes with the heels of my hands. *I know that, Anna. I'm the one who's being run ragged. But this is why I went freelance, so I could build up a reputation as an interpreter who can be available at short notice. The emergency services and social care can't always wait five days. Remember the problems you had when Dad . . .* I stopped, letting my hands drop to the table. I didn't want to think about that day, when my phone went off in the middle of my class, an unknown number that turned out to be a nurse. That day marked a turning point in all our lives – it was the day our dad died, and the last day I spent at uni. It was also the first day of Mum's decline in health, although the cancer didn't appear until a year later.

Anyway, not having an interpreter made everything even worse for you and Mum. I don't want other families to go through that. So I can't tell them to stuff their job, which I know is what you were thinking.

Actually, I was thinking you should tell them to fuck off, Anna replied with a straight face.

101

I raised an eyebrow and she cracked a smile, which made me laugh. *This is exactly the sort of work I was looking for when I left the agency,* I told her. *I can't turn it down.*

You're not sleeping well, I can tell. It's about your connection to the family, not your working hours. This is really getting to you.

Of course it's getting to me; a child is dead!

She was my goddaughter, Anna replied, glaring at me. *I know how bad this is.*

Suddenly, I couldn't contain my anger, and even though I knew it was unfair, I turned on Anna. *Do you? Have you had to sit and listen to details of how they found her dead, of what her body looked like? Have you had to walk through the house where it happened, knowing that her body is upstairs, just metres away? You don't understand the first thing about what I've had to do.*

I stormed out of the kitchen and into my bedroom before she could reply, slamming the door behind me. I'd said too much, I knew I had, but I couldn't take any more. Flopping down onto my bed, I buried my head in my pillow and didn't move when I heard the door open behind me. Anna climbed onto my bed and wrapped her arms around me, lying beside me as we both cried.

Later, we ordered ourselves a takeaway and found a cheesy comedy film to watch. We both needed some light relief to take our minds off the stressful day we'd had. I'd just bitten into my second slice of pizza when my work phone beeped with a new message. My personal phone went off at almost the same time, and I heard Anna's phone vibrate as well. I checked my work phone first, out of conscientious habit. It was from DI Forest.

Please confirm your availability for tomorrow, beginning 9 a.m. if possible.

Before I could text my reply, Anna jumped up from the sofa.

They've found the murder weapon. And they've arrested Alan.

14 hours before the murder

Laura sagged onto a bench next to the ball pool, and watched Lexi clamber up the soft steps and slide down into the pit of coloured plastic balls. Her daughter giggled and shook her curly hair before repeating the action. Knowing Lexi would be amused in this way for a while, Laura pulled out her phone and called her best friend.

Hi, how are you? Anna asked when her face popped up on Laura's screen.

Laura shook her head. *Don't ask. My mum is driving me mad again.*

I've told you before, you need to stand up to her, Anna said sternly. *She'll take over your life otherwise.*

I know, but she makes it hard to say no.

What is it this time?

Laura watched Lexi for a moment. She was sitting in the ball pool, bringing her arms up and down as if she was trying to splash the balls. A little boy was collecting all the red balls, so Lexi passed one to him with a big smile, making Laura's heart ache.

She's pushing me about the court case. She thinks Alan could challenge me and ask for full custody himself.

Really? Anna replied. *Do you think he'd do that?*

Laura shook her head. *He doesn't have time to have all three kids full time, and I can't imagine Elisha would be happy about it. I think she'd be happy if I got full custody then she didn't have to bother with my kids any more.*

Anna pulled a face. *Maybe. It'd serve Alan right if Elisha wasn't there to help out and he had to do everything by himself.*

Laura nodded, her mind drifting towards the idea of Elisha leaving Alan, so he'd be free to come back to her . . . But she knew it was pointless. Alan had always done exactly what he wanted, so if he wanted to come back to Laura, he would, sooner or later.

I've been thinking, I want an interpreter. Mum's taking over, and I can't make any decisions for myself without her interfering, Laura told Anna.

Good idea. Want me to speak to Paige?

Laura nodded. *If she's got the time, yeah.*

I doubt it'll be a problem. I need to get back to work, but I'll call in a couple of days to chat again. Give my love to my gorgeous goddaughter, Anna said before they said their goodbyes and hung up.

Looking up from her phone, Laura's heart leapt into her mouth when she realised Lexi wasn't where she'd left her. She jumped up and moved towards the ball pool, then spotted the back of her head on the other side of the wall. Lexi was sitting with the little boy, and they had a pile of red balls between them. A woman was watching them – Laura assumed she was the boy's mother – and she was talking to both children. She looked up as Laura approached.

She spoke to Laura, who watched the woman's lip patterns. She thought she said, 'Is this your daughter?' so Laura nodded and took Lexi's hand to guide her back to where Laura had been sitting.

The other woman started to say something else, and Laura caught a couple of words, '. . . look . . . better,' but she couldn't understand what the woman was trying to tell her. She pointed to her ear and said, 'Deaf,' which stopped the other woman mid-flow. Some people would simply repeat themselves slower and louder when they realised they were talking to a deaf person, whereas others looked embarrassed. This woman stared for a moment then shook her head and turned back to her son. Laura's face burned; she might not have heard the other woman but she understood well enough that she was judging her parenting.

Leading Lexi back out of the building towards the bus stop, Laura wondered if other people were right. Her mum always told her she wouldn't manage on her own if she moved out, and now complete strangers were telling her she was a crap parent. She was sure her life would have been a lot different if she hadn't had kids.

She sat down at the bus stop and checked her phone. There was a message from her mother, which she considered ignoring for a moment, but she opened it out of habit.

Had a message from Jaxon's school, we need to collect him.

Laura tapped out a reply to say she was on her way back, then sat back to wait for the bus, wondering what had happened this time.

Chapter 9

Tuesday 6th February

I dreamt of Lexi and Caitlin again, the two of them playing on the beach. When I went to give Caitlin a hug, I came away with blood on my hands, then I turned to see the tide rushing in. It swept them both away, while I stood on the sand and watched, once again unable to move.

After another night of broken sleep, I arrived at the police station bleary-eyed but with plenty of time to spare. I'd tossed and turned all night, between the nightmare and going over what might have happened to Lexi.

The text message on my own phone had been from Laura, telling me the same thing she told Anna, that Alan had been arrested for Lexi's murder. She'd texted that I had to tell her everything I knew, but I didn't reply. I didn't know what I could say to help, so it was safest to say nothing.

I sat in the waiting room until they were ready, and got a watery coffee from the machine. I worried I might start getting used to it. Sipping the grey liquid, I reread the posters on the wall to keep myself occupied.

A few moments later, DC Singh stepped into the room and shut the door.

'Morning,' he said. His eyes were bloodshot and puffy with tiredness, and I wondered if this case was taking its toll on him too. 'There are a couple of things I need to discuss with you before we go into the interview.'

I nodded and waited. I realised how much I liked his calming voice and the precise way he spoke.

'You're here to interpret for us in an interview with Mr Alan Hunter. He's been arrested on suspicion of the murder of his daughter, Lexi Hunter. We'll be showing Mr Hunter photographs of the crime scene, and also some of another violent crime. These photographs are of a graphic nature, and you may find them immensely distressing. In fact, I'd be worried if you didn't.'

I bit my lip and swallowed. I was glad he'd prepared me, rather than springing photographs of a murdered child on me, but even so I started imagining the worst.

'Thank you, I appreciate the warning,' I said.

He stood and opened the door for me. 'Mr Hunter's solicitor is already in the room with him. She chose to book her own interpreter for her conversations with her client, but he'll leave before we begin.'

'Okay,' I said, wondering who the other interpreter was. I wasn't surprised the solicitor brought in someone else, and frankly I was relieved. If Alan told his solicitor something that he didn't tell the police, but I knew about it as the interpreter, what would my position be? I had no idea, so it was best that I was kept out of those conversations.

The interview room felt crowded once we were all seated: DC Singh and DI Forest on one side of the table, with me off to their left slightly, and Alan and his solicitor on the other side. Alan looked dreadful, his eyes sunken and his skin an unhealthy grey. He looked like he hadn't slept, and he had a few days' stubble on his chin. His solicitor, by contrast, looked remarkably cheerful, considering we were there to talk about the death of a child.

We made our introductions for the recording, and a shiver ran down my spine as I looked at Alan Hunter across the table. Was it possible that he killed his own daughter, in the horrific way I'd been imagining? There was a pile of paperwork in front of DI Forest, and I expected it would include the photographs Singh warned me about. The brief glimpse I had of Lexi's body would haunt me forever. I was about to be forced to feed those demons. Even thinking about it made me nauseous. I took a deep breath and gulped from the bottle of water I had next to me.

'Mr Hunter, you have been arrested on suspicion of the murder of your daughter, Lexi Hunter. You have been informed of your rights.'

Alan nodded slowly and looked at his solicitor.

'Please can you tell us your movements on Friday the second of February.'

'My client has already made a statement giving those details,' the solicitor cut in smoothly, before Alan had a chance to respond.

DI Forest glowered at her. 'We've received information that suggests your client lied in his statement, so we're now giving him the opportunity to amend it.'

I didn't kill Lexi. I interpreted Alan's signs as he jumped in before his solicitor could speak again. *I would never hurt my child. I love all my children, and I could never do anything to hurt them. If someone's told you I hurt her, they're lying.*

'Mr Hunter, can you explain why your fingerprints were found on the object that was used to kill Lexi?'

I signed this to Alan, though I could feel tremors under my tongue. I wasn't cut out for this. I couldn't do it. They'd have to replace me with another interpreter. I couldn't sit there and sign things like that.

How? What was it? I didn't kill Lexi. I didn't hurt my little girl!

I fought to maintain my composure as I interpreted for him, and told myself to get it together.

Singh pulled a photograph from the file in front of him on the table. 'Mr Hunter, do you recognise this?'

It was a hammer. Nothing special about it, just an ordinary hammer, except for the fact that there was blood on it. I took another gulp of water.

It's a hammer. It could be from anywhere, Alan signed.

'We found this hammer yesterday, on the waste ground at the end of your road, and we have confirmed that it matches Lexi's injuries. She had several wounds to her head and one to her shoulder, caused by someone hitting her with this.' Singh pulled out more photographs and placed them in front of Alan. Hunter let out a low moan at the sight of his daughter's body in close-up. I couldn't help looking – one was of Lexi's head, a thick dark mass of blood tangled in her curls. The other was of her shoulder, a bloody gash running from her spine. She looked so small. I remembered the blood on Elisha's clothes and caught my breath.

'This is Lexi's blood on the head of the hammer,' Singh continued, as tears rolled down Alan's face. 'Can you explain why we found your fingerprints on it?'

The blood drained from Alan's face, and I pressed

my hands to my mouth once I'd finished translating Singh's words.

It looks like mine. I keep my tools in the shed, at the back of the house. It's not locked, though. Anyone could have taken it, Alan explained, his signs slow as if he were in shock.

'Which means my client could have handled the item at any time and his fingerprints would be on it. As he says, anyone could have taken it from the shed in which it was kept. This evidence is circumstantial at best.' The solicitor glared at the two detectives. 'If you're going to charge Mr Hunter, you will need far stronger evidence than this.'

'We found it underneath a pile of rubble on the waste ground. Someone put it there, just far enough away from your house that we didn't find it in our initial search,' Forest said.

There's a passage next to the house, you can get round the back. I don't lock the shed, Alan said, his eyes wide. Beads of sweat were forming along his hairline.

'Have you seen anyone go into your shed recently?' Singh asked Alan directly.

No, but if someone was going to steal something, they could have done it when I was out. Or at night. They could have stolen it that night then broken in.

'You've already said you didn't see any sign that anyone had broken in,' Forest said, her face and voice sceptical. 'Our forensics team couldn't find evidence of a break in, either.'

Alan grimaced and glared at the DI. *Maybe I forgot to lock the back door, I don't know.*

'Elisha insisted it was locked when she checked it. It was certainly locked when our officers arrived.'

I don't know. Maybe she locked it afterwards, so it didn't look like it was our fault. Alan's eyes were wild with panic and I could tell he wasn't thinking about his replies.

Singh made a note while Forest continued to stare at Alan. 'We'll be sure to pursue that line of enquiry.'

I didn't believe her, and neither did the solicitor, who glared at Forest.

'We understand you have a history of violence, Mr Hunter,' Forest continued smoothly.

I never hurt anyone. You're making things up. Alan shifted in his seat and looked sideways at his solicitor, as if to see if she'd back him up.

'What about the caution you received after you were found to be carrying an offensive weapon in March last year?'

Alan didn't respond. He looked to his solicitor, but she didn't say anything.

I didn't know it was in my pocket, he replied eventually. *Maybe someone else put it in there.*

'You're saying someone planted a knuckleduster on you?'

He shrugged again. *Yes. Maybe. I don't know. It wasn't mine.*

'What about the time a man known to be an associate of yours arrived at Scunthorpe General Hospital with injuries that suggested he'd been beaten, but refused to say what had happened?'

Another photograph came out of Singh's file, this time of a man's back. There were huge bruises around the region of his kidneys. A second photograph showed the bloody mess that used to be his face. I shuddered as I

113

realised I was comparing the man's injuries to Lexi's in my head.

'Was there any evidence to suggest my client was involved with what happened to this man? If not, I think we should stop this spurious line of enquiry now.'

'Unfortunately, the man in question died before he could tell us how he sustained his injuries. Witnesses who wished to remain anonymous gave us information about an ongoing feud between the man and yourself, Mr Hunter.'

He owed me money, but I wouldn't hurt him. I never got my money back after he died. It wouldn't make sense for me to kill him.

Forest looked sceptical but didn't push it any further. 'Back to Friday night. Tell us about the fight.'

Alan shifted in his seat and looked over at his solicitor before he answered. *What fight?*

Forest sat back in her seat and folded her arms. 'Several of your neighbours have told us that you had a very loud, public fight with a man outside your house in the early hours of Saturday morning.'

Alan did his best to look like he didn't know what she was talking about, but after a moment his body sagged. *I told him I didn't want him coming to my house.* Anger flashed in Alan's eyes as he signed, and I thought it must be a brave man who crossed him. That, or a stupid one.

'Who are you talking about? Who did you have this fight with?'

Elisha's ex.

It went on for two hours like that, and I reminded myself several times to insist on a second interpreter next time. By the time we finished, I was exhausted, but I felt like

I'd had an epiphany. Alan became more and more emotional the longer he was questioned, but consistently denied hurting Lexi, and I actually believed him. I was almost certain he was guilty of the other crimes the detectives needled him about, but his attitude changed completely every time the conversation returned to Lexi.

I was drained by the time I left the police station, and I found myself thinking about Caitlin again. My emotions about Lexi were getting muddled with my long buried guilt about what happened when I was fifteen. The harder I tried to separate them and remain impartial, the more confused they became. I needed to stay involved with the case and find out what happened to Lexi, then maybe I could put both of them to rest.

Letting myself into the flat later that day, I picked up a pile of post from the doormat and put it on the edge of the kitchen table while I made myself a cup of coffee. I sorted through it, putting the junk mail straight into the recycling box, ignoring the one that was blatantly a credit-card statement. My eyes were drawn to the final envelope, because it had no stamp or postmark on it. Wondering who would be hand delivering me a letter, I opened it, then dropped it in shock. Written in stark, clumsy capitals, the note sent a shiver through me.

WHAT HAPPENED TO LEXI IS NONE OF YOUR BUSINESS. KEEP YOUR NOSE OUT, BITCH.

14 hours before the murder

When Elisha walked in she saw Laura on the other side of the room almost immediately. She considered turning around and leaving again, but Kasey was already tugging at her hand to be allowed to go and play. The soft play centre was huge, and Laura was on her phone, so there was a chance she wouldn't see her.

She found a spot in a corner that put her out of Laura's eye line and let Kasey go off to explore the toddler area. Nobody looked at her and offered a friendly smile; most of the parents there were in twos or threes, chatting and drinking coffee while their children played. When Elisha had found out she was pregnant, she was thrilled, but life as a mum hadn't been what she was expecting. None of her friends had kids, and she spent every other weekend looking after Jaxon and Lexi while Alan did what he wanted. They rarely got any quality time together as a couple, or even as a family. At times she wondered if he'd really wanted a girlfriend or a babysitter.

Laura was still on her phone. She probably had plenty of mum friends, Elisha thought with a pang of jealousy. There was a time when Elisha had thought she and Laura could be friends, as their children were siblings, but she soon realised there was no way that would happen. The hurt and rage Laura felt towards Alan for cheating on her was equally directed at Elisha, even though she hadn't realised Alan was in a relationship when they first met. Okay, her friends had warned her about him and she'd ignored them, but he was the one who'd cheated. It wasn't her fault.

She watched Laura put her phone away then frantically look around. Elisha could see Lexi sitting with a little boy and his mum, who kept looking around to see who this little girl belonged to. Maybe Laura wasn't perfect after all, she thought, with a smug sense of self-satisfaction. At least she always knew where Kasey was and didn't get distracted.

Watching her daughter, she caught her breath as the little girl spotted her sister and began to toddle in Lexi's direction. Should she intervene? Or should she let them meet and just pretend she hadn't seen Laura? Before Kasey reached Lexi, however, Laura took her own daughter by the hand and led her out. She didn't even notice Kasey, Elisha thought, anger beginning to bubble inside her. That's how she feels about my daughter, as though she might as well not exist.

She looked around her, once again hoping for a friendly face, but she was as isolated as she would have been if she were the only parent in the whole room. Pulling out her phone, she texted a couple of friends, though she didn't expect responses any time soon. Since she'd been

117

with Alan it had just been the two of them and the children, her world gradually shrinking. There was a message from her brother, but she didn't reply. She couldn't cope with his ongoing feud with Alan, not right now.

The weekend stretched ahead of her, stressful and boring in equal measure. Just once she'd like to be able to get a babysitter and go out with Alan, but whenever she suggested it he found an excuse. Anyway, Jaxon was too difficult for anyone else to want to look after him, so unless he stayed with Laura for the weekend there was no chance it would happen. Not for the first time, she wondered what Alan would do if she left for a few days, leaving him to look after the children without her. She couldn't leave Kasey, though, not even for a weekend. She'd miss her too much, and worry about her. Alan did so little parenting he wouldn't know what to feed her, or which was her favourite cuddly toy to take to bed.

Her thoughts swirled for a while, until Kasey became fractious. As they walked home, Elisha wondered if Alan would ever realise he needed to take better care of his family, and how far she would be willing to go to make him.

Chapter 10

Wednesday 7th February

The next morning, I was back in the police station with another cup of tepid coffee. The anonymous note I'd received was tucked into a plastic freezer bag, stashed in my handbag. I'd watched enough *CSI* to know I needed to touch it as little as possible, but I also felt a bit foolish.

As soon as Anna had seen the note, she'd taken it off me to read it, so I knew both of our fingerprints would be on it. With any luck, they would find someone else's too. I rolled my eyes at myself, as if a silly note pushed through my door was going to be a high priority for the police. It probably wouldn't be looked at for weeks. Still, I knew I had to come in first thing in the morning and show it to the detectives.

My gut reaction had been to resign, to tell the police I wasn't happy working with them any more, but then I reconsidered. Whoever had sent it wanted me to react that way; they wanted me to be scared and to cut my involvement with the case, and I wasn't about to give them what they wanted.

My sister and I went round in circles last night, trying to work out who could have sent it and why. Anna was still convinced Alan must be guilty of Lexi's murder, but it couldn't have been him, because he was in police custody at the time the note had arrived.

Maybe he got someone to post it for him, she suggested.

But who? And why? And how would Alan have got my address? That idea doesn't make sense, I had countered.

If the note wasn't from Alan, then that means the police could have got it wrong, and Alan didn't do it. So then who killed her? Or could he have done it, and someone sent that note because they want to protect him?

I paced around my kitchen for a minute. *I have no idea*, I said eventually. *Elisha is the only other person who springs to mind, because she was the only other adult in the house. I find it so hard to believe someone could have been in their house, and something so violent could have happened, without either of them waking up.*

Anna shrugged. *They're both profoundly deaf. We can have all manner of adaptations to our houses and other aspects of our lives, but there are still times when we're more vulnerable than hearing people.*

I shivered at the thought. Though I had been around deafness my entire life, I had never actually experienced it for myself, and this particular aspect of the case had shaken me. Could someone have taken advantage of Alan and Elisha's deafness, knowing they wouldn't be heard creeping around the house?

Do you think Elisha did it? Anna asked, going back to

our previous conversation. *Do the police have evidence against her?*

Anna, stop asking me questions you know I'm not allowed to answer. I don't know. I don't know anything!

Someone clearly thinks you know a lot about this investigation, she replied, *and thinks you're getting too involved. If you tell me, who would know? It's stressing you out so much, having to keep all of this to yourself.*

I shook my head and took a few deep breaths. She was right, in a way. Interpreting could be a lonely profession, when you couldn't share any of the details of your working day with anyone else. I wanted to stay professional though, regardless of how it was affecting me, and I couldn't allow Anna to get embroiled in this mess.

Whoever it was, they're barking up the wrong tree. I have no idea who did it, and I'm not going to do anything stupid. I'm going to take this note and give it to the police tomorrow.

Anna huffed. *I wish you had CCTV here, or something like that. We could have at least given them something useful.*

Hopefully whoever sent this note didn't think to wear gloves.

I went to bed early last night, in the hope that I could catch up on some sleep, as well as get away from Anna's questions, but it wasn't to be. All I could think about was Alan's interview, and his revelation about Elisha's ex turning up at the house. I couldn't tell Anna that there was another potential suspect now, and maybe someone who had a motive.

According to Alan, this man, Rick something, had been hanging around recently. There had been some insinuation that he and Elisha were still having an affair, and Rick wanted to find out if Kasey was his daughter.

The last idea was ridiculous, and even I knew that. From the couple of times I'd seen Kasey, you'd know straight away that she was Alan's daughter. Alan's story was that Rick had left, but that didn't mean he hadn't come back later on.

The memory of Lexi's body rose again in my mind, and I shook my head to try to rid myself of those images. I wished I hadn't answered my phone on Saturday morning, and that they'd found another interpreter.

I rubbed my eyes and peered through the doorway of the waiting room. Nobody seemed in a hurry to come speak to me, so I stood and went to see if there was anyone in the corridor.

The first person I saw was DI Forest. She was talking to a man I hadn't seen before, but her body language said he was her boss. Whatever they were talking about, it concerned me in some way, because I saw Forest trying to point at me discreetly. The man looked over at me and nodded when he saw me looking directly at them. He said something to Forest and she shrugged then walked away.

Contrary to popular belief, lip reading isn't easy when you don't know the context of what people are talking about, and only twenty per cent of English speech sounds can be seen on the lips – your brain has to fill in the rest. As I was looking in his direction, the detective came over to introduce himself to me.

'Hi, I'm Detective Chief Inspector Hemmel. You're the sign language interpreter?'

'Paige Northwood,' I said, holding my hand out to shake his.

'Has there been a mix up of some sort? We don't have any interviews today.' His face was wary, and I wondered what Forest had told him about me.

'No.' I shook my head. 'I needed to come speak to someone about this.' I showed him the note in its plastic bag and watched the mixture of surprise and confusion that crossed his face.

'Right. I'll get one of the DCs to come talk to you,' he said, before hurrying off down the corridor.

A few minutes later, DC Singh appeared and led me into a side room.

'DCI Hemmel says you've received a threat?' he said with a frown of concern.

'It arrived yesterday. I found it with the rest of my post, so I don't know who could have delivered it.'

'Has anyone else touched it?' he asked, taking the plastic bag from me and reading the note.

'Anna took it from me, so whoever delivered it and the two of us.'

Singh frowned as he looked at the note, and I realised how tired he was. His eyes were bloodshot and he kept rubbing them.

'You said you live in a flat?'

I nodded.

'What floor?'

'First.'

'Does the building have CCTV? A secure entry system?'

'There's no CCTV, we checked last night,' I said. 'There's a keypad entry system, but some people will let anyone in regardless. I get people coming to my door selling things, when I haven't let them in the building.'

He was silent for a moment as he absorbed what I'd

123

told him, and an anxious flutter started to build in my stomach.

'Thank you for bringing me this. Are you okay?' He looked at me with concern. 'This is understandably worrying, but it also doesn't make much sense to me. You're the interpreter; you're not investigating the case. I don't know why anyone would see you as a threat.'

I'd considered trying to pass it off as a joke, but the intense look he gave me made my stomach churn more. He was right, it didn't make sense.

'I'm not a threat. Whoever it was should realise that pretty quickly.'

'Is there anyone you know who might do something like this as a practical joke?'

I shook my head. 'None of my friends would do something like this. And besides, none of them know I'm interpreting for this case. I haven't talked to anyone about it.'

Singh nodded, then pulled a card from his pocket, pressing it into my hand. 'If anything else worries you, give me a call, okay? My mobile number is on there, so it doesn't matter what time it is. And I'll get someone to come round and check out your building, make sure it's secure.'

'Thanks,' I said, flashing him a quick smile. He gave my arm a reassuring squeeze before disappearing back down the corridor, looking once again at the note.

That afternoon, I was sitting and contemplating a flat felt piece when my phone rang. The distraction was welcome – I'd been trying to finish that particular piece for months, but all I'd succeeded in doing was getting it out, staring at it and eventually putting it away again. Wet felting was my favourite medium when working with textiles, but my perfectionist streak came out when I was working on it. The piece was made by building up layers of coloured wool roving, then using water, a piece of netting and a lot of rubbing to bind the wool together and turn it into felt. There was only so much I could add to it before I ruined other parts of the piece, but I couldn't decide what was wrong with it: the colours? The composition as a whole? Did it need a few extra pieces of wool or other fibres adding, or something taking away?

Answering the video call, I was pleasantly surprised to see my best friend, Gemma, looking back at me.

Hi, I signed, wondering why she was calling during the afternoon. *How are you?*

I've only got a few minutes, she replied, and I could see from the view over her shoulder that she was at work. *Have you remembered we're meeting at mine on Friday?*

I shut my eyes for a moment. I'd completely forgotten. When I opened them again, Gem was watching me with amusement.

I knew it. How you manage to get to your appointments on time, I'll never know.

I'm so organised with work, I think there's no space left in my memory for my social life, I joked. *What should I bring?*

Gem shook her head. *I've got it covered. Come a bit earlier though, Petra wants to see you.*

Of course, I replied with a grin, feeling a sharp jolt of affection at the thought of Gem's little girl. It made me realise more clearly what Anna must have been going through. I'd be devastated if anything ever happened to Petra, and Anna had been just as close to Lexi.

125

Wait, I signed. *Anna's staying with me at the moment.*

Okay, Gem replied. *She can come with you if you want.*

I knew she was only saying this to be accommodating, and if I was honest with myself I didn't know if I wanted to invite Anna. We had different friends and I needed some space, some time to get away from the horror of the last few days. But was it fair to abandon my sister while she was grieving?

I'll let you know, I said in the end. I'd have to think about what I wanted to do, even if it risked upsetting Anna.

Sure, tell me when you see me tomorrow, Gem replied, a twinkle in her eye.

Tomorrow?

Parents' evening, for Petra.

Oh, yeah. It's in my diary, I wouldn't have forgotten.

Paige, what's wrong? Gem asked with a frown. *You're not usually this distracted. Something's happened.*

I sighed. *I can't talk about it, not right now. I'm okay. I'm just a bit . . . overwhelmed at the moment.*

Gem nodded slowly. *Okay. Don't even think about cancelling Friday night, though.*

I won't. Promise, I added when she glared at me.

Once we'd hung up, I slumped down in my chair. I hoped a night with my friends would be enough to get me through what lay ahead.

Chapter 11

Will you take me over to Laura's tonight? Anna signed. She was sitting at the foot of my bed, texting.

Sure, if she's happy to see you.

I think she needs a friend there. I won't stay long, but I think it's important she knows I'm here for her. Will you come too?

I shook my head. *No, I'll drop you off if you want to see her, but I'm not going in the house.*

Are you sure?

I nodded. I'd talked to Anna about Friday night and she was happy for me to go out and leave her, though she asked me to go to the Deaf club with her on Saturday. I had agreed, though I worried about the amount of gossip that would be flying around by then.

I was booked to be with the police the next day, though I had no idea what for, then I had Petra's parents' evening, so it was going to be another busy one. Petra was hearing and went to her local primary school, but Gem needed an interpreter to have discussions with the teachers. I'd hoped for a quiet night, but I thought the least I could do was give my sister a lift.

I don't want things to get confused, I told her. *I can't be there as part of the police investigation and then later trying to be a friend. It wouldn't be right.*

You're not a police officer, Anna said gently. *You won't get in trouble for spending time with Laura. You always interpret for Gemma, and she's your best friend.*

I resisted rolling my eyes at my sister. I couldn't begin to try and explain to her the complications of being an interpreter in a town where most people who used the language knew you by sight.

I just want to rest, I said. *I've had a stressful week. I don't want to get involved with this. She's your friend, not mine, but I'll happily take you to see her.*

Fine, she replied with a sigh. *I said I'd be there by eight, is that okay?*

I checked my watch. *Okay, just let me relax for a bit. Please?*

She nodded and left the room. I flopped back onto my bed to finish watching an episode of *The Good Wife*, but I couldn't concentrate. I couldn't make sense of everything that was going on, whichever way I looked at it.

Forty minutes later, I pulled up outside Laura's house.

Just text me when you want picking up, okay? I could have left her to make her own way home, but if she wasn't staying long I was happy to wait outside for her. She may have been twenty-eight but I still had a protective streak when it came to Anna.

You can still change your mind and come in, she told me.

It's not a good idea, I've already said.

I know your job's important, and of course I don't want you risking anything. I'm just worried that you've got nobody to talk to about this.

I leant my head back. *I know, but I can't talk to Laura either, can I? She's a victim.*

Well you need to talk to someone about it. One of the detectives or someone like that.

As Anna got out, the front door of the house opened and Bridget stepped out. She waved to Anna, a lot more friendly than the last time we were there, then motioned to me to roll my window down, so I did.

'Thanks for coming, Paige. Laura really appreciates your support.'

'I wasn't going to come in . . .' I said, watching Anna stroll past Bridget and straight into the house without waiting to be invited.

'But I thought you were going to help,' Bridget replied, confusion wrinkling her tanned forehead. 'With the court case.'

It was my turn to be confused. Had Alan been charged and I didn't know? Or was there another suspect? Surely they couldn't have a court date already?

'Why would I be helping with the court case?' I asked.

'The case against Alan. Laura wants full custody of Jaxon. She was already in the process when . . . when this happened.' Bridget swallowed, and I stopped myself from contradicting her. I knew Laura's side of the story was a little different, but it wasn't the time, with the grief and turmoil Bridget must be experiencing.

'I don't understand what this has to do with me, Bridget, sorry. What does she want my help with?'

'The solicitor suggested she take an interpreter, rather than using me all the time,' she said, her mouth twisting to suggest she didn't approve of the idea. 'Laura has decided she would like you. Didn't Anna tell you?'

'No, she didn't.' I looked towards the house, where I could see Anna walking into the front room with Laura. Very sneaky of her.

'Well, could you come in and chat to her about it? She doesn't want anyone else, and the solicitor was quite insistent. He doesn't want her to misunderstand anything. It's her right to have an interpreter,' she said, glaring at me as if I had suggested Laura shouldn't have one.

'Of course it's her right. I'm happy to come to any appointments with her. I can forward you a link to my charges on my website,' I added, hoping to make it clear that they would be expected to pay the same as any other client. Another problem with being an interpreter who knew a lot of their clients was that clients started to expect mates' rates, and I had a mortgage to pay.

Bridget waved a hand irritably. 'Fine, fine. She can use her DLA to pay you. Or is it PIP now? Whatever they call it. Just come in now and speak to her, she can give you the background.'

Against my better judgement, I swung the car round onto Bridget's driveway and parked. If I was honest, I was curious about the situation. Could it have had a bearing on what happened to Lexi? Had Bridget told Alan she wanted him to lose custody? If she had confronted Elisha before, I wouldn't have put it past her to do the same to Alan. I pictured him, incensed at the idea of having his children taken off him. But then surely he would have killed Laura, not Lexi. Maybe it had been an accident?

130

But those wounds on Lexi's head couldn't have been accidental.

I followed Bridget inside, accepted her offer of a cup of tea and leant on the kitchen table while she made it. She was dressed smartly, as usual, with flowing peach trousers and a black top, accessorised with lots of gold jewellery. Already slim, she seemed to have lost weight in the days since Lexi's death.

'When did Laura start seeing the solicitor?' I asked, and she started slightly.

She must have been in her own little world as she stood there waiting for the kettle to boil. When she poured out the tea, I noticed her hands were shaking.

'A few months ago. I got fed up with Alan always changing his plans, bringing the kids back stinking of smoke or worse. Jaxon has already learned some inappropriate language, and he's only six.'

'So you persuaded her to seek full custody?' I asked.

Laura had already implied this in her interviews, but I was interested to see if Bridget would take credit for it. Laura was strong in her own quiet way, I'd seen that this week, but she didn't like to upset people or rock the boat. The Laura I knew would never have instigated court proceedings unless there'd been some sort of inciting incident, however much Alan hurt her when he left her for Elisha.

'I convinced her it was the best thing to do for the children.' Bridget's voice was brittle; she didn't like having her opinions challenged, which was clearly how she'd perceived my question. 'It's not good for them, being in that kind of environment.'

'Okay. So why does she want an interpreter now?'

131

Bridget sniffed. 'You'll have to ask her that. I've been there for her as much as I can, supported her throughout her pregnancies, especially with Lexi after Alan left her for that tart, but never mind that. If the solicitor says get an interpreter then I suppose she's choosing to listen to him.'

Having met Elisha, I was surprised to hear her described as a tart. She didn't come across as the sort of person who would deliberately steal a man from another woman, though I supposed Bridget needed to blame both of the offending parties for hurting her daughter.

A cup of tea was plonked down in front of me with enough force to make some of it splash out onto the table. I got up to fetch a dishcloth but Bridget waved me back into my seat. We didn't speak as she mopped up the spillage, then sat down opposite me.

'I don't know what the solicitor is thinking. Maybe he thinks I'm not giving Laura good advice, and he wants to change her mind about something. I've given her as much support as I can, but if she wants to go ahead without me, so be it.'

'I doubt it's personal, Bridget,' I said, attempting a reassuring pat of her hand. 'It's probably just because he wants to cover his back in case the court doesn't give Laura what she's asking for. He doesn't want her to turn around and say she was poorly advised because they didn't have a BSL interpreter. I've seen things like that happen before.'

Bridget appeared to be slightly appeased, and sipped her own cup of tea. Her hands were still shaking, and after a moment she put the cup down and put her hands in her lap. She didn't want me to see these signs of her inner turmoil. I was struck with a rush of sympathy and

I felt the urge to get up and give her a hug, but I knew Bridget would hate such a show of affection, and it would probably do more harm than good.

I made up my mind. I would do my best to help Laura. I couldn't be criticised by the police for getting involved in the custody case – I would be doing what I was paid for. Everything I discussed with a client was confidential. I wouldn't pass Laura any details of Lexi's case, but maybe sticking close to the family would provide me with some more information.

I shook myself. Was I being ridiculous? I wasn't a police officer, nor was I a private investigator. It wasn't my job to find out who killed Lexi. I was getting myself involved far more deeply in the investigation than was good for me.

I was still wondering if I'd made the right decision when Anna came into the kitchen, looking for a bottle of wine. Bridget pursed her lips as Anna headed straight for the fridge, and I resisted the urge to apologise for my sister. It was eight-thirty, not an unreasonable time for a drink, after all.

Come on, Laura wants to talk to you, she told me, tucking the bottle precariously under her arm so she could sign. I gave Bridget what I hoped came across as a supportive smile, and followed Anna back through to the living room.

She's really upset, so give her time, Anna told me before we went in.

Of course she's upset, someone killed her daughter.

Anna glowered at me. *You know what I mean.*

We walked into the room where we sat with the detectives the other day. The atmosphere felt much lighter, despite the weight of the situation bearing down on us.

133

Laura was curled up on one of the sofas, still wearing the huge hoodie, her bare feet tucked underneath her.

Hi Paige. Thanks for coming.

It's fine. Your mum says you need an interpreter next time you see the solicitor?

Yes, please. I really want you, not a stranger. I'll pay.

I nodded. Everyone had their own preferences when it came to interpreters. Some didn't want a familiar face, others did. A lot of women preferred a female interpreter when it came to medical matters in particular. I didn't question, I just took the jobs as they came.

Your mum seems a bit upset about it, I said, hoping to get Laura's side of the story. She rolled her eyes.

She's offended because I want a proper interpreter instead of her. But she can't sign all the legal stuff, and even when the solicitor explains things, she doesn't explain it properly to me. She has a conversation with him, completely ignoring me, then tells me what they've agreed. She's not interpreting for me, she's taking over.

I was pleased by Laura's reaction. I would have half expected her to sit back while her mum sorted everything out for her, especially now, but it looked like she was standing up for herself and taking charge.

I didn't want to take Alan to court in the first place, it was her idea, but if we're doing it then I want to be the one in control. I should be making the decisions about my children, not her.

Laura's face crumpled as she realised what she'd just signed – children, rather than child. Anna rushed over and squashed herself up close to her friend, flinging an arm around her and almost smothering her. I waited patiently as Anna soothed her friend. One thing I can say about my sister is that she's great when someone she cares about is in distress.

You told me everything was okay with Alan, that it was working for you, didn't you? Anna prompted Laura to get her talking again.

Laura sniffed and nodded. *He sometimes changes plans, but so do I. If I have a night out or something I ask Alan to have the kids for an extra night, or whatever. It was fine. But Mum didn't like it because we were getting on with it without her. She wants to have a legal ruling about when he can see Jaxon and Lexi.* Her eyes filled with tears again. *But now this has happened, I don't know what to do. What if he did this? What if he killed our baby girl?*

I'm so sorry, Laura, but I don't know. I don't know what happened, and I don't know who did it. I know the police are working hard to find out, though.

I want to kill them, she replied, her eyes flashing.

Anna stroked her hair and signed, *Me too.*

I nodded. *I know. The police will do all they can to keep them locked up. And if it was Alan, then I'm sure he won't be allowed to see Jaxon. The solicitor will be able to help you with that. But it might not have been him. Why would he hurt Lexi? Didn't he love her?*

Laura blew her nose while nodding. *He's a good dad.*

Well then, it was probably someone else. I can't imagine he'd hurt his daughter like that for no reason.

Laura threw her hands in the air, taking me by surprise. *You don't know what it's like, having to deal with this. My little girl has gone and I'm never going to see her again and I don't know why! Why would someone do this to a child?*

Her fury died down as quickly as it had risen, and she burst into tears again. Anna squeezed her tight and stroked her hair while she sobbed. My heart was breaking for her. I couldn't imagine her pain.

I tapped Anna on the shoulder. *I think maybe we should go. Laura needs to rest.*

She nodded her agreement and I got up to fetch Bridget. She was still sitting in the same place at the kitchen table, staring into her cup of tea, which must have been stone cold. When I walked in she didn't even look up until I said her name. Her eyes were red.

'Where did I go wrong?' she said.

I frowned, unsure what she was talking about. 'What do you mean? This wasn't your fault, Bridget.'

She shook her head sadly. 'It is, it's all my fault. Right from the moment she met that man I knew it was going to end in disaster. I should have intervened then. Now look where we are.'

'Bridget, the police don't know who did it or why, but there's no way you can blame yourself. Nobody could have seen it coming.'

When she looked at me again I was taken aback by how dead and hollow her eyes looked.

'I don't think I'm ever going to sleep again.'

I sat down opposite her and gently placed a hand over hers. 'Is there someone else who can come and stay with you, help the two of you out for a while? You can't be expected to deal with all of this on your own. One of your sons?'

Laura had two hearing brothers, and I was sure Anna had told me Bridget had siblings, at least one of whom was deaf. There was a wider family network I hoped they

136

could get support from, but none of them lived locally as far as I knew.

'No, the boys are busy. Maybe my sister. I don't know though.' Bridget shook herself. 'No, we don't need anyone. Laura and I will be fine. We can see this through, support each other. I appreciate you coming round, Paige, but we don't need any more help.'

A mask had come down, and I knew that we'd outstayed our welcome. 'We're going to go now, give you some peace and quiet, but Laura's quite upset.'

All of a sudden Bridget turned from a meek kitten into a snarling tiger, and she was out of her chair and in the hall before I could move.

'What did you say to her? I knew she shouldn't be having visitors yet! Don't you know she's suffering? You shouldn't have gone to talk to her.'

I didn't bother arguing with her, because I knew it wouldn't have any effect. She was upset and defending her daughter; I couldn't take offence. Behind Bridget, I waved Anna out of the room and we slipped away quietly.

13 hours before the murder

Did they say why they want us to pick him up? Laura asked again as they got out of the car. She usually walked to pick Jaxon up from school, but her mum had insisted on driving.

All they said was there had been an incident and they wanted us to come as soon as possible, Bridget replied.

I hope he's okay.

I'm sure he'll be fine. If he was hurt they would have told us.

Laura nodded. She knew her mum would have to interpret for her when they spoke to Jaxon's teacher, but she hoped Bridget would actually include her in the conversation and not do what she usually did.

As they entered the school, Laura carrying Lexi on her hip, the secretary looked up from her desk and flashed them a brittle smile.

'I'll see if Mrs Folkes is available.'

She scuttled off through another door and Bridget told Laura where she was going.

Why do we need to see the head? Laura asked, her heart sinking. This was happening too often.

We'll have to wait and see what she says. I'm sure it's a fuss over nothing.

They only waited for a couple of minutes before they were ushered through to the headteacher's office. There were two chairs set out for them, so Laura put Lexi down on the floor with a couple of toys from her bag. She'd be happy to entertain herself for a short time.

Sitting behind her desk, Mrs Folkes looked stern.

'Good afternoon. Thank you for coming in.'

'What's happened?' Bridget asked immediately, signing as she spoke.

'I'm afraid there has been another incident with Jaxon and another child,' the head replied, looking between Bridget and Laura. 'We've had to contact the other child's parents as well. Jaxon cut a little girl in his class quite badly with a pair of scissors.'

'I'm sure it was an accident,' Bridget replied.

'One of the staff witnessed the incident and I'm afraid it seems that Jaxon did it deliberately. They didn't have scissors out as part of the activity they were doing. He went to get some from a drawer then turned around and cut the girl's hand. Her mother has taken her to A and E to have it looked at.'

Bridget bristled and sat up straighter in her chair. 'I'm sorry to say I'm very disappointed in the attitude towards Jaxon at this school. He is constantly being blamed for minor incidents that are clearly accidental. He's six years old, accidents like this happen in a busy classroom. The teacher can't control the class properly, so when something like this happens everyone seems to jump to the conclusion that Jaxon is somehow at fault.'

'Mrs Weston, you must understand, we're doing our best to support Jaxon, but the incidents are stacking up. So far this year we have had complaints every week from other children about his behaviour in the playground. We spoke to you in October when he deliberately stamped on another child's neck, then in December when his teacher's wrist was broken.'

'You can't blame a child for an adult getting her wrist trapped in a door,' Bridget snapped.

'Two other adults witnessed Jaxon intentionally slam the door on her.'

Laura looked between her mother and the head, failing to follow the conversation. Bridget hadn't interpreted Mrs Folkes' side of the conversation for her, and in her anger she'd stopped signing her own words as well.

Mum, what's happened? Laura asked, but Bridget waved her off.

I'm dealing with it.

Laura was about to protest, but Bridget had turned back to the headteacher.

'I want to speak to this staff member who allegedly saw what happened today.'

'I'm afraid that won't be possible, they're busy right now,' Mrs Folkes replied smoothly. 'We'd like you to take Jaxon home early today, and then we can arrange a meeting for next week to talk about a plan going forward.'

'A plan? What sort of plan?' Bridget snapped.

'A plan to manage his behaviour. We have various

stages of intervention we can introduce, but something must be done. You understand, we need to safeguard all of the children in our care, which means ensuring Jaxon gets the most benefit from his education whilst also protecting the other children in his class.'

Mum, you need to interpret. What happened? Is Jaxon okay? Laura grabbed her mum by the shoulder, forcing Bridget to look at her.

He's fine. There was an accident with another child and a pair of scissors and they want to blame it on Jaxon, but I won't let them do that.

Let me deal with it, Laura replied.

No, we need to be forceful, Bridget told her.

'Mrs Folkes,' Bridget said, turning back to the head. 'I wonder if I could get a copy of your school's policy on discrimination? Or perhaps I should contact someone on the board of governors to ask why this school is victimising a deaf child?'

'I'm sorry you see it that way, Mrs Weston,' the head replied, her eyes narrowing slightly. 'But you know full well that we've done everything we can with the resources available to us to ensure Jaxon has full access to the curriculum. He has a TA who is a fluent BSL user, and we've provided sign-language lessons for the children in his class so he can communicate with his peers. If you feel his behaviour is purely a result of the communication barrier, when we have the meeting next week we'd welcome any suggestions you have for improving the situation. We'll speak to his teacher of the deaf and invite her in as well, so you can discuss how else we could be supporting Jaxon. However, his behaviour is becoming dangerous, and we cannot allow it to continue.'

Laura could see that whatever the headteacher had said, she'd riled Bridget. Her mum was sitting bolt upright in her chair, almost quivering with indignation.

'I'll be speaking to the council before we have that meeting,' Bridget replied. 'Perhaps I should put in a call to Ofsted as well.'

'You must do whatever you think is best,' Mrs Folkes replied, unshaken by Bridget's threats.

Her lack of reaction needled Bridget further, and she abruptly stood up.

Come on, we're getting Jaxon and going home, she told Laura, who looked at the head in confusion. Laura did as she was told, picking up Lexi and shoving her toys back into her bag. Mrs Folkes offered her a sympathetic smile, then stood and showed them into a side office where Jaxon was sitting with two staff members, a pile of torn paper in front of him.

Once Jaxon and Lexi were secured in the car, Laura asked Bridget to explain what had happened.

I've had enough of them blaming him for things like this, Bridget said, once she'd explained the bare bones of the conversation. *He's only six, it's not like he does any of it on purpose. They're not doing enough to support him.*

Laura thought before responding. She knew that a school for the deaf wouldn't have any communication barriers for Jaxon, and he might be happier there, but it would take away Bridget's favourite excuse. Laura was sure that Jaxon's behaviour would be challenging whichever school he went to, but her mum wasn't ready to accept that yet, and while they lived with her it was hard to go against her will.

Come on, we'll get the children home, she said. *I want to do Jaxon's reading before he goes to Alan's.* Laura turned round to look at Jaxon, who was kicking the back of Bridget's seat, and felt guilty for thinking it'd be a relief if his dad did get full custody. She looked at Lexi, who gave her a big grin and waved a chubby hand at her. She refused to admit she might favour one of her children over the other, but she knew there was no way she'd allow Alan to have full custody of Lexi. She'd kill him before she let him take her.

Chapter 12

Thursday 8th February

The next day, my alarm rang at eight. I'd been awake for a couple of hours anyway, staring at the ceiling. Everything about Lexi's death had been churning around in my mind.

Dragging myself out of bed, I turned on the shower and stood under the hot water for a long time, letting it draw some of the tension out of my muscles. I'd heard Anna stirring a short while earlier, but I didn't want to talk to her just yet. After we left Laura's she asked me more questions about the case – what I'd heard in interviews, what I'd talked about with DC Singh when I took him the note. I didn't really know what to say to her. I couldn't give her any information, and what I knew wouldn't satisfy her anyway. I found myself hoping that the interview I'd been booked for that morning would be more fruitful.

Once I'd showered, I slipped out of the flat and drove into Scunthorpe. I had plenty of time before my next appointment at the police station, so I drove through to the retail park and got myself breakfast and a large coffee.

I sat in the window, watching people arrive for work at the department store next door. My phone rang: it was Anna. I ignored it. She'd text me if it was important.

When I arrived at the station, Forest had a triumphant look on her face when she met me at the door.

'He's refused a lawyer so far, though we've only communicated through written notes. We'll want you to double check that with him when we go in. If he changes his mind, we'll have to wait for one to get here.'

'That's fine. I've got an appointment later on this afternoon, but I'm available until about four.'

Forest frowned, as if she'd forgotten I might have other demands on my time, but I needed to keep taking other appointments, unless she wanted to pay me to sit around the station all day on the off chance that they'd need me.

'Is it the man Alan had the fight with?' I asked, curious.

She gave me a penetrating stare. 'What?'

'I just wondered if the man you're interviewing is the one Alan fought with on Friday night. Elisha's ex.'

'Yes. Rick Lombard.' She gave me a strange look before leading the way to the interview room.

When we entered the room, I took in the scene. Singh was already seated at the table with a folder in front of him, but the other man was leaning casually in the corner of the room. His tracksuit and trainers were all brand new designer gear, and his dark hair was gelled to within an inch of its life. His stubble looked like he was trying hard to cultivate a certain rough-edged look, although it hadn't quite worked, and he appeared to have shaved with a razor that had seen better days. Forest pointed to the seat on the opposite side of the table and he turned his eyes to the ceiling but sat down obediently. I took my seat

145

opposite him, and Forest asked him again if he'd like a lawyer.

I told her before, I don't want a lawyer, the man signed to me, his nose wrinkling in a sneer. *Just get on with it.*

I interpreted this for Forest, who nodded. Singh looked over and shot me a quick smile, just as Forest was opening a brown file and removing a photograph.

'Can you tell us where you were on Friday night?'

You know where I was, he replied. *I was at that house, where the little kid died. But I didn't go inside. It was nothing to do with me.*

'Where were you before you confronted Alan Hunter?' Forest's face remained impassive, but I could tell she was itching to wring the information out of this man.

At home.

'Why did you go there that night?'

A shrug. *I wanted a word with Alan. Man to man.*

'What about?'

Another shrug. *About Elisha.*

Forest waited, though I could feel the frustration and impatience radiating off her. Her tactic paid off, however, as Lombard continued after a moment.

I didn't think he was treating Elisha right. She used to be with me. And there might have been a bit of an overlap, if you understand me.

Forest continued to stare at him. 'No, I don't understand you.'

Lombard sat forward. *It was like this. Elisha and me were still together when she met Alan. We sort of split up, but we still saw each other. We were still shagging.* He flashed a lascivious grin, his eyes flicking to my chest as he looked me over. I managed to keep myself from

146

grimacing. *I thought the kid might be mine, and I wanted to see her.*

'Had you been to their house before that night?'

No.

'Really? We have witnesses who say they've seen you before, on other weekends, when Alan Hunter was out.'

His skin flushed an ugly shade of purple. *Fine. I've been a few times, to see Elisha.*

'Are you and Elisha Barron having an affair?'

No, I just go to see her sometimes. As a friend.

Singh pulled a photograph from the file in front of him. It showed a basic pay-as-you-go mobile phone. 'We found this in Elisha and Alan's bedroom. There are text messages on it between you and Elisha, going back several weeks.'

As I translated this for him, the blood drained from Lombard's face. He chewed the edge of one of his filthy fingernails before replying.

It's not mine. I don't know anything about it.

Forest sighed as I interpreted this response, and I couldn't blame her.

'We know it's not yours. However, it only has one number saved on it, which is under your name. And I'm sure if we traced that number, we would confirm it belongs to your phone. What we're concerned about is the death of Lexi Hunter. Is there anything you can tell us about that?'

Lombard's eyes widened and he sat up straighter in his chair, his signing becoming more frantic. *No, that was nothing to do with me. You can't blame me for that, I didn't do it. I didn't go anywhere near her.*

Singh was quietly making notes, leaving Forest to ask the questions. It sounded like Lombard was a serious suspect, so they obviously weren't convinced Alan had done it – unless they wanted Lombard to give them some evidence against Alan. I shot Singh a sideways look, even though I couldn't ask him anything about it. But what could Lombard's motive have been, if he barely knew the family?

'Tell us about your conviction six years ago,' Forest asked. Ah, that might explain it.

Lombard drew his lips back over his teeth in something closely resembling a snarl. *I didn't do it.*

'Your record shows you spent four years in jail for assaulting your own child. Your ex-partner has a restraining order against you, and you're not even allowed to know which part of the country she lives in. Sounds like you're exactly the sort of person we're looking for, Rick. What sort of man hurts his own child?'

Lombard's shoulders bunched up in rage, but he didn't let rip in the way I was expecting. After a moment, he sagged. *I was a different person back then. Too many drugs. I didn't know what I was doing. I wish I could change it, but I can't.*

'So you're completely reformed, are you? A changed man? I don't really believe that. Your fight with Alan Hunter sounded pretty violent, from the witness statements.'

I'll be violent with a piece of shit like Alan Hunter, yeah, but I'd never hurt a kid. I'm not on drugs now, I've been clean since I was inside.

'We'll ask you again,' Forest said. 'Were you inside Alan and Elisha's house on Friday night?'

Lombard wriggled then nodded. *I went to see Elisha for a bit. To check she was okay. That's all.*

'Did you go upstairs at all while you were there?'

No, Elisha and I stayed in the front room. I didn't go upstairs. I didn't hurt that kid. I didn't even know there were kids in the house until the boy came downstairs!

Singh looked up from his notes. 'What time was that?'

Lombard wrinkled his nose while he thought. *Don't know. But it was a while before Alan came home.*

'Why did he come downstairs?'

He said he wanted a drink or something.

'Did Jaxon see you?'

Yeah, but that didn't matter. If he told his dad I was there I would have said he was lying, Lombard replied with a shrug.

'But Alan came home and found you there, so Jaxon didn't need to tell him anything,' Forest said.

No, Alan saw me outside. I went out the back way before he could catch us, I just wasn't quick enough getting away from the house.

'And your fight took place outside? There was no altercation inside that Jaxon could have witnessed?'

Lombard shook his head firmly. *Definitely not. He'd been in bed for ages by the time Alan got home.*

Singh and Forest conferred quickly, then turned back to Lombard. 'We don't have any further questions for you right now. Is there anything else you think we should know, anything that could help us find out who killed Lexi?'

He squirmed in his seat, and I thought he was going to sign something, but he just shook his head. Forest told him he could go, although I could see she was reluctant.

Once I was back outside I inhaled the fresh air, glad to be out of the interview room. There was no doubting that Lombard was a good-looking man, but his demeanour made my skin crawl. I got to my car, but heard someone calling my name, so I turned around to see Singh crossing the car park.

'Are you okay?' he asked, watching me carefully.

'It's all a bit much to deal with,' I replied, gesturing at the police station to show I meant the case, Lexi's death, the whole situation. 'But I'll get over it. Is there any news on the note?'

He grimaced. 'I'm afraid it might take a bit longer. I tried to prioritise it, but forensics are always snowed under.'

I nodded and turned to go, but then turned back. I wouldn't find anything out if I didn't take a risk now and then.

'Are you any closer to finding out what happened?'

He glanced over his shoulder at the station. 'I wish. Alan can prove the murder weapon belonged to him and his fingerprints could be old, so the evidence against him isn't strong enough to charge him. We don't have anything else on Lombard, and the only other person we want to talk to is proving hard to track down.'

'Who's that?'

But before he had a chance to reply, Forest had stuck her head out of the door and was beckoning to Singh. With an apologetic grimace, he left me standing next to my car, thoughts whirling.

I drove around town for a while after Lombard's interview, trying to make sense of everything I knew. If I went back to the flat, Anna would start asking me questions again, and I needed time to think. What still wasn't clear to me was why. Why would anyone kill an eighteen-month-old?

I had several hours before my next job, so I drove out of town towards Normanby Hall, looking for somewhere to clear my head. The house would be closed, but a brisk walk around the park got my blood pumping and helped me piece together some of the information I had. By the time I'd remembered to have something to eat, it was time to head out to my next appointment – a parents' evening job for a client I would never pass over to another interpreter.

I couldn't find a parking space anywhere near the school, so I ended up parking four streets away and walking back. By the time I arrived, I was verging on late. Battling through the throng of parents hanging around outside the hall, I scanned the crowd for Gemma. She was usually waiting by the door for me, but because of the time she must have gone in. Inside the hall, the headteacher was setting up for her presentation, and I spotted Gemma in the front row.

Sorry, I signed to her. *I couldn't park.*

It's okay! Glad you're here.

What's the presentation? I hadn't had a chance to check in with the headteacher, and she looked ready to start.

Sex education, Gemma replied, giving me a wink.

I groaned. Gem and I used to cause havoc together down at the Deaf club when we were kids. She was the only deaf person in her family, I the only hearing one in mine: we were drawn to each other, even though we were complete opposites. She always had me as her preferred interpreter when I worked for agencies, but that didn't always mean I was given the job. When I went freelance, it meant she could book me directly, and she always did. Her daughter, Petra, called me Auntie Paige, and her teachers knew me well. One of them even stopped me in the street once to tell me how well Petra was doing at school; I had to remind her that Gemma was Petra's mum, not me.

As I was thinking of how close I was to Petra, I thought about how Anna would never get to have that relationship with Lexi. Turning up on my doorstep was probably as much for her to work through her own grief as it was to support Laura, and I couldn't blame her for wanting to know a bit more about what was going on. I needed to be a bit kinder to her when I got home.

Working through the presentation, I reminded myself that I should always check what I was doing before agreeing to interpret for Gem. She knew full well that the one thing I was uncomfortable with was interpreting anything about sex. I preferred to avoid jobs at GP surgeries, in case the client wanted to talk about something sensitive. She was smirking and winking at me, clearly enjoying my discomfort.

It wasn't as bad as I'd been expecting, just explaining to parents the different aspects of relationship education the children learned in each year as they went through primary school, but I still attempted to wind Gem up. As we walked together up the corridor to Petra's classroom after the presentation, I signed to her. *You knew what the presentation was going to be, and you didn't tell me! You're a cow.*

She gasped in mock horror. *I'm paying for your time right now, you can't insult me.*

I raised an eyebrow and signed *Cow* again. By the time we arrived at the classroom we were both giggling and I had to apologise to a couple who were sitting outside waiting.

We occupied the remaining two chairs and chatted for a while as we waited for Petra's teacher to get to Gemma. Petra's dad was killed in a car accident while Gem was pregnant, and she'd done a stellar job as a single mum for the last six years. I kept trying to find people to set her up with, but she told me she wanted to focus on bringing up her daughter.

Did you hear about that little girl? It's awful.

I grimaced and agreed with her, though I'd been hoping I could have a few hours without thinking about Lexi.

Who could do that to a child? Gem asked. *I hope the police find whoever did it. I don't agree with the death penalty, but in some circumstances I could change my mind.*

Do you know the parents? I knew I should change the subject, to avoid the possibility of saying anything I shouldn't, but I was curious to hear Gem's take on it.

I know them from Deaf club. Jaxon is the same age as Petra, so they're in the same group when they do activities for the children.

I should have realised. Gem had always been very active at the Deaf club as an adult and Petra spent plenty of time there.

I always wondered about them, you know, she continued.

About who? I asked. *The parents?* I avoided referring to them by name in case she realised I knew more than I was admitting.

She nodded. *The whole family. Something always seemed a bit . . . off. They always seemed on edge. I wondered if Laura was scared of Alan, but he looked affectionate most of the time. Before he went off with Elisha, I mean.*

153

I made a mental note to suggest the police talked to people at the Deaf club if they wanted to know more about the family. I could maybe persuade DC Singh to join me for a drink, and get some more information out of him that way. Somehow, I didn't think Forest would be interested in my suggestions. I got the feeling she'd reject any ideas that weren't her own.

So what do you think it was, then? What was the problem?

Gemma shook her head. *I don't know. She still has that sort of hunted air about her, and she hasn't been with Alan for nearly two years, so I suppose it can't be him. Laura always hovers around Jaxon, as if she's afraid something will happen to him. She never leaves him unsupervised even for a moment. The whole point of the kids' groups is to give parents a break, so we can socialise as well.*

I was about to ask another question when we were called in to see Petra's teacher, and neither of us brought up Lexi again until we were leaving. Gemma put a hand to her mouth.

Anna knows Laura, doesn't she? This is awful, I'm sorry. I didn't think. She looked at me, and then her eyes widened. *That's what's wrong, isn't it? The police will need an interpreter, for the interviews. It's you, isn't it?*

I didn't need to answer. She could see it in my face, and she threw her arms around me.

No wonder you're distracted, she signed once she'd pulled away. *Oh God, it must be awful.*

It's fine, seriously. I can handle it, I lied.

I'm so sorry, Paige. Especially given . . . She tailed off.

What? I asked, knowing she was talking about Caitlin.

154

I hadn't thought. All of this with Lexi Hunter, it must bring it back.

I shrugged. Gem was the one who was there for me all through what happened to Caitlin, so she knew better than anyone the anguish I put myself through.

Gem gave me a searching look. *You need to come down to the Deaf club this weekend, socialise a bit yourself. You're working too hard.*

I shrugged again, unsure what she wanted me to say.

Promise me you'll think about it?

I've already promised Anna I'll come on Saturday, I replied. But privately I thought I'd like to avoid the Deaf club until it was all over, especially if other people made the link between Lexi and my past.

12 hours before the murder

He parked outside Elisha and Alan's house and turned off the engine, but didn't make a move to get out of the car. Really, he knew he shouldn't be there. It wouldn't do anyone any good. Still, he'd found himself driving towards Scunthorpe on his way home from work instead of turning off to the village where he lived, and his inner autopilot had brought him to their house.

The last time he'd been here, it hadn't ended well. Alan thought he'd got rid of him, but it only fuelled his determination to end it between Alan and Elisha. Elisha had to see that that man was no good for her. He didn't want to be the one picking up the pieces when it all came crashing down around her ears.

As he watched, Elisha appeared in the front window, with Kasey in her arms. The little girl was crying and Elisha looked stressed as she bounced her up and down in an attempt to calm her. If he went and knocked on the door now, would she let him in? Or was she too afraid of Alan? His van wasn't in the driveway so he could safely assume Alan was still at work, but if he came home while he was in the house talking to Elisha, things could get messy.

Not for the first time, he considered just walking in there, grabbing some of Elisha's things and taking her and Kasey away from there. She'd never told him anything specific about the way Alan mistreated her, but he knew it was going on. Even if he wasn't physical with her, he used her as an unpaid skivvy. She spent her days at home alone with Kasey, and her weekends trying to entertain all three children. He'd seen it for himself; she was at the end of her tether and at some point something had to give.

He was about to get out of the car when Alan's van turned in to the street. Quickly turning his head away as if he was looking for something in the glove compartment, he watched the house out of the corner of his eye until Alan had gone inside. Cursing his own indecisiveness, he started the car and pulled away, heading home. Maybe today wasn't the right day, but at some point soon he might have to do something drastic to open Elisha's eyes to the man she was living with.

Chapter 13

Friday 9th February

The next morning found us sitting in my kitchen, going round in circles again.

You know I'm not going to talk to you about it.

Please, Paige. You're being ridiculous. You know Laura will tell me as soon as she knows anything. She just texted me – Alan's been released. She's scared he or Elisha might have done it, and she doesn't know what to think. I just want to help her.

I know you do, I replied, *but I can't tell you anything. Laura can tell you whatever she wants. I'm not risking my job for this. Do you want me to get fired?*

I regretted my words as soon as I'd signed them. I knew she didn't want to put me in a difficult position and was thinking about her friend, and I had to remember how much Anna was grieving. For the last couple of days her PhD research had been spread out on the living room floor, but I doubted she'd been doing anything other than scanning the internet for news.

Of course I don't want you to lose your job, she replied,

looking hurt. *I want to know what happened. I want to help. What if Laura's right, and Alan or Elisha were involved? You said it yourself, it's hard to believe someone was in their house without them knowing.*

I sighed. *You can't help, Anna. Just let the police get on with their jobs, and focus on supporting Laura.*

I'm doing my best. She glared at me for a moment, then snatched up a textbook off the floor and went into her room, slamming the door behind her. I rubbed my eyes and decided to let her cool off for a little while. I sank onto the sofa, but groaned aloud when my work phone beeped a moment later.

I dug it out of my bag, mentally composing what I'd like to say to DI Forest, but the text wasn't from the police.

DON'T TALK TO ANYONE ABOUT LEXI, OR YOU'LL BE NEXT.

My heart leapt into my mouth as I read the threatening capitals, stark against the white screen. Who would have sent me something like that? Bile rose into my throat and I gulped it back down, making myself cough. I screwed my eyes shut. What had I got myself into? Why would someone threaten me? I hadn't talked to anyone about the case, other than Anna, and she didn't know anything beyond what we'd talked about at Laura's the day before. I was just doing my job.

The number wasn't withheld, but I didn't recognise it. No clue to who sent it. I was still staring at the screen when Anna came back out of the spare room. I shoved my phone back into my bag quickly, but she could read the worry on my face.

What is it?

159

I paused before replying, but knew I couldn't hide this from her. *A text.*

Who from?

I shrugged, passing her the phone so she could read it. Her eyes widened. *You have to show this to the police.*

I will.

I can't believe someone is still threatening you! Why would they do this?

I don't know. Singh said it doesn't make sense, and I agree with him.

She sat down, putting the phone down carefully, as if it was dangerous. *Have they found out anything about the note?*

I shook my head. *Not that they've told me. I'll call Singh and tell him about this one today.*

Tell him you need protection. Some psycho is threatening you, probably the person who killed Lexi. They know where you live, and your phone number.

I brushed her comment off. *This is my work phone, the number's on my website. Anyone could have got it.*

She narrowed her eyes. *Fine, but they still put a note through your front door.*

Anna, I know. I know how serious this is. As if to make a point, I picked the phone up again and dialled DC Singh's number. He answered straight away, and he agreed to meet me later that morning.

I could tell by her face that it wouldn't be the end of Anna's questions, but by the time I left she was bent over her studies again.

When I'd spoken to Singh, he'd suggested I meet him at the station, but I'd been reluctant. I wanted to pick his

160

brains a little about the case, and I was convinced he'd be a bit more open with me if DI Forest wasn't around.

Instead, I walked into the cafe we'd agreed on, and he was already there, sitting at a table by the window.

'What can I help you with?' he asked with a wry smile as I joined him. 'I assume there's a reason you didn't want to come to the station.'

'I've had another threat,' I told him, not wanting to beat around the bush. I passed him my work phone so he could read it for himself.

Singh frowned. 'You don't recognise the number?'

I shook my head. 'No. Can you trace it?'

'Yes, but it probably won't tell us anything. I'm sure whoever this is won't be texting you from a phone registered in their own name. We'll check it, but don't hold your breath.'

I had assumed it wouldn't be straightforward. 'Is anyone else being threatened? You or Forest?'

'No, not that I know of. It suggests someone has something personal against you, Paige.' For a moment he placed his hand lightly over mine, then withdrew it as if he'd thought better of the gesture. 'Are you okay?'

I inhaled deeply and sat back in my chair. 'I'm worried, of course I am. But I don't really know what to think. I'm only here because I'm the interpreter who happened to get the call on Saturday morning. It could have been anyone from one of the agencies, if I hadn't been available. So I understand why you say it sounds personal, but I haven't done anything to warrant being threatened. I don't know anything about the case.'

'Perhaps this person thinks you know more than you do.'

'That's why I asked you to meet me here.' I looked at

him over my coffee, wondering what angle I should take to try and persuade him to talk to me. I decided that straightforward honesty would be best. 'I want to know more about the case.'

His face fell. 'I can't give you details, Paige, you know that. I'm disappointed that you've even asked.'

'Can you blame me? I've been thrown into this situation, I'm being threatened, I've barely slept for the last few nights and I don't even know what's happening. Maybe if you give me a bit more information about the case, I can be useful. I understand the Deaf community better than you do.'

Singh looked down at his coffee, then, to my surprise, let out a laugh. 'You're pretty persistent, aren't you?'

I grinned at him. 'Of course.'

He tapped his fingernails on the side of his mug as he thought. 'I can't involve you in the case. There's no call for an expert witness or anything like that at the moment. But I'm going back to Hunter's house after we finish here, and perhaps you could come with me. You can explain the modifications they have.'

I nodded enthusiastically. 'Would Forest allow that?'

He laughed again. 'Hell no. I won't tell her unless I have to.'

'Why is she so horrible?' I asked, and he bit back a laugh.

'I can see why she might come across that way. She had a case last year, an issue with someone who didn't speak English and a mistranslation . . . Anyway, she gets worked up if she can't communicate directly with the people she's interviewing.'

We finished our drinks as I explained the sorts of

modifications available for deaf people to make their daily lives easier.

'The most useful one in our house was the light that hung on the back of the bathroom door. It flashed if someone knocked on the door while you were in there.'

'I'm not sure what Alan and Elisha have, but you'll probably spot them more easily than I will. Ready to go?'

I nodded and picked up my bag, and caught him looking at me appraisingly.

'What?' I asked.

He shook his head. 'Nothing.'

We'd both brought our own cars, so I walked back up Ashby High Street to where I'd left mine. Scunthorpe was formed from five villages, and Ashby was the only one that had retained its own high street, separate from the town centre. I'd parked next to one of several vape shops, opposite a charity shop and a barber's, one of about seven on the street. A couple of lads in tracksuits were having an argument on the pavement in front of me, but they stepped out of the way when I approached.

Pulling away, I cast a glance at the the old market, which had been closed in November. The drab remnants of abandoned stalls were a painful reminder of how close the town came to destitution every time the steelworks was threatened with closure. There was a derelict Kwik Save opposite, though a couple of other budget supermarkets had survived.

Further up the road, I passed a church that had been converted into a gym, and the ironically named Rainbow Hall, a grim-looking community centre, its windows shuttered and with no sign it was still open except for a tattered poster advertising a weight loss group. The council did their best with what little funds they had, but the people for whom the centre was a lifeline could hardly be inspired by its appearance.

I crossed the dual carriageway and drove through the estate where Alan and Elisha lived, pulling up on the street outside the house. Singh was already there, and he got out of his car as I parked. There was still a ribbon of blue and white police tape fluttering across the end of the footpath.

The front yard was overgrown and littered with rubbish: takeaway cartons, cigarette butts and other odds and ends. I hadn't noticed the state of the place in the gloom of last Saturday morning. It was a strange contrast to the stark tidiness of the house that I remembered, though as soon as we stepped inside I realised that what I had thought of as neat was actually quite bleak. The smell of cannabis was stronger than I remembered from that morning, too.

'So, where do you want to start?' I asked Singh as I followed him in through the front door. As I did so, I noticed the door had two handles, one in the usual position and one much higher up.

'I don't even know, really. I wanted to come back here and walk through the house again, try and get a feel for how the family live, and what might have happened. I think better when I'm at a crime scene.'

I raised an eyebrow, but didn't comment, and followed him through the living room, out into the hallway at the back of the house.

'We're working on the assumption that the killer came in by the back door, if they weren't in the house already. If they'd come in the front, there was too much chance they'd wake Alan.'

I glanced back into the living room, looking for the adaptations that Elisha had put in – there was a flashing doorbell, but that was it. There wasn't anything that would alert them to the back door being opened, and the house wasn't alarmed.

'So Elisha and Alan are still suspects, then?'

He threw me a glance, and I gave him an innocent look.

'Fine. Yes, we're keeping an open mind on that front. We still have plenty of evidence to analyse, plus some more witness statements from neighbours to comb through.'

He folded his arms and cast his eye over the back door. I noticed that, like the front door, it had two handles as well, and asked him about it.

'Apparently Jaxon's a bit of an escape artist. Alan put the extra handles in to stop him running out onto the road.'

I nodded. From what I'd seen of Jaxon's behaviour, it made sense from a safety point of view.

'There was no sign of a break in, so either the door was unlocked, or the killer had a key.'

'Or they were already in the house,' I reminded him, but he didn't seem to hear me.

He went into the kitchen and gazed around for a moment. I didn't want to speak in case I broke the flow of his thoughts, but we both turned when we heard a car pull up outside the house.

Singh walked back into the living room and looked out of the window. 'Oh crap.'

Forest was getting out of the car. We saw her cast a glance at both of our cars, then look towards the house, so Singh hurried to open the door for her.

'Rav,' she said, giving him a long appraising look. 'I wasn't expecting to find you here. Certainly wasn't expecting you to be here with the interpreter.'

There was a pause. I didn't attempt to fill the silence, bristling with annoyance at the way she spoke about me but not to me. Singh opened his mouth to reply, but before he had a chance to speak, a movement caught my eye. Behind DI Forest, at the end of the path, was Elisha Barron.

I was instantly suspicious. What was Elisha doing, coming back here? As far as I knew, the police hadn't told her she could go back to the house yet. Was there something she had come to look for, something that might implicate her or Alan?

'Did you arrange to meet her here?' Forest asked Singh. He shook his head, as surprised as she was. Forest glanced my way again, and I thought she didn't believe him, but she didn't say anything.

When Elisha saw the three of us standing in the doorway, she stopped for a moment. 'I wanted to get some things,' she said, looking at the two detectives. Singh looked surprised; I think he'd forgotten Elisha sometimes chose to speak.

I could see from the tension in Forest's jaw that she wasn't happy, but she relented.

'Okay, you can go in and get what you need, but DC Singh and I will go with you,' Forest said. 'We'll make a note of everything you take. Forensics have cleared most rooms now.'

Elisha glanced in my direction for an interpretation, but she didn't make eye contact.

'Can I take things for Alan, or only my things?'

'As long as we see what you're taking and give you permission to take it, you can take things for Alan as well.'

As we trooped through the house, I wondered if I should tell Forest that I persuaded Singh to bring me here. If I told her about the second threat against me, it might make her more sympathetic towards me, and hopefully Singh wouldn't get in too much trouble for letting me tag along with him. I was worried she'd just brush off the threats, however, and I'd dig us into a deeper hole, so I decided to keep my mouth shut.

Turning to Elisha, I asked where she wanted to start. For a moment she looked confused, so I prompted her. *Do you need clothes? Things from the bathroom?* She nodded to both of these, so we headed upstairs, DC Singh leading the way.

At the top of the stairs, she paused outside a room, swallowing as she stared at the door. It was the room where it happened, where Lexi died just under a week earlier. A wave of horror washed through me and I shivered. Forest noticed and frowned slightly, but said nothing. Elisha bit her lip and turned her back on the door, walking across the landing to the room opposite.

The bathroom was dirty and in dire need of modernisation. The mirror over the sink was brown where the silver had peeled off at the back, and several tiles were chipped. The bath had a scummy ring of limescale. There was a threadbare bathmat, and a cabinet with one door hanging off. Elisha collected a number of toiletries and waited while DC Singh made a note of each item.

Elisha looked even worse than she had the last time I'd seen her, and I felt some sympathy. I didn't know her before we met on the morning I was called to the house, but I had known of her. I remembered how outraged Anna was when she found out Alan was leaving Laura for someone else while Laura was pregnant. That was nothing compared to the explosion when she found out Elisha was also pregnant. There was only about six weeks difference in age between Lexi and her half-sister, Kasey.

When we'd finished in the bathroom, we moved back up the hall to the bedroom. Elisha asked if she could take a bag, which Forest agreed to once she had searched it thoroughly, unzipping all of the pockets and carefully feeling along every inch of the lining. I had no idea what she was looking for, and didn't ask.

Elisha packed the bag with underwear and clothing for herself and Alan, opening and closing drawers and the wardrobe seemingly at random. She looked confused and upset, and I wondered if she was actually thinking about what to pack, or just taking things as they came to her. It was possible she'd come back to the house for another reason, then made up a story about wanting to collect things when she saw Forest and Singh were there. She looked over her shoulder at them every time she took something out of a drawer or off a hanger, then handed it over with a defeated look on her face as Singh wrote it down.

A moment later, Elisha knocked a lamp off the bedside table and bent down to pick it up. I frowned and made eye contact with Singh: did he see what I thought I saw? Did Elisha deliberately knock the table with her hip, so the lamp fell on the floor? Singh frowned back; he hadn't noticed. I nodded to where Elisha was kneeling on the floor, replacing the lamp with one hand but scrabbling under the bed frame with her other, and Singh caught on. He stepped sideways to get a clearer view of what Elisha was doing, and Forest followed the direction of his gaze.

'What are you looking for?' he asked.

I interpreted this for Elisha and her face flushed, but she straightened up and signed, *I'm not looking for anything.*

'Really? That's where we found the phone you used to contact Rick Lombard,' Forest said, her voice bone dry.

As I interpreted Forest's response, Elisha's face paled and her shoulders sagged.

'Did you think we wouldn't find it when we searched the house?'

I didn't want Alan to find out, Elisha signed, not looking up.

Forest sniffed and turned away. 'Is that the only reason you came back here?'

I need to get some things for . . .

I paused as I asked Elisha for clarification. I wasn't sure of the sign she'd used, so she fingerspelt it for me: K-A-S-E-Y. Deaf people often have a sign name that is more than just the signed spelling, a sign that represents them to the people they know. Elisha had used the sign name for her daughter, which I wasn't familiar with.

'I need to get some things for Kasey,' I interpreted. 'Clothes, toys, her blanket.'

'Are they in the children's room?' Forest asked. Elisha nodded. 'Well then I'm sorry, but no. There might be more forensics work to be done in there. I can't allow you in.'

What am I going to do about clothes and Kasey's things? She won't sleep without her elephant.

Forest shrugged, and for a moment I bristled with

annoyance at how callous she was. 'I'm sorry, but you'll have to make other arrangements, buy new things for now. Hopefully you can get them tomorrow or the day after.'

Elisha looked distraught and I felt the urge to leap to her defence. It was all I could do to keep my mouth shut.

'Perhaps if she left a list of what she wanted, the forensic team could release those items? If they're not needed for evidence,' Singh said. I was surprised that he had contradicted Forest, but glad he'd spoken up for Elisha.

With a sigh, Forest said, 'Fine, although I can't guarantee they'll agree.'

The DI led us downstairs and into the living room.

'Can you give us the address where you're staying?' she asked Elisha, who nodded and wrote it down. 'As you're here, we'd like to ask you a few more questions.'

I need to get home. My friend's looking after Kasey.

'This afternoon then? Come to the police station.'

A flash of fear raced across Elisha's face, but she nodded. I watched her scuttle out of the door without a backward glance, wondering if the phone was really the only reason she'd come back. When I turned back to the detectives, Forest was glaring at me, so I made my excuses and left.

Before I got in my car, I glanced up the road to the waste ground where the murder weapon was found. Elisha had walked in the opposite direction, but when I turned around I saw she'd stopped and was watching me. She hesitated for a moment, as if she was going to walk back towards me, but then she turned around again and broke into a run as she disappeared around a corner.

Chapter 14

Elisha was sitting in the lobby of the police station when I arrived, and she gave me a fleeting smile. Her eyes were bloodshot and surrounded by dark circles.

Did you know the police wanted to ask you more questions today, when you came to the house? I asked her.

She shook her head. *I don't know why. I've told them everything.* But something about her body language said otherwise. *Everyone is really upset,* she added. *Alan's so angry.*

I reached out to squeeze her hand, but she pulled it away from me sharply.

I'm sorry. I understand how hard it must be for you.

Do you? Have you ever been through anything like this? She glared at me from under her fringe.

Yes, I have, I wanted to tell her, but I kept my comments to myself. It wasn't the time to bring up my past.

I wanted you to know there's support available, that's

all. If you need it. There are counsellors, people you can talk to. And if there's anything you're worried about, you can talk to the police.

She looked at me askance. *The police don't care.*

Why do you say that?

She pulled her mouth into a sneer. *I don't think they're bothered. Not really. They just want to harass us, Alan and me.*

I didn't push the point, because it was clear Elisha would defend Alan even if she thought he might have killed Lexi. *Have you talked about moving back home yet?*

Yeah, but I don't want to, even if the police say it's okay. I've told Alan I want us to stay at my friend's another few days. It doesn't feel right, going back into the house where it happened. Her eyes were shining and I wondered how she was coping. After all, whatever she might have been hiding, it was important to remember she'd been the one to find Lexi's body.

How does Alan feel about that?

Elisha threw another glance over at me. *He's not happy, but he says we can stay there a bit longer. I don't want Kasey sleeping in that room again. What if she has nightmares about it?*

I nodded sympathetically. *Do you think Kasey and Jaxon might have seen what happened? I know the police interviewed Jaxon.*

The look she flashed me took me by surprise, it was so filled with hate. *Don't talk to me about that boy. I don't want him in my house again.*

Why? Did he tell you something about that night? Did he see who killed Lexi?

She let out a snort. *That's all you're interested in, isn't it? You pretend to be friendly, but you just want something to tell the police. Well I'm not talking to you. You know nothing about my family, nothing.*

Please, Elisha, that's not why I asked. I went to touch her arm, but thought better of making physical contact this time. *I wanted to make sure you were okay.*

Piss off, she signed, standing up and turning her back on me.

Several tense minutes later, we were both taken through to an interview room. Singh gave me a sheepish smile, and I wondered if Forest had given him a talking to about taking me back to the crime scene.

Forest sat down and had begun the questions before Singh had finished taking a seat.

'What can you tell us about Rick Lombard?'

Why? Elisha asked, but her eyes gave away that she was keeping something secret.

'He was at your house last Friday night, the same night Lexi died.'

She wrinkled her nose. *I don't know what you're talking about. I didn't see Rick that night.*

'Really? So he didn't come round at any point that night?'

She shook her head and I thought she was starting to look a little frightened, but I didn't know why.

'We know Rick was there when Alan came home. They had a fight. But we have another witness who told us he was there for several hours that evening, when you were alone in the house with the children. Rick himself told us he was there. So think about your answer again.'

Her eyes danced around the room before she replied.

Alan doesn't know, about me and Rick. He didn't know, before that night, I mean. I used to go out with Rick, before I met Alan. Just before. We . . . kept in touch.

'You broke up with Rick to go out with Alan?'

She shook her head. *It wasn't serious, not like that. But Rick got scary when I was pregnant with Kasey, kept saying he was going to tell Alan about us, get a DNA test.*

Forest tensed her jaw. 'Why didn't you tell us this before?'

It has nothing to do with Lexi. Rick didn't hurt her.

'Rick thought Kasey was his daughter. Maybe he went upstairs to try to see her?'

Elisha pulled a face. *No, he didn't go upstairs. He knows Kasey isn't his daughter, she looks like Alan. And she looks like Lexi, and they wouldn't look alike unless they were sisters.*

For a moment, Forest stared at her with her arms folded. Elisha shuffled in her seat and then looked at me as if for reassurance. I waited for the detectives to continue with their questions.

'You know we found the phone you've been using to contact him. We know your relationship is more than just "keeping in touch".' Forest still had her arms crossed, and she watched Elisha to see her reaction.

Elisha hung her head. *I don't know why. I don't want to ruin what I've got with Alan. Rick always talks me into things.*

'Rick Lombard has a history of violence, and you used to be in a relationship with him. You've just admitted that he's coercive, and you were scared of him when you were pregnant. Why are you so convinced he didn't kill Lexi?'

I know him. He's not always a good person, but he wouldn't hurt a child.

Forest raised an eyebrow and looked at Singh. Clearly, Elisha didn't know the full extent of Lombard's history.

Anyway, he didn't go upstairs. Then Alan came in, drunk and ranting. He and Rick got into it, but then Rick left. I watched him leave. He definitely didn't come inside again.

My head was reeling with the different accounts from different witnesses, or suspects, in this case. I was glad I wasn't in Forest's position, trying to make sense of what actually happened that night.

'Tell us about the fight Alan had with your brother the week before.'

This caught my attention. I wondered how much information had been filtering into the police without my knowledge.

Elisha's face turned red and she licked her lips several times, the question making her instantly nervous.

What fight?

'We've been told that it wasn't the first time Alan's had a fight outside your house. The weekend before there was another incident. We know you went to sort it out, and we have it on good authority that the man was your brother.'

Elisha's eyes searched the room again, as if looking for a way out.

I don't know.

'You don't know if it was your brother? The same way you didn't know who Rick Lombard was, even though you had a relationship with him?'

No, no, I knew it was him. I mean, I went outside to see, I went after Alan. But I didn't see them fighting.

175

'Why not? It can't have been that dark. Your road has plenty of street lights.' Forest was getting sarcastic, and I wondered if she'd had enough of Elisha's stories.

No, it wasn't. I mean, they weren't fighting when I went outside. Then he left.

'That's strange,' Forest said, shaking her head. 'The witness who told us about this seems to think you were the one to sort it out, that you stopped the fight.'

That's not what happened. That's not what happened. Elisha repeated herself frantically. *That's not what happened.*

'What did happen then? Why don't you want us to know about the fight Alan had with your brother? We're concerned about this pattern that's developing, of Alan fighting with people in the street. Maybe one of them took things further.

'We'd like to talk to your brother, but we haven't been able to track him down yet. Have you told him to lie low and not get in touch with us?' Forest continued.

Elisha was taken aback by this, and shook her head, but she didn't sign anything.

Singh sat forward in his seat. 'Elisha, you have to understand that we are looking for someone who is very dangerous. This person has murdered a child. They might well hurt someone else. They might hurt Kasey. This is serious. You have to tell us the truth, and tell us everything you know. If you're hiding something, protecting someone, you could get into trouble.'

As I was interpreting, Elisha sat and shook her head over and over, her shoulders hunched, hands pressed between her knees. I could see she was scared and confused, but Singh's words kept coming.

'This person you're protecting, they might have killed Lexi. Do you understand that? You might be protecting someone who murdered a little girl. I don't know if it's Alan, or Rick, or your brother, but you need to tell us the truth. Tell us whatever you're keeping secret.'

'No!'

I was surprised by Elisha's shout. She turned back to me and continued in sign. *You don't understand. He wouldn't hurt anyone. It has nothing to do with him.*

'Who? Lombard? Or your brother?' Forest asked, her face livid.

The effect of Singh's speech wore off as quickly as it came, and Elisha sat back in her chair. *I've told you everything. I don't know why you think I'm keeping secrets. I've told you all I know.*

The conversation went round in circles for another five minutes before the detectives looked at each other, defeat on both their faces. They had no reason to keep Elisha there, and she didn't hesitate once they told her she could go. As the door closed behind her, Forest slammed a file down on the table in frustration.

That evening I arrived at Gemma's around six o'clock, and as soon as she saw the look on my face she led me through to the kitchen and pointed at a chair.

Sit. You look exhausted.

I nodded. *Working hard at the moment.*

She shot me a sympathetic look. *I know you can't talk about it, but if you need to offload at any point, you know where I am.*

I thanked her and leaned back in the chair. The smells wafting from Gemma's oven were intoxicating; a few of

177

us tried to meet up once every month or so, and we varied what we did, but my favourite nights were the ones when Gem cooked for us.

Who's coming tonight?

Jodie and Lucy. Cara has a date. She waggled her eyebrows at me.

Good for her, I replied, not rising to the bait.

She's trying a different website, Gem began, but I was saved from her well-meaning interference by Petra barrelling through the door, her blonde pigtails flying.

'Auntie Paige!' she shrieked, flinging herself into my arms. 'My teacher's having a baby and I want to make her a card, and Mummy said you'd help me because you're good at art.'

I laughed and let her lead me by the hand up to her bedroom, where bits of coloured paper were strewn all over her floor.

'I don't know what colour to use,' she said, a serious frown creasing her six-year-old face. 'I don't know if it's a baby boy or a baby girl, she said it's a secret.'

'Why don't you use yellow?' I suggested. We sat on the floor and sorted through the pile of papers, and she showed me a box where she'd kept pieces of ribbon and buttons.

As we worked, Petra chattered away about school and her friends, telling me she was going to a party the following weekend at the local farm park.

'Is it for one of your friends from school or from the Deaf club?'

She pulled a face. 'I don't like going to Deaf club.'

'Why not?'

For a moment, she concentrated on cutting out the flower I'd drawn for her, a tiny wrinkle forming between

178

her eyes. Without looking up, she said, 'Jaxon always wants to play with me.'

I paused and waited for her to continue, but she didn't say any more.

'Don't you like playing with Jaxon?'

'He hurts me sometimes. He likes to play games where he hits me and I don't like it.'

This new revelation of Jaxon's violent behaviour shocked me, despite what I'd already seen. I tried to hide my sharp intake of breath from Petra, but she noticed. She glanced up at me, a look of concern on her face. 'And he uses bad signs.'

'Bad signs?'

'He signed something to me but I didn't know what he meant, so I asked Mummy and she told me it was a bad sign, for a rude word, and I'm not allowed to use it.' The words tumbled out of her mouth as she looked at me anxiously, and I instinctively gave her a squeeze.

'You weren't in trouble though, you didn't know it was a bad sign.'

She shook her head. 'Mummy was upset that Jaxon signed it to me. She told me to play with someone else, and I tried but Jaxon always wants to play with me and if I tell him to go away he hits me.'

I sat with Petra while she finished her card, steering the conversation round to more lighthearted topics, which led to her adding a picture of the school guinea pigs to her card. When she was satisfied with it, I left her playing and went downstairs to sit with Gemma before the others arrived.

Oh God, did she tell you about that? Gem said, shaking her head when I repeated the conversation I'd had with her daughter. *I know people swear all the time, and she*

179

was bound to learn some unsavoury words and signs soon enough, but I was hoping I could maintain her innocence for another couple of years.

What word was it? I asked out of curiosity.

Bitch, she told me. *I expect he'd seen an adult use it and thought it was funny to copy, but I was a bit taken aback when Petra came up and signed it to me.*

Poor kid, she knows it wasn't her fault but she still feels bad.

Gem nodded. *That's why I've not taken her for a couple of weeks. I want her to mix with the Deaf community, it's part of her heritage, but not if it's going to upset her.*

A light above the door flashed as the doorbell rang, and I jumped up to answer it. Jodie and Lucy had arrived at the same time and we all piled into the kitchen.

Just in time, Gem said, as she lifted the lid off the tagine she'd been making. *I'll get Petra in bed, then we can put the world to rights.*

As we ate, the four of us chatted and signed, sharing gossip and catching up. To outsiders, we might seem like a disparate bunch of friends, but we'd formed our little group over the course of about ten years. Jodie worked with Gem, and had spurred their colleagues on to study some BSL when Gem was first employed. This kindness had led to mutual respect and eventually a close friendship, with Jodie and I working together to support Gem through the year where she lost her husband and gave birth to Petra. Cara, the only one missing from our usual gathering, was my friend from school. I'd taught her to sign so we could communicate across the classroom, and when she'd finished uni we struck up our friendship again.

Lucy was another deaf parent, who had twin boys a couple of years younger than Petra, and she and Gem had made friends at the Deaf club. I didn't know Lucy that well, but she'd fitted seamlessly into our group when she'd moved to the area six months earlier.

Once we'd eaten, we moved through to the living room and the conversation turned to Cara and the reason for her absence.

This is her fourth date in six weeks, so she's certainly working her way through them, Jodie signed.

Paige, why don't you try it? Gem asked, a twinkle in her eye. I shot her a dirty look.

No, thanks. Cara might be having plenty of dates, but she's yet to find a decent bloke she wants to see more than once.

Come on, you might be surprised, Jodie replied, pulling her phone out. *There are free apps, you don't have to pay anything. We could set up a profile for you right now!*

'No!' I said, sharper than I'd intended, earning myself a few raised eyebrows. *Sorry*, I continued in sign, *but I'm just not interested.*

I had only had one serious relationship in my adult life. I'd met Mike when I was twenty-two, and was with him for just over five years. In that time he stripped my self-esteem away little by little, just as relentlessly as he spent my money, and by the time Anna and my friends helped me get him out of my life I didn't even recognise who I'd become. In the three years since, I'd done a lot to repair the damage, but I didn't know when I would feel ready to trust anyone enough to be in a relationship again.

My friends could feel the change in atmosphere, and Gem steered the conversation away from my lack of a love life, but later when I was helping her to clear up, she brought it up again.

You can't be alone for the rest of your life, Paige, just because of one bad relationship.

I pinched the bridge of my nose. I didn't want to talk about it but I knew she wasn't going to let it go.

It wasn't just a bad relationship though, was it? It was five years of my life wasted, with someone who treated me like shit and left me with nothing but debts. You all saw it, but I didn't believe a word you said until it all came crashing down around my ears. I don't want to risk finding myself in that sort of situation again. My taste in men is so bad, I can't be trusted.

There are plenty of men out there who won't treat you like that, though, Gem pointed out. *At some point, you need to give it a chance, even if it's just a date or two here or there.*

You can hardly talk, I said, but it was a cheap shot.

I've got Petra; you know my reasons for staying single, she said, looking disappointed that I'd compared my experience with the loss of her husband. *In a few years, when she's a bit older, I'll be ready for a relationship again. But you've cut yourself off completely from the prospect, and it's not right. I worry you'll be lonely.*

I shook my head, but didn't reply, and she didn't push it any further. As I drove home I wondered if I should be trying to move on, but knew deep down that I couldn't.

182

11 hours before the murder

Laura was playing with the children in the living room, trying in vain to get Jaxon to play nicely with his sister. Bridget hoped he would settle down soon, but knew it was unlikely with his father being such a bad influence in his life.

Crossing the room, she dusted the picture frames on the wall, and her eyes alighted on the photo of her niece. Bridget's brother and sister-in-law had been no good as parents, either, neglecting their child in favour of alcohol and their own social lives. If someone had acted a little earlier, maybe something could have been done to help. She picked up the photo and clasped it to her, deciding to add it to the collection by her bed. It might motivate her when trying to convince Laura that sole custody was the best option.

She turned around and saw Laura sitting against the sofa, her hands across her face.

What am I doing wrong? she asked. *He won't do anything I ask.*

You need to be firm and consistent, Bridget replied. *It's the only thing children understand.*

I am! I am, all the time, but he just laughs at me. She looked over to where Jaxon was ripping up a piece of paper that Lexi had been scribbling on, the little girl looking on in confusion. *She doesn't cry, whatever he does to her. Maybe if she did, he'd learn to be nicer to her.*

Don't blame this on Lexi, Bridget said sharply. *Perhaps she understands him better than any of us.*

Laura sighed and moved to take the paper away from Jaxon, knowing full well he'd hit her and scream when she did. Every time she suggested something that she thought might help Jaxon, her mum shot her down. She should be used to it by now.

Time for tea, Bridget said, before going back through to the kitchen, leaving Laura to tidy up and bring the children through. At least it was Friday, Laura thought, so she got a couple of days' rest. Maybe she'd stop at the Deaf club for a while after dropping Jaxon and Lexi off with Alan. She yawned, then thought perhaps she'd prefer to come home and have an early night instead, but the thought of an evening in with Bridget didn't fill her with excitement, either. If she was honest, she was fed up with her life. It was boring and lonely, and she realised that if she didn't do something about it soon, nothing would ever change.

Chapter 15

Saturday 10th February

I don't know if it was the sound or the smell that woke me. Both crept into my dreams and roused me from a disturbed sleep, but at first I didn't realise what the insistent beeping was. I coughed, and coughed again, and the rank air that filled my lungs helped my brain to make the connection: the smoke alarm.

Grabbing a t-shirt off the floor, I covered my mouth and nose and jumped out of bed. It was still dark, but there was enough light from the street outside for me to see the smoke curling underneath my bedroom door. What was it I'd been taught about fires? Fighting panic, I battled to keep my breathing steady; hyperventilating now would only make me breathe in more smoke. I felt the door with the back of my hand. It wasn't hot, so I risked opening it.

Just inside the front door of my flat was a heap of flames. I couldn't tell what it was and stepped closer.

Oh God, I realised suddenly, Anna wouldn't have heard the smoke alarm!

The fire was closer to her door than mine, but I managed to skirt around it to wrench the door open and shake her awake. She didn't respond. I didn't know how long we'd both been inhaling smoke in our sleep, but she would've had more than me. I redoubled my efforts, and Anna opened her eyes and started to cough heavily. She retched but brought nothing up. I quickly signed *Fire*, and pulled her out of bed.

We were both coughing as we went out into the hallway. The fire was blocking our route to the front door. I'd never considered the possibility of having to get out of my flat another way. Could I fit through one of the windows? Even if I could, it was a long drop from the first floor. I doubled over with another coughing fit, and Anna darted back into her room. She re-emerged with the duvet in her hands and flung it over the fire, stamping down on it. I grabbed her and pulled her back, worried that the duvet would burst into flames, but it didn't, and I wrenched the front door open. I hammered on the nearest door until I woke someone and asked them to call the fire brigade, then rushed downstairs to warn the people in the flat below mine. Anna trailed behind me, coughing loudly.

A few minutes later, we were out of the building, gulping fresh air into our lungs. I could hear sirens approaching and I alerted Anna, earning some curious looks from my neighbours who had also gathered outside. Many chose to stay in the building, but those whose properties were immediately adjacent to mine didn't want to take the risk.

I directed the firefighters to my flat, then stood and waited to be seen by a paramedic who had pulled up in a car. I interpreted for Anna while she was checked over.

'You seem okay, but if you start to cough more, or feel light headed at all, then you need to go straight to A and E,' the paramedic told Anna.

We agreed, and once he'd checked me over, we leant against a wall and waited.

What do you think caused it? Anna asked me.

I didn't want to accept it, but I knew exactly what had happened. *Someone shoved something through the letter box and set fire to it.*

Really? The horror on her face mirrored the feeling in my stomach.

At that moment, a firefighter approached me.

'Miss Northwood? The fire was easy to put out when we arrived, that was quick thinking to smother it.'

I told Anna she'd probably saved my flat from burning down and she beamed.

'First signs do suggest it was arson, so we'll be passing it on to the police. There was charring around the edges of your letter box, and the position of the flammable material suggests that's how it entered your flat. To be honest, it was mainly paper and cotton wool, and your carpet is fire retardant, so it might not have spread much further anyway.'

I nodded. 'I think this might be related to my work with the police,' I said. 'In which case, it needs to be passed to either DI Forest or DC Singh.'

The firefighter frowned, but nodded. 'If you say so. They might just send a PC out to take your statement initially, though.'

I didn't have the energy to argue, and went back to join my sister. She was shivering, so I pressed myself up against her to try and share some body heat. The paramedic came back to speak to us, warning us again about the signs to watch for over the next forty-eight hours, then we were allowed back inside.

The hallway was black with the residue from the smoke. I walked around the rooms, opening every window despite the wintry air that rushed in. I propped open all the connecting doors in the hope that the smell would dissipate. A couple of pictures in the hallway looked to be damaged, including my favourite piece of felt work, but the smoke hadn't penetrated any other room enough to do any more than superficial damage.

We should be thankful they didn't know what they were doing, I said as Anna poked the foamy pile of paper and cotton wool with her toe. The scorched duvet was bundled next to it. I'd have to get her a new one.

Why do you say that?

I doubt they only meant to set fire to my doormat, I replied, then shivered. I didn't want to think about what they'd hoped to achieve, whoever they were.

Picking up my phone, I texted DC Singh to tell him what had happened. He'd probably be fast asleep, it was four-thirty in the morning, but at least he'd be able to look into it when he was back in work. Sending the message made me feel comforted, somehow.

There was a knock at the door, and I opened it to find the firefighter I had spoken to earlier.

'I've reported the incident, so someone will be round to take a statement, but it could be a few hours yet. We've taken samples from the material that was put through the door, and they might want to send forensics out to take fingerprints from the door. It's likely they'll have leaned against it when they opened the letter box, but unless they wore gloves they're going to have a pretty nasty burn. Normally they push stuff through, then drop a match through and set it on fire that way, but your guy did it the wrong way round. Lucky for you they didn't know what they were doing,' he said, echoing my earlier sentiments.

I thanked him, then went back to join Anna in the living room. I sank down onto the arm of the sofa and rubbed my face with both hands.

Who the hell would do this? Anna asked.

The same person who's been threatening me. It must be.

Anna frowned. *Do you think this is all because someone wants to stop you from finding out what happened to Lexi?*

I sat back on the sofa and looked at the ceiling for a moment. *Someone must think I know something. But I can't think of anything that might make me a threat. I don't even know these people.*

Anna came over and put her arm around me, giving me a squeeze. *Do you want to go back to bed?*

I shook my head. *I don't think I can sleep. I'm going to just make a coffee and put the TV on. I want something to distract me.*

Ten minutes later, we'd settled ourselves in front of a DVD when there was another knock on the door. I had no idea who it could be, so we both crept into the hall, Anna standing to the side while I looked through the peephole.

Relief coursed through me, and I opened the door to see DC Singh, looking younger than usual, in jeans and a green jumper.

'I didn't mean you had to come round straight away,' I said, trying to keep my voice lighthearted. I didn't want him to know how relieved I was to see him.

'I was awake,' he said, but didn't offer any further explanation. 'They need to sort out the security on this building. The front door was propped wide open; I just walked in.'

I made him a coffee and he sat on a chair opposite the sofa, listening as I explained what had happened.

He shook his head slowly when I'd finished. 'I'm sorry you've had to experience this, Paige. I didn't take these threats seriously enough, and I blame myself for what's happened tonight.'

'It's not your fault.'

He shook his head again. 'Have you noticed anyone acting suspiciously, hanging around your flat, following you?'

'No, nothing at all. I would have told you.'

'I think we can assume whoever did this is the same person who's been threatening you. I'll make sure we get a CSI down here to see if they can find anything.' He looked up at me, his brown eyes full of concern. 'Do you want to reconsider working for us on this case? I completely understand if you want to withdraw. We can find another interpreter.'

I thought about his suggestion for a moment. I was torn. These threats were starting to scare me, especially now they'd involved Anna by setting fire to my flat while we were both asleep. I didn't want anything worse to happen, but I also didn't want to give up my connection with the police. I was desperate to help, to know what was happening. And something about his tone of voice made me think he didn't want me to quit.

'No,' I said firmly, making my mind up. 'Whoever it is wants to scare me off, and I'm not prepared for them to succeed.'

Singh gave me a small smile. 'Okay. But if you change your mind at any time, please tell us. And keep hold of my number, in case anything else happens.'

Are they going to give you police protection? Anna asked, but I waved her question away. Singh looked between the two of us, so I interpreted her question for him.

'I'm not sure we can do that at the moment,' he replied. 'But I will look into it.'

I nearly laughed, thinking he wasn't serious, but the look he gave me said otherwise, so I thanked him instead. He got up to leave, but as we reached the front door he turned to me. 'Do you have any idea who it might be? It does look like whoever this person is, they know you're working with us, and they see you as a threat. They must think you know something.'

'I have no idea, I'm sorry. None of the people involved really know me, other than Laura.'

Singh nodded, holding my gaze for a moment, then said goodbye. Once he'd gone, I leant against the door, deep in thought, until Anna came through to find me.

I don't think they're taking this seriously, she said.

They are, they just have no idea why someone would want to hurt me. Neither do I. Maybe they're just trying to scare me. I didn't believe it, but by saying it I thought I might allay Anna's fears.

But when they realise you're not quitting, what then? They could have killed both of us. What do they need to do for the police to believe someone wants to hurt you?

I glared at her. *Don't say things like that. Anyway, you saw him, he believes us. But he's a DC, he's not in charge, and I doubt DI Forest will want to waste any resources on me.*

A jolt of anger coursed through me. How dare this person think they could threaten me and stop me from doing my job? I wasn't weak. I wasn't a coward. And I would not let them intimidate me or push me away from this case. They'd threatened my life, and the life of my sister, and I wouldn't let them get what they wanted.

Do you still want to know what I know about the case?

Anna's eyes lit up. *Of course. Why?*

Because I'm ready to tell you. Get a notebook or something. We're going to find out who did this.

Chapter 16

Anna and I didn't go back to bed, instead we started sorting through all of the information I'd learned about the case, the suspects so far and the distinct lack of an obvious motive. I felt lighter after sharing it, and I knew Anna would feel more empowered to support Laura if she knew what was going on. I knew there was a chance it would jeopardise my job if anyone found out I told her, and that worry still niggled at me, but the relief of sharing finally outweighed this concern.

Do you want to come out with me this morning? I asked, knowing I needed to clear my head after everything that had happened.

No, she shook her head. *I need to send some emails and have a chat with my supervisor.* She gave me a side-ways glance and I wondered how much of her PhD work would actually get done, but I didn't comment.

Driving into town, I knew exactly where I wanted to go. The Scunthorpe Arts Centre was based in a converted church, flanked by the steelworks and several council buildings. There was something incongruous about the beauty of the old building directly opposite the ugly rear of the library, with the glow of the industrial chimneys behind, but to me it was an oasis in the desert.

I'd seen the exhibition advertised for several weeks and kept meaning to go, but I'd never found the time. Today, however, I needed some beauty to detract from the threats and violence. It was a free exhibition, and I took my sketchbook with me in case it inspired any ideas.

Heading into the main body of the church, I stopped to drink in the colours of the work around me. This particular exhibition was a mixture of glass and metalwork, but the ways the colours blended and complemented each other sparked ideas for my own textile projects.

I spent an hour wandering slowly around the exhibition while people around me came and went. Sometimes I felt self-conscious, pulling out my sketchbook in public, but for once it didn't bother me. An idea came to me of a piece I could do to represent the local landscape, and I sketched it out with notes at the side about colours and textures.

When I was satisfied with what I'd come up with, I wandered through to the cafe area, only to see a familiar face on the other side of the room. DC Singh was sitting opposite a blonde woman in her fifties, and as I watched they both stood, she gave him a hug and a kiss on the cheek then left. Singh sat back down to finish his drink, and on impulse I wove my way through the tables towards him.

'Hi,' I said, hovering next to the chair the woman had just vacated.

'Paige,' he said, smiling. 'What are you doing here?'

'I've just been in to see the exhibition. How about you? Hot date?' I asked with a smirk.

He laughed. 'Not quite, that was my mum.'

My surprise must have been written all over my face, because he laughed again. 'What, think I'm too brown to be half white?'

'I . . . I don't know . . . No, I don't think . . .' I stopped, flustered, as he tried to keep a straight face and failed. I took a deep breath. 'I made an assumption, and I apologise.'

'No harm done. My brother and sister are paler than me. Genetic quirk I suppose.'

'Are you close to them?' I asked, taking the seat opposite him.

He nodded. 'Pretty close. My sister still lives at home, so I see her and my parents regularly. My brother's at uni in Birmingham, doing a PhD in pharmacology.'

'Anna's doing a PhD too, in London. She comes to visit pretty often though.'

'Is it just the two of you?'

I nodded and told him about our history, the deaths of our parents within a few short years and how we'd become closer since.

'I find myself trying to replace Mum sometimes, though. Anna's only two years younger than me, but I still feel responsible for her.'

He sat back and folded his arms. 'She can take care of herself, she's clearly a capable young woman. Maybe you should cut her a bit of slack, relax a bit. I get the feeling you spend too much time worrying about her instead of living your own life.'

I shuffled in my chair and looked down at the table, not wanting to let on that he'd hit on an uncomfortable truth. The awkwardness was broken by a waitress coming to clear the plates left over from Singh's lunch with his mum. I used the interruption to get up and fetch us a coffee each, hoping he'd change the subject when I returned.

'What do you do for fun?' he asked after I sat down again.

'I'm pretty busy with work, but I try to see friends at least once a month,' I replied. As I said it, I was aware of how sad it sounded, but work had been my necessary priority for the last three years. Mike left me with huge debts that I was still repaying, and it affected my life to a massive extent.

Singh waited expectantly, so I racked my brains for something else to say. 'I love going to art galleries, and I usually come to see the exhibitions here, whatever they are. I love all kinds of art, seeing different people's interpretations of the world around them.'

I found myself explaining to him about my aborted textiles degree, how I sometimes pulled out my felting and made some progress on my own art work, but life got in the way and I never seemed to finish anything. Or if I did finish it, I had no confidence in its quality as a piece of art, and it ended up sitting in a drawer.

When I paused, I realised he was watching me intently, his eyes dancing.

'What?'

He shook his head. 'You're really passionate about this, so why are you settling for a job you don't enjoy?'

I shifted my weight uncomfortably. 'I don't hate being

an interpreter. I find it rewarding, a lot of the time anyway. It would be too difficult to go back to uni now. I'm too old.'

He burst out laughing. 'People study when they're in their seventies. How old are you? Late twenties?'

'Thirty,' I told him, feeling defensive. 'I need to pay my mortgage, though, and I can't work full time and study.' It wasn't the time to bring up my last relationship, the financial control that had left me with almost nothing. It was a miracle I'd managed to keep my flat.

'Okay, I won't push it,' he said, smiling at me and laying a hand over mine for a brief moment. 'I'm sorry. But I think you should look into it.'

'What about you?' I asked, moving the conversation on as quickly as possible. 'What do you do for fun?'

'Fun? I'm a police officer, I don't have time for fun,' he joked.

'You're not working right now,' I pointed out.

'True, but I usually use my time off for sleeping and seeing family. Sad, but there you go.'

I smiled at his self-deprecating shrug. Clearly, his family meant a lot to him. I wished things had been different, and that Anna and I had grown up surrounded by a large extended family. Both of our parents were only children, so when they died, our family halved in size. I wanted to know what it was like; maybe I'd have children of my own one day, and Anna too, so they'd at least have cousins. That brought my thoughts around to my friends' suggestions that I tried dating again, but the mere idea brought me out in a cold sweat. I didn't want to lay myself bare on a dating site, but I had no idea where else I was going to meet an eligible man who might be interested in getting to know me. Also, I'd been such a bad judge of men in the past, I couldn't trust myself not to get sucked in again.

'I'd better go,' Singh said, with a regretful grimace. 'This was nice, though. We should do it again, when there isn't a murder hanging over us.' He frowned, as if he was blaming himself for having some down time when Lexi's death was still unsolved.

'Maybe,' I replied, unsure of what he was asking. If he was just being friendly, I could cope with that, but if it was something else . . . I felt my face flush.

He nodded and stood up, then hovered awkwardly for a moment before squeezing my shoulder and walking away. I turned to watch him leave and he turned back as he reached the door, raising a hand in farewell before zipping his coat up to his nose and pulling on a hat.

I sat there for a while longer, hands wrapped around my coffee mug, staring into space. I felt like there'd been a shift in the last week, as if everything in my life had suddenly changed, but I couldn't put my finger on why I felt like that. With a sigh, I bundled myself up and prepared to go back into the bitter February air.

It was already getting dark, and at first I didn't notice the two people in front of me as I crossed the square. They were clinging to each other, and it was only when one of them glanced over her shoulder that I realised it was Elisha. The man didn't look like Alan from behind, though; he was shorter and slimmer. I realised it was Rick Lombard, the man she couldn't seem to keep away from.

She didn't notice me, and turned back to snuggle in closer to her companion. They were walking in the direction of the car park, so I told myself I wasn't following them, they just happened to be going the same way as me.

They got into a grey Golf parked two rows away from where I'd left my car, and I pulled out after them. At the roundabout, they turned right, which was the direction I was taking to go home. I wasn't following them, I told myself again. It was coincidence that I'd ended up behind them.

As we drove in the direction of the steelworks, an unearthly glow lit the rapidly darkening sky – coke being pushed out of the ovens and flaring in the cold night air. It was a sight you grew up with around Scunthorpe, but today something about it made me shiver. A couple of cars had moved between us at a junction, but ahead of me I saw Lombard indicate and turn into an industrial estate. I knew I shouldn't follow them and it could get me into trouble, but curiosity got the better of me, and I did the same.

I pulled into the estate to see the car turning behind a warehouse, but I hung back and slowed down. Driving past the turning, I saw their car stop next to a small hut, so I carried on up the road and pulled into the kerb by the next warehouse. Before I got out, I grabbed a torch from my glove compartment, then shut the door as quietly as I could and walked back up the road.

Peering around the corner, I could see a light on in the hut, so I hugged the fence and walked nearer, keeping the torch in my pocket for now. The outside of the warehouse wasn't lit, and I wondered what they were doing there at this time. As I got nearer, I could see the hut was some sort of office, with a bank of CCTV screens flickering with grainy images. The sight made my heart sink, realising I'd been caught on camera, but neither Lombard nor Elisha were looking at the screens. He was sitting in a chair with her on his lap, and they might not have noticed if I'd walked in the door.

Elisha pulled away and stood up, so I backed away, hoping to still get a view through the window whilst remaining hidden in the darkness outside.

Come on, show me the new stuff, she signed.

Lombard rolled his eyes, but he got up and took a bunch of keys off a hook on the wall, and the two of them walked to the door. I scuttled back against the fence, out of sight of the door, and waited for them to pass. They came out of the office and crossed over to the warehouse, pushing the door closed behind them. I didn't hear the sound of a key turning, and I only hesitated for a moment before creeping after them.

The door creaked as I opened it, and I held my breath, but nothing happened. Inside a warehouse, I knew the acoustics would play havoc with Elisha's hearing aids, so hopefully she wouldn't be able to pick out the sound of the door amongst other noises. The place was stacked with huge shelving units from floor to ceiling, full of pallets and wooden packing boxes. I could see a light down the end of one aisle, so I headed towards it, keeping to the shadows as much as possible.

As I got closer, I could see Lombard and Elisha leaning over a packing case. They both had their backs to me, and he leaned over to show her something in the case.

Is that everything? she signed, frowning.

No, there are more in those three, Lombard replied, indicating the other boxes on the end of that row.

Can I see?

He thumped the lid down. *Why? Trust me, it's all there. It won't be a problem.*

She looked like she was going to argue, but before she did he came up to her and wrapped his arms around her, lifting her up onto the packing box. Within seconds, they were tearing at each other's clothes, and I started to back away. I had no idea what was in those boxes, but I didn't want to stick around for the show.

Hurrying back the way I'd come, I felt my way along the shelves. My eyes hadn't readjusted to the darkness after watching Lombard and Elisha, and I couldn't remember where I needed to turn to get back to the door. My heart hammering, I picked up speed as I hurried along the aisles, but then my foot caught on a stack of pallets. They wobbled precariously, and for a second I thought I'd been lucky, but then they started to fall. I ran out of the way just in time as they clattered to the ground, shattering the silence in the warehouse.

Would they have heard that? I wasn't sure if Lombard wore hearing aids, but Elisha couldn't have missed such a commotion. Sure enough, I heard movement behind me and threw caution to the wind, switching on my torch and sweeping it around until I spotted the door, then lunged towards it.

As I burst out into the night air I didn't stop to look back, racing across in front of the warehouse and back up the road to where I'd left my car. I leapt in and threw it into gear, turning around with a screech of tyres as Lombard raced around the corner after me. He tried to get in front of the car but I steered around him and raced back to the main road, tearing through the traffic lights as they turned red and heading for home and safety.

I'd been so stupid, following them in there. Had they recognised me? What would I do if they reported me to

Chapter 17

What had I been thinking? When I got home, I paced around the flat for a while. Anna was engrossed in her thesis, and I didn't tell her where I'd been. It would only lead to more questions. But what had Elisha and Lombard been up to?

A couple of hours later, I drove Anna to the Deaf club like I'd promised. I'd been reluctant at first, but then I took one look at my scorched hallway and decided I could do with an evening out. I was deep in thought while Anna made notes in a little book she had in her handbag, and I wondered if she'd spoken to Laura again. Laura had seemed convinced that Alan couldn't have hurt Lexi, but I was keeping an open mind. Anna had told me she was sure Laura was still in love with him, whatever she might have said, and we all had blind spots where our loved ones were concerned. The number of suspects had grown since we'd last seen Laura, however: along with Alan and Elisha, there was Rick Lombard, and Elisha's brother who the police were struggling to track down. I was becoming more interested in what Elisha was up to.

When we arrived, the main room of the Deaf club was half full. Scunthorpe was lucky to have kept this amenity, when so many towns had been reduced to hiring a room in a community centre once a week. It was one of the few Deaf clubs that were still a dedicated centre, and it was the best place for the Deaf community to socialise, particularly on Saturday nights. We went up to the bar and Anna ordered while I scanned the room. There was no sign of Laura, but Alan was surrounded by a group of men at a table nearby. It surprised me that he was here so soon after his daughter's death, but if that was where his support network was, maybe it helped him. I knew Anna would want to spend some time with her friends, but I would've preferred it if we sat on the other side of the room so Alan didn't see me. What if he was the one who'd been threatening me? The last thing I wanted was further scrutiny or suspicion from him.

Gem waved to me from the other side of the room and we went over to join her. She was sitting with Lucy and a couple of other people I vaguely knew. We pulled up chairs but Anna looked around anxiously, her eyes narrowing when she saw some of the people Alan was talking to. Part of me wanted to ask what she was thinking, but it was probably better if I didn't know.

You're out late, I teased Gem.

My mum's looking after Petra. I needed a bit of adult time, she told me.

No kids' club tonight?

Not any more, not enough volunteers. She pulled a face. *They only run it on Tuesdays now.*

The Deaf club received funding from the local council, though the building was owned outright by a trust. Mostly it was run by volunteers, with funds raised by renting out a couple of rooms for anything from yoga to Gamblers Anonymous. If there weren't enough volunteers to help with certain events, they couldn't run.

We were just talking about you, Paige, Lucy signed with a wink. *Think we can find you an eligible man tonight?*

I pulled a face. *I think if there were any eligible men at the Deaf club I would have found them by now.*

Lucy and the others laughed, though Gem gave me a knowing look, and said, *I know you think you've known every man here since you were a toddler, but you might be surprised. We'll see.*

I didn't protest, knowing the quickest way to get them to change the subject was to pretend their talk didn't bother me.

While we chatted, Anna carried on watching the group around Alan.

Is everything okay? Gem asked, picking up on the tension we were both feeling.

I glanced around to check nobody else was watching us. *It's this business with Lexi. It's awful. We're trying to get our heads round it still.*

She nodded her understanding. *It's terrible. I don't know who could have done something like that. I heard Alan was arrested,* Gem said, following Anna's line of sight. *They didn't keep him in for long, though. Do you think he killed Lexi?*

With that, I realised the rumours were already under way. They'd been trickling along under the surface for days, but something about the atmosphere tonight made them swell to a raging torrent. Everywhere I looked, people were glancing over their shoulders at him, then turning back to sign or speak to their friends. I wondered again why he'd come.

I turned back to Gem. *I really hope this is over soon, and whoever did it is caught. It's horrible to see them going through this.*

I know. The committee want to hold a memorial for her, on Tuesday evening. They know it could be a while until Laura and Alan can have a funeral, so they thought it might be a good way to show how much the community are thinking of them.

I thought this was a really nice idea, though I also made a mental note to mention it to Singh. It could be a good time to find out what other members of the Deaf community really thought about the family, and give any new witnesses a chance to come forward and tell what they knew.

Do you think it was Alan? Lucy asked as well. I shrugged and left it at that. She knew I couldn't talk about what I'd heard, but it didn't stop her fishing.

I heard Laura's trying to get full custody. Do you think that's why Alan killed Lexi, to stop Laura taking her away from him?

No! I signed suddenly. *I don't know. Nobody knows what happened. It could have been someone who came into their house in the middle of the night. It could have been anyone. Maybe we'll never know why they did it. Whoever it was.*

The others looked at me sceptically. *I know you know more than you're telling me,* Gem signed. *You've been in all the police interviews. Tell me, if you had a child, would you let them near Alan Hunter right now?*

I didn't reply. What could I say?

We sat there for a few moments, absorbed in our own thoughts, before Gem told us she needed to leave. *I have to work tomorrow, and if I stay much later I'll be shattered. Will you be at the memorial?*

Hopefully, I told her, thinking it would be a good opportunity for Anna to say goodbye to her goddaughter. She would need my support, and I wanted to go.

My best friend knew me too well not to notice my mood, and raised her eyebrows at me. *You don't want to get involved. Heaven knows what has been going on in that family. I feel for Laura, I really do, but Alan . . .* She shook her head and didn't elaborate.

When Gemma had left, Anna slipped away to talk to someone at another table, and I sat with my drink for a while. Over at the bar, I noticed a man looking in my direction. He was tall, with a wiry build, like a runner, and his brown hair had a copper tinge to it. He saw me looking over at him and grinned, and I felt a pleasant shiver run down my spine. It was a good job Gem had left, or she'd have me eating my own words. Before I had a chance to think about what I might say to him, I noticed Elisha getting herself a drink. It wasn't the time for me to be flirting with attractive men – I needed to make sure Elisha hadn't seen me following her and Lombard earlier. I watched her for a moment and she glanced around the room, but she didn't look at me. I hoped that was a sign she hadn't made the connection.

I turned around and saw the man from the bar walking towards me, shirt sleeves rolled up, his copper hair tousled in a way that must have taken particular effort.

Can I buy you a drink? he asked.

I looked over at Anna, wondering if she'd notice and come to my rescue. *I'm here with my sister*, I told him, hoping he'd get the hint and leave me alone. Across the room, Anna crooked an eyebrow at me but didn't move to see what was happening.

I turned back to him with an awkward smile. *Okay. What can I get you?*

Just a lemonade, thanks. I'm driving.

He pulled a mock sad face and walked over to the bar. I wasn't sure whether to follow him or sit down; he'd completely derailed my train of thought, and I resented Anna for leaving me with him. I'd enjoyed entertaining the idea of flirting a few minutes earlier, but now it came to holding a conversation with him I felt sick. The quickest way to get rid of him would be to accept the drink then make my excuses, so I joined him at the bar.

What brings you here tonight? he asked. *I don't think I've seen you here before.*

Do you mean, do I come here often? I replied, giving him a look.

He looked sheepish. *Was it that bad?*

Nearly. He laughed, and I joined in despite myself. *I don't come here very often these days, but my sister's visiting and she wanted to come. I said I'd come with her.*

You're both deaf?

No, she's deaf, I'm hearing, I replied.

Ah, an invader, he said with a grin that showed he didn't mean it. Some deaf people disliked hearing people coming to the Deaf club, though it was usually when a group from a BSL course came trooping in, wanting to practise their signing. Most people accepted them happily, but others resented what they saw as an intrusion into their social space.

I'm Paige, I said, trying to think of something interesting to say.

Nice to meet you, Paige. I'm Max.

I found myself blushing as he looked at me, embarrassed at how a conversation with a good-looking man could turn me into a teenager again.

What do you do for a living? he asked. *Don't tell me, you're hearing, with a deaf family member, so fifty-fifty chance you're an interpreter.*

My blush deepened, but this time it was because I felt completely transparent. He laughed at my obvious discomfort.

I'm sorry, I was only teasing. I didn't mean to stereotype you. Are you really an interpreter?

I nodded. *I'm afraid so. And my whole family are deaf, not just my sister. I'm the odd one out. What about you?*

I'm a TA. I support deaf children in a school in Hull. It's a mainstream school, and I take the kids out of class each morning and do one-to-one support for maths and English.

I smiled and took a drink, my heart thumping. *Why did you want to work with children?* I asked, trying to steer the conversation away from my own career.

He leaned back and thought about his answer for a moment. *When I was at school, I remembered the people who helped me the most, the people who tried to sign even if they didn't know much BSL, and the people who helped me to understand what it meant to be deaf in a hearing world. I want to be that person for someone else, so young deaf people can grow up and reach their potential.*

I was impressed, and it must have shown on my face because he ducked his head, embarrassed. *I know it sounds cheesy, but it's the truth.* He paused. *And you get better holidays than any other job.*

We both laughed, and I felt myself relaxing more in his company. Glancing past him, I saw Anna sitting with some people she knew. She looked like she was trying to catch my eye, and when she succeeded she beckoned me over. A few minutes earlier I would have jumped at the excuse to leave Max behind, but I found myself reluctant to end our conversation. Anna glared at me, however, so I excused myself and crossed over to speak to her.

What's wrong? I asked when I reached where they were sitting.

Anything you want to tell me? Anna asked, looking pointedly at Max.

Is that why you called me over? It's nothing, I just said I'd have a drink with him. If I was honest, I didn't know what to tell her, because I didn't know myself what was going on. I'd only accepted the drink to be polite, but now I found myself wanting to return to his company. I waved away her protests and turned, intending to go back to where Max was sitting, but she grabbed my arm.

Don't you know who he is?

I shrugged. *He's called Max.*

Yeah. Max Barron, Anna told me pointedly. *Elisha's brother. The one you told me the police want to question.*

My stomach performed a forward roll. Bloody typical, the one time I get chatting to an attractive man, it turns out he's a suspect in a horrific murder.

Oh God. I need a way to get out of this conversation, I told her.

Why? You might find out something useful, she pointed out, but I shook my head.

No, I don't want to talk to someone who might be involved. I can't risk it.

They wouldn't fire you for that, would they? Anna asked.

I don't know, but I'm not going to give them the opportunity.

Anna looked at her watch. *Come on then, we can make up some story about a personal crisis and get you away from him.*

I looked over to where Max was still leaning on the bar, and felt a jolt in my stomach as he gave me a lopsided smile. This was why I'd given up on dating, because the only men I met who I found attractive were completely unsuitable.

I signed across the room to him, *I'm really sorry, I need to go.*

He looked confused, but I turned my back on him before he had a chance to reply. Anna and I walked towards the door, and I resisted the urge to look back at Max. As we left, we passed Elisha, who narrowed her eyes at me.

We stepped outside the building and walked over to my car. Behind us, I heard the creak of the door and automatically looked to see who it was, but by the time I turned, they'd disappeared. I shivered and pulled my coat tighter around myself.

Did you get a chance to talk to Elisha? Anna asked me once we were in the car.

She isn't going to talk to me. I still didn't mention having seen her earlier in the day. I needed to figure out what I'd seen, first. *I think she knows something else, but she doesn't want to say.*

What do you think she knows?

If I knew that, I wouldn't need to ask her, I replied.

Anna gave me a withering look. *You know what I mean.*

I don't think she knows who did it. If it was Alan she'd be afraid of him, and I don't know if there's anyone else she'd protect.

I don't think we can rule him out, though, Anna said, and I nodded my agreement. *But don't forget Elisha's brother is involved in this somehow. It could be him she's protecting.*

She had a point, and I told her as much.

Anyway, there's plenty of gossip going around, but I didn't find out anything new, she continued. *Everyone knows Alan's always good for weed, sometimes something a bit stronger, so there are often people going in and out of the house. Nobody's heard anything about anyone going round last Friday, though.*

So was it someone who broke into the house when everyone was asleep? Or was it someone who was already in the house? I asked. Anna frowned as if she'd had an idea, but she didn't share it.

Did you get the impression that Alan knew who it was? she asked.

Not really, I replied, thinking back to Alan's interviews.

I was about to turn on the engine so we could drive home, when my phone vibrated. I picked it up and looked at the screen.

Police? Anna asked, her face hopeful.

I shook my head. *No, definitely not them.* It was a text, and my heart sank as I saw it was from the same number as before.

DON'T THINK I'VE FORGOTTEN ABOUT YOU.

10 hours before the murder

Laura tried to grab Jaxon's hand, dropping the bag she was holding, but he was too quick for her. She couldn't chase after him with Lexi held against her hip, so she grabbed the bag and trotted towards the Deaf club as quickly as she could. By the time she reached the door, Jaxon had already run inside, and she sagged with relief that at least he was out of the car park.

In the main hall, Jaxon ran over to Alan and flung himself at his dad, grabbing Alan by the arm and tugging until he turned round and picked the boy up, swinging him round. Laura's stomach did a somersault; she always worried Alan would drop Jaxon when he did things like that. She'd told him off for doing the same thing to Lexi just the other week, but he'd brushed off her concerns.

Where's your girlfriend? she asked pointedly when she reached Alan, sitting Lexi on a chair opposite him. Usually Elisha was there to take the kids' stuff off her. Laura couldn't stand her, but she was better at keeping the kids to a routine than Alan was, which Laura grudgingly appreciated.

Not here tonight, Alan replied.

Are you taking the kids home soon? Laura asked, knowing Alan liked to stay late on a Friday night.

He shrugged. *Whenever.*

You know they should be in bed at seven. It's already gone six. Jaxon needs to keep to his routine.

Alan rolled his eyes, but didn't reply, instead turning back to his friends. Laura wasn't going to push it, but then she thought about the court case, and Bridget's suggestion that she couldn't look after the children by herself.

Don't do that, she told him. *It's important. They're only little, they need lots of sleep. Jaxon always comes back tired, and his teacher said his work isn't as good on Mondays.*

Are you saying that's my fault? Alan asked, now giving her his full attention.

Laura took a deep breath. *Yes. You have to think about these things. Just because you don't have him on school days doesn't mean you can ignore his problems he's having at school.*

This again. Alan pulled a face. *He's just a normal boy, boys get into trouble.*

Not as much as he does. We're his parents, we have to take responsibility for him.

Alan waved a hand dismissively. *Whatever, Laura. Stop nagging me. I'll take them home when I'm ready; one late night won't do them any harm.*

She clenched her jaw but didn't reply. Whenever she tried to assert herself with Alan he made her feel stupid.

Maybe I should take them straight round to yours, she said, putting a protective arm around Lexi.

Elisha might have taken Kasey out, he replied, with a smirk that told her he was lying.

So? I've got a key, I can wait there for her to come back.

Alan's lip twitched. *Don't be stupid.*

They stared at each other for a moment before Laura looked away.

Fine, she told him, turning away quickly so he couldn't see the tears that pricked her eyes. Sometimes she believed she was still in love with Alan, that she wanted him back, but at that point she thought, no, I don't love him. I hate him.

Chapter 18

Sunday 11th February

I forwarded the message on to DC Singh once we were home, but didn't get a reply. When we got up the next morning I tried to put it to the back of my mind, settling down with the most boring paperwork I could find, a job I always put off until the last minute, while Anna worked on her thesis. Around three in the afternoon, the doorbell rang, setting off the flashing light I'd had connected for Anna when I bought the flat. We looked up, each seeing our anxiety reflected in the other's face. Neither of us was expecting anyone.

Be careful. Check who it is first.

I'm not stupid, I told her, checking the video entry system. *It's Elisha.*

Anna's face went white. *What does she want?*

I grimaced. *I followed her yesterday, and I'm pretty sure she saw me.*

What? Why didn't you tell me?

I don't know. I was still trying to figure out what was going on.

She nodded at the door. *Do you think she's come to confront you about it?*

We won't know unless I let her in.

Wait. Anna came closer. *What if she's involved? She was the one who had the easiest opportunity to kill Lexi.*

I shivered, but shook my head. *I'm going to let her in. We won't know why she's here if we don't.*

Fine, but I'm not leaving you alone with her. Not while someone's threatening you.

I pressed the button to unlock the outside door and opened my front door so I could see Elisha approaching. We both watched the door leading to the stairs but stepped back when she appeared and marched towards us. Her jaw was squared and she glared at me.

Why were you following me yesterday?

I was about to deny it, but Elisha must have read this on my face. *You've got a fucking bright yellow car, Paige. I know it was you.*

I glanced at Anna, who was blocking the doorway. It was clear she wasn't going to let me invite Elisha inside.

We wanted to know what you're hiding, Anna replied, pushing her shoulders back and standing up straighter, and I was impressed with her bluffing skills. Anna was the tallest of the three of us, and Elisha took half a step back.

I'm not hiding anything, Elisha snapped, but her hands were shaking as she signed. *You have no right to follow me. I haven't done anything wrong.*

Other than cheating on Alan? I said, giving her a pointed look.

Elisha looked like she was going to slap me, and I tensed.

218

Look, Elisha, you've been really cagey when you've talked to the police. We want to know what happened to Lexi, so we wanted to know what it is you're not telling them.

She sneered at us. *Why would it be any of your fucking business? My life is nothing to do with you. You know nothing about me. I've told the police all they need to know about that night, everything I know that might help.*

I held my hands up to try and placate her. *The police have interviewed Rick, though, so clearly they thought he might have been involved. You didn't tell them he was in your house that night. And what's this about your brother?*

Elisha sighed. *I don't know why they want to involve Max, he hadn't been round for nearly a week when Lexi died. Someone is shit stirring, trying to make it look like we're up to something. But I promise, I had nothing to do with this.* Her shoulders sagged and the fight went out of her. *I want them to find out who did it so this all stops, and we can try to have our life back.*

Anna moved to sign something but I gave her a sharp look. I thought this might be our opportunity to get Elisha to talk.

Why don't you come in? I'll put the kettle on.

Elisha hesitated, but Anna moved out of the doorway and gave her some space, so she relented.

Once the three of us were seated in the kitchen with a cup of tea each, the atmosphere was less tense. Anna was still glaring at Elisha occasionally, but she trusted me enough to not raise her objections.

It's all such a mess, Elisha blurted out. *I don't know why I keep going back to Rick. Alan looks after me, and Kasey, but whenever Rick texts me I can't help myself.*

She looked like she was about to burst into tears. *I don't want Alan to leave me, but I can't blame him if he does now. I can't face moving back into that house, not yet, but Alan's getting fed up of staying with my friend.*

I patted her hand. *Maybe he'll understand, if you talk to him about it. You'll need to stop seeing Rick if you want things to work with Alan, though.*

I'm worried Alan will go back to Laura, she replied, looking at Anna, who shrugged.

He's done that before, Anna said, and I winced at the harshness of it, *but unless you sit down and talk to him, you won't know how he's feeling.*

I'm not sure I even know what I want. Maybe Kasey and I would be better off on our own. She looked at me with glistening, red-rimmed eyes. *What if Alan did it? What if he killed Lexi? I can't trust him around Kasey. And there's Rick, too. I don't think it was Rick, but God knows. Maybe it was him. How am I supposed to know who I can trust?*

I had found myself thinking the exact same thing, but I had included Elisha on my mental list of suspects. There was something about the way she was appealing to us that made me suspicious. Could it have been her? Was she so fed up of taking care of another woman's children that she murdered one of them in cold blood? The idea sent a sting of ice through my veins.

What do you think happened that night? Anna asked.

Elisha blinked. *I don't know. Lexi was fine when I went to bed. When I got up in the morning and checked on her, she was dead.* She looked over at me. *I told the police the truth. I didn't see anyone. I don't know what happened.*

Surely you must have some idea, though? You must have your suspicions. Someone acting strangely, or someone telling lies?

Elisha picked up her cup of tea and drained it. *I need to go now. Alan will be wondering where I am. He wants to know what I'm doing all the time at the moment.* She only looked at me as she said this, and didn't make eye contact with Anna. *I'll tell Rick I made a mistake, that I don't know who it was. He wanted to come round here himself, but I stopped him.*

From her facial expression, I didn't know if she expected me to be grateful that she hadn't brought him with her. Elisha scuttled towards the door and left before we could ask her anything else.

Once we'd seen her leave the building, Anna and I went back into the living room.

So, do you want to fill me in?

I looked at my sister and winced. *I'm sorry. I should have told you yesterday, but I wanted to figure out what it meant first.* We sat down and I told her about seeing Elisha and Rick in town before deciding to follow them, and about the strange conversation they had in the warehouse.

Well. That wasn't suspicious, Anna said sarcastically.

I know. I have no idea what they might be up to, or what he showed her.

Could you tell the police, get them to have a look in the warehouse?

No, I replied. *I have no evidence there's been a crime, so there'd be no reason for them to look.*

There's definitely something dodgy going on, and Elisha's lying about it, Anna said.

221

I'm more confused than ever, I replied. *Is she protecting someone, or was it her and she's trying to make us suspect Alan or Rick?*

It was her, Anna said firmly. *I'm sure of it.*

I don't know, I replied. *I can't read her.*

Think about it. The murder weapon was at her house, so she could have killed Lexi spontaneously. Something happened and she lashed out with whatever was to hand. Then she covered it up, but she's not been very good at it, which is why the evidence doesn't point to any one person. If she'd planned it, everything would implicate Alan and he'd be locked up by now, I'm sure of it.

But why would she kill Lexi in the first place? I asked. *If she'd had enough of Laura's children, why wouldn't she kill Jaxon first? He's much more difficult to look after than Lexi was.*

Maybe Alan favoured Lexi? Anna suggested, getting up and pacing as she thought. *Maybe Elisha was fed up of Laura's daughter being given priority over hers, or being loved more by her father. So she decided to get rid of Lexi, because she was the rival for affection that should have been Kasey's.* She gave me a triumphant look.

Nice theory, but we have no evidence of that at all. Nobody has said anything about Alan having favourites. And if Elisha wanted to implicate Alan, the obvious plan would be to tell us the opposite, that Alan loved Kasey a lot more than he loved Lexi.

She pulled a face and carried on pacing for a moment, deep in thought.

What about the threats? I asked. *Why would Elisha threaten me? She barely knows me. We'd never spoken before the night I was called to the house.*

As I signed, Anna stopped, and I could see the moment a thought crossed her mind.

What? I asked, but she held up a hand.

The threats, she said.

Yes, exactly.

How does Elisha know where you live?

I hesitated.

How does she know where you live, Paige? If you didn't know each other before this case started, how would she know your address? Your work phone number is on your website, but not your address.

I didn't have an answer for this. When she'd turned up at the door it hadn't crossed my mind to wonder how she'd found me. Even if she'd seen the car outside by pure chance, she wouldn't have known which flat was mine.

And when you buzzed her in, she walked straight to the right flat. How would she know where to go, unless she'd been here before?

As Anna's words sank in, a feeling of horror filled me. *Do you really think . . . ?* I didn't finish the thought, but she nodded anyway.

It makes sense, Paige. She found out where you lived from someone else, shoved a note through your door, and when that didn't put you off she came here in the middle of the night and tried to burn the flat down. She's scared and irrational. You saw that today.

I shook my head slowly. *I still don't understand why she would threaten me, though. Why me?*

You're the one link between her and the police. You're the interpreter, so maybe she feels like you're the one asking her all these questions. Without you, they'd need to find someone else, someone who wouldn't care as much about what happened to Lexi, so might not be as vigilant in their work.

She could have seen you talking to the police and felt threatened by you, Anna continued. *Maybe it's just because you know Laura. Who knows? Elisha herself might not even know. But I'm convinced, Paige. I'm sure it must be her.*

I didn't say anything, and she came to sit next to me. *Think about Caitlin.*

I flinched. *No, I don't want to compare Lexi to Caitlin,* I said, ignoring the fact that my subconscious had been doing that for days.

You know what I mean, though. When a child dies like that, and it's nothing sexual, it's most likely to be a parent. Someone who was meant to care for her.

Tears welled up in my eyes and I squeezed them shut. I didn't want to go there. I couldn't let myself relive that time.

Anna gave me a hug. *Promise me you'll talk to the police about Elisha.*

What on earth can I tell them? I replied, sniffing and blinking rapidly. *We don't have any proof.*

Tell them she came here, that you don't know how she knows where you live. Tell them you think she's suspicious, whatever, but at least point them in her direction. They might ignore you, but if they take you seriously and start looking at Elisha more closely, perhaps they'll find the answer.

I looked at my sister, and realised that despite her grief she was finding a purpose in this, investigating and digging into people's lives. She hadn't been on the raw end of it, though. She'd not been there and seen Lexi's body. She hadn't been there when Caitlin died, either. I wished I could have Anna's positivity that it would all end soon, but I still felt like there was something we were missing, something crucial that would point us in the direction of a killer.

9 hours before the murder

DI Forest was sorting some paperwork when there was a knock on the door. She hoped whoever it was would piss off quickly; she actually wanted to leave at a decent time on a Friday, for once.

'Mel, you got a minute?' One of her colleagues, DI John Stevens, stuck his head around the door.

Forest nodded to the chair opposite her desk and Stevens sat down.

'We've had a name come up in a sexual assault case I'm investigating,' he said, shifting his weight slightly. 'I think he might be familiar to you.'

'Who?' she asked, but from the look on his face she already knew.

'David Osario.'

Her heart sank. Goddamned Osario, back to haunt her. The one case she'd truly fucked up.

'What do you want to know?' she asked, leaning back

in her chair, trying to look casual and hide the tension she was feeling.

Stevens spread his hands wide. 'It's a difficult situation. I'm pretty sure he's the bloke we want, but I'm struggling for evidence. He's sly.'

'Have you got an interpreter?'

Stevens shook his head. 'He said he didn't need one.'

Forest groaned inwardly. At least she could help Stevens to avoid the mistakes she'd made.

'Get one anyway. Have someone read him his rights and tell him the charges in his first language, and if he says he doesn't want an interpreter make sure you get it in writing and on video.'

'What happened?' Stevens was curious now, she could see. 'His record isn't clear.'

Forest made a low growling noise in the back of her throat. 'He claimed that I hadn't asked him if he wanted an interpreter. I asked him in the car, so there was no formal record. We got a confession out of him, but his lawyer realised he could claim Osario didn't understand what we were asking him because his first language was Greek. My own bloody fault, of course, but I didn't think he'd manage to get the case thrown out.'

'He did,' Stevens said, and it wasn't a question. Forest nodded.

'Once we'd got a confession, things slowed down, we weren't as worried about the evidence. I know, it was our responsibility, and I certainly won't make the same mistake again.' She grabbed some papers on her desk and shuffled them to cover her anger and embarrassment. Mel Forest was known for her ability to solve a case quickly, or at

227

least as quickly as the bureaucracy allowed, and that case still ate away at her two years later.

'I can't help you regarding your evidence, John. Just make sure you find something incontrovertible, then you can put him away. And get an interpreter. Cover your back.'

Stevens nodded, and left, seeing that he'd touched a nerve. Forest reached into her bottom drawer and pulled out the case file that had been buried in there. It was still open – she knew Osario was guilty of three separate sexual assaults, but she'd never been able to prove it. His confession had been real, she knew that, but after the case was thrown out she couldn't prove it. She knew it was only a matter of time before he reappeared, and she was glad she wasn't the one who'd been given the case. Her strengths lay in her interviewing skills, in her ability to tease information out of suspects, but that case had shown her talents were no use if she wasn't able to communicate directly with the people she was interviewing.

Chapter 19

Monday 12th February

By the next morning, I was jittery. Singh had replied that evening, asking me to come into the station the next day. I'd already arranged to interpret for Laura at her meeting with the solicitor in the morning, but I was regretting it. I wanted to talk to Singh, and find out if they'd made any progress on the threats on me. Despite Anna's insistence, I still didn't know if I should mention Elisha's visit, for fear of being accused of interfering.

I was due to meet Laura at the solicitor's office at ten, so I left Anna bent over her PhD work and drove into town. My stomach was turning somersaults at the thought of the meeting, and I'd lain awake for a couple of hours the previous night thinking about it. I was worried I was too distracted by my own memories to support Laura through this. Whenever I closed my eyes, all I could see was Caitlin's face, as she was when she was alive, and then afterwards . . . It was disturbing my sleep, my subconscious refusing to let me rest.

Laura was waiting outside the solicitor's office when I

arrived, smoking with shaking hands. I thought she'd given up, but I understood the stress and grief might have made her lapse. As I approached, I heard a yell and looked over to see Jaxon thundering up and down the pavement. Laura made a half-hearted move to stop him, but he dodged past her and careered towards the road. I dived in and got my arm around his waist moments before a car came past.

Oh God, thank you, Laura said, taking the struggling boy from me. *You need to be careful,* she told him, but I could see from his face that he was looking for his next chance to escape. Bridget was nowhere to be seen.

My mum's busy, she explained, in answer to my questioning look. *She was going to look after him, but she had to go somewhere. She got a phone call this morning and she looked really worried, but I don't know what it was about.*

Shouldn't he be at school today?

She shook her head. *Half term.*

How are you doing? I asked, although my eyes gave me the answer. Her face was drawn, her skin pale and translucent, with a yellowy tinge around her eyes.

She didn't reply, and busied herself getting Jaxon into the building. I followed her in and looked around. The offices looked recently refurbished and I wondered how Laura could afford this solicitor. I assumed Bridget was funding it, though I didn't know where she would get the money from, either.

When Laura first met Alan, Anna would call me with stories of the blazing rows that Bridget and Laura had, sometimes in public. All that ever did was push Laura further towards Alan. Even when she was twenty-two,

Bridget treated her like a teenager, and then along came Jaxon, tying Alan and Laura together forever, much to Bridget's horror. There was a rumour that she took Laura for an abortion, insisting it was what Laura wanted, but Laura kicked and screamed until the medical staff refused to even give them the consent forms, and Bridget was escorted off the premises. Back then it should have been clear that Bridget wasn't the best person to interpret for Laura; her personality was so forceful, so domineering, that she didn't even realise when she was putting across her own point of view instead of her daughter's.

The receptionist greeted us and asked us to wait in the seating area in the lobby, giving Jaxon a sideways look as he tried to grab something off her desk. We didn't wait long before a young man with very shiny hair strode towards us across the room. He shook Laura's hand, and gave her a sympathetic look she must be getting sick of by now, but what do you say to a woman whose child has been murdered? Looking down, he gave Jaxon a broad smile that didn't reach his eyes, then introduced himself to me as Jeremy Braggins.

'Thank you so much for stepping in. I do feel we should have a qualified interpreter at these meetings.'

I nodded, and interpreted this for Laura, but she didn't see, her attention fully on Jaxon. He was squirming to get away from her again, and I wondered how successful this meeting was going to be.

Braggins must have been thinking the same thing, because he gave Jaxon a worried look. 'Perhaps I can get some colouring for Jaxon to do while we talk.'

Thank you, Laura said, *but I've got his tablet in my bag. He should be okay with that.*

The solicitor led us into a small but well-decorated room, with low padded chairs. I sank into one and Laura took the chair opposite, lifting Jaxon up to sit next to her. She fished his tablet out of her bag and he snatched it off her the instant he saw it, and at last was still.

After another wary look at Jaxon, Braggins turned to me. 'Has Laura filled you in on the background of the case?'

'I know the basics, yes.'

'Okay. We'd been putting together a case for Laura to apply for full custody of her children, Jaxon and Lexi, on the basis that their father, Alan Hunter, has neglected them in the past. We have statements from family members who are willing to testify to that effect. We also have a number of text messages from Mr Hunter that are suggestive of his lack of care for the children.'

Laura seemed to grow smaller as I interpreted this.

'Now, of course, things are very different.' The solicitor battled with a few facial expressions, then settled for something between serious and sympathetic. 'We will cooperate with the police, and if anything pertinent to the custody case emerges during the course of the investigation, we will of course take it into account. However, the fact that one of your children tragically died whilst in his care will make it far easier for us to ensure you are awarded full custody of Jaxon.'

I was revolted by this line of conversation, however true it might be. I saw his point though: whether or not Alan was involved in Lexi's death, surely no judge was going to assume he was a fit parent if one of his children was murdered in his house while he slept.

'The question I have to ask, Laura, is whether or not you

232

want to continue with proceedings right now? Going through a court case like this is stressful, and you're grieving.'

There was a pause before Laura answered. *I don't know. I don't know what's best.*

Braggins and I waited for her to continue. She looked at Jaxon, who was kicking the chair leg as he played a game, his eyes glued to the screen.

I don't want to believe Alan did this to Lexi, but what if he did? What if he killed our daughter?

'I don't know anything about the police investigation, I'm afraid.' Braggins shifted uncomfortably on his chair.

I didn't want to take Alan to court in the first place. It was my mum's idea, and I went along with it because it was easier that way. She can get so angry if I don't do what she wants. Before this happened, before Lexi died, I'd told her I'd changed my mind, that I didn't want to go through with it. But now I don't know what to do. She looked at me. *Paige, what do you think?*

I can't help you make the decision, I'm sorry.

Jaxon made a frustrated noise and jabbed harder at the screen, his little face screwed up, and Laura put a hand on his arm. He shook her off and carried on scowling at his game.

If we wait, it might not matter, Laura signed. *If Alan did hurt Lexi, he'll go to prison and he won't get out until Jaxon's grown up. Is that right?*

Braggins hesitated. 'If he were to be found guilty of murder, yes, I'm sure you're right. Do you have any reason to suspect he did kill Lexi? If you do, you should speak to the police.'

No, I don't, but everyone else thinks he did it. I think . . . She broke off as Jaxon roared in annoyance and threw

233

his tablet on the ground. It was covered by a tough rubber case, and I could see why. Laura bent to pick it up and he grabbed her wrist, trying to wrestle it off her. She kept hold of it and gave him a quick telling off before handing it back. There was a livid red mark on her wrist from where he'd grabbed her.

I need to think about this, she said, and Braggins nodded.

'I agree. Perhaps we should put the custody case on hold for now, while the police investigation is ongoing. When that's concluded, we can meet again and decide how you want to proceed. Is that okay?'

Laura agreed, and the meeting drew to a close. I was pleasantly surprised with how reasonable the solicitor had been – rather than pushing for a case that would undoubtedly bring in more money for his firm, he saw that Laura couldn't take any more emotional stress.

I offered to give Laura and Jaxon a lift home, but she wanted another cigarette first, so we stood outside the solicitor's office, sheltering against the wall from a bitter wind that had blown up. Laura leant against the wall while Jaxon kicked at a corner of a paving stone that was sticking up.

Alan is the only one who can control him, she said, watching her son.

What do you mean?

She gestured to Jaxon with her free hand. *You've seen him. He's very . . . active. He's hard work, and I don't know how I'd cope with him on my own.*

You've got your mum.

Laura laughed. *Yeah, but I can't live with her forever, much as she'd like me to. I don't know.* She paused. *I still keep thinking Alan and I will get back together one day.*

I knew from Anna that this had been on Laura's mind, but I didn't say anything.

Things were good between us, she continued. *Our relationship was great until Elisha came along and ruined everything. He didn't have to move in with her.* She pulled a face that made her look like a sulky child. *We could have made up, Kasey could have come to stay with us. I would have forgiven him like I did every other time.*

But if he cheated on you, things can't have been that good, I said gently.

It wasn't perfect, but nobody's perfect. Even Mum said that if it wasn't for Kasey, Alan and I would have stayed together. It's only because he got Elisha pregnant that he felt he had to leave.

This didn't make sense to me, because Laura had also been pregnant at the time, but I decided not to argue.

I know he cheated, but he always came back to me. Every time, he preferred me to whoever his new woman was. They were new and exciting, but he'd get bored quickly, then he'd be really loving and appreciative of me for ages afterwards. I'm the one he wanted to be with.

I didn't know what to say, and at that moment Jaxon ran up, signing, *Tablet. Tablet.*

Not now, Laura told him.

He pulled a face and launched himself at her, trying to grab her bag, and when she held on to it and told him *No* again, he kicked her. I stood there, stunned, as the little boy lashed out at his mother, not knowing if I should intervene. A moment later, Laura had pulled the tablet out of her bag and given it to him, not looking at me.

235

We stood there for a few moments while Laura finished her cigarette, watching Jaxon sitting on the pavement, absorbed in another game.

I think maybe it's best if we walk home, Laura signed, not making eye contact with me. *He needs to let off some steam, I might take him to the park for a bit.*

Okay. I was secretly glad, worried what Jaxon might do once we were in the car. As I walked back to my car, I wondered what was going on in Jaxon's young mind to make him so angry.

Chapter 20

I drove straight to the police station, wondering if this was what my working life was going to look like for a while. As I pulled up, I noticed a familiar figure leaving the station, and I hurried to get out of my car and catch up to her.

'Bridget?'

She started and turned to look at me, her eyes wide. 'Oh. Paige. Are you here for an interview?'

'I have a meeting with one of the detectives,' I said, not wanting to give her too much information. 'Why are you here? Laura told me you were busy so you couldn't look after Jaxon, but she didn't mention you were with the police.'

Bridget paused for a moment, and I wondered if she was going to refuse to answer my question. Just as it was about to become awkward, she blurted out, 'I came to report Alan.'

'Alan? What's he done?'

'He's been hanging around my house. Well, I've seen a black van that looks just like his. Sometimes it parks outside a house up the road, sometimes it drives past slowly. I don't think Laura's noticed, so I didn't mention it to her. I don't think she needs to be any more worried than she already is.' Bridget glared at me, daring me to contradict her.

I nearly kept my mouth shut, but I couldn't help myself. 'Laura needs to know something like this, Bridget. What if she's alone in the house with Jaxon and Alan turns up? You should tell her.'

She drew herself up as tall as she could and looked at me down her nose. 'I think I'm the best judge of what my daughter needs.' Turning away from me, she marched across the car park, her heels clicking on the tarmac as she went. I watched her go, then went into the station, wondering what she might be up to.

DC Singh stuck his head in the waiting room and shot me a smile. He was as smart as usual, but the case was taking its toll on him, judging by the bags under his eyes.

'Hi, Paige,' he said. 'We're no further on with the text messages, I'm sorry.'

My face must have shown my disappointment, because he came and sat next to me, putting a hand gently on my back. 'I know it's scary, and we're doing all we can, but as it's a pay-as-you-go phone we can't track the owner. The tech guys are going to try and get information on where the phone was when it sent those messages, which might help. We're taking this seriously, it just isn't as easy as it's made out on TV.'

'It's just so frustrating,' I replied.

238

'I understand,' he said, and I could see my annoyance mirrored on his face. His mouth twisted, and he looked as if he was weighing something up. 'I'm not supposed to tell you this, but DI Forest isn't convinced the messages are from Lexi's killer.'

'What? Who else would be sending them?' I felt heat rise in my face, a mixture of embarrassment and anger. Did they think I was making it up?

Singh held up a hand to placate me. 'I don't agree with her. But I'm not in charge of the investigation, so if she won't push for further information about the phone, there's not a lot more I can do.'

I could see from his face that he was torn between following orders and doing what he was convinced was right.

'I just want to get on and do my job,' I told him, 'but I'm scared of what's going to happen to me if you don't find out who it is soon.'

'I know, but we're making some progress. In fact, I didn't call because I knew you were coming in anyway, but we've finally tracked down Max Barron, Elisha's brother.'

'You've arrested him?' I asked, worried he might mention our drink in the Deaf club on Saturday night.

Singh shook his head. 'No, nothing like that. We don't have any evidence that he was even at the house that night. We need to talk to him though, and he turned up about forty-five minutes ago.'

'You want to interview him now?'

'Is that okay? You don't have another job, do you?' He looked worried, and I could imagine the look on Forest's face if he went back in and told her I'd left.

'No, don't worry. I can stay.'

239

He led me through to the interview rooms and while we walked, something occurred to me. Max Barron. MB. The strange Facebook post about Alan's previous arrests, the one Anna and I read then couldn't find again, was written by someone who used the initials MB. Could it have been him?

When we entered the room, Forest was already sitting opposite Max Barron, and I swallowed at the sight of him, trying to keep any sign of recognition from my face. Today he was dressed in jeans and a black shirt, his sleeves rolled up. I could see the definition of the muscles in his arms, and when he smiled at me I found myself looking away. His eyebrows twitched in surprise when he realised who I was, but he didn't show any other sign that we'd met before, for which I was grateful.

Forest began without greeting me. 'Mr Barron, can you confirm your relationship to Lexi Hunter, please?'

Barron frowned and pulled an exaggerated thinking face. *Is this a brain exercise? I'm Elisha's half-brother. If Elisha is Lexi's stepmother, does that make me her step-half-uncle?* He looked amused and I couldn't blame him. It was a stupid question.

Forest cleared her throat. 'And where were you on the night of Friday the second of February?'

I went to the Deaf club, then I went to the pub for a bit, then I went home.

'Can anyone confirm this?'

Plenty of people saw me in the pub, but nobody came home with me, unfortunately, he replied, one corner of his mouth lifting slightly in a wry smile.

'When was the last time you were at Elisha and Alan's house?'

The weekend before, the Saturday night.

'Were you invited?' Forest asked, which I thought was a strange question.

Not as such. I texted Elisha in the afternoon to ask if I could come round later, and she said it was fine.

'What was Alan Hunter's reaction to you coming round that night?'

Barron shifted in his chair slightly. *He told me to . . . go away.* From the pause I assumed those weren't the exact words Alan had used.

'What is your relationship like with Mr Hunter?'

As I signed to him, I found myself avoiding meeting Max Barron's eyes, instead looking at a point just above his eyebrows.

It's okay. We put up with each other.

'What does that mean?' Singh asked.

It means I don't like him. I'm worried about the way he treats my sister, but I have no proof he's done anything to her. But if I push her to leave him, I'm worried she'll be angry with me and won't want to see me. She's not ready to hear a word against Alan at the moment, so I make sure I see her regularly, in case anything happens and she needs me.

'Are you concerned Mr Hunter is abusing her?' Singh seemed to choose his words carefully.

I am. Maybe not physically, but emotionally. Her self-confidence has dropped since she met him, and she hardly goes anywhere without him. She had post-natal depression after Kasey was born, and Alan didn't do anything to help her. I was the one who took her to the doctor and got her some help.

A couple of weeks ago I might have been more

241

surprised by this, but the more I heard about Alan, the more these revelations seemed in keeping with what I'd learned about him. Given my own history, I was pleased Elisha had someone in her life who had noticed Alan's treatment of her.

'What about the children?' Forest asked.

Barron nodded slowly. *I've been worried about them as well, because Alan has a temper, and he's a regular drug user. I don't think it's a positive environment for kids. I've never seen him lay a finger on any of them, though.*

Forest scowled at him. 'Why didn't you report any of this earlier?'

What could I have said? Barron replied, spreading his hands. *I have no proof he's anything other than a loving partner and father. You wouldn't have listened to me if I'd walked in here telling you I don't like him.*

Making a noise in the back of her throat, Forest turned over a page of the file in front of her. 'We've been told that you and Mr Hunter had a fight the weekend before Lexi was killed. Can you tell us what that was about?'

Alan doesn't like me. I think he's realised I'm keeping a close eye on Elisha's wellbeing. Normally, I go round when he's not there, or Elisha meets me in the park so I can see Kasey. He'd had a bit to drink that night, and he was probably high. He sighed and rubbed his face. *It was my own fault, really. I wound him up. I made a comment about how I hoped the kids were in bed before he started on the drugs, and he went for me.*

'Were you trespassing?' Forest asked, her face hard.

He frowned. *No, my sister lives there and she said it was fine to come round. Where is this going?*

Forest looked like she was about to reply, then gave a tiny shake of her head. 'We need to make sure we have all of the details,' she said vaguely.

Barron leant forward. *The details I'm concerned about are the ones where an adult sits smoking drugs in the same house as my baby niece. It stinks of weed in there, and the kids can't help breathing it in. Elisha's told me she's worried about Jaxon going to school on a Monday reeking of the stuff and social services getting involved. I'm not the bad guy here. I'm just looking out for my sister and the kids.*

'Have you ever taken drugs in your sister's house?' Forest asked. I was surprised by the question; she was clutching at straws.

What? No, never. I have no interest in drugs. Anyway, I work with kids, and my job means a lot to me. I'm not going to ruin my health and my career. Barron looked at me while signing this reply, rather than the detectives, though I didn't know why.

'And you didn't visit Elisha on the Friday that Lexi died?'

No, I told you, I hadn't been to the house for nearly a week.

'What time did you leave the pub that night?'

Midnight, maybe a bit later.

'Is there anyone who can confirm your story?'

I said goodbye to a couple of people before I went. They might remember what time it was.

'Did you go straight home?' Singh asked.

No, Barron replied. *I got a taxi back to Brigg, then I went for a kebab before I went home.*

'We'll need the name of the shop.'

Fine. I can't remember it, but I can let you know. Barron tapped his foot, clearly fed up and ready to leave.

'When did you next leave your house?'

I don't know, it's over a week ago now. Some time on the Saturday morning, but I was at home when Elisha sent me a message to tell me what had happened.

Singh and Forest exchanged a glance, the latter with a sour look on her face. 'That's all for now, Mr Barron, but we might want to ask you some more questions. Return our calls next time, please.'

I told you, my phone was broken. I was using a replacement until this morning. I came as soon as I got your messages. He was wide eyed, keen to show he was cooperating.

Forest said nothing, only nodded, and left the room quickly. Singh saw us out, promising to be in touch if they got any further with the threats, then I found myself walking back to my car with Max Barron.

This is why you ran away from me the other night, isn't it? he said. *You're interpreting for the police, and you found out I'm Elisha's brother.* He looked sad rather than annoyed.

I'm sorry. I don't really think I should socialise with anyone involved with the case. At least until it's over.

He nodded. *Do you think this is my fault?* he asked me suddenly.

Lexi's death? Why would it be your fault?

He stopped and faced me. *I didn't try hard enough to keep Elisha and the children safe. What if Alan killed Lexi, and I could have prevented it?*

I shook my head. *You said you didn't have any proof he'd harmed her, and you'd never seen him hurt the children.*

244

He nodded and carried on walking, but stopped again a moment later and looked at me. *Are you at the Deaf club often?*

Sometimes. I haven't been much recently, I told him, then stopped. Why was I telling him anything about myself? I barely knew him.

He smiled shyly. *Well, once they catch the bastard that did this, maybe we could continue our conversation.*

We shook hands, and the pressure lingered a little longer than was professional. He turned away, still smiling, and I felt the blush rising up from my chest to spread across my face. I took a deep breath and told myself to get a grip, but I found myself watching his car as he drove away.

Later that day, Anna and I sat on her bed. I'd begun to think of it as her room, rather than my spare room. Pages of a notebook were scattered across the covers, where we'd been writing down our thoughts about who could have killed Lexi, and who was threatening me.

You need to remember, I explained to Anna as she sifted through the notes I'd made, *Laura might be involved somehow. So you can't talk to her about any of this.*

Seriously? She's one of my best friends. I know she wouldn't do anything like this. I can't believe you'd even say that! Anna glared at me fiercely, but I stood my ground.

The police don't seem to have a clue, I told her. *I thought they were fixated on Alan, but right now I can't see that they have a solid suspect. So it could have been anyone, and you know there are all sorts of reasons people come up with to hurt children—*

Anna didn't let me finish. *I can't believe you. Why are*

245

you trying to pin this on Laura? Just because of what happened with Caitlin.

I'm not! I clenched my fists for a moment, holding back what I wanted to say. There was so much Anna didn't understand about what happened to Caitlin, and I wished she'd stop bringing her up. *I don't believe Laura did it, not for a minute, but we can't be biased about this. She's still a suspect, so we need to be careful.*

Have they said anything about Laura being a suspect? This is all coming from you, isn't it? It's bullshit.

I ignored her comment, even though she was right. I didn't know why I'd included Laura on our list of suspects, but I felt her name needed to stay.

What I mean is that we need to be careful who we talk to about this. The police are groping in the dark at the moment, and if anyone finds out we're sticking our noses in, it could mean a hell of a lot worse than me losing my job. I glanced out of the door to the blackened hallway and shivered. The text threats were bad enough, but was the murderer only biding their time until they did something worse?

The things I've seen and heard are horrifying, I continued. *It's been going round in my head all week, and I would've gone mad if I hadn't talked to someone about it. Does that make sense? I shouldn't have, but that's why I told you. You're my sister, I can trust you, and only you.*

It was true – I did trust her, despite my warnings. She understood the implications of talking to Laura or any of their mutual friends about this.

Anna leant back against the headboard and gave me a searching look. *There's something you're not telling me.*

246

You still feel guilty about Caitlin, don't you? Fifteen years, Paige. It's been half your life. You can't keep blaming yourself.

I couldn't deny it. I could have protected her, but I didn't. It would always stay with me, no matter how many years passed.

You have to let it go, Paige.

I nodded and looked down at the papers strewn around us. For a moment, I wondered if my subconscious was linking the two cases for a deeper reason, but I couldn't think of a connection other than the tragic deaths of two little girls.

I want to go to the Deaf club again tomorrow, Anna told me, jumping off the bed.

I nodded. *It's the memorial for Lexi tomorrow, isn't it?*

Her eyes were bright. *Exactly, and it's the only time everyone is likely to be together in the same room, so we can see how people are behaving. We can try to narrow down our suspects.*

Don't get too obsessed with this. Something about her attitude worried me.

Right, how are we going to organise these? She flicked through her notebook, ignoring my last comment, tearing out pages and reordering them, making some notes as she read, and I marvelled at her. All of the horrors I'd told her about she'd taken in her stride. All of the information she'd suspected, but I previously wouldn't tell her, she'd simply nodded and made a note of. Even though she was devastated by Lexi's death, she'd put that energy to good use, and I'd never been prouder of my little sister. It was my job to make sure she didn't get carried away with it.

We need to work out how someone got upstairs and

into the children's room without waking anyone up, Anna said.

Alan said someone could have slipped in the back door and he probably wouldn't have noticed. I remembered that Anna hadn't been to the house, and described the position of the stairs, leading down into the rear hallway by the back door. *They wouldn't have walked past him that way, they would have gone straight up the stairs. Everyone in the house was deaf, so they wouldn't have been worried about making a noise.*

Anna nodded. *It suggests it was someone who already knew the layout of the house. Could they have got round the back easily without being seen? If they'd hidden earlier in the evening, or in case someone was looking out of the window?*

I thought about the house and its layout. *Possibly. There's a passage down the side of the house, leading to the back garden, and when it's dark I doubt you'd see anyone going down there.*

The forensics people might have discovered something when they went over the house, Anna said. *I wish we could have access to what they've found.*

DC Singh said there was no evidence of a break in, I told her, exasperated.

What if they missed something? She chewed her lip for a moment. *I've got an idea, but you're not going to like it.*

Can I say no right now, without knowing what it is?

She went on as if I hadn't replied. *I think we've got a small window of opportunity here, and we should take advantage of it. Elisha told you they're still staying at her friend's house even though the police have finished with theirs. So it'll be empty now.*

248

I shook my head slowly. *No. Oh no, no, no. I know exactly what you're thinking, but it's not happening.*

Come on, Paige. Don't you want to know what happened to Lexi?

Of course I do, I replied. *I want the police to follow the evidence, and I want the threats to stop. But that's not a reason to break into someone else's house!*

I didn't mean we should break in, as such, she replied, spreading her hands wide in an attempt to look innocent. *But we could go and have a look around outside. Anyway, you said you don't think DI Forest has a clue, and the police are no closer to catching the murderer. Well, here's our chance to look for clues, to decide for ourselves whether or not there should be any other suspects.*

I stood up and gave Anna a brief hug before stepping back and looking at her. *You're my sister, and I love you, but this is complete madness. You can't do it. I'm not letting you put yourself into a dangerous situation. I won't help you, and I'll do my best to stop you doing it by yourself.*

She looked like she was about to argue with me, so I put up a hand to stall her. *I tell you what I will do. I'll call DC Singh and ask him to meet me tomorrow. He was close to giving me a bit more information last time, so I'll see if I can get any more out of him. Will that satisfy you?*

Anna pursed her lips and glared at me, but eventually she nodded. I was going to have to work hard to get some information out of Singh, if only to prevent my sister doing something stupid.

8 hours before the murder

Max leant against his car, his breath fogging in the cold night air. He knew it wouldn't be long before Alan came out for a cigarette, and he'd confront him then. This wasn't a conversation he wanted to have inside the Deaf club – too many witnesses.

He watched the door open and someone step outside, but it wasn't Alan. Max shrank back into the shadows and waited. Ten minutes later, he was about to talk himself out of it, when Alan stepped outside. Instead of sheltering by the door for a smoke, he had his coat on and looked to be leaving. Making his way across the car park, Max intended to head Alan off before he got to his van, but he stopped short when he saw Alan had the children with him.

What the hell do you want? Alan asked as soon as he saw him.

To talk to you, but now isn't the right time, Max replied, indicating the children with a tilt of his head.

Alan laughed. *Fucking coward. Using my children as*

an excuse to back off. He stepped forward and into Max's personal space.

Thoughts of Elisha rushed into Max's mind, telling him not to get into it with Alan in front of Jaxon and Lexi. The little boy was tugging on Alan's arm and complaining he was cold, but the girl just stared at him with big brown eyes. He smiled down at her and thought about Kasey, his niece, and was about to walk away when Alan poked him in the chest with his index finger.

I know you're trying to get Elisha to leave me. It's none of your fucking business what she does. She's an adult, and if she leaves me she's not taking my daughter.

I'll do whatever I need to do to get Kasey away from you, Max said, returning Alan's glare. *Does Elisha know about your little side line with Rick Lombard?*

The night air seemed to drop several degrees.

I don't know what you think you know, but you need to keep your fucking nose out of other people's business.

When it comes to protecting my sister and niece from a scumbag like you, I'll do whatever I have to. I don't give a shit if I have to ruin your life to do it.

Alan lunged for Max, but he dodged out of the way and backed off. Jaxon watched the two men with interest, but Lexi's bottom lip began to tremble and within moments her face had transformed as she burst into tears. Her father glanced at her for a moment, then looked back at Max, who'd stepped out of his reach.

Look after your daughter, Max signed, *before someone takes your children away from you for good.*

He stalked off through the car park, heart pounding, steeling himself for the blow from behind that he was expecting, but nothing came.

Chapter 21

Tuesday 13th February

I was woken the next morning by my phone, and I answered it to find Gem looking frantic.

Paige, are you busy today?

No, why? I'd arranged to meet Singh for a coffee, but apart from that I wasn't booked for any jobs.

Oh thank God, could you have Petra for a few hours? I've been called in to work, it's half term and I can't find anyone else to look after her.

Gem worked for the local council and was one of three people responsible for the online chat support service, so she dealt with everything from queries about benefits to complaints about changes to the bin collection schedule.

Of course. Want to drop her round here?

Fifteen minutes later, Gem appeared at my door with a bag of clothes and shoes. Petra grinned and hugged my waist before running through to the living room and grabbing the remote.

Thank you so much for this. The other two called in

sick today so they needed me. I'll give you some money to take her out.

Don't be ridiculous. Get off to work, and just text me when you're finished. With that, I practically pushed her out of the door and went to join Petra on the sofa.

'What are we watching?'

'*The Make-it Show.* They make things out of rubbish.'

I nodded appreciatively and sat with her for ten minutes until she was absorbed in the programme, then went to make us some breakfast. Anna came into the kitchen, rubbing her eyes.

Is that Petra?

I nodded and explained what had happened. *I'll take her out somewhere in a bit, let some energy out.*

Anna switched on the coffee machine and chose a pod out of the selection in the cupboard. *I really need to get some more work done today. If I'm going to be here any longer I'll need to send some more work for my students, too. I don't know how long they'll be willing to cover my seminars.*

I gave her shoulder a quick squeeze. *Hopefully this will be over soon.*

Pulling the neck of my coat up a bit higher, I huddled into my seat. The air inside the trampoline centre felt colder than it did outside, yet Petra was happily bouncing away with very few layers on compared to me. Maybe I should have joined her and warmed myself up that way, but I didn't fancy breaking a wrist.

I'd texted Singh earlier to postpone our coffee, so when my phone beeped I was expecting a message from him. I froze when I saw it was from a number I didn't recognise, assuming it would be another threat, but this time the message had been signed.

Hi Paige, got your number off your website, hope you don't mind. Wondered if I could take you for that drink tomorrow? Max.

I caught my breath. A treacherous part of me wanted to throw caution to the wind and say yes, but I knew it wasn't worth the risk.

I'm sorry, I can't. I replied, then berated myself for being rude. I followed it up with *Ask me again when the case is over.*

Why did I say that? I didn't want to date anyone. Max's text made me think back to Singh's comment about getting a coffee once they'd solved this case, and I wondered again what he'd meant by it.

I put my phone back in my pocket and looked over to where Petra was playing with another child, and I realised they were signing to each other. The other girl looked a little bit older than Petra, but her responses were quite shy. Scanning around, I saw a woman sitting in front of me who was watching the two girls intently, so I got up and went over to join her.

'Is that your daughter?' I asked, nodding at the little girl with Petra. For a moment the woman looked confused, and I was about to repeat the question in sign in case she was deaf too, but then she nodded.

'Yes. Is there a problem?'

'No, I just thought I'd come and say hi. It's nice to see them playing together.'

'Is your daughter hearing impaired?' she asked. It's not a phrase I would normally use but I didn't comment on it.

'She's my friend's little girl, and no, but her mum's deaf. Petra grew up signing, and she has a lot of friends at the Deaf club.'

The woman nodded her understanding and her shoulders relaxed slightly. I wondered if her daughter found it difficult to socialise, or if she was anxious about something else.

'I think I recognise her. We used to take Aysha to the Deaf club, to the children's activities, but we haven't been for a while.'

We lapsed into silence, my attempts at small talk not making much headway. Five minutes later, the woman beckoned to her daughter and they left. The girl waved at Petra and her mother gave me a brief smile, and I wondered if something else was bothering her.

Petra got bored soon enough, and we went through to the cafe for some lunch. Gem was sparing with the junk food she let her daughter have, but I caved and got us burgers and chips. We sat and munched our way through them happily, Petra daintily licking ketchup off her fingers.

'Do you know that other girl from the Deaf club?' I asked her, still curious about them.

'Yeah. Aysha doesn't go any more, her mummy doesn't like it there.'

'Really? Why not?'

Petra took a careful bite of her burger before replying. 'Because of Jaxon.'

I raised my eyebrows but Petra was too focused on her food to notice.

'What about Jaxon? Does he try to play with Aysha too?'

She shook her head. 'He's not nice to her. He's a bully.

He called Aysha names because she's from Pakistan. Then when her mummy told Jaxon's daddy, he got cross and said she was lying. Jaxon's daddy's scary,' she added, frowning. 'So they don't go any more.'

'That's a shame. I wonder if Aysha's mummy told the people who organise the kids' club.' I made a mental note to ask Gem about it later, see if she knew what had been done about it.

Petra kicked her feet on her chair and picked a bit of gherkin out of her burger. 'Aysha told me her mummy was upset because people knew she was telling the truth, but they wouldn't do anything about it.'

I chewed my food in silence for a moment, turning the story over in my mind. Had Alan been intimidating people at the Deaf club? Or was it just a case of a father not wanting to believe in his son's poor behaviour?

As we finished up our lunch, I got a text from Gem telling me she'd finished at work, so I offered to drop Petra home. When we arrived, my friend hugged me.

Thank you so much for stepping in.

It's fine, we had a good time, I replied.

What have you been doing?

I told her about our day, including the chance meeting with Aysha and her mum. When I told Gem what Petra had said, her face grew grave.

To be honest, I'm not sure I'm happy with Petra going at the moment, either. We've missed a couple of weeks because she's not enjoying it, and I don't know if I'll be taking her back.

Really? Why? I was surprised Gemma said this, as she'd always been keen for Petra to spend time with both the Deaf and hearing communities.

She looked down into her drink. *It's related to the problems that family had. I'm worried about how it's supervised. Petra keeps telling me she doesn't like Jaxon's daddy, because he's grumpy. And he argues with other grown-ups.*

She told me he was scary, I agree. *So Alan's been arguing with people at the kids' club?*

Gemma nodded. *I assume so. Kids aren't the most reliable witnesses, but she's definitely seen something she's not comfortable with, and that makes me uncomfortable too.*

Who does he argue with? I asked.

I'm not sure. She came home with this story about how a man had told Jaxon off, grabbed his arm, and he and Alan ended up fighting. I don't know who the man was. Petra tells me these stories but she can't give me a name or a decent description.

Have you told anyone about it? I asked.

Gem made a huffing sound. *I've tried, but they're only volunteers. There's only so much they can do, and I think everyone's a bit wary of Alan. They don't want to be the one to rock the boat.*

If it carries on, there won't be much of a kids' club left by the sound of it, I pointed out.

She nodded. *Are you going to the memorial for Lexi tonight?*

Yeah, I think it'll be good for Anna. She's too busy trying to figure out who did it to grieve properly.

I said my goodbyes and went back out to the car, feeling my phone vibrate in my pocket as I sat down.

If I can prove my alibi, then will you meet me? ;)

I smiled. *Nice try. You'll have to be patient.*

Max Barron was certainly persistent, but I couldn't decide if I found it charming or intrusive. Driving home, I found myself thinking about him – could he be the person threatening me, trying to throw me off the scent? I didn't exactly have a positive track record when it came to attracting decent men. Or was his interest completely innocent? I knew only time would tell, but the stress of suspecting everyone was starting to take its toll on me. It was exhausting, not knowing if the person I was talking to was the sort of person who could kill a child. I couldn't wait until this case was over, though I was worried this level of suspicion would have a lasting impact on me. Who could I trust?

Chapter 22

Chairs were laid out in rows in the main hall of the Deaf club, and most of them were full by the time the memorial began. The Deaf community wasn't huge, and even those who didn't really know Laura and Alan felt the loss of such a young child. The service was led by two of the senior members of the club's committee, one who spoke and one who signed, to make sure everyone could follow what was being said.

There had been tension when Alan and Elisha arrived. Laura was already seated on the front row, with Jaxon fidgeting on the seat next to her. Alan and Elisha made their way to the front, and she moved as if to sit at the opposite end of the row, but Alan took the seat next to Jaxon, leaving Elisha standing awkwardly at the front of the room, Kasey on her hip. After a moment's hesitation, she sat next to Alan. Laura stared straight ahead, not acknowledging either of them.

Laura told me they asked if she wanted to say anything,

but she couldn't face it. Alan refused as well, Anna signed to me. One of the volunteers for the kids' club read out a poem, tears running down her face.

There was a huge picture of Lexi at the front of the room, and some people had placed flowers and teddies next to it. I hadn't thought to bring anything and felt bad for a moment, then I looked over at Laura's ashen face and reminded myself that she probably couldn't care less about the gifts and tributes. None of it would bring her little girl back.

When the service was concluded, people milled around the bar. There was a sombre air to the place, and I didn't want to stay, but I'd promised Anna, so I didn't make any move to leave until she was ready. I left her to talk to her friends while I drifted aimlessly around the edge of the group, not really wanting to talk to anyone.

Walking over to the bar, I was about to get myself a drink when Anna came running up to me.

I need your help.

I followed her without asking for more details as she ran back through the hall towards the exit. When she opened the door, I could see it was lashing with rain outside and I hesitated on the threshold.

In the car park, Laura and Elisha were backlit by a lamppost, grappling with each other in front of the Deaf club. I hesitated for a moment but Anna dashed out into the rain, running towards where the two women were locked together.

I followed Anna and we ran to intervene together, Anna grabbing Laura by the shoulders while I put my arm across Elisha's waist and held her back. It took a moment to separate them, both of them drenched, their hair sodden

260

and wild. Laura's eyes blazed as she tried to get past Anna, but my sister held her friend back.

You killed my daughter! She's dead because of you! Laura signed around Anna.

I still had a tight hold of Elisha, and I could feel her breathing hard. There were tears in her eyes, and I tensed myself in case she tried to break free from me, but she had stopped struggling. She bent her head into my shoulder and sobbed.

Behind Laura, I could see Bridget huddling in her car, Jaxon strapped in the back seat. Why hadn't she tried to intervene? I hadn't noticed her at the memorial, which surprised me, but maybe she didn't feel like she was part of the Deaf community. She saw me looking at her and looked away.

At that moment, I heard a wail, and my gaze snapped towards the open door of the Deaf club. Kasey had got away from Alan and was standing there, her curly hair tousled, her head thrown back as she screamed for her mother. I spun Elisha round so she could see her daughter's distress, and she ran to the child, scooping her up in her arms and holding her close, soothing her as best she could. Kasey tried to pull away from her mother's soaked clothing, but Elisha kept a tight grip on the girl, looking over her head to where Laura stood with Anna.

Laura's face twisted into an anguished snarl. *Why does she get to keep her daughter when my little girl died? It's her fault! She should have looked after Lexi. How could someone get into her house and kill my daughter without her knowing? I don't believe her!*

Anna did her best to soothe Laura, but she wasn't having any of it. She shook herself free and ran towards

261

the door, but I headed her off and got between her and Elisha.

Please, you have to tell me what really happened, Laura begged, tears flowing down her face, indistinguishable from the rain. *You must know something. You have to know what happened.*

Elisha shook her head and buried her face in Kasey's curls.

'I don't know anything!' she cried. She was holding her daughter with both hands, so I signed her response for Laura.

Bullshit!

I moved to fill the doorway as much as possible, in case Laura tried to get past me, but instead she slumped down on the tarmac. I caught Anna's eye over Laura's head and she nodded, helping her friend to her feet and leading her towards Bridget's car. Behind me, Elisha stepped back into the Deaf club, and once I was sure Laura wasn't going to follow, I went in after her.

Are you okay? I asked, and she shook her head, the tears falling again. *Come and sit down.*

I need to go home and put Kasey to bed. She picked up her daughter and held her close, then fetched her pushchair from where she'd left it in the corridor outside the main hall. I wanted to make sure Elisha was okay before I left; I knew Anna would be looking after Laura.

I want this to be over. I want everything to go back to the way it was last week. She took a big shuddering breath as she signed.

I know.

It won't be the same, will it?

I shook my head. *I'm sorry.* There was nothing else I

262

could say. I paused for a moment, thinking of what Laura had been saying. *What happened out there?*

Elisha rubbed her face. *I don't know. Laura was out there having a cigarette. I went out to clear my head, to get out of that hall, and she started having a go at me. She thinks I know what happened, but I don't. I'm telling the truth.*

She turned imploring eyes on me and I reached out and squeezed her arm. *She's grieving. She wants to know what happened, and she can't process everything right now.*

My mind was whirring. Did Laura have a point? Was there something Elisha knew, that she hadn't told the police?

You know, if you remember anything about that night, anything you haven't told the police, you need to tell them straight away.

She frowned at me. *I know, I'm not stupid.*

I held up my hands. *I'm not saying that.*

Her lip curled. *You don't believe me, do you? I should have known. You're friends with Laura, you don't care what I say. You'll believe her. Maybe it was her! Maybe she came to my house and killed her daughter because . . . I don't know, because she's insane.* Elisha's eyes were blazing. *Go on, go back to your friend.* She nodded towards the door and glared at me until I backed away.

I want to help, Elisha. I want to find out the truth, the same as you.

My words were futile, however, and she turned her back on me, so I slipped out of the door to the car park. Bridget's car was still parked outside, but when I came out of the club Anna got out and Bridget and Laura drove off without a backward glance at me.

263

Anna and I crossed over to my car and got in, shivering.

Laura's going crazy. She thinks Elisha did it, or that Alan and Elisha are in it together.

I shook my head. *I don't know what to think any more.*

We sat in silence for a moment, the engine running to warm up the car.

Paige, what's going on here? Anna asked, and for the first time I thought I saw fear in her eyes.

I don't know, I replied. *But at least one person isn't telling everything they know.*

7 hours before the murder

Where are you going? Elisha asked as Alan walked towards the door.

Pub.

Are you serious? You only just got back from the Deaf club!

Yeah, I had to bring the children home.

Elisha glared at him. *You stayed there too late, the kids are knackered, and Jaxon takes ages to get into bed. You can at least stay until he's asleep.*

Alan shook his head. *He'll be fine, just let him watch TV or something if he's not tired.*

You have no bloody idea, do you? Elisha was furious. She'd refused to go to the Deaf club with him this evening because she only ever got to stay for about an hour, then Alan expected her to take his kids home while he stayed out with his mates. When was she supposed to spend any time with her friends?

Why do you have to be such a drama queen? Alan

265

asked, turning back to face her. *Laura was never like this when I went out.*

I bet she was, Elisha thought. She knew Laura got just as annoyed as her about him paying no attention to the kids' routines and letting Jaxon do whatever he wanted.

One night I'm going to go out and leave you with all three kids, and see how you manage it, she signed. *You can't just let Jaxon stay up, because then he'll be exhausted and overstimulated and he'll never want to go to bed.*

Let him fall asleep on the sofa then, Alan said with a shrug. *I used to do that all the time as a kid. Didn't do me any harm.*

Elisha couldn't think of a response to this that wouldn't make him angry so she just shook her head. *You don't get it.*

They're kids, Elisha. It's not that hard. His lip curled unpleasantly. *Jaxon's upstairs, what more do you want?*

You know he won't stay there, and I'll spend the next three hours putting him back to bed, probably getting hit and scratched while I do it, she snapped.

I don't know what you want me to say. You need to learn to control him. He's my son, I'm not going to stop having him here. He raised his eyebrows, as if she'd been suggesting Jaxon couldn't stay, and she had to take a couple of deep breaths before replying.

I didn't say the kids couldn't stay. I know they're your kids, and when you moved in I knew Jaxon and Lexi were part of the deal. What I'm asking is that you actually behave like a parent and look after them for once, rather than leaving me to do it all.

Alan thumped the wall. *It's Friday night, I need time with my mates to relax. I've been working all week so you don't have to, and now you want me to sit at home and not see anyone? I'll spend time with the kids tomorrow, right now they're asleep so I don't see what good it'll do them if I sit here all night.*

He glared at her until she turned away. Elisha knew there was no way she could win that argument. Alan refused to see her point of view, and nothing she said to him would change that.

The security light by the front door went off as he stepped outside, and she watched him walk away up the road until he was out of sight. She pulled a phone out of her pocket and sent a quick text. Maybe it wouldn't be long until Alan regretted using her as his free babysitter.

Chapter 23

Wednesday 14th February

Anna was in the kitchen, clutching a coffee, when I went in the next morning. Her hair was limp and her eyes bleary, and she looked off-colour. She winced when I pulled up the blind on the kitchen window, shielding her eyes.

What time did you go to bed last night? I asked.

Not sure. Maybe half two? I think I finished off that bottle of vodka you had at the back of the cupboard, she replied, waving a hand to suggest she didn't really remember much about it.

What were you doing up so late? I wasn't going to offer her any sympathy for her hangover.

Scrolling through stuff on social media. Seeing what the gossip is. Trying to figure out what happened. She put her head on the table and didn't elaborate.

My phone vibrated on the table, making Anna wince. I wanted a day off, without any police work and without even thinking about Lexi, but I opened the message and found myself smiling when I read it.

Hi, it's Max. I know the rules, but I need your help

with something. Nothing underhand, I promise. Meet me at Marco's for lunch?

Nothing had changed since the night before, however, and I tapped out a reply politely turning him down. I didn't send it, and stared at my phone for a minute before deleting my reply and typing a new one. It wouldn't hurt to meet him just once, surely? I wasn't going to get involved in anything, and whatever he wanted my help with might be connected to the case.

Still unsure, I didn't send my reply right away, giving myself time to mull it over. I left my phone on the table while I went to take a shower, but when I was finished I found Anna standing in the doorway to my room, holding it out.

What the hell is this? You've been texting Max Barron?

I snatched the phone off her and threw it on my bed. *You have no right to read my messages*, I fumed.

You are such a hypocrite, Anna signed, her eyes flashing. *You keep telling me not to get involved, not to be reckless, yet you're going out for lunch with one of the suspects.*

Come off it, Anna. He's not a suspect, he has an alibi.

She curled her lip. *Really? Because you fancy him, you believe him.*

That's not true! He said he needs my help with something, I replied, defensive.

That's just a line to get you to meet him! How can you be so naive?

I shook my head. *Keep your nose out of it, Anna.*

No. Why should I? You keep treating me like a kid, like I couldn't possibly understand what's going on here. I'm twenty-eight, Paige! I'm not your baby sister who needs protecting, not any more. There's one rule for you and one for me, just like after Dad died.

Her words stunned me and I couldn't respond. Was that really what she thought of me? I'd done my best for her, and I knew I'd made mistakes, but she'd never told me she felt like this before. We stood there for a moment, neither of us moving.

Is he still a suspect? she asked.

I glanced back at my phone, wondering what to do. *He's only been interviewed once. He'd fought with Alan before, that's why they wanted to talk to him. I don't think he's a suspect, no.*

Anna shook her head at my reply. *Don't you get it, Paige? He could have killed Lexi, if he was that desperate to get his sister away from Alan. Nothing else he'd tried had worked, you told me that. Maybe Max just lost it, thought that if Elisha didn't have these other kids to look after she'd see sense and leave him?*

He wouldn't. I'm sure of it.

She threw her hands up in despair. *You've floated stranger theories this week. We both have. Maybe he wanted to get back at Alan for something. Punish him by killing his child.*

Things like that don't happen in real life, I told her. *You'd have to be really sick to do something like that, to kill an innocent child to get revenge on someone.*

Anyone who kills a child is sick, she replied. *So what are you going to do? Are you going to go and meet this guy, knowing he could be a killer, or are you going to listen to me for once?*

I shook my head at her. *Don't be so dramatic. You've always been like this, making something out of nothing.*

270

There you go again, talking to me like I'm still a teen-ager. I've had enough of this. I came here because I wanted to support my friend at the worst time in her life. From now on I'll do that, and I'll keep out of your way, because you obviously don't give a shit what I think.

My bedroom wall shuddered as she slammed the door, then again a moment later as she stormed out of the flat.

I sat and brooded for a couple of hours, debating whether to call Anna and apologise. I'd eventually replied to Max, agreeing to meet him, although I was already having second thoughts. I was curious to know what he wanted my help with, but I stood firm in my assertion that I didn't want to get involved with anyone.

An hour before I needed to go out, I began to pace around the flat. I was nervous, so I laid out a few outfits on my bed before throwing them all into the bottom of the wardrobe. In the end, I settled for jeans and a pink-and-grey striped jumper. I didn't want him to think I'd made too much effort, but I still put a bit of make-up on before I went out.

The drive up to Marco's was an easy one, but the car park was rammed. It was a popular place for families in the winter, because it had a huge indoor soft play area. I found a space at the end of the overflow car park and I huddled into my coat as I walked back across the gravel to the main building. The wind was bitter, a weak sun doing nothing to take the chill out of the air.

I breathed in the fuggy smell of the farm as I crossed the car park, which changed to a wonderful aroma of cheese, spices and jams as soon as I stepped into the shop. I glanced through to the restaurant area but I couldn't see

271

Max. I was early, so I looked over the deli counters, sampling a few of the local cheeses.

When I checked my watch and realised it was 12:40, my heart sank. He was ten minutes late. Had he changed his mind? It seemed strange that he'd stand me up, when he was the one who asked me out in the first place. I'd started to think of it as a date, especially as it was Valentine's Day, but I shook that thought out of my head.

I wandered around the shop for another ten minutes, then decided to give up. If I left straight away, I wouldn't feel too humiliated. It was probably for the best anyway.

Heading for the front door, I pulled my phone out of my bag to check I hadn't had any messages, but there were no notifications. He could at least have let me know if he wasn't coming. Suddenly, I remembered the texts and the attempted arson, and I was struck by an idea – what if this was a ruse to get me out of my flat? I flung open the door of Marco's to run back to my car, and promptly walked straight into Max.

Sorry! he signed the moment he realised it was me. *I'm really sorry, I was stuck behind a tractor.* I raised an eyebrow, and he pulled a sad puppy face. *Forgive me?*

I sighed, but couldn't stop myself from laughing at his expression. Was it this case making me paranoid, or did my past mean I would always be distrustful of men and their motives? *Fine. But now you have to buy me cake.*

Of course! I can stretch to more than that, if you ask nicely. He grinned at me and I tried to keep a straight face, but the fluttery feeling was back in the pit of my stomach.

Finding a table, we spent a few minutes looking at the menu. It had obviously been a busy morning, and we were lucky to get a table in the crowded restaurant. At least one of the advantages of sign language is that you can have a private conversation in a public place. I glanced around at the other customers: a couple of young families, the children starting to get restless and demanding more time in the play areas; some older couples, too.

After we'd ordered, I realised Max was watching me intently and I gave him a quick smile. *What did you want to talk about?*

He looked down at the table, fiddling with the pot of sauce packets in front of him for a moment before he replied. *Can I trust you?*

My heart picked up speed. *Of course you can. I want to help, you know that.*

He nodded. *I like you, Paige.* He didn't make eye contact as he signed this, and looked faintly embarrassed to have said it. *I mean, I would like to get to know you better, but we need to trust each other.*

I eyed him carefully, wondering where this was going. *It's difficult for me, being involved with this investigation. I don't know who I can trust. Someone's lying.*

I understand that, but I need you to believe it wasn't me. If you think that I could have hurt a kid, I don't know what to do. You're not going to be able to help me.

He was asking a lot, and he knew it. I'd only just met him, so I had no reason to take his word for it that he wasn't involved in Lexi's death, but could he really be so obsessed with getting Elisha away from Alan that he'd hurt a child to do it? My gut told me that I could trust him, but was that only because I was attracted to him?

Do you know something about what happened? Because if you do, really you should be talking to the

273

police, not me, I told him, knowing it was the right thing to say. He'd caught my interest, though, and I was keen to hear anything he knew.

He shook his head. *I don't know anything concrete, they won't listen to me. I only have my suspicions.*

Why do you want to talk to me about it? I asked, wondering if he hoped I'd pass his ideas on to the police.

I said, because I like you. He risked looking at me that time.

I nodded, but didn't say anything. I didn't trust myself.

So, will you listen to me? Because I really want you to believe me.

I took a moment to consider what he was saying, and decided to take that risk.

Okay. What is it you want to tell me?

I've been trying to get Elisha to leave Alan. For the last six months I've been working on her, telling her all the stories I hear about him, making notes of all the things she tells me about how he leaves her to look after the children. The problem is that I can't get through to her.

I had to admit I was disappointed. I was hoping for something a bit juicier, to be honest. Still, it could give me a bit more insight into the family.

She used to bring the kids round to mine at the weekends, you know? he continued. *Jaxon is a real handful, but if you let him know the rules he soon calms down. Kasey is my niece, so I love her to pieces, and it was worth having Jaxon around in order to see her. But Lexi . . .* He tailed off, shaking his head, his face darker. *She was such a good kid, and Elisha loved her about as much as she loved Kasey. The two of them were like peas in a pod – they both look like Alan, rather than their mums. All this crazy curly hair that took forever to brush. Kasey hates having her hair done, and Elisha always has a hard job with it. If they're coming to mine at the weekend, she waits until then to do Kasey's hair, then she gets me to sit in front of her and pull funny faces to distract her. Lexi loved it, though; that was the main difference between them. She used to giggle the whole time.* A sad smile crept across his face. *I know she wasn't my blood relative, but I'm going to miss that kid as much as if it was Kasey who had been . . .* He stopped again, unwilling to sign the word.

Our order arrived, which broke the tension. I put my hand over his and we sat like that for a moment. I hadn't considered that he had also been close to Lexi, and maybe he was taking her death as hard as Anna was.

He sniffed, then carried on with his story. *I always offer to go over to see them, rather than her coming to me, but she refuses. She gives excuses – the house isn't tidy, she wants the children to get outside, she prefers a change of scenery, things like that. But I think she doesn't want me in the house when Alan's there. She's my half-sister, but we lived together growing up, so I just think of her as my sister. Alan's sick in the head if he thinks there's some-thing going on, but he won't let any other man near Elisha so I guess I fall into that category.*

I grimaced. *Seriously? Alan is jealous of you spending time with Elisha?*

He shrugged. *I think so. It's either that, or he doesn't like me spending time with his kids.*

I thought back to some of the other things he'd told me. *If he's mistreating Elisha, could he be worried she's confiding in you? Maybe he knows you want her to leave him, and doesn't want you influencing her.*

275

Max nodded slowly. *That sounds likely, I think you might be right. That might be why he squared up to me last night at the Deaf club.*

What happened? I asked.

He told me to get lost, leave Elisha alone, Max signed, spreading his palms wide as if to suggest it was pretty minor stuff. *He does it most weeks, but hasn't taken it any further. The only time I'm around him is when we're at the Deaf club. I don't live in Scunthorpe, and I work in Hull, so it's not like we hang around in the same places. I think he just needs to maintain his image, you know? If he stops telling me to fuck off, maybe people will think he's gone soft, something like that.*

It makes sense. But if you've been trying to get Elisha to leave him for six months, surely he knows it's not working? I mean, she's still with him, isn't she? He's a suspect in the murder of a child and she's still with him.

Max frowned and looked down at his coffee, stirring it slowly. I wondered if he was processing what I'd said, or trying to think of a way to answer. He grimaced, put the spoon down then slowly sipped his coffee. I took a bite of my sandwich while I waited, although I felt a bit guilty for eating when we were talking about something so serious.

He put his cup down and looked at me. *The only reason they moved in together was because she was pregnant. If that hadn't happened, she would have just been another conquest and he would have gone back to Laura, like he always did.*

Yeah, he cheated on Laura a lot, I agreed.

Max nodded. *And I'm sure he's cheated on Elisha too. That's another reason I want her to leave him, but she refuses to believe me. She can't carry on turning a blind eye to the way he treats her or the children, even though she makes excuses, but she absolutely won't believe that he has cheated on her.* He shook his head in disgust. *She's a hypocrite really, considering how they got together. Elisha knew that Alan was with Laura when they first started seeing each other, but it didn't stop her. He flattered her, told her she was special, and she was sucked in. It'll come back to bite her, though. I know it will. It's only a matter of time before he gets someone else pregnant, and then she won't be able to deny it any more. She'll be devastated, though maybe then she'll leave him.*

He chewed his bottom lip then took another swig of his coffee. *I don't want her to go through that, though.* Max pulled his lunch towards him and took a big bite, again not making eye contact.

Do you know about Elisha and Rick Lombard? I asked.

He pulled an expression of disgust. *Yes, and that bastard's no better than Alan. I was hoping I could convince her that neither of them were any good for her, but I thought she'd stopped seeing Rick.*

No, there's still something going on. I stopped short of telling him Lombard was in the house the night Lexi died, as I doubted it was common knowledge.

She's a bloody fool. Lombard and Alan are into some dodgy shit together.

Really? I asked, wondering if this was related to whatever Lombard was showing Elisha in the warehouse.

Max nodded. *Receiving stolen goods. Mostly shoes and handbags stolen from other warehouses. I think it was one of Alan's drug contacts who got him involved. I've been keeping an eye on them, and I intend to go to the police as soon as I've got something incontrovertible to show them.*

I was stunned. I hadn't realised just how much criminal activity Alan was caught up in. That made sense. But did Alan and Elisha each know the other was involved? Or was Lombard somehow stringing them both along? Max hadn't mentioned Elisha's part in all of this, but I didn't know if he was protecting his sister or didn't know she was mixed up in it as well.

There's something else, Max said, his head bowed. *I'm not proud of it.*

What?

I lied to the police. I went to the house on that Friday, the day Lexi died.

I was stunned, and didn't reply for a moment. *Why would you lie about something like that?*

Because I was scared! He looked at me earnestly. *I've never made a secret of how much I dislike Alan, and if I'd told them I was there it would have looked bad. And now I can't exactly tell them the truth, because they'll think I've lied about everything. But I was only outside that afternoon. I didn't go in, and I didn't go back that night. I promise. All I want is to get Elisha to see the truth about Alan.*

Something triggered in my memory, something I wanted to ask Max. *Anna and I were looking at a Facebook group about Lexi, and there was a post from someone called MB. When we looked for it again, it had disappeared. Was that you?*

He nodded. *I wanted people to know what Alan was capable of. But then a friend saw it and told me it was libel, because Alan was never charged, so I took it down.*

Not necessarily suspicious, as it turned out. *So what is it you want my help with? I don't know Elisha, there's no way she would listen to me. And I can't vouch for you to the police. I've only just met you.*

He shook his head. *I know, it's not that. I want to know how likely it is that Alan is going to be put away for Lexi's murder.* He grimaced as he signed the last word.

I have no idea, I told him, sitting back in my chair and glaring at him. It was my connection to the investigation that he was interested in, not me personally. In a way it was a relief, but part of my treacherous mind had started to like the idea of having an admirer. *I'm not privy to any of the evidence other than the interviews with the deaf people involved. When Alan saw his solicitor, she employed a different interpreter, so I don't know what he talked to her about.*

Do you know the other interpreter? he asked, interrupting me and sitting up straighter. *Could you ask them what happened, what Alan said?*

I gave Max a stern look and he sat back again, hanging his head.

Sorry, I shouldn't have asked that.

No, you shouldn't. *Would you be happy if I talked to another interpreter about your statement to the police? Or if you employed me to go to a medical or legal appointment with you, would you be happy for me to share your personal information with anyone?*

He shook his head, grimacing at the telling off he knew he deserved.

Seriously, Max, if that's the only reason you asked me to meet you today, I'm leaving right now. I reached for my bag and started to stand up, but he grabbed me by the arm.

No! Don't go, please. That's not the only reason, I promise.

I took a deep breath. *Fine. But if you ask me something like that again, I will leave. Understand?*

He gave me an apologetic look. *I'm sorry. I just need to find a way to get Elisha to listen to me, and if Alan was locked up she would have to believe me. I'm desperate. I'd do anything to get her away from him. She's not the same person she used to be; she's a shell of the Elisha I know, my little sister. I want the old Elisha back, and I'm running out of ways to make that happen.*

A dark look crossed his face, and I caught myself wondering just how far Max would go to get his sister away from Alan Hunter. Shaking the thought off, I took another bite of my sandwich before asking him again what he wanted me to do.

I want you to ask Laura to talk to Elisha.

I nearly choked on my food, and had to take a gulp of coffee to wash it down before I could answer. *Are you serious?*

Absolutely. His face said it as well. *She knows better than anyone what Alan Hunter is really like, and she can talk Elisha into leaving him, I'm sure of it.*

I shook my head slowly. *It'll never work, Max. Laura will never talk to Elisha. Anyway, there's a big part of Laura that wants Alan back, so she's hardly going to slag him off when she's in denial over what a scumbag he is.*

Doesn't Laura think Alan killed Lexi?

I shrugged. *Your guess is as good as mine. I think part of her thinks he did, the part that listens to everything* her mother says and takes it as gospel, but I also think there's part of her that is still obsessed with him, and that part can't ever believe anything bad of him. Like I said, she's in denial. She's focused on Elisha, not Alan.

But that's good, if she wants Alan back. It would give her more of a motive to get Elisha to leave him, Max replied.

I laughed. That's not the way it works. We women can be very calculating, and I'm sure Laura would love to split them up, but she wouldn't go about it that way. I'm sure she wouldn't. She'd want him to make the choice, to choose her over Elisha, rather than come back to her because he didn't want to be on his own. And if we went to her and asked her to split them up, because it would be the best thing for Elisha, she'd probably do her best to keep them together.

Max looked confused. Why? I don't understand.

Because if we tell her it's the best thing for Elisha, she won't want that to happen. She wants Elisha to suffer, to be unhappy, because in Laura's opinion it serves her right. She stole her man, and if she's unhappy in the relationship now, it's justice. Laura will revel in that. She won't be able to see past her hatred of Elisha to the bigger picture.

But surely if we tell her that's what we want, she'll see it? If we say we want Elisha and Alan to break up, and ask her to talk Elisha into it, won't she do that? Max leaned forward, his eyes bright with enthusiasm.

I doubt it, I told him. Anyway, if Laura comes to Elisha and tells her what a terrible person Alan is, won't Elisha just defend him even more? She told me she's already worried Alan will leave her and go back to Laura. That would just reinforce the idea.

Max's shoulders sagged. *You're right. I hadn't thought of it that way.* He kicked the table leg in frustration, making me jump. *Sorry. I really thought it might work.*

I put my hand over his, and he turned his over and gave mine a squeeze. We sat like that for a few seconds. Sign language has its disadvantages too – you need both hands free.

I would do anything to protect my sister. Anything. I could see his concern for Elisha in his eyes.

I'm sorry. I would love to help you, but getting Laura involved won't work.

Max seemed to deflate in front of me. *She has to leave him,* he told me. *I'm worried she isn't safe.*

I nodded, and agreed with him that Elisha could be in danger, but I wanted him to get the idea of trying to separate her and Alan out of his head. The more he tried to force her, the deeper she'd dig her heels in until she was ready to see the truth. I should know; it took years for me to see what my friends and Anna had been trying to warn me about.

I decided to steer him away from the subject and squeezed his hand again. *Do you want to go for a walk, clear your head?*

He sighed. *I'd love to, but Elisha is bringing Kasey over.*

I nodded. *Okay. But if you want to talk any more about this, you know where I am.*

As we walked out to the car park, Max reached for my hand again and the butterflies went mad. We stayed like that until we reached my car.

Can I see you again? Maybe take you out for dinner one night?

I shook my head and pulled my hand away. Anna was right. I'd broken all my own rules because this guy had sweet-talked me, and I was doing exactly the sort of thing I'd told her not to do. I made a mental note to apologise to her as soon as I got home. My relationship with my sister was too important to damage over something like this.

What's wrong? Max asked, taking a step towards me.

I rubbed my eyes with one hand. *I'm exhausted. This situation is overwhelming. I'm an interpreter, I do hospital appointments and parents' evenings, and now suddenly I'm in the middle of a murder investigation. Someone is threatening me, and I have no idea who. I'm suspicious of everyone, I'm not sleeping properly, and now suddenly you're here asking me out, and it's all too much for me.*

Someone's threatening you? He gave me a look of genuine concern.

Yeah, notes through my door, weird texts. Someone tried to set fire to my flat.

He leaned forward and touched my arm. I could feel the warmth of his hand even through my coat.

I understand what you're saying. This isn't a good time. I'll still be around when this is all over. He gave me a gentle smile and I leant more of my weight on my car.

But, Paige, whoever has been threatening you, I promise it wasn't me.

He squeezed my hand lightly before turning and walking away. I watched until he reached his car, half hoping he'd turn and look back, so when he did, my heart somersaulted.

* * *

283

As I drove home, my mind was spinning with a million thoughts about Max, Lexi, and the situation with Alan and Elisha. I'd missed a call from Anna while I was talking to Max, but I decided I'd rather speak to her in person when I got home. I was distracted when I pulled into my road, so at first I didn't notice anything unusual, but when I did it sent my heart plummeting. Two police cars were parked outside my flat.

I pulled into my parking space and approached the cars on foot. I was shaking, and it felt like forever before I reached them. Before I could speak to one of the uniformed officers, DC Singh got out of a car and hurried over to me. The expression on his face made me lean against the nearest car for support.

'What happened?' I asked.

'Paige, I'm so sorry.' He reached out and squeezed my shoulder. 'Your sister's been involved in an accident. She's been taken to Scunthorpe General.'

The street began to spin. Singh caught me as my knees buckled, and somehow opened the door of the police car and guided me to sit down.

'What sort of accident? Is she okay? What happened?' My voice sounded quiet and far away, and I had the presence of mind to put my head between my knees before I fainted. Oh God, was Anna going to die? I thought of the argument we'd had earlier. That couldn't be the last memory I had of my sister. I pressed my lips together to stop myself being sick.

Singh crouched in front of me, his voice low. 'She's alive, but in a serious condition. It appears to have been a hit and run.'

'Where? Here?'

He shook his head. 'Do you know if your sister had any plans today? Was she meeting anyone?'

'I don't know. Why? Where was she?'

'Outside Alan and Elisha's house.'

My head swam. Why hadn't she told me she was going there? Is that why she called me? Had she found something?

'Why didn't they stop?' I risked looking up at Singh. I wanted to make sure he was telling me everything.

He rested a hand on my arm. 'We believe it was deliberate.'

Chapter 24

I couldn't remember how I got to the hospital. I remembered being in a vehicle, but it wasn't my car. There's no way I was in a fit state to drive.

When I arrived at the hospital, Anna was in surgery and nobody could speak to me. There was no family to call, nobody I wanted there with me, so I paced until I wore myself out. Singh stayed with me until he was called away, then I sat for two hours, staring blankly at the walls, until a doctor finally appeared.

'She's out of surgery and we're taking her up to Intensive Care. Once she's settled, you can go up and see her, but she won't be conscious. She had a severe bleed in her abdomen, and a nasty head wound that has caused some swelling in her brain. At the moment we're hopeful that she will regain consciousness, but you need to be prepared for the possibility that might not happen.'

Her words were like a knife to my heart. I thanked her, my voice shaking, and she promised to keep me informed of any changes in Anna's condition, but it was another hour until I was allowed to see her. The ward was eerily quiet except for the hum and hiss and beeps of the apparatus. I barely recognised my sister, surrounded by tubes and machinery, as I stood at the foot of the bed. Who could have done this to her? It had to be connected to the investigation, and to the threats I'd received. Why had she gone to the house, and what had she found there?

As if he'd read my mind, I heard footsteps approach, and turned to see DC Singh. He gave me a sad smile and asked if he could speak to me. We sat down next to Anna's bed, where he began to talk in hushed tones.

'I wanted to come and fill you in on a few more details. We have a witness who heard the impact and saw a black van pulled up on the pavement next to the house. It drove away moments later, and the witness saw your sister on the pavement and called for an ambulance.'

I put my face in my hands as I took his words in. Someone had tried to kill my sister, my gorgeous little Anna. I should have protected her, especially after the fire. I should never have let her get involved. My heart gave a lurch as I remembered our argument, her accusation that I was being *over*protective. I couldn't get it right.

'Was it Alan?' I croaked. 'He's got a black van, and it was outside his house.'

'We don't know anything right now. I'm sorry, Paige.' He looked away quickly. There was something he wasn't telling me.

'You think it was his van, though, don't you?'

Singh didn't look at me when he replied. 'I can't talk to you about it. You know that.' He reached over and squeezed my hand quickly. 'Is there anything you can tell me that might help us? Do you know why Anna was there?'

I couldn't speak. Tears welled up in my eyes and I shook my head. Singh put an arm around my shoulder and held me as I sobbed.

It took me a couple of minutes to compose myself, but when I did I looked up at him, and he pulled away awkwardly.

'It must be whoever has been threatening me. You need to trace that phone! Why hasn't it been done yet?'

Though I knew it wasn't his fault, he was there in front of me and he bore the brunt of my anger.

'If you'd done your job and found this lunatic, they wouldn't have had the chance to attack Anna. They probably meant to kill her! They might have succeeded; she still might not wake up.'

The tears began to flow again, and I cursed myself for being preoccupied with Max Barron when I should have followed my sister. If I had gone after her, maybe this wouldn't have happened. It was my fault, just as much as the police's.

I apologised to Singh, and he was about to speak when he received a text.

'I've got to go, I'm sorry. I promise I'll call you as soon as we know anything.'

I watched him walk away, wondering how this would all end.

I stayed for another two hours before I was told visiting time was over and I could return the following day. I was anxious about leaving my sister, but the nurses were strict and wouldn't bend the rules.

Instead of going straight home, I found myself turning off towards Bridget and Laura's house. I needed to ask them some questions, and I didn't feel like going back to stare at the walls of my empty flat just yet.

Bridget answered the door, and she looked at me in shocked silence for a moment.

'Paige. You look terrible,' she said.

'Can I come in?'

She nodded, and ushered me through to the kitchen where Laura was washing up. I sat down and slumped over the dining table, but turned down the cup of tea that was automatically offered to me.

You look terrible, Laura told me, echoing her mother.

'Anna's in hospital,' I replied, speaking and signing together. 'Someone ran her down.'

What? What the hell happened? Is she okay?

I shook my head, swallowing hard to try and stop my voice from cracking. 'They don't know. She might wake up. She might not.'

I put my head in my hands and took several deep breaths. I didn't even know why I'd come to Laura's. I should have gone to Gemma's, got some comfort from my closest friend, but part of me felt I didn't deserve to be comforted. I could have just texted Laura to let her know what had happened to Anna, and to ask about Alan's van, but maybe I thought I'd get more answers in person.

'Bridget. It was a black van,' I said, fixing her with a firm look.

Her eyes widened. 'Why would that have anything to do with me?'

Laura looked between the two of us, a frown of confusion on her face.

Your mum's seen someone watching your house, I told her without hesitation. *A black van. She's seen it parked along the street, or driving past. That's where she was on Monday. She went to report it to the police, because she thinks Alan's stalking you.*

Bridget's face darkened as I signed all of this to Laura. 'This is none of your business! I told you I wanted to keep this from Laura. Just because you and Anna have been sticking your noses in where they don't belong, that's no reason to get my daughter involved.'

Mum! Laura jumped up. *That's not fair! I want to know. What else haven't you told me?*

Bridget shook her head, signing as she spoke. 'What, and have you end up like Anna? No! I don't want anything else to do with you, Paige. It's Anna's own damn fault this happened, and yours.'

I took a few deep breaths as my vision clouded slightly, the force of Bridget's words stunning me into silence. Laura was standing between us with her mouth open, a horrified expression on her face at her mother's words.

Without another word, I stood up and crossed the kitchen. Bridget stepped back against the worktop, her eyes wide. I glared at her, but couldn't trust myself to say anything, so I turned swiftly and left, slamming the front door behind me.

Back home, I sat in my living room in the dark, fretting over details, wondering how I could have prevented this. I should never have involved Anna, shouldn't have told her anything about the case. Eventually, exhausted, I climbed into bed, but stared at the ceiling for ages. I heard a beep from the other room and got up to check my phone. My heart leapt in my chest as Anna's name flashed up on the screen. Could she be awake already?

I tapped on the message to open it, and made a strangled noise in my throat.

You'll be next.

My heart pounding, I dialled DC Singh's number without thinking. He picked up after the second ring.

'Paige?'

'Rav, I need your help.' I didn't elaborate, but he must have heard the fear in my voice.

He barely paused before he replied. 'I'll be there as soon as I can.'

It was less than ten minutes until I buzzed him into the building, and I guessed he must have broken every speed limit on the way there.

'What is it? Are you okay? Is it Anna?'

I stood in the hallway, my arms wrapped tightly around myself. I could feel I was shaking, but I couldn't do anything to stop it. Singh noticed, closed the door behind him and guided me into the living room, where he sat me on the sofa and draped a throw around my shoulders.

'Is it Anna?' he asked again.

I shook my head, and showed him my phone.

'Who sent this?' He stared at the phone in confusion. 'Anna can't have sent you those messages. Was her phone stolen?'

I took a deep breath before answering. 'I assume whoever ran her over took it.'

Singh's frown deepened. 'The witness said the van had stopped after the impact. Whoever it was could have got out of the van and taken Anna's phone. They would have been taking a huge risk though, in case someone had seen them.'

He got up and paced for a moment, then slammed his hand into the door frame. 'How the hell haven't we found them yet?'

I didn't reply. I didn't need to.

He stood in the doorway for a moment, his head bowed, and I found myself taken aback at the emotion I could feel flowing from him. A moment later, he turned round to look at me.

'Do you have somewhere else you can stay?'

I thought for a moment. The only close friend I had was Gem, and I wouldn't put her and Petra in danger.

'No. We don't have any family.'

'Okay. Well, I'll stay here then.'

'What?'

He sat down next to me again. 'I can't leave you here on your own. It's not safe, that much is clear. And if there's nowhere else you can go, I'll stay with you.'

Gripping his hand fleetingly, I nodded. 'Thank you.'

'Don't worry,' he said with a grin. 'I'll sleep on the sofa.'

I gave a half-hearted laugh. My mind couldn't have been further from the idea of him sharing my bed.

'Is there any news from the hospital?'

'No, nothing yet.' I pulled the throw tighter around my shoulders and glanced at my phone. 'Why don't we call Anna's number? See who answers?'

He shook his head. 'They won't answer. And you might scare them into dumping the phone. Give me the number, and I'll pass it on to the station, make sure it's a priority for getting it traced in the morning.'

'Why can't they do it now?' I asked, frustration making my voice shrill.

He smiled gently. 'A lot of departments work normal office hours. They won't be back in until the morning, I'm sorry.'

'Fine. I don't think I'm going to be able to sleep tonight though,' I said, rubbing the bridge of my nose.

Singh squeezed my shoulder gently. 'I understand, but you should try.'

'Do you want a drink?' I asked, getting up and shuffling through to the kitchen. I knew coffee would be a terrible idea, but I thought there was some hot chocolate at the back of the cupboard.

After digging it out and checking it was in date, I made mugs for both of us. We sat at the kitchen table, not speaking, staring into our drinks. Something was nagging at the back of my mind, but it took its time to come forward. When it did, I leapt out of my chair and dashed into Anna's room, locating her tablet under a pile of paper.

'Anna was always putting her phone down in stupid places,' I told Singh, sitting opposite him again. 'So she signed up for one of these apps that can locate your phone. I know her password, she uses the same one for everything,' I added.

'Will it show you where the phone is now?'

'It only works if it's turned on. Hopefully whoever has it hasn't thought to turn it off.' After a moment of scanning the home screen of Anna's tablet, I brought up the app and logged on.

'It must have been turned on when they sent you the message, at least. Won't it show you where the phone was then?'

We both peered at the screen, but the only thing we saw was a message in red telling us there was no data to display.

'Damn. Anna only got the free version, so it doesn't store tracking information,' I said, after clicking on an icon in the corner of the screen. 'But if they turn it on again, this can help you to find it, can't it?'

'Definitely,' he replied, taking the tablet from me eagerly. 'Can we keep this?'

I nodded. 'If it'll help. I'll write her password down for you. Then when all of this is over I'll make her change all of her passwords.' I didn't want to think about the fact that Anna might never wake up. I had to continue as if she was going to get better, or I'd collapse.

We watched the screen for a few moments, as if we were willing the phone to burst into life spontaneously, but nothing happened. The adrenaline had worn off, and my head felt heavy, my neck drooping.

Singh put a hand over mine. 'You need to try and get some sleep.'

This time I agreed. I pulled a pillow and a spare duvet out of the cupboard in my room and left them on the sofa for him, then crawled into bed. Tonight, of all nights, I was dreading the nightmares that might come. Despite my exhaustion, I didn't expect sleep to come as quickly as it did.

5 hours before the murder

Jaxon was bored. He didn't want to go to bed. Elisha had told him he wasn't allowed to stay up, but he wasn't sleepy. Climbing out of his bed, he looked around for a toy to play with, but she'd taken them all away. He would have to go downstairs and get one.

He opened the bedroom door and looked out. There was nobody on the landing or on the stairs, so he started to creep down. When she tidied up, Elisha put all his toys in a box by the back door, he knew. If he could get to the box without her seeing him, he could find something to play with and take it back upstairs with him.

Jaxon made it to the bottom step before Elisha caught him.

What are you doing? Come on, back to bed.

Where's Daddy? I want to say goodnight.

Daddy's gone out, Elisha said, and she had that look on her face that grown-ups have when they're annoyed with someone.

I want to see Daddy, he repeated. He knew Daddy would let him stay up and watch TV with him.

No. Bed.

He kicked Elisha but she picked him up and carried him up the stairs, putting him back into bed. He tried to bite her hand, but she moved too quickly. Jaxon knew that Elisha wouldn't go downstairs straight away, so he couldn't go back to get a toy. He waited until she'd closed the door and he saw her shadow move away, then he got back out of his bed and climbed onto Lexi's.

Lexi wriggled in her sleep, but she didn't wake up. He stepped on her as he crawled across her bed, but he didn't really care. He didn't like either of his sisters; they were boring. From Lexi's bed, he knew he could see out of the window, so maybe he could wait for Daddy to come home. Then he could get up and watch TV.

Pulling back the curtain, Jaxon peered out into the street. The houses opposite were a bit bigger than this one, and he saw a trampoline in the garden of one. He wanted a trampoline but Elisha said no. He hated Elisha, she never let him have anything he wanted. He wanted to go back to Mummy and Grandma's house. Grandma would let him have a trampoline.

There was a man walking towards the house, but it wasn't Daddy. He stopped outside, then came down the path to the front door. He didn't know who the man was, but he'd go down and find out later. He disappeared from view, and Jaxon looked out across the street again. When Daddy came home he'd ask him about the strange man, and he'd tell him something else he'd seen too: someone was standing in the bushes outside the house opposite, watching him.

Chapter 25

Thursday 15th February

The following morning, I woke late. I heard the kettle boiling and for a moment I thought it was Anna in the kitchen, until I remembered what had happened the day before. A grey wave of depression rolled over me and I buried my face in my duvet, trying to hold back my sobs.

Knowing Singh was in my kitchen, I battled to compose myself. I quickly checked my phone, in case I'd had a call from the hospital, but there was nothing. It was gone nine, but I still had a couple of hours before I would be allowed to see her.

Singh was making toast when I joined him. There was a crease on the side of his face from the pillow, which I found endearing. He looked surprisingly well rested, considering he'd slept in his clothes.

'Hope you don't mind, I was hungry.'

'Course not. Help yourself,' I said, yawning. I slid into a chair and rubbed my eyes. 'Did you manage to sleep?'

'Sort of. There's a lamppost right outside the window that shines through the blinds, right onto the sofa.'

'Sorry,' I said, but he laughed.

'I'm teasing. Did you sleep okay?'

I nodded and yawned again. 'Better than I expected. I feel like I could sleep all day. But I need to be up, then I can go to the hospital as soon as it's visiting hours.'

'No news?'

'Nothing yet.'

Singh busied himself making tea and toast, and I thought he probably didn't know what to say. What could anyone say? We had no idea if Anna was going to make it.

I stared at the table, my mind elsewhere, until I was dragged back to the present by a beep from my phone. Anna's name flashed across the screen.

'Quick, get the tablet.' I didn't have to ask twice. He brought up the app and I opened the message.

You'd better be looking over your shoulder.

I shivered and passed the phone to Singh, who scowled. The logo for the app swirled around for what felt like an hour, before it was replaced by a map of Scunthorpe. A little flashing red dot showed us where Anna's phone was: somewhere in the town centre, near the high street.

'I need to call this in,' Singh muttered, but I put a hand on his arm to stop him.

'Why? If we go now, we might be able to catch them.'

'You mean if *I* go now,' he said sternly.

'No, I mean we. I'm coming too. This is my sister we're talking about.'

He made a frustrated noise in the back of his throat. 'Paige, this isn't a game. We're talking about someone who has tried to kill Anna and probably killed a child, too. We need back up and it needs to go through the proper channels.'

I snatched the tablet off him. 'You're not going to talk me out of this. If we waste time arguing about it, the phone will be turned off again. We need to go now.'

We stared at each other for a moment. I hoped he'd back down, but he was stubborn and kept silent until it became too much for me. I went into the bedroom and shut the door.

'What are you doing?' he called through the closed door.

'Getting dressed. I'm going to look for this damn phone.'

'Paige, you're being ridiculous. It's not safe.'

I struggled into my jeans and threw on a jumper, grabbing some socks before I wrenched the door open again. We collided in the hall, but I pushed past him to grab my boots.

'I told you, you can come with me,' I said, keeping my body between him and the tablet, in case he tried to take it back. 'But I'm not letting you lose me this chance.' I looked him in the eyes. 'They hurt my sister. They're not getting away with this.'

Singh threw his hands up. 'Fine! But I'm calling it in on the way.'

I shrugged. 'Whatever. But we're going. Now.'

Singh drove as I followed the little dot on the tablet. It moved up and down the high street, continuing to blink as we got closer to the town centre. I couldn't believe our luck. I had no idea how accurate the GPS was – would we be able to find whoever had Anna's phone in a crowded shop? Or would it just give us a general idea about where they were?

We parked as close as we could to the pedestrianised high street and he looked over at the screen. 'Still here?'

'Yeah. It's moved around a bit, but they haven't left yet.'

He peered over my shoulder. 'Looks like it's up at the far end. If we walk up there and keep an eye on the app, we can see if there's anyone we recognise around. Some uniforms will arrive in about ten minutes, too.' He gave me a pointed look, as if hoping I'd change my mind and wait for the police to take over, but I ignored him.

We crossed the car park and walked up between the market and the library. It was busy for a Thursday morning, and we scanned the crowds for familiar faces. I clung to the tablet, bumping into people as I followed the little flashing dot past the pound shops and the ones selling discount clothing. I led Singh down a side street to the left. A moment later, however, the dot jumped slightly and I wondered about the quality of the GPS.

'It's back down the other end now, in Oldrids,' Singh pointed out, and we turned around and walked back to the other end of the high street. A couple of people gave us odd looks but I ignored them, keeping my eye on the dot.

'It's stopped moving,' I muttered, looking anxiously at the department store ahead of us. 'What if they've dropped it?'

'Maybe they're looking at something, or they stopped for a coffee,' he said, nodding at the sign in the window advertising a breakfast deal. 'But you're right, they might be dumping the phone.'

Now that we were getting closer to the source of the signal, fear washed over me. It wasn't too late to relent and let Singh take over, with the back up he was still waiting for. But then I wouldn't know what had happened, who it was, and I couldn't bear the uncertainty.

'What do we do when we find them?' I asked.

Singh stopped and gave me a stern look. 'We don't approach them, whoever it is. You don't do anything. Depending on who it is, I might speak to them, but I might just observe them. Even if we see someone we suspect, we won't have any evidence that they have Anna's phone. I'll take the information back to DI Forest, and we'll take it from there.'

'You'll just let them walk out of here?' I asked, incredulous.

'Unless I see them committing a crime, yes. I don't have any other choice. And remember, we're probably talking about the person who killed Lexi, and who tried to kill your sister. They're dangerous, and we can't take risks.'

I opened my mouth to argue with him, but then glanced back at the tablet and my heart sank. 'It's gone.'

Singh grabbed the tablet from me. 'What happened?'

'It must have been turned off.' I was quite glad he'd taken the device from me, because I wanted to smash it on the ground. 'Shit,' I said, loudly enough to earn me a scandalised look from a man walking past.

'Whoever it is might still be in there,' Singh pointed out, glancing up towards the department store. It had three floors, and they could be on any one of them.

'Okay, we'll go in and have a look around. We can split up and meet in the middle to cover more ground,' I suggested. 'See if we can spot anyone who it might be. I know, I know,' I continued, holding my hands up. 'I won't approach anyone. But we might see someone we know, who you can then find a reason to question, or search, or something.'

He considered it for a moment. 'If we split up, can I trust you not to do anything stupid?'

I glared at him. 'I'm not an idiot. I just want to know who attacked my sister.'

He nodded, and we set off into the shop, separating at the escalator. I scanned the faces of shoppers as I travelled up to the second floor, but nobody familiar appeared. When I got up there, the floor was relatively empty, and it didn't take me long to scan the homewares and glance around the coffee shop. Only a couple of tables were occupied, one by a mother with two small children and the other by an elderly couple.

Heading back to the escalator, I went down to the first floor, which was the men's clothing department. I walked round in a square, looking behind me occasionally as I scanned the faces of the shoppers. Again, there was nobody I recognised. I wasn't sure if I was relieved or disappointed – when it came down to it, I didn't want to creep up on someone who might be a murderer.

I turned towards the escalator, intending to meet Singh back on the ground floor, when I saw he was already on his way up. Stepping back, I bumped into someone and turned to apologise, but the words stuck in my throat. It was Max.

Hey, sorry! What are you doing here? he asked, his face split by a charming smile.

I swallowed and shook my head, completely lost for words.

Singh arrived at the top of the escalator and came over to join me, standing next to me and looking at Max. The men sized each other up for a moment, both wondering why the other was there, then they looked to me for an explanation. My mind went blank.

What have you done? I blurted out to Max.

What? His brow wrinkled in confusion. *What are you talking about?*

We tracked my sister's phone. Have you got it?

Why would I have your sister's phone? Max took a step back and looked at Singh again, who was confused, unable to follow our signed conversation. *Are you on a date with him or something?*

'It must be you. Who else could it be?' I realised I was yelling at him as well as signing, because Singh put a hand on my arm to try and calm me down.

'Paige, remember what I said. We need to leave now.'

I shook his hand off and glared at him. 'You want me to leave, and ignore everything that's happened? Forget that my sister is lying in the hospital, that she still might die?' A sob caught in my throat and I covered my face with my hands.

I took a deep breath and gave Max a searching look. He stepped back and held his hands up. *I have no idea what's going on here, but I need to go. Paige, text me if you feel like explaining, okay?*

I didn't turn to watch him leave.

'Why aren't you doing something? Call your team, get someone to follow him!' I spat, rounding on Singh.

'This was a stupid idea,' he said, with a low growl at the back of his throat. 'I shouldn't have trusted you to control yourself. You need to go home and let me deal with this.'

'Deal with it how? What exactly are you going to do?' My raised voice was attracting stares from shoppers, but I didn't care.

Singh shook his head. 'I'm taking you home.'

* * *

We didn't speak in the car, and I slammed the door when Singh dropped me off. My mind was in turmoil, driven by frustration. Could it have been Max? I couldn't deny the evidence of my own eyes. But why? Why would he kill Lexi or attack my sister? He'd lied to the police, he'd told me so himself, so I should have realised then that he couldn't be trusted.

I paced around the flat for a while, my fingers itching to throw something. Eventually the clock ticked closer to visiting hours and I drove to the hospital, where Anna still lay unconscious. I sat by her bedside for hours, only leaving to get coffee. She was well cared for on the ward, but I was worried about the lack of police protection. What if someone tried to finish what they'd started?

By mid-afternoon, one of the nurses suggested that I get myself something to eat, but the thought of food turned my stomach. Visiting wasn't permitted between four and six, but I couldn't face my empty flat, so I went outside and sat in my car. It was only when I was alone there that I let myself cry.

I sat for an hour, getting colder and stiffer, but I barely noticed. I was being threatened, my sister was fighting for her life, and I didn't feel like I had anyone I could turn to for help. Gem would be sympathetic about Anna, but I couldn't explain the complexity of everything else that was going on, and there was nobody else I could trust. Nobody could protect me.

My phone rang, startling me, and I recognised the number for the police station.

'Hello?' I answered warily, wondering if Singh was going to tell me off again.

'Hi, Paige.' I was surprised to hear DI Forest's voice. 'We really need your help.'

'What's happened?' I hoped she was going to tell me they'd made progress in the investigation.

'We have an interview we need to conduct as soon as possible, and we can't get another interpreter.'

My heart sank. 'I can't work at the moment. My sister is still in a critical condition. I can't even think about anything else right now.'

There was a pause. 'I understand that, I do, and as I say, we've tried to get another interpreter but nobody is available until the middle of next week. Given what has happened to your sister, we wouldn't ask if it weren't important. I'm sure you understand that in an investigation like this, time is of the essence.'

I swore under my breath. 'I can come first thing in the morning, but I won't stay beyond eleven. I have to be back at the hospital. And if Anna's condition changes, I'm reserving the right to leave at any point.' A week ago I wouldn't have dreamed of speaking to DI Forest like that, but a lot had changed. I didn't care what she thought of me any more.

'That's fine,' she said quietly.

I hung up and rested my head against the steering wheel, shivering as I noticed how cold it had become in the car. It was no good, I told myself. I couldn't help Anna if I was a gibbering wreck myself. Heading back into the hospital, I followed the signs for the canteen. It was only when I'd sat down with a sandwich that I realised I hadn't asked who the police would be interviewing.

305

4 hours before the murder

Rick tweaked the curtains and peered out onto the road.

You're sure Alan won't be coming back?

No way, Elisha replied. *I pissed him off before he went out, so he'll stay for last orders and then go round someone's house to carry on drinking. I know what he's like.*

All the more time for us, then, Rick signed, flashing her the grin that always made her stomach flip. He pulled her close and she kissed him, running her hands up into his hair. Moving away from the window, he pushed her onto the sofa, his hand finding its way under her top and snaking round to unfasten her bra.

Elisha knew she shouldn't do this, especially when Alan could be home at any moment, but part of her was excited by the risk. It would serve him right if he came home and found her with Rick, right here on their sofa. Arching her back, she pushed her body into his and ran her fingernails down his back, feeling his grunt of pleasure deep in his chest.

She felt rather than heard the living room door bang open, and both of them jumped off the sofa to see Jaxon standing in the doorway, a frown on his six-year-old face.

I want a drink. He was fidgeting, hopping from one foot to the other as if he were nervous.

Okay. I'll get you a glass of water, Elisha said, standing between Jaxon and Rick, but the boy peered around her.

Who's he?

He's a friend of Daddy's. Come on, I'll get you a drink.

Where's Daddy?

Elisha didn't reply as she steered Jaxon out of the living room and into the kitchen. She pulled a glass from the cupboard and ran the tap, then turned to hand it to Jaxon, but he didn't take it from her.

Don't want water. Want Coke.

You can't have Coke, it's time for bed. Coke will keep you awake.

I want Coke.

She looked at the set of Jaxon's jaw, knowing that if she gave in to him he'd never learn, but also wanting to get him back to bed as soon as possible so she could spend time with Rick.

Orange juice? she offered, hoping for a compromise.

He shook his head. *Coke.*

Making a quick decision she knew she'd probably regret, she grabbed a can out of the fridge and handed it to him, putting her hand on his shoulder and guiding him to the stairs. Once he was back in his bed, she tucked him in, checked on the two girls then went back downstairs to find Rick sitting on the sofa.

Now, where were we? she asked, cosying up to him, but he sat back.

We can't do this, not here.

Why not? You didn't have a problem ten minutes ago.

He shook his head. *You didn't tell me the kids were upstairs.*

She frowned. *Where else did you think they'd be?*

Rick looked blank. *I don't know.*

Alan's other kids are here every other weekend, but even if they weren't here, I'd still have Kasey.

Nodding, Rick looked towards the living room door. *Can I see her?*

Kasey? No, she's asleep, Elisha replied. *Why do you want to see her?*

He shrugged. *I want to see what she looks like now.*

She rolled her eyes. *Not this again. She's not yours. She looks like Alan, not you, and she couldn't be yours, not from the dates.*

I don't believe you. You think you've got everything you want here, but I'd treat you both better than Hunter does. I'll pay for the DNA test if that's what you're worried about. He sat forward again, looking at her eagerly.

She squeezed his hand. *I wish I could say I was wrong, and that Kasey was yours, but she's Alan's daughter. If I left him and moved in with you, we'd still have to see Alan. He might even try to get custody.*

Elisha stood up and walked over to the window, but didn't draw back the curtains. She turned to face Rick, hoping he could understand the situation she was in.

I can't do anything that would take Kasey away from me, you see? I love her more than I ever thought I could love anyone. If I left Alan and he tried to take her, I'd die.

Rick chewed his lip and looked down at his hands for a moment as if he was thinking.

What if he wasn't around any more?

What do you mean?

What if we could get rid of him, for a long time?

She shook her head. *I don't know what you're trying to say.*

He held her gaze for a moment, then looked away. *No, it wouldn't work. Ignore me. I thought I might be able to help.*

Elisha breathed deeply to calm her racing heart. *I'd leave with you today if I thought Alan wouldn't come for my daughter,* she told him.

He nodded. *Okay. It won't be today, but let's make a plan.*

She knew in her heart it would never happen, but as he explained his idea she smiled and let herself live in a fantasy world, if only for one night.

Chapter 26

Friday 16th February

I didn't sleep well that night, my dreams full of Caitlin and Lexi again. I woke up with one thought central in my mind – Caitlin's death was tragic, but I had always been convinced it hadn't been premeditated. It happened on the spur of the moment, and whilst it could have been prevented it couldn't have been foreseen. Lexi's murder was different in that it felt planned, of that I had no doubt, but I just couldn't understand how someone could have such rage and hatred towards an eighteen-month-old. So who was her death meant to punish, and what could anyone have done to deserve such a punishment?

I called the hospital as early as I thought was acceptable, but there had been no change in Anna's condition, so I headed to the police station. As I was signing in at the desk, the door opened and Max walked towards me. The floor lurched as I realised he was the suspect Forest had been desperate to interview, and I held on to the desk for support, but he didn't seem to notice.

I was hoping you'd be here, he said, standing next

to me. *I have no idea why they want to talk to me again. Have they told you anything?*

I shook my head but didn't offer any more information.

Is this something to do with you and Singh following me around town yesterday? His question seemed light-hearted, but his eyes watched me closely for my response.

I don't know.

He reached for my hand but I pulled it away. His face showed a mixture of hurt and frustration, but I shook my head again.

I'm here in my professional capacity, I told him, because it was the easiest excuse I could think of, easier than admitting I suspected him of murder, and after a pause he nodded. We sat and waited for the detectives without exchanging another word. I felt sick just sitting there next to him; he might be the man responsible for all of this.

Half an hour later, Singh opened a door and asked me to follow him, telling Max to wait a bit longer. He looked exhausted as he led me into a small side room.

'I told her not to call you.' He rubbed his face with a hand, and I knew he was referring to Forest. 'I haven't told her you were with me in town yesterday. All I've said is that you gave me the tablet, then I left and tracked the phone myself. We were wanting to interview Barron anyway, but I told her we should get a different interpreter. It's not appropriate for you to be here.' His face was anguished, and I felt sorry for him.

'I know. She told me she couldn't get anyone else until next week.'

'Still. That doesn't make it any less of a conflict of interest on your part.'

I shrugged. 'I'm here now. You can cancel if you want,

move your interview to next week and get another interpreter. Or we can get on and do it now.'

He sighed. 'Fine. But if I think it's getting too close to your personal involvement, I'll say so.'

'Are you going to ask him about the phone?'

'No,' he said. 'We have no evidence that he had it. This is related to Lexi. Look, if you want to stop at any time, just tell us. Okay?'

I agreed, and he took me to the interview room before going back for Max. DI Forest joined us a few minutes later and the interview began.

I had to force myself to concentrate on what was being said and signed. I was scared of missing even the tiniest detail that might help the police to get to the bottom of this.

'Mr Barron,' Forest was saying. 'We'd like to ask you some more questions in relation to the murder of Lexi Hunter on the night of Friday the second of February.'

Max nodded.

'We have received a report from a neighbour that a car was seen parked outside Mr Hunter and Miss Barron's house in the early hours of the morning Lexi died. The make and model described match your car.'

Max frowned and shook his head. *I wasn't there. I told you when I was there last.*

I narrowed my eyes. He had lied to the police about being there on the Friday, even though he'd told me about it; how was I to know he wasn't lying about this? Should I tell the police what he'd told me?

'We wanted to give you this opportunity to tell us if you wish to change your statement,' Forest said, her arms folded, eyes boring into Max.

No, I've answered all of these questions. I didn't leave my house after I went home from the Deaf club that night, and I certainly had nothing to do with Lexi's death. Max bristled, leaning forward in his seat. *This is complete bollocks. Someone has made this up because they don't want me interfering with the family.* He sat back again, breathing heavily.

'What do you mean, interfering with the family?'

I signed this for Max and he took a few deep breaths before replying. *I've said all this before. I was trying to get Elisha to leave Alan, and he knew it. I haven't made a secret of how much I dislike him, and the way he treats my sister. This is Alan trying to get back at me, trying to get me out of Elisha's life. I bet he put that neighbour up to this.* He shook his head and gave a short, bitter laugh. *I would have preferred it if he'd beaten me up, because if he'd done that, Elisha would see what he's really like.*

I hated to admit it, but his explanation made sense to me. After all, why only bring this up now? All the neighbours were questioned straight after Lexi's death, and it seemed a bit suspicious to remember seeing a car nearly two weeks later.

'We'll be investigating this claim fully,' Forest said, her face impassive. I wasn't sure if she'd even taken in what Max said. 'We may need to question other people in your life, including your employer.'

Max leapt out of his seat. *You can't do that! I could lose my job.*

'Sit down, Mr Barron,' Singh barked, and Max did as he was told, but perched on the edge of his chair.

I'm a teaching assistant. If anyone thinks I might have

313

done something like this, I'll lose my job and I'll never get another one.

Singh seemed moved by this, and I wondered if he believed this sighting of Max's car was bogus. Forest didn't look impressed, however, and she leant forward to speak to Max.

'All we have is your word that you haven't done anything wrong. We need to make sure, and if we have to follow this up in order to protect the children you work with, then so be it.'

Despite my confusion about Max and what he might or might not have done, I was shocked by what Forest said and forgot myself for a moment.

'What happened to innocent until proven guilty?'

Forest frowned, realising that I wasn't interpreting for Max. He picked up on what I'd said and immediately signed something to the same effect, but I could see that Forest was fuming.

'Are you aware that Anna Northwood is critically ill after being involved in a hit and run?' Forest asked Max, ignoring my comment.

He nodded, then turned to me. *A friend told me. I was going to call you, but I thought you'd need some time.*

'Your car also matches the description of the car that ran down Anna Northwood two days ago,' Forest continued, ignoring Max's aside to me. Her words were like a punch to my stomach, and I had to catch my breath before I could interpret them. Singh looked stunned; I assumed they hadn't discussed this. I thought the witness had said it was a van. Max's car was large, a 4x4, and dark blue, but it couldn't be mistaken for a black van.

Max stared at me, open mouthed, before he replied.

314

His words were directed at me, not the detectives. *I was with you when it happened. You're my alibi, so you know I didn't do it.*

I stuttered as I interpreted this for the detectives, my voice shaking. He was right, of course. The police were waiting for me when I got home, so it must have happened whilst I was with Max. It couldn't have been him. I'd been so preoccupied with Anna, praying she would be okay, that I hadn't thought about the timeline. Though he was late, a little voice in the back of my mind reminded me.

Hurriedly, Singh stepped in. 'For now, we're following a number of lines of enquiry. We'll be looking for evidence to corroborate the statement about your car, Mr Barron. For now, we simply ask that you make yourself available for future interviews whenever we request.'

Max agreed, and the interview ended. My head swirling, I collected my things and made to leave, but Forest stopped me.

'A word, please, Miss Northwood.'

My heart sank, but I stayed behind as Max and Singh left the room.

'It is not your place to comment on the content of interviews in which you are present,' she snarled at me the moment the door was closed. 'I understand the situation with your sister has affected you emotionally, but you need to remember your role. Is that clear?'

'Absolutely,' I said, swallowing the lump in my throat. I wanted to point out that I simply reacted to her bullying tactics, that I was justified in what I said, but self-preservation made me keep my mouth shut.

'You are here as an interpreter, not an advocate for

those being questioned, and I suggest you remember that if you wish to work with us in the future.'

I gave her a curt nod, but the stress of the past few days had built up and I couldn't help myself. 'What about my sister? Who's going to be her advocate, now she's lying unconscious in the hospital? You called me and asked me to come here when you knew what had happened to Anna, so don't be surprised that I'm emotionally involved now. You're the one who brought up her accident and blindsided me with it.' Forest's nostrils flared and she looked like she was about to respond, but I jumped in before she could. 'Why aren't you doing more to find out what happened? And what's this about the description of the car? Max drives a dark blue 4x4, not a black van.'

'The witness statements vary,' Forest said, wrinkling her nose. 'We need to check all possible leads.'

'Well as far as I can see, you're doing a piss-poor job of it.'

I stood quickly and walked out before she could reply.

As I left the building, I saw Max waiting by my car and my heart sank. I didn't want to talk to him, even though he'd been telling the truth – he was with me on Wednesday afternoon. By all accounts, Anna's attack happened when Max and I were having lunch together. Unless that was why he was late.

He looked up and saw me coming, then flashed me a wan smile. *That was a hell of a lot worse than I expected. Thanks for sticking up for me.*

I nodded, unsure of how to react to him. *I don't like her tactics, but I need to be careful. She could make it a lot harder for me to get work.*

Max ran a hand across his face. *When did this become*

such a mess? Isn't it bad enough that a child died, without her threatening our livelihoods? His expression was grim.

If there's no evidence you did it, they'll stop looking into you, I told him.

What do you mean, if? Of course there's no evidence. Paige, I didn't kill Lexi and I didn't attack your sister.

You know what I meant, I replied. *I wasn't accusing you. I'm not here to judge, just interpret.*

I'm sorry, he said, reaching for my hand, but I pulled away again. *What? Nobody can see us out here, it's fine.* He tried to put a hand on my shoulder but I shrugged him off and took a step back so I was out of his reach.

He looked hurt. *Right. Is it like that? Do you believe them, then?*

I shook my head and let out a frustrated noise. *I don't know what the hell to believe any more, Max. Everything is too confusing. It's too much for me right now.*

Well, I'm sorry if me being wrongly accused of murder is too difficult for you, he said, taking a step towards me. *How can you believe that awful woman over me?* he continued, gesturing back towards the police station. *I thought we had something good here. I thought this might go somewhere.*

You're reading too much into this, I snapped. *I told you I wasn't willing to do this until after the investigation is finished.*

You mean until you know for sure whether or not I killed a child?

I couldn't look him in the eye.

If you don't believe me now, Paige, how can we ever get over that? It won't work if you won't take my side.

That's not fair, I replied. *It's not that I'm not taking*

317

your side. I barely know you. I'm not taking anyone's side. My job is to be impartial, and that's what I have to do right now. No, I don't honestly believe you'd do that, from the little I know of you, I told him, realising it was true, *but I also know the police have to do their job, and that means following every lead. It's not about us right now, it's about finding out who killed Lexi and who tried to kill Anna.*

And once you know it's not me, then you'll go out with me? He shook his head. *I've had enough of this.*

He stalked off through the car park in the direction of the road. I thought about going after him, but I was too exhausted, emotionally and physically.

Visiting hours had started by the time I arrived at the hospital, so I spent the rest of the day at my sister's side. I barely noticed the time passing as I sifted through the events of the last two weeks. The doctor came to speak to me – the swelling in Anna's brain had reduced, and they were a little more hopeful that she would regain consciousness in the next few days. My heart leapt; I hadn't dared to hope until then. If she came around soon, I wondered if she'd be able to tell us who did this to her.

I sat in the canteen between four and six, watching hospital staff, patients and visitors coming and going. As I sat there, I turned over the events of the day Anna had been attacked. Anna had left the flat before me that morning, and I didn't know the exact time the witness had reported the attack to the police. Could Max have tried to kill my sister and then driven to Marco's and had lunch with me? I went back to sit with Anna, my thoughts going in circles.

At eight o'clock, I was forced to leave, with kind but

firm words from the ward manager. As always, I made them promise to call me if there was a change, even if it was the middle of the night.

Before I headed home, I sat in my car for a few minutes, taking some slow, deep breaths. The lamppost opposite where I'd parked was flickering, and after a few moments it went off. I shivered, and set off home.

Scunthorpe was strangely quiet for eight o'clock on a Friday night and, as I passed the steelworks, the sky was glowing again. I was accustomed to the rotten egg smell of sulphur that hung around parts of the town but, even after living most of my life around there, I was still fascinated by that glow.

As I pulled off the roundabout and onto the dual carriageway to get out of town, I saw a black van pull out behind me. A flutter started up in my stomach, even though I told myself it was only a coincidence, and I kept my eye on the van until I indicated to turn onto the road that would lead me home. The van followed me onto the slip road, and stopped so close behind me that my own brake lights almost dazzled me in my rear-view mirror, reflected off the van's bonnet.

I called the driver a couple of choice names and waited for a car to pass on the opposite carriageway, so I could turn off.

My heart thundered, the sound of it muffling the noise of the engine.

I braked, and the van slowed down to match my speed. I couldn't see the person behind the wheel; it was too dark and the headlights dazzled me.

I picked up to sixty as the road wound through Twigmoor Woods, hoping I could make the van back off, but it stuck behind me. If I slowed down, he'd hit me. I had to lose this van somehow, but my frantic mind was blank.

Ahead, I could see the lights of Greetwell, where the speed limit reduced to forty, so I braked slightly out of habit. The van bumped into the back of me and I gasped with the shock of the impact, minor though it was. Wondering if I could reach for my phone and dial 999 whilst driving, I realised my bag had slipped down the side of the passenger seat and I couldn't get it without pulling over. I didn't want to stop, for fear of who might be in the van. The driver continued to tail me all the way through the village, until we were back on the deserted country road.

The van bumped me again, harder this time. Anna had been collateral damage, I knew it. It was me they were after, and now they were going to finish the job. I couldn't afford to panic. I needed to think. If I sped up, there was a chance I'd lose control of my car on one of the winding bends, or the van would run me off the road. If I slowed down, he'd keep bumping me.

To my left, I saw a layby. Without slowing down, I waited until I was immediately level with it, then yanked my steering wheel, pulling off the road and slamming my brakes on. The emergency stop took the wind out of me and set my heart hammering harder, but the van sailed on past. For a moment, I thought I was going to be sick, especially when I heard a screech of brakes and the sound of the van reversing. I threw my own car into reverse but I wasn't fast enough. The van swung around and rammed the front end of my car, pushing it back onto the metal barrier. I heard the glass in my headlights shatter and they both went dark, then the van driver turned off their own lights, plunging us into blackness. Out here there were no street lights and no houses, and I was as good as blind. I punched the button to lock the doors. There was no space for me to pull out, nowhere to reverse into and the van had blocked me in at the front.

I sat in horror for a few seconds. The van's driver's door opened. My night vision was fuzzy after being dazzled by the van's headlights, and all I could see was a vague silhouette. I couldn't tell anything about who they might be, male or female. I couldn't even judge their height as I cowered in my seat. There was something in the figure's hand. A crowbar or metal pipe.

Panicking, I tried to reverse, but my bumper clanged off the barrier marking the edge of the layby. I tried to drive forwards, but the power of my little car was nowhere near enough to shift a van. Reaching over to my bag, I grabbed the strap and tugged, but it was stuck and I couldn't work it free. Without my phone, I was fast running out of options. I considered climbing over to the passenger side, getting out and running across the fields, but it was at least a mile to the nearest village, and I wasn't a natural runner.

There was a crash as the crowbar smashed down onto my car's bonnet and I shrieked. They hefted the piece of metal, aiming for my side window. I ducked and waited for the impact.

Before the blow landed I heard the sound of engines and three motorbikes came around the corner, one after the other. They slowed when they saw the scene in the layby, and there was a screech of tyres on tarmac as one of them veered towards us. The figure jumped back into the van and gunned it into life, spinning the wheels as the driver turned back onto the road, nearly knocking over one of the bikers in their haste. I glimpsed part of the number plate, but it was too dark for me to read the whole thing when it was moving. Thumping the steering wheel in frustration, I repeated the portion I'd seen to myself so I didn't forget it.

'Are you okay?' another of the bikers shouted at me through my closed window, and I nodded, already putting my car into gear to get out of there. He tried to ask me what happened, but I pulled away before he could finish the sentence. I couldn't stop to thank them; I didn't want to risk the van driver coming back. In my rear-view mirror I saw the motorbikes turn around and race off after the van, probably more concerned about the driver nearly hitting one of them.

I broke the speed limit the whole way home, and when I reached my parking space I finally managed to free my bag from beneath the passenger seat and ran into the flat. I didn't know why someone was after me, but it was pretty clear that whoever ran Anna down also wanted me dead.

Chapter 27

I paced around my flat for a few minutes before grabbing my phone and calling Singh. He didn't answer, so I left a message describing what had happened, including everything I could remember about the van. I hoped the portion of the number plate I'd seen would be of some use.

When I'd finished my message, I flung my phone down on the table. Who was doing this, and why? There was no way I wanted to go out again, in case the person who attacked me was lurking outside, but nowhere was safe, really. They knew where I lived, so there was no sense waiting there for them to try a different way of getting to me. If it was a choice between being at risk in my flat or somewhere else, I'd rather be doing something productive.

The first thing I could do was try to identify the driver of the black van. I knew Alan had a black van, and he knew what my car looked like – he'd watched me get into it at the police station on the morning Lexi was found dead. But would he be careless enough to use his own van?

If it was someone connected to the case and the Deaf community, there was one place I might find them on a Friday night, and that was the Deaf club. Perhaps it wasn't likely that they'd turn around and go out socialising after attempting to kill me, but if I went I could at least find out if there were any more rumours, any more pieces of information filtering through the layers of gossip. I needed to feel like I was doing something, and sitting around in my flat wasn't going to achieve that.

I ordered a taxi and kept pacing until it arrived. I couldn't risk going out in my car again; the person in the black van might be waiting for me. Anyway, my headlights had shattered and I'd need to get them repaired before I drove anywhere. Giving the taxi driver the address of the Deaf club, I watched the roads around us warily the whole way back into town.

When I got out of the taxi, the car park was deathly quiet. Nothing moved, and the shadows loomed menacingly. I took a deep breath to steady my hammering heart, wrapping my coat more tightly around myself to keep out the bitter night air. I walked between the rows of vehicles towards the door, checking them all for signs of a black van.

There were three large black or dark blue vehicles that could have been the one that chased me an hour or so earlier. I was sure it had been a van rather than a people carrier or 4x4, but I had the full beam of its headlights in my eyes most of the time, and I remembered Forest's words about the witness statements differing. I was willing to accept I could have made a mistake, in the stress of the moment. I looked at each of the three in turn, checking the bumpers for damage and looking at the number plates, but none of them seemed to be the one. They were all cold, two of them already bearing some frost from the freezing night air. I recognised one of them as Max's car. It had definitely been a van I'd seen, but this didn't prove anything; Max could have access to a van as well. If Anna had been there, I knew exactly what she'd say – I couldn't trust him just because I'd felt some attraction towards him. I felt my body sag; I wished I had her there to help me.

Steeling myself, I crossed the car park and walked inside the Deaf club. A rush of warm air greeted me as I opened the door. Being there without Anna felt strange, even though I'd been alone plenty of times before. I missed her so much. I looked around the room. Laura was sitting at a table by the wall, and I wondered if she had always come every night, or if she was just trying to keep herself occupied, to take her mind off the horror she'd experienced. As I watched her, Laura looked up and caught my eye.

Taking a seat next to her, I noted that she was looking even more tired and gaunt.

How's Anna? Laura asked me, concern in her eyes, and I felt a rush of affection for her.

She's still unconscious, I told her. *The hospital said they'd call me as soon as she wakes up. If she wakes up,* I added, my hands shaking slightly.

Do you know what happened? Laura was fidgety, not looking directly at me as she signed, and I glanced over my shoulder to see what she was looking at, but I couldn't detect anything specific.

325

Not yet, I said. *They think it was deliberate, but I don't know why anyone would want to hurt Anna.*

Deliberate? Laura's eyes widened in shock.

I nodded. *I think they were trying to kill her.*

Why?

I don't know. I couldn't risk telling Laura that my sister might have found out something about the investigation, might even have discovered who killed Lexi. My head was a mess and I didn't know who I could trust.

That's terrible. I hope the police can find them, but they haven't found who killed Lexi yet. Her face darkened, and I wondered why she hadn't linked the two events in her mind, considering the way Bridget blamed me and Anna for sticking our noses in.

Laura glanced over my shoulder again, then down at her drink. Making my excuses, I slipped off to the ladies', looking around me as I went.

I stood in front of the mirror, scrutinising my reflection. My eyes were bloodshot, and there was a puffiness to the bags beneath them. What was I doing here? What would I actually be able to find out? There was nothing for me here that would help the police find out what had happened to Anna. Giving a deep sigh, I made my mind up to leave and go home.

Stepping back into the corridor, I approached the hall when a group of people caught my eye. Max was there, with some others I didn't recognise. He was laughing and chatting, calm and relaxed. He didn't look like someone who had been questioned by the police that morning.

As I watched, a child came up to the group. It was nearly ten o'clock; children shouldn't have been allowed in at that time. It was Jaxon. I expected nobody wanted to take on Alan Hunter and tell him his son couldn't be there; it wasn't worth the aggravation. Jaxon was tugging at Max's sleeve, trying to get his attention, but Max ignored him.

I stood still, watching their interaction. For another few seconds, Max continued to ignore Jaxon, chatting with his friends, then he turned towards the boy, so his back was to me. Suddenly, Jaxon was on the floor. I caught my breath, unsure of what I'd just seen.

Not moving from my spot, I watched as Max helped Jaxon up. As he did, I saw him gripping the boy's arm tightly, Jaxon wriggling to free himself. Max signed something with his other hand, but I couldn't see what he was saying. He released Jaxon, then turned back to his friends.

For a moment I was frozen. What just happened? Did Jaxon fall over, and Max was only telling him to bugger off and leave him alone? Or did Max push him? As I turned the incident over in my mind, I realised that Max was walking towards the passageway where I was standing, and I panicked. I backed away until I came to where the corridor branched off. There were no lights on down there, and I hid in the shadows. Once Max had gone into the gents', I'd be able to leave without him seeing me.

Before he got there, however, Max stopped. I risked leaning out of my hiding place to see Alan Hunter squaring up to him. Both men looked angry, their hands signing furiously.

The argument seemed to get more heated. Max stepped towards Alan and I braced myself for the first punch, but then he backed away and turned down the corridor. I ducked back into the shadows as Alan stormed after Max, grabbing him by the arm and spinning him round.

I'll kill you, you bastard, Alan signed, gripping Max's arm with his left hand and signing only with his right.

Is that something you're making a habit of? Max replied, his bold question not hiding the fear flickering across his face.

Alan shoved Max into the wall. *I don't want you anywhere near my family, ever again!*

Why? What are you afraid of? Max continued to bluster, then Alan hit the wall next to him.

Next time it'll be your face.

You think I won't tell her what I know? Huh? What did Max know? And who was he going to tell?

Alan scowled at him. *You won't tell her anything, you cowardly little shit.*

That's what you think, Max signed. *I told you I'd ruin your life if you hurt my sister. Didn't you believe me?*

Alan roared with rage and lunged for Max, who darted away and back into the main hall, presumably in the hope that Alan wouldn't beat him up in front of witnesses. Shaking, I leant against the wall and waited for five minutes before emerging from my hiding place.

When I hurried back through the main hall, there was no sign of Alan, but Max was back with his group of friends. He looked rattled, but he was covering it well. His last words ran back through my mind. What did he mean?

I rushed back out into the car park and took a few deep breaths of the cold night air. My phone beeped, and the sight of Anna's name on the screen didn't surprise me. My breath caught in my throat as I read the message, but I steeled myself and refused to give in to the fear. Until I'd worked out what was going on, I couldn't let anything scare me any more.

2 hours before the murder

Shit. Shit, shit, shit. Elisha jumped up from the sofa when she saw the glow through the curtains. The outside light had come on.

What? Rick asked.

Alan's home! Quick, you need to go out the back door. She shoved him out of the room, past the stairs and towards the back door. It was locked, but she grabbed the key from a low shelf to the right of the door, and fumbled with it for a moment until she got the door open. Rick tried to protest but she gave him another shove into the back yard and shut the door behind him.

What's happening? Alan came through from the living room to find her standing with her back to the door.

Nothing. I was just locking up.

Alan frowned at her. *Is there someone outside?*

Elisha shook her head, but Alan was no longer looking at her. He turned round and went back the way he'd come, sticking his head back out of the front door. She tried not to let her anxiety show, though she knew her hands were shaking. Would Rick have had the sense to get out of there quickly? Or was he hiding somewhere at the back or side of the house?

'Hey!' Alan shouted, and Elisha squeezed her eyes shut in fear. She had no idea what Alan would do if he realised she'd been with Rick.

She followed him out of the door to find him dragging Rick out of the passage next to the house. Alan was much bigger, and he flung the other man on the ground.

What the fuck are you doing here? Alan asked Rick, his foot pinning Rick to the ground. *I told you not to come to my house.*

It's not like that, I was just passing!

Alan aimed a swift kick at Rick's ribs and Elisha rushed forward and grabbed on to his arm.

Don't!

Why not? Why was he here? Alan asked, rounding on her.

He just wanted to talk, that's all, she replied, trying to pull Alan away from where her lover was scrambling to get to his feet.

Talk? Alan spat on the ground. *I know what he wanted. If I find out you've cheated on me . . .*

He didn't finish the sentence, but the threat was clear in his eyes. Elisha watched him, willing herself to only look at Alan, and not at Rick, who was now on his feet and backing away.

Alan stepped towards Rick and swung a punch, which landed square on his jaw and floored him again. Elisha winced as Alan stepped on one of Rick's legs, leaning his

330

weight onto him as the other man tried to drag himself away. Alan stepped back, then gave him another couple of kicks to the ribs. Curling up on himself, Rick covered his head, as if anticipating further blows. Alan grabbed Rick's hands and pulled them away from his face, so the two men were looking each other in the eye.

Fuck off, Alan told him. *I don't want to see you here again.*

Elisha held her breath, expecting more as Rick scrambled to get up and out of reach. Alan wasn't the sort of man to back away from a fight, and she knew he'd love this excuse to give Rick the beating of his life. Was he storing up his anger for something worse? She trembled at the thought.

Casting a last glance at Elisha, Rick turned and walked away, his sense of self-preservation too strong to let him stay any longer.

Once Rick was out of sight, Alan grabbed Elisha by the shoulder and steered her back into the house. She winced at the strength of his grip but didn't complain. He pushed her towards the stairs and sneered at her.

Go to bed.

Alan, it wasn't anything, he—

I don't want to hear your excuses. I'll sleep down here.

Don't, she pleaded. *Come up to bed, please.*

He didn't reply, but walked back into the living room and slammed the door behind him. Elisha took a few deep breaths to try and stop herself from trembling before carefully climbing the stairs. At the top, she paused outside the children's room, wondering how she had managed to get herself into this situation. The first time Alan had

Chapter 28

Saturday 17th Feb

I got a taxi into town first thing in the morning and picked up the hire car I'd reserved online the night before. I couldn't really afford it, but I didn't want to be waiting around for taxis if the hospital called me about Anna. From there I drove to the police station to give a statement about the van that tried to run me off the road. I didn't think there was much that forensics could get from my car, but a team was sent to my flat to take some samples anyway. Forest and Singh were both there, despite it being a Saturday, and I showed them the most recent message I'd received.

YOU WON'T BE SO LUCKY NEXT TIME.

Forest chewed her lip while she read through the texts, then folded her arms. 'We think we're getting close to identifying who's been threatening you.' She held up her hand at the astonished look on my face. 'This doesn't mean it's the same person who tried to kill your sister, nor does it mean this person is Lexi's killer, but it looks like there is certainly a connection.'

'Who is it?'

She and Singh both shook their heads. 'We can't discuss that with you right now. We'll be interviewing a suspect very soon, but we've managed to find another interpreter who's coming over from Sheffield. Given the current developments, it's not appropriate for you to be working with us on this case any longer.'

Annoyed that she was repeating exactly what I'd said to her the other day, one detail stood out to me. 'So, this suspect is deaf?' That didn't really narrow it down, as Alan, Elisha, Rick Lombard and Max would all have required an interpreter, but it pointed towards it being someone I already knew.

'We can't give you any more information,' Forest said, her face impassive, although I could tell from Singh's less guarded expression that I'd hit the right note.

'When were you going to tell me this? You might have identified my sister's attacker.'

'Until we question our suspect and finish working through the evidence we've gathered, there's nothing concrete. It would be irresponsible of us to discuss it with you before we know anything definite.'

Singh reached forward and laid a consoling hand on my arm. 'Remember, you've gone from being a professional whose services we hired, to the family member of a victim. There's a conflict of interest and you can't be involved. We're going to put a uniformed officer outside your flat, just in case.'

I was seething, but I knew they were right. That didn't mean I was going to go home and sit in my flat like a good little girl.

Once I'd finished giving my statement, I went back out

to the car park, but I didn't leave. I sat in my hire car and waited. Outside, it began to rain.

After three hours I was frozen and stiff, but I was finally rewarded with the sight of one of my former colleagues from the agency pulling up to the building. The presence of another BSL interpreter proved that this suspect was deaf, and my heart started to pound. I slid down in my seat to prevent him seeing me, and carried on waiting.

My breath kept fogging up the windscreen as the rain turned to sleet, and I had to wipe it clean every few minutes. Fifteen minutes later, a police car pulled into the car park and two uniformed officers got out. They opened the back door and helped someone out, but from that angle I couldn't see who it was. I got out of the car, my joints protesting after sitting in the cold for so long, and I approached the door of the station from the opposite side. Before I reached it, I could see who the police were escorting.

It was Laura.

When she saw me, her eyes widened in panic. *It wasn't me, Paige. Please believe me. It wasn't me. I didn't hurt Anna. I didn't do it, any of it.*

I stared at her as she continued to deny it and the officers escorted her inside the building. When the door closed, I leant on the wall and sank to the ground, ignoring the freezing drips running down my neck. I didn't know what to believe any more. Laura? How could Laura be involved in any of this? None of it made sense. Of all the people it could have been, I'd never truly believed Laura was capable of hurting her own daughter, but was it possible she was a far more accomplished actress than any of us realised?

One of the officers escorting Laura must have told Singh that I was still outside, because he came out with a giant umbrella and crouched down next to me.

'You need to go home.'

'I know. But I can't cope with doing nothing.'

'Go back to the hospital then, or spend some time with friends. Do anything to take your mind off this place. We're doing our best, and you can't help any more.'

I clenched my fists as I tried to control my anger. 'How can Laura be involved in this? I can't believe I've trusted her this whole time. I felt sorry for her!'

He took a deep breath, clearly wondering what he could and couldn't say to me. 'We traced the phone, the first one. It was a pay-as-you-go phone, bought with cash, but the credit was topped up using Laura's bank card.'

It took a moment to sink in. 'So Laura sent me those messages? But why?'

Singh shook his head. 'Nothing is definite. It was her bank account, but that doesn't mean it was her. We haven't yet found any other evidence to link her to these crimes. That's why we're questioning her today.' He squeezed my hand, feeling how cold my skin was. 'Paige, go home. Before anyone else finds out you're still here.'

I knew he meant Forest, and I knew he could be in deep trouble over what he'd just told me. He got up and helped me to my feet, then gave my hand a final squeeze before I walked back to my car and drove away.

Instead of going home, I drove to the hospital and made my way up to the Intensive Care ward. A doctor and a couple of nurses were standing by Anna's bed, so I waited until they'd finished. I tried to ask them some questions as they left, but all I got was another promise that they'd let me know if anything changed.

She looked so small, lying in the hospital bed, surrounded by machines and tubes. There was no trace of the Anna I knew, no life or animation, and I hunched over as the fear of losing her hit me, knocking the breath from my body. I sank into the chair by her bed and tried to hold back the sobs, but they were too strong for me to resist. My little sister might die, all because she chose to come and stay with me and get mixed up in this case. She came to support a friend, the same friend who was being questioned by the police. I should have stopped her from getting involved. I should never have allowed my professional and personal lives to merge.

What made it worse was that we'd argued the last time I'd seen her before she was hit by the van. I couldn't remember ever having an argument that fierce, one that cut so close to the bone. And I knew now that she was right: I had never quite got past the role I'd taken on when Dad died, as my little sister's protector and extra parent. When Mum wasn't able to process what had happened and could barely look after herself, I stepped in, and even ten years later a part of me still thought of Anna as a teenager who needed my advice and guidance. I made a promise to myself to be a better sister if she got through this.

Wiping my eyes, I took her hand. 'I'm going to find out who did this. You're going to get better, and we're going to be okay.' I still couldn't believe that her best friend could have done this to her. Kissing my sister softly on the forehead, I left.

Back in the flat, after a cursory nod to the PC in his

car outside, I flopped down on the sofa and stared at the ceiling for a while. Nothing made sense, and I still couldn't form any coherent ideas as to why Laura would have sent me those messages. The only thing I could think was that Anna suspected something, something important, but hadn't told me. Then she went to the house looking for something – clues, evidence, I didn't know – and she'd somehow surprised whoever ran her down. I pushed aside the guilt I felt about not going to the house with her, and forced myself off the sofa. I needed to be proactive. There was nothing I could do to help Anna get better, so I could at least help the police find who was responsible.

The spare room was a mess. Anna had never been the tidiest of people. There were piles of articles and textbooks that she was using for her PhD research, along with a novel and some notebooks. I flicked through the notebooks, but they were all related to her academic work. I hunted around for another couple of minutes, then sat down on the bed in frustration. I had no idea where to look, or if Anna would have written her suspicions down in the first place.

I started to search the room again, being more methodical this time. I began at the door and worked my way around the room until I got back to the door again. When I'd finished, there was still nothing, and I kicked the door in frustration. It swung shut, to reveal a mass of Post-it notes in different colours, stuck in columns on the back of the door. Laughing softly at my sister's methodical approach, I read through Anna's investigation board.

Perhaps I'd been wrong about Anna being disorganised – she had all of the suspects on pink sticky notes, observations about possible motives on yellow ones, and green ones with notes about the investigation. One of the green sticky notes had fluttered off and I picked it up from the carpet. All that was written there was a phone number, and under it a name: Hannah Lachlan. The name was familiar, but I couldn't place it, so I scanned the rest of the notes for a reference to a Hannah Lachlan, but there was nothing else.

Going back through to the living room, I sat and stared at the sticky note. Could she be someone Anna mentioned to me in passing, a friend or colleague? In which case, could the note have fallen out of her PhD work when I was searching? I racked my brain for a minute, until it came to me: she was Jaxon's TA. I met her when the police interviewed Jaxon, or at least tried to. Why would Anna have her number? There was only one way to find out, and that was to call her.

I picked up my mobile and dialled the number, feeling anxious as I listened to it ringing. It went on for a while, but just as I thought nobody was going to pick up, the ringing stopped.

'Hello?' Her voice was clipped and wary. She probably thought I was a spam caller about to ask if she wanted to claim back her PPI.

'Hi, is that Hannah Lachlan?'

'Speaking. Who is this?'

'My name's Paige Northwood, we met at the police station.'

'Oh, yes!' Her voice became warmer. 'When they interviewed Jaxon. What can I do for you?'

'I was wondering if you'd spoken to my sister at all, Anna Northwood. She's in hospital, and I found your phone number in her room, so I wondered if you could tell me what she wanted to talk to you about.'

There was a pause. 'We met one evening in the Deaf club. She told me who she was and that you were trying to help the police find out what happened.'

By the sounds of it, Anna had implied I was consulting directly with the police. 'What did she want to talk about?'

Another pause. 'I'll tell you the same thing I told her. I can't talk to anyone about the pupils I work with. It's not professional.'

'She wanted to talk to you about Jaxon,' I replied. I'd already worked this out, but I wanted to know where Anna's thoughts were heading. 'I understand you can't tell me anything about him, but what did Anna ask you?'

Hannah Lachlan clicked her tongue. 'She asked questions about his behavioural problems. She seemed to know a lot about him, which I assume Laura told her, but I refused to answer any of her questions. I'm sorry to hear she's not well, but I can't really tell you any more than that.'

I thanked her and let her go, knowing it wouldn't do any good to push her further. The conversation hadn't really helped; I felt like I was even more in the dark about what was going on. Surely the thought rising in my mind couldn't be accurate?

There was one way to check what Anna might have been thinking, so I went back through to the spare room to look over her notes on the back of the door again. I scanned the pink ones, where she'd written her list of suspects, and sure enough, there was one at the bottom that I'd never considered before.

Anna thought Jaxon Hunter killed his sister.

Chapter 29

It was dark by the time I got to Laura's, and for a while I sat outside in the car. I could see Bridget bustling about in the kitchen, and upstairs there was a glow behind one set of curtains. After what Bridget said about Anna and me last time I was there, I had no desire to speak to her.

Was Laura still being held by the police, or had they released her? I wanted to go in and talk to her if she was there, ask her about Jaxon and if she thought he could be the one responsible for Lexi's death. I wanted to look her in the eyes when I asked her if she'd been threatening us to protect her son, but I had no idea how I was going to broach that conversation.

What would I do if it turned out it was Jaxon? Now that I was sitting outside, I didn't know what I wanted to say. So many little things I'd heard about Jaxon ran through my mind, about how difficult he was to handle, how Laura couldn't cope with him on her own. The comments I'd overheard in the police station, and the behaviour I had witnessed myself. Max, Laura, Elisha – all of them had told me about Jaxon's problems, but we'd been so busy looking for an adult killer that I'd never paid much attention to him.

Bridget looked out of the kitchen window and spotted me. She watched me for a moment before disappearing, then reappearing at the front door. I took a deep breath before I walked up the path towards the house.

'Paige. Laura didn't tell me we were expecting you. I thought I'd made it clear I didn't want you coming back here?'

I gave her a cold look and pushed my way inside. Bridget didn't protest, but stood in the doorway of the kitchen and watched me.

'Is Laura around?' I asked as Bridget didn't seem to be about to volunteer any information. I hadn't interpreted for Laura's interview, so I could pretend I didn't know she'd even been questioned, unless she had told Bridget about seeing me in the car park.

'She's upstairs, putting Jaxon to bed,' she said, jutting her chin upwards. For a moment I thought Bridget was about to tell me to leave, but to my surprise she relented. 'You'd better wait for her down here. I don't know if she'll want to talk to you. She's had a dreadful day.'

I followed her through to the kitchen and sat down at the table, curious as to why she'd allowed me to stay. Was she going to put forward her case for Laura's innocence, in an attempt to protect her daughter?

'Do you have news?' Bridget asked when she had her back to me.

I could tell she'd been dying to ask this from the moment

she opened the door, but her self-control was too strong for her to ask me while I could see her face.

'Not exactly. I just need to talk to Laura about something,' I said. Bridget shot a look at me over her shoulder, one that was almost calculating, as if she was trying to read my mind and understand what I might want with Laura, and how much I knew.

Bridget didn't attempt to make further conversation, but sat at the table, watching me. Every time we heard a thump or a noise from upstairs that suggested Laura was struggling with Jaxon, she glared at me, as if daring me to say a word. I wondered how Bridget felt about Jaxon, really. She wasn't the sort of woman who gave away her true emotions if she didn't want to. Did she feel he was getting out of hand, at the age of six? Did she either know or suspect that he could be responsible for his sister's death? The thought was too huge for me to contemplate. Was I doing the wrong thing? Surely, one of the adult suspects must be Lexi's killer, not her six-year-old brother.

'How is Anna?' Bridget asked abruptly, her face solemn. She watched me carefully as I answered.

'No change,' I said quietly.

Bridget nodded. 'She's not been able to tell you anything then?'

I frowned. 'No. She's still unconscious,' I explained, assuming she had misunderstood the seriousness of Anna's condition. 'She hasn't come round since the accident.'

Bridget didn't reply. We lapsed into silence again, me swirling the dregs around the bottom of my cup of tea, her staring at her own hands on the kitchen table.

Eventually, Laura came downstairs looking worn out, a large red welt blooming on the side of her face.

He threw a toy at me, she explained when I asked her what happened.

Bridget glared at me, as if challenging my right to ask Laura a question.

Laura, can we talk? It's about Anna.

Laura licked her lips, fear flashing in her eyes, but she agreed and we went through to the living room, a sour-faced Bridget watching us go.

Your mum really doesn't like me, does she? I was trying to lighten the mood, but Laura didn't laugh.

No, but I don't know why. I think she thinks you're working against me or something, because you're helping the police with their investigation. She picked at a thread on the chair for a moment. *And then because I asked you to interpret for me with the solicitor. She really didn't like that. She wants to be the one doing everything for me, but she takes control and I don't like it.*

I nodded. We'd had this conversation before, but it meant I could delay asking about Jaxon.

What was it you wanted to talk to me about? she asked, curling up in the armchair like I'd seen her do so many times.

What do you think?

She shook her head. *I didn't do any of this, Paige. I haven't done anything to you, or Anna. I don't know who sent you those messages, but it wasn't me.*

They topped up the phone using your debit card.

Someone must have taken it, or stolen my card number. I gave her a sceptical look and she flared with anger. *Do you think the police would have released me and let me come home if they thought I'd tried to kill someone? They've searched me and the house, and I don't have that phone. I've got proof I couldn't have hurt Anna. If the police believe me, you should too.*

The news that Laura had an alibi was a relief and I sagged in my chair. I was still wary, but a big part of me wanted to believe her. Still, there was the question of Jaxon.

I'm just so worried about Anna, I said, rubbing my face. I was so tired. *She's still in Intensive Care, but they don't know yet if she's going to wake up. There was a lot of internal bleeding, including a bleed on her brain, so even if she does wake up she might not be the same. She might not be the Anna we knew.* It was the first time I'd articulated this and as it hit home, the tears started to flow. *The police won't tell me anything now, and I don't know who to trust. All I know is that it was a hit and run. A black van.*

A dark look crossed Laura's face. *You said that the other day. Are they sure it was a black van?*

I nodded. *Yes. And I know what you're thinking – Alan has a black van.*

Alan's van was stolen.

I stared at her for a moment, taking in what she was saying. *What? How do you know?*

I've been texting him, she confessed sheepishly, a light in her eyes at the mention of him. *He'd left his van outside the house while he and Elisha were staying with friends. He went round yesterday and it had gone. Mum was wrong about him hanging around outside here. Do you think whoever stole his van might have done it?*

I could tell from the look on her face that she didn't want to think he could be involved, but I found myself nodding. *It's possible, I suppose. Do you know the van's number plate?*

345

To my disappointment, Laura shook her head, but I was convinced the person chasing me was driving Alan's van. My mind was racing. Either his van was stolen by the person who hit Anna and was threatening me, or he'd fabricated the theft to cover his tracks. Laura looked anxious, and I wondered if she was trying harder to convince me or herself that Alan couldn't have done this. If Anna was right and Jaxon was responsible for Lexi's death, there must be an adult involved who would stop at nothing to protect him. That adult could just as easily be Alan as Laura.

It's the person who's been threatening me. Anna must have found something when she was at the house, that's why she was attacked. But why threaten me in the first place? I'm not a police officer. I haven't done anything. I don't know what the police are doing, I don't know much about the evidence they've found.

I watched Laura carefully as I told her all of this.

Can't the police protect you? Why would someone threaten the interpreter? She threw questions at me, but she looked genuinely concerned rather than just trying to find out what I knew.

Maybe they think I've heard something when I've been in the police station, or in interviews. I have to keep a lot of information confidential as part of my job, so maybe they think I know too much. I'm scared for Anna.

She nodded and chewed her sleeve for a moment, looking like a scared teenager rather than a woman in her late twenties.

Did Anna tell you what she'd found out?

I frowned and sat up in my chair. *What do you mean? Do you know something?*

No, I promise, I'd tell you if I knew. She told me she was asking questions at the Deaf club, trying to find out what people knew. Maybe she asked someone the wrong questions? Maybe someone thought she was close to finding something out, and they attacked her for it?

I paused, trying to take in what Laura was suggesting. The way she signed, it didn't seem like this was a new thought to her. It was more like she was reciting something she'd said before, or something someone had said to her. I thought about what she was saying, and realised she could be right; Anna's own investigations could have taken her into danger. I knew from finding the notes in her room that she hadn't shared all of her suspicions with me.

Can I go and see her, in the hospital? she asked.

I'm not sure. It might be family only at the moment, I stalled. I didn't trust anyone other than me at Anna's bedside. *I can check when I go tomorrow, and let you know.*

That would be good, thanks.

We sat for a moment without saying anything, and I knew this would be my only chance to broach such a terrible subject. I gritted my teeth and thought of a way to bring it up. I needed to see Laura's reaction, to see if she'd been lying to us and covering things up for the last two weeks, or if she was as innocent as she made out.

Anna's been talking to a few people, making notes about what people have said to her. I think she came up with a theory about what happened to Lexi.

Laura frowned and looked at the living room door, as if she was afraid her mother would walk in and interrupt our conversation. *What do you mean? What sort of theory?*

347

She got it into her head that the police wouldn't find the right person, so she's been investigating on her own. I told her not to, but you know Anna once she gets an idea in her head.

Laura nodded, obviously not sure where the conversation was going.

Anna came up with a theory, like I say, and I wanted to talk to you about it. I want to know what you think.

A theory? She knows what happened? There was a wary look in Laura's eyes, and she glanced at the door again.

Not necessarily, but she had an idea. You mustn't get angry, Laura, because it might not be true, but I want your honest answer.

Answer about what? You're scaring me. Her eyes were wide and she was poised in her chair as if she was going to run at any moment. I needed to deal with this carefully. If she was the one who attacked Anna, and then me, she could do the same again.

Laura, how bad are Jaxon's behavioural problems? I know you've said to me that you can't cope with him on your own. I've seen how he behaves.

There was a long pause and I watched the mixture of emotions that swept across Laura's face – confusion and anger, but first surprise. Whatever she was expecting, it wasn't that.

Jaxon? He's a handful, you're right. But he's only six. I was being stupid when I said that. Grief, stress. They're getting to me. She let out a laugh, as if to show how ridiculous an idea it was, but it was forced and I could see fear in her eyes.

He's hurt quite a few people though, hasn't he? The children at school, and his teacher.

348

That was an accident. She trapped her hand in a door. Laura was starting to look frantic. *He's a little boy, he couldn't hurt anyone deliberately!*

I knew I couldn't tell her what I'd overheard at the police station on the day they tried to interview Jaxon, so I tried another tack. *Maybe it's because he's frustrated at school, because the other children can't communicate with him. Or maybe it's something else. But you can't deny he has problems.*

Laura narrowed her eyes at me but didn't move.

I took a deep breath. *What if he was playing, after the girls had fallen asleep, and it happened by accident? Don't you think that could be a possibility? Then an adult tried to cover it up, so Jaxon wasn't blamed.*

She shook her head, but I could see that her mind was whirring. Whatever she said, I could tell she was considering this possibility. I couldn't trust her.

No, she said eventually, her eyes blazing. *He loved Lexi, she was his sister.* She shook her head again, more vehemently this time. *No. He loved Lexi. He didn't like Kasey, she was the sister he didn't like.* She glared at me, breathing heavily.

I think Anna was worried about Jaxon, about what he might have done, I said gently. *I don't know if it's true, but I wanted to know what you thought. Has he ever hurt Kasey?*

No! Well . . . No. Just little things. Kid things. She didn't elaborate, and I wondered if she was playing it down to make Jaxon seem less aggressive. Laura shuddered as she continued talking about Kasey. *I saw Elisha with her yesterday. It's horrible, how much she looks like my little girl.* The tears started to fall, but my treacherous

349

mind couldn't feel sympathy for her, deflecting the conversation away from Jaxon. *Why does she get to keep her little girl when I lost mine?*

I waited for a few moments, and she realised I wasn't going to be put off. Squaring her jaw, she glared at me. *If it was Jaxon, who's been threatening you? It can't have been a child.*

No, you're right. There must be an adult involved. Maybe they're trying to protect Jaxon.

It has nothing to do with my son. It must be Alan, she said, sitting forward in her chair again. *He must have lied about his van being stolen.*

Why would he use his own van, though? It doesn't make sense. Even if Anna was attacked on the spur of the moment, he wouldn't use his own van to try and run me off the road.

Now that I thought about it, I wondered if that was the whole point. Whoever ran me off the road and tried to kill Anna wanted the police to think it was Alan, by using his van. Did that mean Alan wasn't involved at all? That only left Laura, because who else had such a strong motive for protecting Jaxon? Or was I on the wrong track entirely?

I can't believe you think Jaxon might have done this, Laura said, and I was surprised to see fear in her eyes.

I honestly don't know what happened, Laura. I'm trying to work out what Anna was thinking before she was attacked. I've seen Jaxon's behaviour, and I don't think he realises that it's wrong to hurt other people. Maybe he doesn't understand what happened? Children don't think in the same way adults do.

You're wrong. Jaxon couldn't do something like that.

350

He knows right and wrong. She paused and looked me dead in the eye. *Don't tell anyone about this, Paige. They'll take my little boy away from me if they think I can't control him, and then I won't have anything left.*

Could I possibly keep this to myself? It would mean that someone else might be blamed for Lexi's death. Forest and Singh were playing their cards close to their chest, but I had a feeling they were still focused on Max. I didn't know if I could allow that to happen, in all good conscience. But how could I go to the police and tell them that I thought a six-year-old might be guilty of murder? I wasn't sure they'd believe me. And Jaxon would have to grow up with the stigma of being the boy who killed his sister, even if it was written off as a tragic accident. He might not even remember doing it, yet he'd have to live with it for the rest of his life.

I don't know, I told Laura. *I don't know if I can keep this to myself.*

Laura's face hardened and she snarled at me. *Get out. Get out of my house now.*

I'm just trying to find out what happened to your daughter.

You don't know anything. You're just trying to ruin my life! Get out!

She launched herself at me and I managed to dodge out of the way, backing towards the door.

Bitch, get out!

I darted out of the door before she could aim another swing at me. When I reached my car, I looked back at the house and saw her watching me from the window.

15 years before the murder

Just you and me today, Paige, my dad told me.

Why?

Your sister's not feeling very well, so Mum's going to stay at home with her.

I was sad for Anna that she was going to miss the trip to Cleethorpes, as I knew she'd been looking forward to it, but I was glad it didn't mean I had to miss it too. The night before, Matthew had asked me if I was going, and when he smiled at me I almost melted. Some of the other girls gave me dirty looks when he was talking to me, but I didn't care.

The Deaf club had hired a coach for the trip, and we all piled on early in the morning. Caitlin's parents sat at the front, where everyone could see they were already drinking. I willed Dad to say something to them, but he wasn't one for confrontation. I asked Caitlin if she wanted to sit with me, and her eyes lit up. She was only eight and I knew she looked up to me. Her parents used the Deaf club as a large group of babysitters while they propped up the bar, and over the last few months she'd gravitated towards me.

Two weeks earlier, Caitlin had found me in the toilets of the Deaf club and shown me some marks on her body. There were bruises in different shades of blue, green and purple, and small red marks she told me were from cigarettes. When I'd asked her about it, she told me her mummy and daddy got angry with her and hurt her. She tried to be good, but they still hurt her.

I was sick to my stomach. I'd known her parents weren't great, but I hadn't realised how far things had gone. She asked me not to tell anyone and I nodded in agreement, even though I knew I couldn't keep it to myself. I'd mulled it over for a couple of weeks though, wondering who I should tell and how. What if all the adults knew about it, and nobody was going to help? I didn't want to make things worse for her. I decided to try and persuade Caitlin to talk to my dad about it that day.

Cleggy isn't somewhere to go if you want a paddle, because the tide goes out so far your chances of even seeing the sea are slim, and on that day we found ourselves faced with seemingly miles of sand and a strip of water in the far distance.

We had a good morning, Caitlin hanging around with me and my dad while her parents worked their way through the bottles of cider they'd brought with them. She stayed with us over lunchtime, Dad buying us both fish and chips, knowing full well her parents weren't going to get her anything. In the afternoon, Caitlin and I set to building a sandcastle, but before we'd got very far a group of other kids my age wandered up.

Paige, want to go for a walk? Matthew asked.

I'd had a crush on him for months, and I didn't give Caitlin a second thought. There were loads of other people we knew on the beach who'd keep an eye on her. Telling Caitlin to go and check on her parents, I brushed the sand from my hands and joined the group.

We wandered along the beach for a bit, then once we reached the pier Matthew took me by the hand and we peeled off from the group. I was fifteen, and I'd kissed two boys before but I hadn't been any further than that. They had both been boys I knew from school, but neither of them made my insides shiver the way Matthew did. He was seventeen, with dark floppy hair and warm brown eyes that made you feel like he only ever wanted to look at you, and when he kissed me I felt a sensation almost like an electric shock. His hand slipped under my top, and I didn't even consider stopping him.

A little while later, blushing from our clumsy fumble under the pier, I sauntered back over to our group, only for several people to rush up to me.

Where's Caitlin?

Is she with you?

The questions kept coming, and when I shook my head and said I'd left her building a sandcastle, their expressions turned to panic. She was missing.

We divided up and searched everywhere we could think of, some people taking the arcades by the pier, others walking the length of the seafront to the leisure centre. My dad and I stayed with those searching the beach. I don't know where she went after I walked away with Matthew, but I know where we found her. Her little body was curled up on itself at the end of one of the breakwaters, blood all over her head and the back of her dress.

When the police arrived, they didn't have an interpreter, and as most of the potential witnesses were deaf, I stepped in to help them establish what happened, until they could get an interpreter to take official statements. It was exhausting and harrowing; by the end of the day I was numb. I hadn't cried – I don't think I had really processed what had happened.

Caitlin's parents claimed they hadn't seen her all day, and that she hadn't come back to them. They said she must have slipped and fallen, but the post-mortem concluded she'd been hit repeatedly on the back of the head. Some people came forward to say Caitlin had gone back to her parents after I left, but lack of evidence meant nobody was ever convicted of her murder. I knew it must have been one of her parents, or both, and it transpired so did everyone else at the Deaf club. When the evidence of long-term abuse came out, nobody was as surprised as I thought they would be. It seemed many people had suspected something, but nobody had ever reported them; nobody wanted to get involved, and many people in the community distrusted social services. I still felt the crushing weight of my own guilt for not saying anything to anyone, though. If I'd told my parents when Caitlin showed me the marks on her body, I could have forced them into doing something and prevented her death.

It was made clear that Caitlin's parents were no longer welcome, and they moved to Newcastle. Caitlin had told me she had a cousin who was also deaf, but her parents never let her see her because her dad had fallen out with her aunt. I lay awake every night for weeks after her death, wishing I could turn back the clock and that her family would come to rescue her.

Chapter 30

Sunday 18th February

My head was spinning and, against my better judgement, I didn't tell anyone about my suspicions that night. I needed time to think it through again. The way Laura had reacted was only natural, but it had made me wonder if she suspected the same thing and was protecting Jaxon, and so she had actually been threatening me. I went home and considered getting drunk, but I didn't have the energy. Picking at some food, I soon gave in and climbed into bed.

All morning, I mulled over the issue, then made my decision: I'd go to the police with this theory and let them decide what was true, and if they needed to look into anything further. It would be devastating for the family, but the truth was the most important thing, and if someone else was convicted of a crime they didn't commit, I'd never be able to forgive myself.

This was something I needed to discuss in person, not over the phone. I considered calling Singh and asking him to meet me somewhere, but it was too serious for a coffee shop; I needed to go to the station. On the drive over, guilt gnawed away at my heart, but I had to do it. Someone had tried to kill me and nearly succeeded in killing my sister. It if was someone who was protecting Jaxon, be it Alan or Laura, I needed to tell the police what I knew so they could find out who it was and arrest them.

'I need to speak to DC Singh,' I told the woman on the desk when I arrived at the station.

She looked me up and down and raised an eyebrow. 'Why?'

'I need to talk to him about the Lexi Hunter case.'

She gave me a long, searching look, as if she was trying to decide whether or not I was wasting her time. Eventually, she called to a PC, who trotted off to find Singh. I stood at the desk, shifting my weight from one foot to the other. Now I was there, I was worried that my information would sound ridiculous, but I was sure Singh would hear me out.

The PC returned. 'DC Singh isn't here today, but DI Forest says she'll speak to you.'

My heart sank. I'd lost track of what day it was, and it hadn't occurred to me that Singh might have a day off. I'd also hoped I could avoid speaking to Forest. Still, I was there, and if I turned tail and left I'd never be taken seriously. I was led through to an interview room, where Forest was already waiting.

At the sight of me, her face fell. 'Miss Northwood. This is a surprise. I was told someone was here who had information about the Lexi Hunter case. Would that be you?'

'Yes,' I replied, swallowing hard. There was something about her that brought on my fight or flight reflex. I felt more like fleeing, but I stood my ground. 'But I don't have information, as such. I wanted to talk through some of my thoughts, that was all. I can come back another time, when Rav's in.'

'You might as well tell me, now we're here. Sit down,' Forest told me, nodding to one of the chairs.

For a moment, I thought she was going to stay standing, to use that power over me, but she moved the second chair further away from the table and sat opposite me. We looked at each other for a moment, as if we were opponents, rather than sharing a professional relationship.

'So, Paige,' Forest began, her voice calm and precise as she took time over her words. 'I was under the impression from our conversation that you weren't going to involve yourself any more in this case. How naive of me.' The sarcasm dripped from her words. 'Before you tell me anything, I must advise you that if it turns out you've withheld information from us in the course of this investigation, we'll be forced to take further action.'

Forced? She'd be thrilled. I took a deep breath and tried to prevent myself from responding sarcastically.

'Of course. This is something that's just come to my attention, something Anna was trying to work out. I couldn't keep it to myself, in case it turned out to be important.'

'Your sister told you this?'

'I found some notes she'd made. She's still unconscious.'

Forest sniffed and looked down at her hands. 'What is it you'd like to report?'

I noticed that she didn't have a notebook out, nor had she started the tape recorder. She didn't think I was going to tell her anything of consequence.

'It's a theory rather than definite information,' I said,

pausing as I wondered how to word it. 'Is it possible Jaxon Hunter killed his sister?'

There was a long pause. Forest stared at me, unblinking.

'It may have been a horrible accident,' I went on. 'Perhaps he didn't understand the consequences. If Laura knows what happened, it would explain why she's been threatening me and my family. She's trying to protect him. It would explain the attack on my sister as well – Laura's her best friend, I'm sure Anna would have said something to her about this.'

Forest continued to stare. I shifted uncomfortably in my seat. 'All I've heard for the last two weeks is how difficult he is to handle, how he can be violent and only Alan can control him.'

She sucked in her cheeks then leant forward, putting her elbows on the table. 'You came here to tell me that you think a six-year-old is a murderer?'

'No, that's not what I'm saying. Obviously, Jaxon has issues that need addressing. He has a history of violent outbursts and behavioural problems. He's broken a teacher's wrist and deliberately harmed several other children at his school.' She frowned at me, clearly wondering where I'd got my information, but I ignored her. 'He needs help.'

'I think you're the one who needs help,' Forest muttered.

'Excuse me?' I couldn't help myself.

'This is pure insanity. Walking in here and claiming you know what happened to that child, then telling me this pile of bullshit? You don't have a clue what you're talking about.'

'Will you let me finish?' I said, interrupting her tirade.

'No, I will not!' Her face had gone red, and I sat back in my chair, prepared for her to explode. 'Not only is

359

your story preposterous, it is presumptuous. Just because you've been present in a few interviews doesn't mean you have any in-depth knowledge of this case and the evidence that's come to light. The information you've heard, in your professional capacity,' she added, spitting the words at me, 'is only a small part of our investigation.'

I clenched my jaw, willing myself to stay calm in the face of her condescension.

'You don't know all of the facts of this case,' she continued, enunciating each word clearly for emphasis. 'It is not your job to know all of the facts, nor is it your job to be making accusations. Lexi Hunter had cracked ribs. Jaxon may be bigger and stronger than a toddler, but he's not strong enough to break bones without the help of a door.' She saw the frown on my face and gave me a withering look. 'Oh yes, we know about Jaxon's history. We do actually make a habit of gathering as much information as we can in a case like this. We're not as incompetent as you seem to believe, Miss Northwood.'

I sat in stunned silence. I didn't know Lexi had cracked ribs as well; it had never been mentioned in any of the interviews I'd been in. Maybe they thought the parents didn't need to know every minute detail of Lexi's injuries. I saw their point.

'Do you think we're on a TV soap?' Forest's voice rose in pitch. 'Are you suggesting a six-year-old got up in the early hours of the morning, went downstairs, unlocked the back door, went into his father's shed, picked up a hammer, then decided to go back inside and attack his sister with it?'

'I didn't—' I began, but Forest continued speaking, ignoring me.

'I was actually going to call you later, as we have evidence regarding your sister's attack. Laura Weston's debit card was used to purchase the phone that sent you those messages, but she has an alibi for the attack on Anna. Yes, I know you loitered outside yesterday to see who we were interviewing, and you're lucky we haven't arrested you for interfering with a police investigation. We've also found the van that Alan Hunter reported stolen yesterday, burnt out on some waste ground. Did you know that the paint chips from your car matched those found on the pavement where your sister was hit, and that both matched his van? Someone threatened you, stole Alan Hunter's van, attacked your sister and then you, because of your insistence on prying into the details of this case. You need to accept the fact that your sister's attack was completely your fault for getting involved in something that had nothing to do with you, and that you had no understanding of.'

I opened my mouth, but Forest cut me off. 'No, Miss Northwood. I think you've said enough. It's been clear to me throughout this investigation that you have not been acting professionally. You should have excused yourself from this role the moment you were aware of who the victim was, but I also take responsibility for letting you carry on. From now on, your services will no longer be required by Humberside Police, and I'll make sure neighbouring forces know you're unsuitable.'

I was stunned, and her words took a moment to sink in. I'd been fired, and she was going to ruin my reputation as an interpreter. I knew it would happen if they found out I'd talked to Anna about the case, but I hadn't expected it to happen this way, when I genuinely thought I was helping.

Forest stood, and held the door open for me to leave. Without looking at her, I got up and walked out, careful to keep my pace measured and even until I was out of the building and across the car park. When I reached my car, I leant on it for a moment to catch my breath.

It's okay, I told myself. *There will be other jobs. You probably weren't cut out for working with the police anyway. It's too stressful.* I tried to ignore the voice telling me that Forest was right, that my suggestions were completely ridiculous, and I'd behaved like a naive child.

I managed to get in the car before the tears started. The accusation that Anna's accident was my fault had started to sink in. The emotion and tension of the last two weeks came pouring out and I leant over my steering wheel, unable to control the sobs. A child had been murdered. A family had been torn apart. I'd been attacked, my sister had nearly been killed, and we'd had possibly our biggest ever fight right before it happened. All I'd done was try to help people, and everything had backfired. I'd made mistake after mistake, both in my job and in my relationship with my sister, and it was time to give up. The police didn't want me working with them any more, and who could blame them, after everything I'd said and done?

Taking a few gulps, I prepared to drive home when my phone rang in my bag. I considered ignoring it, but I thought it could be important.

'Hello?' I said, trying to clear my throat inconspicuously. My voice sounded stuffy because of how much I'd been crying.

'Hello, is that Paige Northwood?'

'Speaking.'

'This is Doctor Thassos from Scunthorpe General. I'm calling to let you know your sister has regained consciousness. You can come and see her as soon as you like.'

I put my head back and closed my eyes as I took it in. Anna was awake. My little sister wasn't going to die. For a moment I couldn't breathe as the relief flooded through me. I'd thought I was out of tears, but a few more flowed before I pulled myself together and raced to the hospital.

Chapter 31

The sight of Anna shocked me. I think I was expecting her to be sitting up in bed, smiling and looking cheerful. As it was, she was pale and her skin was clammy, and the whooshing tubes and beeping machines were still doing their jobs.

'She's still very weak,' the nurse who took me in told me in a hushed voice. 'She might not be up to much yet, so don't be surprised if she falls asleep. She hasn't spoken yet.'

I raised my eyebrows at the nurse, considered a sarcastic response, but then stopped. At some point, someone would remind her that Anna was profoundly deaf and never spoke, but I didn't want to embarrass her.

The nurse left, so I pulled up the chair next to the bed and held Anna's hand. She blinked at me a few times, and I wondered how strong her pain medication was. Did she even realise it was me?

After a moment, she squeezed my hand, then slowly

lifted her other hand to her chest. I thought she was trying to sign *Sorry* but I shook my head at her.

The police think the person who's been threatening me did this to you. You've got nothing to be sorry about. I'm the one who should be apologising to you.

Gone were the notions of giving up that were in my mind only fifteen minutes earlier. Whatever Forest said, I needed to know who hurt Anna, and I believed someone in the family was hiding something. One of them was responsible for Lexi's murder, and they nearly killed my sister.

Anna was trying to sign something to me, but she was so weak I couldn't understand her at first.

Did you see who did this to you? I know you went to Alan and Elisha's house but I don't know what you were looking for.

She shook her head and signed *Don't know. Saw someone, don't know who.*

I had known it was a long shot and I squeezed her hand.

I worked out what you were thinking. You thought Jaxon might have killed Lexi, didn't you?

Anna nodded, the tube from the ventilator rattling as she did. I started to tell her everything, from what I worked out after finding her notes on the back of the door, my argument with Laura, to my conversation with DI Forest. I wasn't sure how much she was taking in, because her eyes drooped occasionally, so I stopped.

A thought had been niggling at me since Forest's tirade. *It couldn't have been Jaxon*, I told Anna. Much as I loathed Forest, I realised she was right – I didn't know all of the evidence. What about Lexi's broken ribs, for a start?

I looked up to see Anna watching me, her eyes open and more alert. She took a deep breath and raised her hands. I realised she was signing *door* and asked her if she wanted me to leave, but she shook her head fiercely.

Back door. Handle.

The back door was locked?

Anna took another deep breath, and I felt a stab of guilt for asking her a question when every sign took so much effort.

High. She stretched her arm up, then dropped it onto the bed next to her. I thought for a moment.

The handle on the back door. Of course, the second handle, it's quite high up. Jaxon couldn't have reached it. I remembered Singh's comment about the strange position of the handle, there to prevent Jaxon getting out of the house. I didn't think anything of it at the time, but Anna must have realised its significance when she went poking around Alan and Elisha's house.

Anna nodded, and I saw her shoulders relax a little. I didn't want to stress her out any more, so I sat and thought for a moment.

You knew Jaxon couldn't have got out the back door without help, so he can't have got the hammer that killed her. You thought he was a good suspect until you worked that out, right?

She nodded.

I cursed myself for being so stupid. I thought I was making amends for the way I'd treated Anna by looking at her notes and running away with my own ideas, but I'd only made things worse. What I should have done was waited until she could tell me her ideas, instead of assuming I knew best, as always. She'd already worked out why she was wrong, but I'd gone off on one without taking the time to think.

In which case, it must be one of the adults the police have interviewed. I sat back. Whoever it was must have been worried we were asking too many questions and might have discovered the truth. *Laura is going to hate me, but I was so convinced it could have been Jaxon.* I shut my eyes, trying not to think about how badly I'd screwed up. *Alan has a history of violence, but I don't think it was him, Anna.* I took her hand and briefly squeezed it. *By using his hammer, and then using his van to attack both of us, I think someone tried to make it look like Alan had killed his own daughter.*

Anna's eyelids fluttered as she drifted off again, so I sat and thought. My eyes wandered over the machines and wires she was attached to, and I listened to the regular beep of her heart monitor. I found myself wondering if Anna had needed CPR, and if the person who witnessed the van driving off had gone to help her after calling 999.

The thought triggered something in my brain. Lexi's broken ribs. What if they'd been broken when someone tried to perform CPR? I chewed my lip as I thought. Elisha hadn't said anything in her statement about trying to revive Lexi, and if anyone else had found her body before then, surely they would have been the one to call the police. So if CPR had been performed, who else could have done it, other than the person who killed her? What if they changed their mind? What if they realised, as they were doing it, how horrific it was? They tried to bring her back, but they were too late.

I looked back at Anna, ready to tell her what I thought, but her eyes were still closed. One question remained.

Why? Why would someone kill a child then immediately try to revive her? Unless they had only meant to hurt her, not kill her.

I repeated that last idea, muttering it aloud to myself, wondering why someone would want to hurt Lexi.

Then, something clicked.

I changed the inflexion of the sentence, and thought back to comments various people had made – Laura, Max, even Elisha – and something dawned on me. I tested out the theory in my head, trying out all of the different stumbling blocks we'd come across, but it worked. It made sense.

Anna's eyes flickered open again, and I turned to her. *I think I've got it,* I told her excitedly. I could tell she was battling to stay focused as I explained my theory to her.

Her eyes widened in shock.

It all makes sense. I need to tell someone about this.

Anna started to nod, but then her eyes rolled back in her head and her body began to jerk. I jumped back from the bed as the pitch of the machines' beeping changed, becoming more urgent, and two nurses rushed to Anna's side. I backed up against the wall, watching in horror as my sister's body bucked and rolled on the bed, and the nurses tried to keep her from hurting herself. They shouted things to each other that I didn't understand, and one of them injected Anna with something while another hustled me out of the room. My eyes blurred with tears as I was thrust into the corridor and could no longer see what was happening to my sister.

I sank to the floor, crouching on my heels as sobs racked my body once again. A passing doctor stopped to ask if she could help, but I shook my head and tried to control my breathing.

I waited in the corridor for half an hour, pacing and staring at the door to the ward. Eventually, a nurse came out to see me: Anna was back in a stable condition, but it was probably best if I let her sleep.

'Can I sit with her?' I asked.

'Okay. But don't disturb her.'

I nodded, and followed her back through.

Anna's skin looked greyer than before, and my breath caught in my throat at the sight of her. I sat on the chair and laid a hand on her arm, but she didn't stir. The nurse told me she'd been sedated, so she wouldn't know I was there, but I stayed anyway.

At the end of visiting hours, they practically had to throw me out of the door. I would have stayed with her all night if I was allowed, but they were strict with the rules. I had to use this time to get to the truth.

The police wouldn't help me. Anna couldn't help me. Leaving the hospital, I went back to my hired car, which I had more or less abandoned on a side road in my haste to see my sister, rather than drive round the car park for ages hunting for a space. As I got in, a flood of rage rose within me. How dare someone do this to us? How dare they think we wouldn't retaliate? I grabbed my phone and fired off a text to the one person I thought might still help me, and shifted my car into gear. If nobody was going to trust me, I needed to do this by myself. I was going to confront a murderer.

Chapter 32

Sitting in my car, I waited to see if I got a reply to my message. I wondered if I was doing the right thing. I should go to the police, speak to Singh and try to talk him round to my way of thinking. But by then he would have spoken to Forest, and if I turned up for the second time in one day, with a second theory about who killed Lexi, there was no way they'd listen to me. I needed proof, something incontrovertible.

My hands drummed against the steering wheel as I stared at the house, wondering how someone who'd killed a child could just go on with their day-to-day life afterwards. My phone remained stubbornly silent. I needed to get out of the car and do this by myself.

The path to the door was twice as long as I remembered it, my footsteps heavy with reluctance. If I'd thought there was any other way to bring the truth out into the open, I would have seized that opportunity with both hands. As I knocked on the door, I remembered

Anna's body spasming as the seizure took hold of her, and I shivered.

I heard footsteps coming to the door, and when it opened I forced my friendliest smile.

'Hi Bridget, is Laura home?'

'No, she's out. She doesn't want to see you, anyway.' Bridget watched me with a suspicious frown, her black hair falling in her eyes as she looked down at me. 'What do you want?'

I took a deep breath. 'Can I come in and talk to you?'

She considered, then relented with a shrug and held the door open for me. I walked past her and into the kitchen, which was where we normally talked. I didn't want her to think this time was any different. Behind me, I heard a click from the Yale lock as she pushed the front door closed. I was sure she suspected something. My heart increased its pace.

Once we were in the kitchen, Bridget busied herself making the obligatory cup of tea that all visitors were offered, then turned to face me.

Folding her arms, she looked at me sternly. 'Laura told me what you talked about last night, about Jaxon.' She sighed deeply and shook her head. 'I was afraid of this, if I can be honest with you. I knew that, some day, there would be something we couldn't talk our way out of.'

I frowned, confused. She'd wrong-footed me. 'What do you mean?'

She sighed again, and this time I recognised it for the charade it was. 'Jaxon. He's always been . . . troubled. Laura can't control him. Neither can I. Alan's the only one who manages to keep him in line, and even then it's with a very firm hand. Some of the methods Alan uses aren't exactly what I would agree with, but sometimes these things are necessary.'

I nodded, pressing my lips together, wondering where to go from there. 'Did Laura tell you how I worked it out?' I asked, seeing how long we could play it out.

'She said you'd talked to his school about the problems we've had there.'

'Well, not exactly. I've heard about it, though. And a few people have mentioned how difficult Jaxon can be.'

She nodded, then spread her hands wide. 'But what can we do, Paige? If we go to the police, Jaxon will have to live with what he's done for the rest of his life. He's only six. I don't want to put him through that.'

I leant back in my chair. 'Nothing's going to happen to Jaxon,' I said, hoping to reassure her and put her at ease. It was true, anyway. 'I think we need to talk. You should know what I've figured out. There are other things that have happened, you know. Things that couldn't have been Jaxon.'

She frowned, but moved to sit opposite me with our cups of tea, though I had no intention of drinking mine. 'What do you mean, other things?'

'Let me start from the beginning. We know that Lexi was killed by several blows to the head. As I said to Laura, it could have been Jaxon in a temper, or he could have killed Lexi by accident if he was messing around. The police have been looking into all of the adult suspects, but nobody seems to have a motive to harm Lexi – she was eighteen months old, just a baby. Why would anyone want to hurt her?'

'Exactly,' Bridget interrupted. 'Jaxon would never have meant to hurt her, I'm sure. It's a tragedy.'

I held up my hand, asking her to let me speak, and she fell silent with a sour look on her face.

'But there are parts of the story that don't make sense. Lexi also had some broken ribs. That couldn't have been Jaxon. But what if an adult caught him and knew what he'd done? That adult might then try to protect him.'

Bridget nodded, and I could almost see the cogs turning in her mind.

'Then there are the threats and attacks on myself and Anna.' I watched her carefully, and there was a delay before her nod turned into a concerned frown. She knew exactly what I was talking about. 'They certainly couldn't have been carried out by Jaxon, so again I thought maybe someone was protecting him. Someone who thought Anna and I were getting too close to the investigation and might find out who was responsible. Whoever it was wanted us out of the way, permanently, if necessary.

'But he couldn't have done it. Jaxon couldn't have gone outside and picked up the hammer, taken it back upstairs and hit Lexi with it. He couldn't get out of the back door by himself, because the handle's too high. Anyway, the police would have found some evidence on his clothes, and they haven't found anything. So without Jaxon as the culprit, a lot of the other events don't make sense.'

Bridget leant back in her chair and folded her arms, a crease forming on the bridge of her nose. 'Are you now saying Jaxon didn't do it? Because it's pretty presumptuous of you to march in here and accuse my grandson of killing his own sister, then take it back a day later.'

'Maybe, but that's exactly what I'm saying. Jaxon didn't kill his sister, but someone did.'

One of the problems with this case had always been

motive – why would someone want to hurt Lexi? If it was to send a message to either Alan or Laura, why not hurt them instead of killing their child? If Elisha was fed up with having to look after another woman's children, surely she would have killed Jaxon first, as he was by far the more difficult of the two to look after? Even the suggestion that Max killed Lexi to get Alan away from his sister seemed too far-fetched, another attempt to lay the blame on someone else.

I paused. 'It was pretty clear that someone wanted Alan to be blamed for Lexi's death. The hammer, which only Alan had used, so would have traces of him on it, was meant to implicate him. But what possible motive could Alan have for killing his own daughter?'

'I don't understand where you're going with this, Paige,' Bridget said, standing up and walking over to the kitchen window. 'All you seem to be telling me is what you don't know. How about something you do know? Or don't you know anything at all? Have you come here to show off your skills at interfering in something that has absolutely nothing to do with you? Because that's all I can see evidence of so far.'

I gave her my sweetest smile. 'I'm just coming to that, Bridget.' I enunciated her name in a clear and sarcastic tone, mimicking the way she said mine. It had come to me when I was sitting in the hospital with Anna, when I'd thought to myself, 'Maybe someone only meant to hurt her. They didn't mean to kill her.' They didn't mean to kill *her*.

'Lexi wasn't the intended victim, was she?'

Bridget's hands were trembling. She clenched her fists by her sides. 'What on earth do you mean by that?'

374

'I don't know how it took me so long to realise, to be honest. Everyone's said it to me at some point: Lexi and Kasey looked so alike they could be twins. From the back, Laura said she could easily mistake Kasey for her own daughter, and if a mother can do that, surely anyone can make the same mistake.'

'I think people have been greatly exaggerating,' Bridget spat at me, her voice shaking. 'Lexi and Kasey looked nothing alike. Nothing.'

'I know you're lying. But don't you see? Now everything makes perfect sense. The person who killed Lexi didn't mean to kill her. They meant to kill Kasey. And as soon as they realised they'd attacked the wrong child, they tried to revive her, using too much force in their panic and distress. Then they set about trying to frame Alan for the crime, which they'd always been planning to do anyway, with the murder of Kasey. I'm relieved they didn't turn around and then kill Kasey – maybe they were interrupted, or they'd just lost their nerve, but at least one of the girls survived.'

I'd worked it out as I sat by Anna's bedside. Who would want Kasey out of the picture, and Alan locked up? I thought it through logically – if Kasey had died, and Alan was in prison, what would happen? Elisha's life would be ruined, certainly, and Laura would end up with sole custody of her children.

I stared at Bridget, willing her to say something. She swallowed and waited for me to continue, but I held on, knowing she'd want to fill the silence.

The light of an idea flashed across her face. 'Are you suggesting Laura did this? Because that's even more preposterous. Laura was here with me that night, and never set foot in Alan's house. The police released her yesterday because they know full well she didn't send those threats or attack Anna. This is pure fabrication on your part, and you know it.'

I shook my head slowly, maintaining eye contact. Getting to my feet, I crossed the room to stand opposite her. 'No, Bridget, I'm not suggesting Laura did it. Because that's not really the outcome Laura wanted, is it? You know she's only fighting for custody because you forced her into it. You've browbeaten her until she doesn't have the energy to argue with you any longer. Laura loves Alan, despite everything he's done to her, and whilst she might want Elisha and Kasey out of the picture so she can have Alan to herself, I'm sure this isn't the method she'd choose. She certainly wouldn't frame Alan, because he can't come back to her if he's in prison. All Laura wants is to go back to her illusion of a happy family. But she can't have that now, can she? Because you killed Lexi. You killed your own granddaughter, by accident, because the room was dark and you mistook her for Kasey.'

Bridget's calm veneer slipped and her face twisted into a sneer. 'How dare you come into my house and accuse me of something like that? If you think you've got it all worked out, why aren't the police here?' She raised an eyebrow. 'You can't prove anything. You've come up with a crazy story that fits your twisted version of events, and now you're trying to accuse innocent people. You've been nothing but trouble, you and your sister, sticking your noses in where they don't belong!'

'That's the one thing I haven't been able to figure out. Why have you been threatening me? What did I do that made you think I knew what had happened?'

'It wasn't what you did, it was what you *didn't* do.'

'What the hell is that supposed to mean?'

She glared at me, her eyes flashing. 'Caitlin.'

I stared at her. Caitlin? How was Caitlin connected?

'I know she told you her parents abused her, but you did nothing,' Bridget continued. 'You probably told Anna that in confidence, didn't you? Well, she told Laura all about it, how you were still haunted by Caitlin's death. It was your fault, Paige. Your fault she died, and your fault that her feckless parents got away with it.'

I was speechless for a moment. 'What has Caitlin got to do with this? You didn't even know her, she died before you moved here.'

'She was my niece!'

My mouth gaped in shock. How had I not known this? I'd never been in Bridget's house before Lexi's death, but Anna had. We'd been adults when I'd finally told Anna what I had known about the abuse Caitlin suffered, my guilt plaguing me. Had my sister known all along but not told me? Or had Bridget and Laura deliberately hidden their relationship to Caitlin's family from the Deaf community when they moved to Scunthorpe?

'And now here you are, getting yourself involved in this case,' Bridget spat. 'I hadn't even realised you'd known Caitlin until Anna told Laura about it, telling her you'd stop at nothing to find out what happened to Lexi because you still felt guilty about letting Caitlin down. I'd told Laura never to mention our connection to that family. I didn't want to be tarred with the same brush. My brother and his wife were drunks, and I cut them out of my life, but I always hoped I'd be able to help Caitlin. You were her friend, Paige. You knew her parents didn't care for her, but you left her on that beach anyway.'

'That's why you've been threatening me? Because of Caitlin?'

'I knew I could steer the police towards Alan. It would have been so easy to frame him, he was such an obvious suspect. But then the two of you couldn't stop interfering, and I couldn't let you find out what I'd done. You were so hell bent on helping the police to solve this, just to ease your conscience after you let my niece die.'

My body trembled, the adrenaline coursing through me and making me reckless. 'You're lecturing me about my conscience? You bloody hypocrite! You were prepared to let your own grandson take the blame! You looked so relieved at the idea that the police might believe he was responsible. He's a child, and you would have ruined his life simply to save your own neck.'

'You don't know anything! Jaxon woke up and touched Lexi, he got blood on his hands, but I cleaned him off. If I'd wanted the police to suspect him, don't you think I would have left him covered in his sister's blood?' she raged.

I shook my head. 'You think that makes everything better? You disgust me,' I spat at her, and that was when she flew at me.

With hindsight, I shouldn't have confronted her in the kitchen. I saw the knife in her hand too late, and shrieked as she dragged it across my arm. Blood bloomed through my torn sleeve as Bridget slashed at me, but I grabbed her wrist and twisted hard. She screamed and dropped the knife, which skittered away across the tiled floor, but she used her position to bear down on me. She was slim, but several inches taller than me, and she used that against me, forcing me down onto the ground, pinning me down

378

with a knee to the stomach that took my breath away. Fighting to inhale, I clawed at her, but she got one of her hands round my throat.

My vision started to darken at the edge as she leant all her weight on me, cutting off my breath, her other hand grabbing my flailing wrist and twisting it around painfully.

'Did you really think I would let you carry on with this? Did you think I would allow you to leave my house after you've told me everything you know? I'll pin your death on Alan, and then at least one good thing will have come out of all this. I don't want that man anywhere near my daughter, or Jaxon, ever again. He's dangerous scum, but Laura can't see that. I needed her to see that!'

Engrossed in her tirade, she'd slackened her grip with both hands and I took a ragged breath. Pushing up with a foot and hooking an ankle round her leg, I flipped over and slammed her into the ground, trapping one of her arms underneath her. Using what was left of my remaining energy, I straddled her chest, kneeling on her free arm.

'I need to know something, though,' I panted, trying to breathe through my bruised windpipe. 'Why not just kill Elisha and frame Alan for that murder? Because then Laura might get saddled with someone else's child? Or was it just because Kasey would have been easier to kill than Elisha? Easier to murder a defenceless toddler than a grown woman?'

Rage flashed in Bridget's eyes. 'Elisha was as bad as Alan. She was the reason he left Laura, and why this whole thing began. I wanted her to suffer! If I'd killed her, her suffering would be over. Without Kasey she'd suffer for the rest of her life.'

I saw the horror in her eyes as she remembered that,

through her mistake, she'd meted out this terrible fate to her own daughter. She struggled beneath me, and I could feel her wriggling her arm free. I shifted to try and hold her down, but she was ready for me and caught me off balance. I fell back, cracking my head against the corner of the worktop.

My vision clouded for a moment as pain burst in my head. I squeezed my eyes shut and retched, half kneeling, half sitting on the kitchen floor. I opened my eyes in time to see Bridget grab the knife and launch herself at me. Twisting before she could drive the knife into my chest, I felt a searing pain in my shoulder. My head throbbed and the room swirled around me as Bridget pulled the knife out and prepared to strike again, then I heard a splintering crash and something rained down on top of me. I thought I saw a familiar face, then everything went black.

After the murder

Lexi. How could it have been Lexi? It was supposed to be Kasey!

Bridget couldn't remember leaving the house, hoped she hadn't triggered the security light in her daze. She had walked there, didn't want to risk her car being seen anywhere near that road, and her feet automatically took her in the direction of home.

She was halfway down the road when she realised she still had the hammer in her hand. It was too risky to go back and leave it outside the house as she'd planned, so she dropped it by the side of the road, at the edge of the waste ground.

It was nearly five by the time she got to her own house and slumped down in the kitchen, her head in her trembling hands. What had she done? All she had wanted was to keep her own grandchildren safe, to get Alan Hunter away from them for good.

She remembered how her hands shook as she washed

the blood off Jaxon after he touched Lexi's body. Moving carefully, she'd cleaned him up in the glow from her torch, not wanting to risk Elisha or Alan waking and seeing the bathroom light on. At least she didn't have to worry about them hearing her.

A bad man did this, she had told Jaxon. *A bad man hurt your sister.*

He hadn't contradicted her and had gone back to bed quite willingly, which was unusual, so perhaps he hadn't been fully awake. Even if he was, hopefully he didn't realise what he'd seen. It might not have gone this far if Laura had been more dedicated to the court case, to making sure Alan didn't get custody. Hadn't Bridget done enough for them all over the years? Didn't she deserve to have her grandchildren in her life?

Alan didn't deserve to have children, the way he treated them. He was as bad as her own brother had been, neglecting his child in favour of drink and drugs. Even before her death, Caitlin's childhood had been ruined. She didn't want the same thing to happen to Jaxon and Lexi. Oh God, Lexi . . . What had she done?

Chapter 33

Monday 19th February

The last time I was in hospital, I was being treated for a deep gash on my arm after breaking a window in my flat. Until then I had put up with Mike's gambling, sticking my head in the sand about how much of my money he was throwing away, but Anna and Gem finally made me see sense when he locked me in the flat and took my phone. It took me four days to accept I would have to break the window to escape. At the time, I had felt like my life was ending, and some aspects of it had been on hold since then. Maybe it was time to get him out of my head for good and move on.

I was still groggy from the pain medication I'd been given overnight, but I managed to pull myself up in the hospital bed when I saw DC Singh coming through the door. He took the chair next to my bed and moved it around to the side so he could see me. I wasn't sure if he was going to berate me or not, but I didn't have the energy to defend myself if he did.

Singh cleared his throat. 'If you're feeling up to it, I'd

like to take your statement regarding the events of last night.'

I nodded, taking a shaky breath. I had to do it. I chose to go in there alone, so I had to be the one to relate what happened.

I started from where I left Forest, telling Singh how I realised I was wrong, and that Bridget was the only person who could have killed Lexi.

'Once I realised Lexi wasn't the intended victim, it made so much more sense. Nobody wanted Lexi out of the way, but Bridget couldn't stand Kasey's existence. She felt Kasey was the reason her grandchildren were being taken further from her – if Elisha hadn't become pregnant, Alan would have eventually gone back to Laura, like he always did, and there would have been no concerns over the custody of Jaxon and Lexi.'

Singh was recording me with a pocket voice recorder, but also taking notes as I spoke. 'Did you share your suspicions with anyone?'

I nodded. 'I told Anna, but she was so out of it, I'm not sure if she'll remember.' I looked over to the door. 'I want to see her, but they've told me to stay in bed.'

'Her condition's improving,' he replied with a gentle smile. 'I checked on my way in.'

'Thank you,' I said quietly.

'Did you tell anyone else?' he asked, getting back to my statement.

I bit my lip before replying. I needed to tell the truth. 'Yes. I sent a text to Max Barron, telling him what I'd worked out, and that I was going to Bridget's house. We'd argued, so I didn't expect him to respond, but I didn't know who else I could trust.'

'You were certain he wasn't involved?'

'Yes,' I said, relieved to realise I was telling the truth. I think I knew it all along, but I didn't know whether to trust my gut instinct about someone I was attracted to. Self-sabotage, probably.

I finished telling him my story, up to the point where I passed out on Bridget's kitchen floor. The detective shut his notebook and sat back in the chair. 'I can fill in some more details there. Mr Barron received your text message. He contacted us using the emergency text alert system and told us you were in danger. He also relayed the contents of your text message to us.'

I flushed, remembering the plea for forgiveness that I began the message with.

'After contacting us, he drove to Bridget and Laura Weston's house. He was going to wait for us, but he saw what was happening through the kitchen window and tried to get in. He couldn't break the front door down, so instead broke the kitchen window and got in that way. He pulled Bridget off you and restrained her until we arrived.'

A half-smile crept onto his face, and I wondered if he'd forgive me my recklessness. I should have called him, let him know what I was doing, but I'd assumed Forest would have already told him about my humiliation and warned him not to speak to me.

'We arrived moments later and an ambulance brought you straight here.'

I nodded. The doctor had been in earlier to explain I'd had minor surgery on the wound to my shoulder. Along with a concussion and bruising to my windpipe, I felt like I'd been hit by a bus, but I'd been told it shouldn't take too long to recover.

'Thank you,' I said, and I meant it. I was glad he'd filled in the gaps, though I shuddered to think what would have happened if Max had chosen to ignore me, or if he'd waited for the police to arrive before coming in.

'We needed to check your story matched with Mr Barron's, and it does, so neither of you will be charged with anything.' He saw the surprise on my face and elaborated. 'Criminal damage, on his part. Possibly wasting police time, for yourself, Paige. Although as you got it right the second time, DI Forest has told me she's willing to ignore your original accusation. I think her words were, "I'm prepared to forget the discussion we had regarding the termination of her contract, provided that in future she sticks within the boundaries of her professional role." Or something like that.'

I nodded and thanked him again. It wouldn't do much for my professional reputation if it got out that I'd come close to accusing a six-year-old of murder.

'What about Bridget?'

'Mrs Weston confessed once we had her in custody. On the morning in question, she had left her house in the early hours, when Laura was still asleep, and driven to Mr Hunter's house. Laura has a key to the house, which she'd taken. She went through the back garden, picked up the hammer from inside the shed and crept up to the children's room.'

We sat in silence for a moment, contemplating the sheer evil of the woman.

'What about the van?' I asked.

'She was getting desperate because we hadn't charged Alan with Lexi's murder, and went back to the house to try and plant some more evidence. When she saw Anna

386

there, she panicked. Alan kept a spare key for his van by the back door, so Bridget took it and tried to kill Anna so she couldn't tell anyone she'd seen her there. We found Bridget's fingerprints in the van. She didn't do a very good job of destroying it.'

He gave me a look, as if to tell me they could have done it without me. I knew I'd been reckless, but the truth was out there now, and that was all that mattered to me.

'And Anna's phone? She took that after she'd hit her, I assume.'

Singh nodded. 'She was out shopping when we were tracking the phone. As we entered through one door, she saw us and left by another. If the battery in the phone hadn't died, we might have been able to continue tracking her and caught her sooner.'

'Would we have believed it was her, though? It's horrific. Even now I can't get my head around it.'

'If I'd seen her, I might have had my suspicions. We had previously questioned Mrs Weston,' he replied. 'We found evidence that she had been in the house, one of her earrings under Jaxon's bed, despite Laura insisting her mother had never been there. But she came up with a plausible explanation about Jaxon taking things from her, and we couldn't take it any further.'

'That was the day I bumped into her outside the police station,' I guessed. 'She told me she'd been to report Alan for stalking Laura.'

'She did claim she'd seen Mr Hunter outside the house, but we checked and he was at work at the times she gave us. Those lies made us suspicious as well, but without much more to go on it was difficult to proceed.'

'Poor Laura. Her mum killed her daughter.' I shook my head, trying to fathom how awful she must feel.

'She took it better than I would have expected, you know,' Singh said. 'I think part of her was afraid her mother might have been the one responsible. One of her brothers is coming up to collect her and Jaxon, and they'll go down to London to stay with him for a while. The two sons more or less cut ties with her and Bridget because their mother had made their lives hell, demanding to see their children and making up lies about their wives. If we'd reached out to the wider family perhaps we would have seen her for what she was a little sooner.'

'She's a good liar. She had us all convinced.'

Singh nodded. 'Right, that'll do,' he said. 'I'm sorry you got caught up in this, Paige, though I have enjoyed working with you.'

I gave a wry smile. 'It was certainly eventful. I'm not sure I'll be looking forward to working with CID again.'

He laughed. 'We'll keep your number on file, just in case. Though next time, perhaps you and your sister should do less of your own investigating.'

His mention of Anna gave me a pang in my chest. 'I need to see her. You were right, you know.' He gave me a questioning look. 'When you said I spend too much time worrying about her. We fought about it right before the accident.'

He put a hand over mine. 'I'm sure all that will be forgotten now. You're both on the mend, and once you're out of here you can sort things out.'

I nodded. 'I hope she'll forgive me.'

Laughing, he stood up. 'She's your sister. Of course she will. But right now, I believe you have a visitor waiting.' He cleared his throat again, looking at his feet awkwardly.

There was a tentative knock at the door and I looked up. Max was standing in the doorway looking sheepish. He and Singh looked at each other for a moment and I was struck by the juxtaposition of these two men, both of whom I liked very much but who had been on opposite sides of the investigation. I remembered Singh's comment when we'd had coffee in the arts centre, and wondered again if he'd been asking me out, but I didn't have much chance to think about it before the DC glanced back at me, gave me a strange sort of smile and left the room.

Once he'd gone, I smiled at Max and patted the sheets at the end of my bed.

Be careful, I said, indicating my shoulder when he leaned in to hug me. He gingerly perched on the edge of the bed.

Thank you for saving my life, I told him, wanting to lead with the most important issue. *If you hadn't come, Bridget would probably have killed me and tried to frame Alan. I'm not sure she would have succeeded, but I'd rather be alive to see her go to prison than dead on her kitchen floor.*

He frowned. *Don't joke about something like that. There was blood everywhere, all over you, and you were so pale. I thought you were dead.* He reached for my hand and I gave his a squeeze.

I'm okay, I promise.

Don't do anything like that ever again.

I know, I know. We held each other's gaze for a moment, then I looked away, feeling my face flush. *I'm sorry about the other day. I hope you can forgive me.*

He looked down at my bedsheets for a minute, deep in thought. *It must have been hard for you to know what was really going on, what to believe. I hope you realise now that I would never do anything like that. I'd never hurt anyone, certainly not a child. And not you.*

His words reminded me of when I'd seen him at the Deaf club, when Jaxon had fallen over. I couldn't relax until I knew what had happened, so I asked him about it.

Elisha sometimes brings all three kids over to mine, he explained. *Jaxon was asking me when they could come again, because I'd promised to take him to the trampoline park. When I said I wasn't sure when, he got cross and jumped at me, then he slipped. It's a laminate floor and he was boisterous,* Max signed looking concerned. *I picked him up and told him to be careful, and said I would take him, I just had to talk to Elisha and find out when. I promise it was nothing sinister.* He squeezed my hand again, and I got a pleasant fluttering in my belly; I knew he was telling the truth.

Max sighed. *All I wanted was to protect my sister from an emotionally abusive relationship, and I found myself mixed up in this.*

It sounded like we'd both learned our lesson about being too protective of our sisters – we'd unwittingly pushed them into more danger.

I have one question, though, I said. *What is it that you were threatening to tell Elisha?*

Max looked confused, so I explained that I saw him fighting with Alan in the Deaf club on Friday night.

Oh, that. He made a dismissive gesture. *I told you, remember? Alan and Rick Lombard were dealing in stolen goods, and they were selling counterfeits too.*

I grimaced. *But she already knew about that.* I told him about following the two of them to the warehouse.

Max nodded sadly. *I've been pretty naive where my sister's concerned. Elisha gave me this watch for Christmas, and I never even thought that she might have been in on it with Lombard. Apparently he had a plan to back out and grass Alan up, so he and Elisha could run off together with the money. But the police found the stash yesterday, while you were getting stabbed. Alan and Lombard have both been arrested and charged, so they're probably going to prison. Hopefully Elisha will be able to claim she didn't know the goods were dodgy, just thought they were setting up a market stall.*

I frowned. *If the police charge Elisha as well, what will happen to Kasey?*

He shrugged. *I doubt Elisha will get more than a fine. Alan and Rick were much more heavily involved, so might face charges for the original thefts, hence why they'll probably get jail time. But if it comes to that, I'll look after Kasey.*

I smiled at him. *Next time, I promise I'll ask you before jumping to conclusions,* I said.

Next time? I hope we're not going to go through anything like this again.

We sat for a moment, neither of us saying anything. It would take time for us to heal, and for the community to get over this tragedy, but I wanted to begin that process as soon as possible.

I'd better go, Max told me. *I need to go and see Elisha. She's really upset about the whole thing, blaming herself for not waking up and catching Bridget in the house. And knowing that it was nearly her own daughter who was killed has shaken her even further.*

I nodded, wanting to ask if I could see him again, but

not wanting to push my luck. I was physically and emotionally strung out, and my mind was whirling once again with thoughts of Lexi and Caitlin. If I'd acted on what I'd known, and I'd saved Caitlin, would I also have prevented Lexi's death fifteen years later? No, I couldn't start thinking like that. Bridget was the one responsible, nobody else. I was just a handy person for her to blame. Still, the idea niggled at the back of my mind and I knew it would take some hard work to dispel these thoughts.

As Max walked to the door, he turned and signed, *I'll text you*, before he disappeared into the corridor. I sank back onto my pillows and smiled. Maybe something good could still come out of all this.

Acknowledgements

Many people have had a hand in making this book what it is today, and I am in awe of the support I've received from so many people I know.

Firstly, huge thanks to my fabulous agent, Juliet Mushens, for seeing the potential in an early draft and spurring me on to make it better.

Thanks also to the gorgeous Debi Alper, for her keen editorial eye and for having faith that I would get here one day.

Much love and gratitude to Rachel Faulkner-Willcocks and Tilda McDonald, fantastic editors who saw how to make this a better book when I had lost all objectivity. Everyone at Avon has been amazing: thanks to Sabah Khan, Ellie Pilcher, Rebecca Fortuin, Dominic Rigby, Kelly Webster and Catriona Beamish for the many roles that come together to make a book a reality. Thanks also to Sarah Whittaker for such a fantastic cover, and Jo Gledhill for copy editing.

Also, thanks are due to David Bishop, for reading an early draft and giving excellent feedback; to fellow writers Liz King and Mette Thobro for always being willing to have ideas bounced off them, however strange they are; to Faye Robertson for advising on police procedure but also allowing me plenty of creative licence when necessary (all mistakes, inaccuracies and flights of fancy are my own); and to friends Hannah Bowman, Rebecca Page and Jen Clapp for being endlessly supportive and putting up with my eccentricity.

To my parents, Glynis and Mark Hutchinson, thank you for surrounding me with books from a young age and taking me to the library every weekend, for nurturing the writer in me and always supporting me. To Gary, Edna and Julia Pattison, thank you for welcoming me into your family and cheering me on through the publishing process.

And lastly, thanks to Stuart, who is the best husband, father and partner-in-crime I could have ever wished for.